THE CURSE OF A

CADES COVE

AIDEN JAMES

Acclaim for Aiden James:

"Aiden James has written a deeply psychological, gripping tale that keeps the readers hooked from page one."
—Bookfinds review for THE FORGOTTEN EDEN

"Not only is Aiden James a storyteller par excellence, but his material for his story is riveting."
—Huntress Reviews

"Aiden James writing style flows very easily and I found that CADES COVE snowballed into a very gripping tale. Clearly the strengths in the piece were as the spirit's interaction became prevalent with the family… The Indian lore and ceremonies and the flashbacks to Allie Mae's (earthly) demise were very powerful. I think those aspects separated the work from what we've seen before in horror and ghost tales."
—Evelyn Klebert, author of A GHOST OF A CHANCE and DRAGONFLIES

"Aiden James is insanely talented! We are watching a master at work…. Ghost stories don't get any better than this"
—J.R. Rain, author of MOON DANCE and THE BODY DEPARTED

BOOKS BY AIDEN JAMES

WITH FIONA FRASER
Toxicity
They Fought Like Men

CADES COVE SERIES
Cades Cove
The Raven Mocker
Devil Mountain

DYING OF THE DARK VAMPIRES
With Patrick Burdine
The Vampires' Last Lover
The Vampires' Birthright
Blood Princesses

THE JUDAS CHRONICLES
Immortal Plague
Immortal Reign
Immortal Destiny
Immortal Dragon
Immortal Tyranny
Immortal Pyramid
Immortal Victory

THE RODERICK CHRONICLES
Immortal Supremacy
Immortal Storm

NICK CAINE ADVENTURES
With J.R. Rain
Temple of the Jaguar
Treasure of the Deep
Pyramid of the Gods
Aiden James only

Curse of the Druids
Secret of the Loch
River of the Damned

CLASH OF COVENS
The Witches of Denmark
Witch Out of Water

THE GABRIEL FILES
With J.R. Rain
The Soul Taker
The Ghost Maker

THE SERENDIPITOUS CURSE
With Lisa Collicutt
Reborn
Reviled
Redeemed

NASHVEGAS PARANORMAL
With Patrick Burdine
Deadly Night
The Ungrateful Dead

THE TALISMAN CHRONICLES
With Mike Robinson
The Forgotten Eden
The Devil's Paradise
Hurakan's Chalice

Published by
Manor House Books

Cover Art: Blue Sky Design ~ Boston

Printed in the United States of America.

Third Edition ~ Fully revised, April 2017

CADES COVE

AIDEN JAMES

To Fiona, forever my love, my muse, and my mentor.

"No place, indeed, should murder sanctuarize;
Revenge should have no bounds."
~ William Shakespeare, "Hamlet"

Chapter One

"Yep… I believe this must be it!" David Hobbs motioned for Miriam, his wife, to join him on a rock ledge overlooking a secluded ravine, roughly a mile's hike from John Oliver's famous homestead in the Smoky Mountains of Tennessee. He smiled like a kid with a dirty secret.

It's here… right where Ned said it would be!

"Are you sure?" Miriam panted as she caught up to him.

Her tone clearly announced a desire to end this unexpected adventure off the beaten path. For the moment, David ignored her lack of enthusiasm.

"Wow, just look at this place…. Welcome to the Smokies' oldest 'Lover's Lane', darlin'!"

He tipped the bill of his ball cap toward the view. A lush carpet of grass covered the ravine, where colorful wildflowers lay nestled in the shade from tall pines, elms, and maples.

She glanced down into the ravine and shrugged.

"I guess it's nice, but a horseback ride through the cove would've been better." She removed her backpack, letting it fall to the ground, and sat on a small boulder nearby. Her lovely sky-blue eyes peered at him through long, dark hair while she massaged her tired legs and ankles.

"I thought you wanted romantic." David worried his planned surprise might fall flat. After carefully maneuvering their venture to this remote destination, he was hoping for a new way to sweep her off her feet. "How much more romantic can it get than being here, in this beautiful place, *and* on a day like this?"

The weather was perfect for October, with clear skies and the temperature hovering in the mid-sixties. He winked and she giggled in response.

He stepped over to Miriam and lifted her backpack, adding it to his own. Then he gently helped her to her feet. His knees felt weak, reminding him of when they first dated, back in college. "Let's have a look around."

They stepped down from the ledge together into heavy brush, wading toward the heart of the ravine. From the looks of things, no one had been there in quite awhile. A feeling of serenity surrounded him. Immersed in waist-high grass and thistles, he tried not to think about what might be slithering along the ground near his feet. Miriam pulled back, reluctant to go further.

"Aren't you afraid of being bitten by a snake or something?" she asked. "The park ranger back at the Cable Mill said timber rattlesnakes and copperheads are out here."

David nodded but pressed on, hoping she would follow and muttering a quiet prayer that the snakes had already gone into hibernation. Miriam's hushed curses echoed lightly across the ravine as she scurried along the path he'd created to catch up.

"What do you think? It's pretty cool, isn't it?"

Beneath the canopy of ancient trees, wildflowers thrived in abundance. It was as if they had stepped into a small section of paradise, even more beautiful than what they had seen thus far in Cades Cove. His hunch about the snakes seemed correct so far, and he felt relieved that the out-of-the-way locale mentioned by his boss, Ned Badgett, just might be worth the trouble of finding after all.

In addition to the pines, elms, and maples he had viewed from the ledge moments ago, majestic oaks, chestnuts, and maples towered along both embankments. The leaves had already embraced the season's change, offering a brilliant sea of red and orange amid towering evergreens. Wild roses, geraniums, and orange jewelweed added even more splendor.

"It is." She grinned as if pleasantly surprised.

David wrapped his arm around her waist and pulled her close. His trimmed blonde beard brushed against her cheek as she reached up and kissed him.

"Sorry I was a bitch."

"It's all right, baby." His hazel eyes twinkled, mischievous. "You can make it up to me after lunch."

"You think so, huh? We'll have to see about that!"

She playfully jabbed him in the side, and he feigned injury before moving across the ravine to a large oak, where he set the backpacks down. Miriam remained where she was, distracted by the carvings on many of the trees surrounding them.

"Ned told me about them," he said, upon his return.

A multitude of scrawled names covered more than a dozen tree trunks. Carved hearts enclosed most of them. It sort of reminded him of a guestbook, like a giant version of the one they signed when they picked up the keys for their rented chalet in Gatlinburg the night before. Ned told him the ravine was the spot most frequented by the area's young lovers during the late 1800s, and into the early1900s.

"This is really something," marveled Miriam, scanning the list of names. "Didn't you say there's supposed to be like a thousand names here?"

...Mary Ellen + Joshua, Milton + Anna, Shannon + Edmond...

"According to Ned, that's true." He joined her in studying the names inscribed upon the nearest tree. "He called it the home of Cades Cove's star-crossed lovers. Apparently, his ancestors once lived around here, before everyone moved out in the 1930s."

...Johnny Lee + Pauline, Samuel + Bertha, Thelma Lyn + Adam...

"Here's one with a date." She pointed to one of the fainter inscriptions. *Walter Smith + Marylee Oliver, June 13, 1908.* "It's more than a hundred years old... They're long gone from this earth by now."

"Probably their kids are long gone, too." David glanced around the ravine. A yellow poplar caught his attention. *Harold Potts + Samantha Pope, September 14, 1932.* "I'll bet we can find even older names back in there."

He pointed past to a heavily wooded area beyond the forgotten streambed.

"Maybe later," she agreed. "I'm starting to feel a little weak. My stomach's been growling for the past half hour."

"Sure, it can wait."

David grew concerned as her smile continued to die, morphing into a worried frown. She looked around her in a way that made him wonder if the place suddenly creeped her out. He gently grasped her hand, bringing her attention back to him.

"Let's go eat... I think you're gonna enjoy what I've got planned for lunch."

David led her to the other side, settling on a spot below the shade of one of the immense oaks. So far, the secluded ravine from years past seemed like the perfect spot to rekindle the passion that had been missing as of late. Their marriage of fifteen years stood on solid ground, but over the past few years, intimacy had waned. He regretted that it had taken a waning sex life to finally open his eyes to what was missing. In his focus to be an excellent financial provider for his family, he had neglected the sincere affection that a healthy marriage needed to survive, where the couple's daily emotional and physical contact didn't always mean intercourse lingered on the horizon.

Keeping her in his loving gaze, he removed the contents of his backpack, laying out a large picnic blanket next to the oak tree's base. She seemed especially surprised when he produced two elegant place settings. Cold, fried chicken from a local deli was the main entrée, since easiest for him to pack and serve. But, to ensure she fully understood his romantic intent, he brought a bowled candle to light along with two crystal wineglasses and a bottle of expensive chardonnay—Miriam's preference for special occasions.

With everything arranged as best he could, he motioned for her to join him on the blanket.

"David, this is *really* nice!" she enthused as she sat down.

"To our fifteenth *fantastic* year together, my love!" he said, pouring her a glass of wine, and then one for himself. They tapped the glasses together, and the pitch resounded throughout the ravine, carried by a gentle breeze moving among the trees.

"Well, how about that?" She smiled as she watched the wind's diffusive caress enfolding the ravine. "Maybe it's a good sign, like the next fifteen years will be even better."

"I'd love that." He lifted his glass towards hers again, and they clinked softer this time.

Afterward, they snuggled close, lying upon the blanket. As they discussed how to spend the rest of their afternoon, David noticed something faint that was carved upon the oak's trunk, and rose to investigate it. It was another name, but unlike the others they had seen, this solitary inscription was cruder—like whoever made it did so in haste.

"What does it say?" Miriam came up next to him for a closer look.

The bark had curled around the edges of the wound inflicted long ago, forming an imperfect heart. Carved inside was the name 'Allie', and below it was either a '+' or a 'T'—difficult to say which. They mouthed the name together, glancing at each other before looking at it again.

"It looks like someone got stood up," he said dryly.

"Or, maybe she changed her mind before it was too late… and, she didn't let the boy carve his name inside the heart," said Miriam, her tone becoming sad as she mentioned the last part.

David smirked.

"Oh, I'm sure it's just wishful thinking she wasn't spurned by whoever her beau was," she added, forcing a laugh.

It made the mood awkward, and as David looked past the oak to the ravine's streambed, an idea occurred to him. Something to brighten things up a bit.

"What are you looking for, hon?" she asked, after returned to his backpack.

"This seems like the perfect location to try out my new zoom lens." He carefully removed a camera from its case. "I'd like to take your picture, my love. How about you go stand in the ravine again?"

At first she protested, thinking about the snakes again. But she relented to David's persistence, posing where the wildflowers were most abundant. He stepped under the ledge at the mouth of the ravine and knelt, attempting to position the camera to also catch the treetops. He prepared to snap the picture, and then hesitated.

"What's wrong, David?"

"It's not the right angle—hang on a moment." He climbed onto the ledge and aimed the camera, but wavered again. He frowned.

"I guess I'm too ugly, huh?" she deadpanned. "I'd hate to put a crack in your precious lens."

"That's not even funny."

But it was, and he smiled. Scanning the area, his gaze was drawn to the oak again. It seemed inviting, and it occurred to him that it might offer the perfect point for his intended shot of Miriam.

"Now where are you going?"

"Up here." He started climbing the tree. "I think this will work, but you'll need to back up just a bit."

"David, don't do it." Her faint smile disappeared as she stepped toward him. "I've got a bad feeling about this."

"It'll be all right."

He found it surprisingly easy to scale the tree and was soon fifteen feet above the embankment. After straddling two large branches, he prepared to take the shot, but still wasn't satisfied. He ventured onto a smaller branch above the ravine's basin.

"David, you're really scaring me! Just leave it *alone!* I'm scared to death you're going to fall and break your neck!" Her voice cracked.

"I'll be okay—just relax!" The branch creaked beneath his weight. "It's gonna be perfect and I'm almost there."

He leaned toward her and positioned the camera to his eye. *Yes this is the perfect shot! If only she didn't look so damned worried….*

"Smile, baby!"

A sudden strong gust distracted him, and he placed more weight on the branch. It cracked loudly and splintered.

"David!"

The branch gave way, taking him with it. Desperate to avoid a free fall to the ground, he threw his arms around the tree's trunk, surprised when something unseen shoved him up against it. Sliding to the ground, his sweatshirt ripped, and the oak's sharp bark scraped his arms and hands.

"Oh, baby, are you all right?" Miriam scrambled up the embankment and gently helped him to his feet. His initial grimace turned to a sheepish look as he brushed himself off. "You're hurt!"

"Well, at least I got the picture, huh?"

He retrieved his ball cap and camera. Surprised the camera wasn't broken, even his prized lens was spared. A slight scratch to the camera's casing was the only damage. Curious to find out what had pushed him against the tree, he gazed toward the spot he'd vacated. The broken branch was next to the thickest one on the tree, with no evidence of anything unusual. Still, he squinted, wishing he had brought his prescription-tinted eyeglasses, instead of the cheap sunglasses he purchased that morning in Gatlinburg. As far as he could tell, nothing was there, despite the peculiar sensation that something unseen was glaring back at him. He shivered.

Get a grip, man. It's just an empty old tree.

"I can't believe you did that!" scolded Miriam, her eyes briefly following his gaze before she attended to his injuries.

The scrapes on his arms bled, and his hands ached. Miriam guided him to the blanket and opened her backpack, pulling out a small first-aid kit. A dozen years as a successful pediatrician came in handy at a time like this. She helped him remove the sweatshirt, and dressed his wounds, relieved that the injuries were largely superficial. Their painful sting told David otherwise.

"You stubborn, stupid man," she said, kissing his hands. "You could've been killed just now, do you realize that?"

She looked into his face. Her eyes were soft and misty.

Another breeze blew through the trees, much cooler, and it raised gooseflesh on his bare back and chest. Meanwhile, his wife's kisses moved up his arms. She kissed his neck, and then his mouth with fervor. Powerfully aroused, he saw urgent longing in her eyes. He pulled her down onto the blanket, where they gave in to their passion.

* * * * *

Miriam awoke in panic, looking at her wristwatch.

"Oh shit!"

"Huh?" Roused from a dark and fragmented dream, David looked around him, disoriented. "What in the hell happened?"

Long shadows crept into the ravine. The sun almost finished with its journey across the autumn sky had left a cool crispness in the air.

"It's almost five o'clock. *That's* what happened!" she announced, sharply. She grabbed her clothes. "We must've fallen asleep."

He stood and moved to his clothes, piled at the end of the blanket, as chilled air embraced his naked body. He turned to face Miriam, who scrambled to fix her bra and pull on her panties. The sight of her vulnerability stirred his desire, and he thought about taking her in his arms once more. But, the waning sunlight told him that it wouldn't be prudent, not to mention she looked distressed. His well-toned body and powerful arousal would have little influence. It didn't help matters that the opportunity to do anything else in the park was now lost, on account of their scheduled flight back to Denver from Knoxville the following morning.

"Are you going to just stand there and admire yourself, or do you think you can be dressed by the time I'm finished here?"

She smiled, but he knew better than to test her current mood. He dressed, wincing from his wounds as he pulled on his sweatshirt. He finished just before she packed the remaining wine and glasses.

Miriam motioned for him to step off the blanket, so she could fold it. Something metallic jingled… an object fell onto the ground where his clothes had been. A golden glint caught David's eye, and he reached to pick it up. It was his wristwatch.

"This is really strange." He shrugged and pulled the watch over his wrist, snapping the band shut. "You know I almost never take this off, and only in the shower. I don't recall removing it from my wrist."

Still puzzled, he looked at the spot where it had fallen.

"What in the hell's this?"

A small cloth bag with a leather drawstring lay nestled in the grass. He picked it up. Near the top, the words *Allie Mae's Treasures* were cross-stitched on one side in light blue thread.

"Let me see that," said Miriam, setting the blanket down.

"It's got to be some sort of prank." David handed the bag to her, while looking up at the tree's inscription. "The name stitched on the bag is almost identical to the one up there."

"That's really weird." she agreed, peering at the bag. David watched her warily look around, before examining the bag more closely. She held it by the knot at the end of its leather drawstring, and another metallic jingle soon resounded from within the bag. "I wonder what's inside?"

She loosened the drawstring and opened the bag. A musty, earthen scent rose from within. Gingerly, she poured the contents into one hand and sifted through them with the other. Four items rested in her palm: a steel sleigh bell, a broken, solid gold locket attached to a chain made from a lesser grade of plated gold, a blue, silk hair ribbon, and a folded letter.

The bell and hair ribbon looked ordinary, although the ribbon seemed to be of fine quality. The locket appeared torn at the hinges, and may have contained a picture at one time.

"I wonder what this is about." Miriam opened the letter. She ran her fingers over the paper, admiring its texture.

"Do you think it's such a good idea to be prying into someone's personal business like this?" It made David uncomfortable, watching her casually skim over the letter's contents.

"It can't be too private, since it was left on the blanket while you and I were sleeping—in the nude, no less."

Miriam spent the next few minutes silently reading the letter while he looked on. When finished, she refolded it and stood silently.

"Well, what does it say?" he asked, finally.

"I believe it's definitely a love letter," she advised, after another moment's hesitation. "The penmanship is so graceful, as if from another era altogether, which sort of contradicts the occasional misspellings. And, the ink has definite stops and starts, as though an old-fashioned fountain pen was used. Part of the letter is unclear, as if this girl named Allie must've read it over and over, until some of the writing faded over time."

She opened the bag and placed the items inside, the letter being the last thing in before she closed the drawstring.

"It's from a boy or man named Seth," she continued, handing the bag back to him. She finished folding the blanket and placed it inside her backpack. "It seems he was on his way to some war. The words are too dim for me to make out which one it was. It doesn't seem possible that the bag could belong to the same girl whose name is on the tree, since the carving was obviously made a long time ago…."

"The chances for that are probably less than winning the lottery," he said, when she didn't go on. This crazy scene made no sense whatsoever. As much as he prided himself on being straight minded and very practical, being a CPA by trade, Miriam was even more so. Meanwhile, she busily searched the immediate area.

"You're not thinking it's the same person, are you?" he asked, after she took the bag and moved to the tree. "You do realize how crazy that sounds—especially if the carving on the tree is actually as old as it looks."

"I guess you're right… this is silly." But she didn't give it up yet, taking a closer look at the crude inscription and comparing it to the bag. "Yet, we both know a lot of things these days can be made to look a certain way with the right props and equipment."

"Who in the hell would go to such trouble?" he asked.

She sighed, and looked toward the tree's carved image. "I guess seeing how lonely the name looks on the tree, along with the letter from the bag, somehow pulled on my heart…. It's made me feel really sad, and I hope this girl's heart wasn't broken too badly."

"I'm sure it's just some prankster trying to yank our chain," said David. He moved over and wrapped his arms around her. "Who better to pull one over on than a pair of unsuspecting tourists like us?"

He gave her a wry smile and then looked around the ravine again, scanning for clues as to where a hoax perpetrator could have come and gone from. Only the broken grass and weeds from when he and Miriam had moved through the area earlier met his gaze. He suddenly thought about the unseen force that pushed him against the tree.

"We probably should be on our way, darlin'," he said, when she began looking at the bag again. *Definitely time to go. Time to get far, far away from this frigging creepy place.*

"Yeah…. Is there anything else near where you found this?"

He wanted to say 'no'. But, an imploring look flickered in her eyes. He bent down and groped through the grass. The cool blades brushed against the scratches on his palms, eliciting a brief tingle. He patted around to make his effort appear more convincing, and then touched something that almost made him jerk his hand back. *A small nut or pebble?* Ready to leave the object in the depths of the grass roots, it turned over in his grasp, and a sharp, jagged edge lashed at his fingers. Reluctantly, he lifted it out of the grass.

"Holy shit!" he gasped in surprise.

A broken bicuspid lay in his palm, covered by dried, crusted blood along one side.

Miriam walked over to him, her eyes wide in amazement as she looked at the tooth. "There's something really wrong here, David. We need to take this stuff to the visitors' center and have someone look at it.... We'd better tell them about the inscription on the tree, too."

Chapter Two

The blood drained from Tyler Hobbs's face as he looked toward the second floor of his family's spacious home in Littleton, Colorado.

"You're *so* busted, Ty!" Twelve-year-old Jillian Hobbs adjusted her oversized Denver Broncos sweatshirt, and turned to leave him in the backyard.

"Hey, *wait!*" he called after her. "Jill, come back here! *Please!*"

His sister didn't respond until she reached the deck, and only to show a tattletale smile. Despite the brisk weather's effect on her hip due to a chronic condition, she limped gleefully to the back door.

"Stop her, Chris!"

Tyler's urgent plea to his brother sitting on a bench next to the door went ignored. By the time Christopher looked up from his game device, she was already inside the house.

Damn it!

Frustrated, Tyler shook his head. Yes, he had just done the one thing his dad warned them to never do in the backyard. He kicked a football. Dad always said you could throw it. But, you could never, *ever* kick it.

"You shouldn't have kicked the ball, Ty," said Christopher. His nose reddened from the autumn chill, he waited for Tyler to step onto the deck and join him at the door. "Jill's right. Dad's going to *kill* you when he and Mom get home tomorrow!"

The youngest of the Hobbs children, he would be nine in November. He was five years younger than Tyler, who turned fourteen the past August.

"Yeah, I'm sure he will." Tyler sighed. *Just frigging great!* He opened the back door and motioned for Christopher to come inside. "Thanks a lot for being so helpful, you little twerp! Next time I need a favor—like stopping Jill from telling Auntie Jan what just happened—I'll be sure to keep you in mind."

Christopher looked at him with a pained expression. He began to sniff, which annoyed Tyler all the more. The older Hobbs boy ran his hands nervously through his thick brown hair. His brother was a sure bet to tell Auntie Jan the name he just called him. And right then in the living room, he heard Jillian give her a full report on the football incident.

Tyler hung his jacket on the hall tree in the foyer, and followed Christopher into the living room. Jillian stood next to the sofa where Janice Andrews sat. Auntie Jan was

Mom's best friend. A freelance editor, Mom once told him that the two of them had been friends since their freshman year at the University of Colorado, nearly two years before Mom met Dad, who attended the same school. Tyler's buddies considered Auntie Jan sort of hot—at least that's what they told him whenever they came over and she was around. Not bad for a thirty-something divorcee. Pretty and petite, with sandy hair and big brown eyes… he tried not to think of her that way.

"All right, Ty, tell me about the window," she said, frowning. She set aside the latest mystery galley she was working on. "Before you do, I want all three of you to stand in front of me, so I can see each of your faces. That way, I'll know who's telling me the truth about what just happened."

Janice motioned for them all to line up on the other side of the coffee table. When ready, she told Tyler to begin. He hesitated, glancing at his sister and brother. They stood on either side of him as troll-like sentries blocking the only path for escape, between the loveseat and coffee table. They were mini-versions of Dad, with the same blonde hair and deep hazel eyes. Tyler alone favored their mom, with blue eyes and dark hair.

Jillian and Christopher looked up with innocent, expectant eyes. They seemed detached from their roles in causing the world of doggy-doo Tyler found himself in.

"Well," he began, coughing nervously. "We were playing with the ball out back, and… I kicked it." The confession slipped out, but brought immediate relief. It was much better this way, instead of prolonging the inevitable. "I know none of us are supposed to do that, but I never intended to kick the ball so hard, or for it to go so high. But it did."

Janice nodded in response, her lips a thin line. "There's probably no way you can afford to fix the window, is there?"

He shook his head and lowered his eyes.

"He's going to be in *big* trouble when Dad finds out!" said Jillian, her tone solemn and worried, and for the moment devoid of the tattletale joy she spoke with earlier.

"Well, hopefully we can keep that from happening," said Janice, as she stood. "Let's take a look at the window, and go from there. All right?"

Tyler shrugged. Her stern look from a moment ago softened. It gave him hope things might work out after all.

"You really should be more careful," she continued, on the way upstairs. "But we all make mistakes. Just never make the same one twice."

They moved past Jillian and Christopher's bedrooms on the left side of the landing. Tyler's room sat at the end of the hallway. He insisted on going first. His two younger siblings rarely got to visit his private domain. Christopher, wide-eyed, surveyed the array of posters covering the walls. A couple of scantily clothed females made Jillian blush and Janice raise an eyebrow.

"Mom knows about them," he advised, after noticing their reaction. "There's the window."

He pointed to a large French-paned window facing the backyard. The damage wasn't as extensive as he had feared. Only one corner of the window was broken, the panes directly above and below bore small, web-like cracks.

"This might not be too bad." Janice moved to the window and took a closer look. Most of the glass shards were large enough to pick up safely, and only a few splinters remained on the windowsill and Tyler's desk. "Jill, would you mind grabbing the scissors and masking tape from the bottom shelf in the pantry downstairs?"

While Jillian left the bedroom, Tyler retrieved a cardboard box he no longer needed from his Guitar Hero game stashed inside the closet. His sister soon returned with scissors and tape.

"Now, give me a hand here and let's see if we can't repair this bad boy," said Janice.

She moved to the window and tested the strength of the two cracked panes. When satisfied they would hold for the time being, she turned her attention to the broken pane, making a rough estimate of the cardboard patch needed. With the kids' help, she completed the patch and secured it in place within fifteen minutes, and cleaned up the remaining glass shards and splinters.

"If David decides to dock your allowance for this, I'll pick up the tab, Ty," she offered. Grateful, he smiled and thanked her. "Since this is our last night together before your mom and dad return home, how does pizza and a movie sound?"

"Yeah-h-h-h! Thank you, Auntie Jan!" the younger kids shouted, followed by a hearty "Woo-hoo!" from Tyler.

* * * * *

Janice waited downstairs while the kids finished getting ready. She returned to her spot on the sofa in the living room, next to the fire that slowly died in the fireplace. The late afternoon sun had begun to set behind the foothills at the base of the Rockies. Its light diminished to a mere trickle through the main floor's back windows.

After turning on a table lamp, she pulled out a note from her galley that also served as a bookmark. It contained all of the pertinent memos and phone numbers Miriam had given her two days prior. On impulse, she picked up the phone, prepared to dial the number. But she noticed the 'EST' memo next to the phone number, and remembered the two-hour time difference between Littleton and Gatlinburg.

"Probably out on the town right about now, I imagine," she said quietly. "Enjoy yourselves, because there's a little surprise waiting here when you get home."

Chapter Three

"Hey, hon, what are you thinking about?"

Miriam reached across the table to gently grasp David's hand, bringing him back to the present.

"Huh? Sorry, babe," he said, sitting up in his seat and taking another sip from his beer.

Spending their last Gatlinburg dinner in one of the more expensive steak establishments, he smiled as he set the bottle on the table. She smiled and urged him to tell her what was on his mind.

He honestly didn't know where to begin, as the day's strange events filled his head like a spinning Roulette wheel. After they left the ravine and Cades Cove's forgotten Lover's Lane, and reached the edge of the meadow that separated John Oliver's property from the path leading to the ravine, she suggested they stop for a farewell photo. They hoped to find a passing tourist to take their picture. However, since it was almost the park's closing time, they found themselves alone.

Sunset approached quickly, and David insisted Miriam pose first. He managed to get two excellent shots of her standing in front of an incredible backdrop of the Smoky Mountains. She captured a great shot of him posing in the same place. The sun fell behind the mountains just as she snapped the picture. When they reached the parking lot adjacent to John Oliver's place, it sat deserted, except for their rented Chevy Malibu….

"Well… I'm waiting, Mr. Music."

"I'm still trying to put today's experience in its proper perspective," said David, once he defined the main theme fueling his rampant thoughts.

"I'm sure it's just a strange string of coincidences, which only seemed connected in some weird way," she said, and looked away. It was as if she'd already filed the event away in the recesses of her mind, and was unhappy to deal with it again. "Like we talked about earlier, maybe we just happened upon some stuff that had already been there for awhile."

David shrugged and took another sip.

"But, now that you've turned the bag and tooth over to the park service," she continued, "we no longer have to worry about it."

Ah… therein lies a problem, thought David, smiling at her. When they reached the visitors' center next to the Cable Mill, he was the one elected to give the items to a ranger.

For efficiency, he opened the bag and dropped the tooth inside. Once he stepped inside the building and up to the main information desk, he held out the bag for the park service employee behind the counter to take. The pudgy, middle-aged woman with thick eyeglasses was filling out a report.

Unsure if she was an actual ranger or not, David intended to give her the bag anyway. Right before she finished the report and would finally acknowledge his presence, a peculiar sensation came over him. He pulled his hand back, and by the time the woman looked up, he'd deposited the bag inside one of his coat pockets. The pocket already contained a pair of Indian arrowheads and an odd shaped piece of pyrite he found on the way to the ravine. Without saying a word, he turned and walked out of the visitors' center.

"So, what did they tell you?" asked Miriam, when he returned to the car.

He started to tell the truth, but sensed he shouldn't—or, more like *couldn't*—without somehow incurring a terrible consequence for doing so. With his mouth open and saying nothing for a moment, he lied.

"The lady I just spoke to said she'd take care of the bag and tooth."

Miriam frowned, and David feared the ruse would be uncovered.

"What did she think about what happened? You did tell her everything. Right?"

"Yeah, I told her," he said, worried he hadn't stayed inside the visitors' center long enough to make the story believable. "But, I'm not sure she took me seriously."

He hoped the clipped explanation sufficed, still wondering why he couldn't give the items away. And worse, he felt terrible lying to his beloved wife.

"Well, that takes care of it, then."

Miriam seemed relieved, and by the time they were on the main road, they were making dinner plans. They returned to the chalet, took a quick shower, and headed back into town to look for one of the nicer dinner venues….

"Thanks a lot for reminding me about that poor girl and her lost beau," said Miriam, as he nodded in silence across from her. "Can you picture how lonely she must've been out there in the cove?"

"Yeah, I imagine it was no picnic for her," he concurred, pausing to brush his fingers through his thick, blonde bangs. "I wonder when our food's coming?"

Ready to move on to other business, he wanted to forget about the strange afternoon, and enjoy their last night together in the quaint mountain town. Miriam seemed lost in her own thoughts as she stared at the flickering candle in the center of the table. When she looked up again, he could tell she had more questions. Luckily, their food arrived.

The conversation shifted to more pleasant subjects, and before long the issue of Allie Mae and her mysterious bag of treasures seemed truly behind them. After dinner, they walked along Gatlinburg's historic strip, where they picked up a few souvenirs for the kids and Janice. They walked back to the car hand in hand, enjoying the town's ambience and the crisp autumn evening.

The embers from their earlier passion were still warm upon returning to their secluded chalet, nestled on a heavily wooded hillside above the town. David thought it especially nice not having to worry about what the kids and neighbors might hear or even see, and Miriam soon let her desires run wild with his. They retired to the master suite just before midnight, holding each other close. The only interruption in their intimacy was when she set the bedside alarm for 7:00 a.m., as they planned to find a nice place for breakfast in Gatlinburg before flying home.

* * * * *

Ping!

David awoke.

Pi-i-i-n-n-ng!

There it was again. The sound came from the kitchen, located down the hall from the bedroom and across from the living room.

Ping!... Pi-i-i-n-n-ng!

Two distinct rings... like someone's fingernails were being flicked against a drinking glass in the kitchen. *An intruder?* He checked on Miriam, who slept soundly.

Ping!... Pi-i-i-n-n-ng!... PI-I-I-N-N-NG!

The rings were ominously spaced apart, and the loudness of the last one quickened his pulse. He slipped out of bed, quietly putting on his jeans, and grabbed one of the hiking boots to serve as a weapon. He ventured out of the bedroom, creeping down the hall toward the kitchen. Miriam had left a small nightlight on in the living room.

Ping!

Softer this time… whoever made the sound must've heard his approach. The small hairs along the back of his neck sprang to life. Danger was near. He checked inside the game room and bathroom, fearing a second intruder might also be in the chalet. Both sat empty.

Once he reached the living room, he tiptoed to the front door and then over to the sliding porch door. The extra bar restraints were still in place, and the locks set. As far as he could tell, nothing had been tampered with. That left only the back door in the kitchen as a possible breach.

Ping—

The last ring was abruptly muted once he walked through the dining room and peered into the kitchen. He flicked on the overhead light and stepped under its bright glare.

Nobody was there.

"What in the hell?" he whispered in bewilderment.

He moved to the far end of the kitchen, where the chalet's washer and dryer were hooked up, next to the back door. It was locked tight. Mystified, he prepared to leave the kitchen and investigate elsewhere. Two wineglasses from the previous afternoon were sitting on the counter next to the sink. He'd assumed that Miriam had already washed them and placed both inside the cupboard with the fancier glassware.

He picked up one of the glasses to examine it, flicking a finger against the side. A ring similar to the one he heard filled the air. He set the glass next to its mate and walked out of the kitchen, turning off the overhead light. Perplexed, he returned to the living room.

As he reached the hallway, one of the wineglasses slid noisily across the Formica countertop in the kitchen. A loud crash resounded as the glass exploded on the kitchen floor, waking Miriam.

"David? Are you all right?"

He didn't immediately answer, creeping toward the kitchen with his boot raised in readiness. Had the intruder been hiding beneath the dining room table? He glanced under the table. Only a toddler could successfully hide here, as the chairs were pushed in tightly.

"David?"

Miriam ran down the hall.

"I'm all right!" he called. "Stay back there!"

Knowing she'd ignore the warning, he moved quickly to secure the area, hoping to get the upper hand on whoever was in the chalet with them. The intruder had to be inside the kitchen. He turned on the kitchen's overhead light again just as Miriam reached his side. The only thing different from his last visit was the shattered wineglass upon the floor.

"What in the hell happened here?" she asked.

"I don't know."

He stared in disbelief. It was unmistakably the same glass he handled earlier. *Maybe I left it too close to the counter's edge, and it slipped off.* That would make logical sense, and a hell of a lot easier to go back to sleep after he cleaned up the mess. But the stem and larger pieces of the glass rested closer to the doorway where he and Miriam stood, nearly four feet from its mate on the counter.

"I thought I put those away."

She bent down to pick up the stem. Her hair disheveled and the nightgown loose, her shapely form and lovely nakedness were clearly visible. It made him especially worried about a depraved sexual predator cleverly hiding. Despite the likelihood of an earlier attack while they slept, it didn't mean one wasn't forthcoming. Someone *had* to be in the chalet… hiding somewhere.

David stepped carefully around the glass fragments and moved to the washer and dryer. He checked the back door again, and opened the pantry. When he looked inside the dryer and washer, it drew a curious look from her.

"What are you looking for, hon?"

"Just checking for something," he said, and opened the larger cabinets beneath both counters in the narrow kitchen.

"So, I take it that you weren't in here when this happened?"

She looked worried, and he realized she thought he made the mess, as if his nighttime clumsiness sent the glass tumbling to the floor.

"Actually, the glass is my fault," he told her, determined to ease her concern before it grew worse. If that happened, there would be no more sleep for her tonight.

He glanced at the clock on the stove. 12:46 a.m.

"I need to find something to clean up this mess."

The last cabinet revealed two rows of pots and pans.

No place to hide, which means no one's in here.

"The broom and dust pan are behind you," she said. "So, what's really going on here?"

"I just told you." He forced a lighthearted smile while moving to the broom and dustpan, next to the trash container. "I got up to get a drink, and I guess I set the glass too close to the edge before it fell onto the floor."

The look on her face said she didn't believe it, at least not entirely.

"And you needed *two* glasses for that?" She placed her hands on her hips.

Why does a woman notice everything?

"You must've forgotten to put them back up in the cupboard." To him it sounded plausible. "Since they looked clean, I decided to go ahead and use one."

From her expression, it appeared she believed him… almost. To further sell it, he cleaned up the mess. By the time he finished, she had placed the other glass back inside the cupboard and left the kitchen.

"We're going to have to pay for the glass, you know," she said. From the sound of her voice, she was on her way to the bedroom.

"Yeah, I guess so," he called after her.

The floor was clear of glass chips, and he surveyed the kitchen one last time. Clean and empty. He turned off the overhead light and stared into the darkness, waiting for whatever caused the disturbance to creep out from its hiding place. *Maybe,* he thought, *it was just a chipmunk rummaging for breadcrumbs.*

David backtracked through the chalet, making sure all the rooms were empty and every entrance secure. When satisfied, he crawled into bed with his wife. Miriam snored lightly, and he took that as a good sign. He stared into the bedroom's darkness for nearly half an hour. Every shadow had become suspect, and remained that way until his eyelids finally grew heavy enough to drift off to sleep.

All remained quiet, with only the steady breathing and occasional snores of David and Miriam Hobbs. Neither heard the glider rocker in one corner of the bedroom as it moved back and forth silently in the darkness. Nor were they aware of the shadowy figure sitting in the chair, keeping watch until the dawn's light peered in through the bedroom windows that Sunday morning.

Chapter Four

"Mommy! Daddy!"

Late Sunday afternoon, Christopher and Jillian ran to the front door of their Littleton home, upon seeing the edge of the first suitcase poke into the foyer. Tyler scrambled downstairs from his room once he heard the commotion, followed by Janice and the Hobbs' Yorkshire terrier, Sadie, from the kitchen. The dog demanded immediate attention, pawing at Miriam's pant legs while the youngest children hugged her tightly.

"I've missed you all *so* much!" Miriam embraced and kissed each of her children before moving on to hug Janice and give attention to Sadie as well. Meanwhile, David finished bringing in the rest of the luggage.

"Here, Dad, I'll help you carry these upstairs," offered Tyler, picking up one of the suitcases and a backpack. He hoisted them up the tall stairway to the second level. Not to be left out, Christopher asked if he could help, and David let him handle a smaller bag. That left one backpack for David, as Miriam wanted to keep the carry-on bags downstairs until everyone received their souvenirs.

Weary from the return trip home, David began to remove his coat while upstairs until he discovered several small lumps inside the front pocket. He pulled out the arrowheads and pyrite he brought home for the kids, and felt something else.

Oh, Jesus, I almost forgot!

Hurriedly, he fished the little cloth bag from Cades Cove out of the pocket. For some reason, the bag looked older, and the cross-stitched Allie Mae's Treasures in blue thread seemed to have faded as if it had been years since he discovered it by the oak tree, less than twenty-four hours earlier.

"Honey, are you ready to join us down here?"

Miriam's voice from the base of the stairs pulled his attention. From what he could tell by the other voices, his boys had returned downstairs.

"I'll be done in a minute."

Quick! Where to hide this frigging thing before she finds out I never gave it back!

He considered hiding the bag somewhere in his closet, or slipping inside a guestroom to hide it.

No, Miriam will find it for sure if I do that.... Ah, but this might work!

Moving to his dresser, he threw open the middle drawer. Home to all the handkerchiefs, neckties, and cufflinks he never used, it seemed perfect. He closed the drawer after tucking the bag deep inside, beneath the most hideous necktie of the bunch.

"Ooh, you scared me!" Miriam nearly lost her balance after he almost bowled her over coming out of the bedroom.

"Sorry, babe, I was on my way down. Couldn't forget the other souvenirs, right?" He showed her the arrowheads and pyrite in one hand while wrapping his other arm around her waist.

"Oh, I forgot about those." She seemed pleased he remembered. "Everyone's waiting on you, hon. Once we give the kids and Janice their souvenirs, how about we take them out for a nice coming home dinner?"

"Sure, why not."

David forced a broad smile, not sure why he felt like bad a little boy who had jus hid a cherished family keepsake he'd broken. Taking his wife's hand, he squeezed it tightly as they returned downstairs.

"Okay, Dad's here, everyone!" Jillian enthused. "So, what did you bring us from Gatlinburg?"

Jillian and Christopher's excitement made it easier to slip Tyler's leather coat to him without the younger kids noticing the obvious disparity between souvenirs. David had rehearsed a lame explanation to justify the more expensive teenager gift as compared to Jillian's handcrafted, Smoky Mountain rag doll and Christopher's authentic, Indian headdress and deerskin drum and mallet. He hoped the younger kids wouldn't immediately notice… but Jillian did. Once she saw the coat, her frown deepened and she started to cry.

"Tell you what, sweetie," he said, gently. "How about you pick the place where we'll go for dinner?"

It was the best he could think of on the fly, and she seemed uninterested. But then she started to smile. David suspected his wallet was about to pay more than just the difference between Jillian and Tyler's souvenirs.

"Casa Bonita!" she shouted.

"That's a wonderful idea," Janice agreed. "I'll pitch in some cash if you'd like."

He almost accepted until Miriam waved her off and shot him a perturbed glance, reminding him of an anniversary promise to lighten up on the kids and the budget. Instead of a less expensive outing to a burger or pizza joint, the restaurant known throughout the region as a Mexican food mini-Disneyland would deepen the dent in their expendable income.

After Miriam gave Janice her souvenir and a half-pound of Gatlinburg fudge, David handed an arrowhead each to Jillian and Christopher, while the pyrite piece went to Tyler.

Before long, the family piled into their minivan and headed north to the older section of Denver's sprawling metro area.

With the house to herself, Sadie jumped onto the sofa and curled up in front of the TV, which Jillian had changed to the Cartoon Network for her just before they left. She began to doze off… until a creak resounded on the stairway. Sitting up with ears perked high, she listened. A hazy form drifted into the living room and passed in front of the television, eliciting a low growl from the dog. Jumping down from the sofa, Sadie followed the shadowy presence into the kitchen with her teeth bared, launching a full assault of angry barks.

* * * * *

"Sadie? Oh, Sa-a-d-i-e-e-e!"

It was nearing eight o'clock. The Hobbs family returned home after dropping Janice off at her townhouse, where she had joked about gaining five pounds before morning from the Gatlinburg fudge.

"Sadie?" Jillian called again. She checked the kitchen, dining room, and the den before returning to the living room. "Where's the dog?"

The Cartoon Network blared loudly on the TV, but the sofa sat empty. David followed Miriam and Tyler into the house, with Christopher carried upon his shoulder.

"Sweetie, she's probably somewhere upstairs," David assured her. Christopher was fast asleep, and he laid him on the loveseat.

Jillian had already headed upstairs to look for the dog. Tyler paused long enough in the living room to change the TV channel to a gaming network before joining his sister in the search.

"Hey, son, we're not watching that stuff... not tonight!" David called after him. Tyler's groaned *'Oh, Dad!'* resounded mournfully from the second-floor landing. "I imagine he's had free rein around here since Thursday night."

"Who needs television when you've got me?" Miriam snuggled up to him, pressing her face beneath his jaw while caressing his neck with tender kisses.

"Hey, I found her!" Jillian announced shrilly from atop the stairs. "She's hiding under my bed, and I can't get her to come out!"

"Hold that thought, my dear," David whispered. He returned her kisses until Jillian called again. "We're coming!"

From downstairs, they heard the dog's whimpers along with Tyler's urgings for Sadie to come to him. By the time David and Miriam reached Jillian's bedroom, Tyler was halfway underneath Jillian's canopy bed.

"She's *not* going to come to you!" said Jillian confidently, crouched next to her brother. "I bet the only person she'll listen to is Mom."

"Oh, yeah?" Tyler retorted, his voice muffled.

"Maybe Jill's right, guys." Miriam lifted the bedspread to take a peek. Sadie lay curled in one corner panting, on the opposite side of the bed from where Jillian's and Tyler's faces peered at her. "Come here, baby girl."

The dog whined until Miriam pulled Sadie out and gathered her in her arms.

"Oh my God, she's shaking!" Miriam looked over at David. "Come here and feel how she's trembling."

He came to where she stood, near Jillian's nightstand. A beautiful purebred Yorkshire terrier, Sadie's long brown hair covered most of her body, except for her head, which was a mixture of rust and blonde. Her dark brown eyes always seemed to sparkle in the light, but they were half-open as she continued to shake.

"Is she sick?" David lovingly stroked the dog's neck, which usually brought a soft grumble of pleasure, where Sadie would lean into his hand for a good scratching. Not this time.

"I'm not sure," said Miriam, worriedly. "It's almost like something scared the hell out of her."

She started to carry Sadie out of the bedroom, and immediately the dog clawed to get down. Miriam stooped and released her, and Sadie immediately crawled under the bed.

"Maybe we should call the vet." David watched Tyler and Jillian resume their contest to see whom the dog preferred most.

"No… I don't think that's going to do any good." Miriam glanced around the room nervously. "Would you mind taking a look around to make sure nothing's out of place?"

"Sure." He could tell that she wanted him to check the entire house for evidence of a break-in, which might've happened while they were gone. A string of burglaries had hit their peaceful community two months earlier. "I'll be right back."

David thoroughly checked both floors and the garage, and took a quick stroll around the yard. Nothing seemed out of place, although it felt a little eerie walking through leaves up to his ankles in the darkness and hearing them crunch beneath his shoes. Next weekend would be spent raking the leaves, if his self-absorbed teenager didn't miraculously offer to do it before then.

Satisfied there wasn't a prowler hanging around, he went back inside. He checked all the doors and windows on the main floor, and returned to the living room to get Christopher. Groggy and disoriented, David assisted him in negotiating the long stairway to his bedroom. Soon after, Tyler retired, promising to wind down before his ten o'clock bedtime. Jillian often fought to stay up later, but that night she didn't put up a fuss.

"It's just you and me now, my love," David whispered from behind Miriam. He blew softly on her neck, as she stood waiting for him with her back to him, in their bedroom doorway. She pulled him inside, and after he closed the door and locked it, they embraced. Their foreplay intensified, and he carried her to the bed, where they made passionate love for the second night in a row.

Chapter Five

"Billy Ra-a-a-y-y-y...."

"Huh?" David woke lying on his back.

Miriam had already moved to her side of the bed. They had made love for more than an hour before calling it a night. He remembered that much. But something had changed in the room. The bedroom door stood ajar, and the glow from a light source carved a narrow sliver up to their bed.

"Damn it, Ty!" he hissed, thinking his son had left the hall light on, after visiting the bathroom or getting a drink from the kitchen downstairs.

His wife stirred briefly and rolled away from the light. The digital clock on her nightstand read 12:33 a.m. He rubbed his eyes and looked again, irritated at being awakened at half past midnight for the second consecutive night. *Tomorrow's really going to suck!*

"Come he-e-r-r-r-e-e-e!"

"Who said that?"

David got out of bed and pulled on his pants. The words had been whispered, and the voice sounded as if it belonged to a young woman standing in the hallway outside the bedroom.

He crept to the doorway, suddenly remembering the door had been locked. He tried to recall if Miriam unlocked it after they had made love, which she often did, in case the kids needed her during the night. However, she almost never left the door open, since she struggled to fall asleep. Peering into the hallway, there was no sign of anyone on the landing. That's when he noticed the light above the stairway was also on.

What in the hell? I turned off everything up here earlier. I'm certain of it.

Pushing the bedroom door aside to slip through, he stepped into the hallway and quietly closed the door. He checked each room on the second floor, starting with Jillian's bedroom. She slept soundly. Sadie, curled up at her feet, lifted her head when he opened the bedroom door and then rested it on Jillian's shin as he shut it again.

Christopher snored from exhaustion, and when he checked on Tyler, he noticed the cardboard triangle on his window under the hall light's illumination. The camouflage of the orange-eyed, black spider gracing the patch made the cracked panes look like a believable Halloween spider-web creation.

Satisfied his oldest son lay asleep, he closed the door and moved to the guestroom and bathroom. Both were empty. Bewildered, he stroked his beard while walking back to his bedroom. He heard the girl's voice again.

"I'm not up th-e-e-r-r-e. I'm down he-e-e-r-r-e!"

A chill ripped across his spine. The voice sounded hollow, as if the words were spoken from far away. Yet, the voice also sounded as if it resonated from beneath the landing, perhaps the dining room on the main floor. His first instinct was to grab the handgun stashed in his nightstand, but his machismo took over. He ran downstairs.

The entire main level was immersed in darkness. The kitchen and living room nightlights were off. The security system was armed. David turned on the dining room chandelier and the living room's overhead light.

"Are ya afraid, Billy Ray-y-y?"

Billy Ray? Who in the hell is that?

"Who's in here!" he called out, gruffly.

Except for an incredibly cold breeze embracing his face and torso, there was no other response. Just unnerving silence, as if the house itself held its breath in anticipation of what would come next. He walked into the kitchen from the living room, flipping on a row of fluorescent lights. The kitchen was empty. There was no one in the laundry room, either. Ditto for the den.

"Come out and show yourself, damn it!"

He grabbed one of the larger knives from a wooden cutlery block next to the stove, and wielded it menacingly. After circling through the main floor, he explored the garage. Nothing. Worried the mysterious female might harm his family while they slept, he raced to the foyer and up the stairs. He almost fell down the staircase when the mysterious voice cackled gleefully from a few feet behind him.

David whirled around. There wasn't anyone else on the stairs.

The knife ready, he slowly moved downstairs. For the moment, the evasive female kept silent.

Despite several more trips around the entire floor in hopes of drawing her out from her hiding place, she remained hidden. Weary of the game, David waited in the living room. The clock on the mantle read 1:05 a.m. With too much adrenaline flowing to allow him to go back to sleep, he turned on the TV and set the volume low. Perched on the edge of the sofa, he suffered through three late-night infomercials while waiting for something else to happen.

Just before two-thirty, after one last uneventful tour of the main floor, he returned the knife to the cutlery block in the kitchen and turned off the television, along with all of the downstairs lights. The earliest morning birds outside began singing in earnest as he trudged upstairs. But before he reached the second-floor landing, a high-pitched ring emanated from the dining room.

P-i-i-i-n-n-g-g-g!

With his heart racing, David tiptoed down the stairs again and crept to the dining room. He half-expected the ringing sound to stop when he flicked on the switch to the chandelier. It didn't. The noise resonated from a large crystal bowl gracing the middle of the dining room table. Dumbfounded, he stared at the bowl, listening to the reverberations until they died.

Why in the hell is this happening to us?

The room grew chillier as he stood there.... David felt as if unseen and menacing eyes suddenly surrounded him. He shivered as he considered the connection between tonight's events and what happened in Gatlinburg. As much as his pragmatic mind hated the idea, too many similarities said so.

What about the voice, and who did it belong to? Was it even real? If it wasn't, was this what happened to someone at the onset of insanity? Maybe all the tireless hours he'd worked the past few months had finally caught up with him.

"This is just *too* crazy." He laughed uneasily and turned off the chandelier, backing slowly from the dining room. The unsettling feeling followed him, hovering as a thick heaviness as he paused in the foyer's darkness.

Looking over his shoulder, no one followed him upstairs. Even so, the hairs on the back of his neck didn't stop tingling until he climbed back into bed and pulled up the covers. When he heard the mischievous female's laughter again, coming from downstairs, he told himself over and over it wasn't real. Thankfully, it became harder to keep his eyes open. Once he succumbed to sleep, it seemed like a matter of minutes before Miriam's alarm signaled the start of the new week.

Chapter Six

"Come on, kids, we don't want to be late!" urged Miriam, motioning for Jillian and Christopher to gather their book bags and lunch boxes.

She walked briskly up to David, who stood next to the coffeepot in the kitchen. Sipping his second cup of coffee, he paused to give her a kiss.

"I had a great time this weekend," he whispered in her ear. "If you're up for some fun later tonight, you know where to find me." He added a wink.

"Oh, yeah, big boy? It looks like you could use some serious rest."

She gazed into his eyes, and he was painfully aware she noticed the redness under them from the few hours of sleep he had missed last night.

"A few more cups of petrol, and I'll be good for the entire day!" He forced a wry smile.

"Yeah, right."

She turned away and headed for the foyer.

"Bye Daddy! Bye Ty!" said Jillian and Christopher, just before they exited the house. Jillian stuck her head back in through the doorway. "I like your coat, Ty!"

"Wow, son… now that looks great!" Miriam agreed, just before leaving. She stopped to admire her eldest child decked out in his new leather jacket as he sauntered into the kitchen. "The girls won't be able to keep their hands off you, and your buddies will wish they had it so good, huh?"

Tyler blushed, smiling shyly as he pulled out a package of chocolate Pop Tarts from the pantry and pouring himself a glass of milk from the fridge.

"Well, we'll see you both tonight," she said, prodding Jillian back outside. "'Love you!"

Tyler and his dad echoed her sentiment, and soon the sound of the minivan faded into the distance.

"We should be on our way, too, Studly." David patted his son on the shoulder. "I'll take Sadie outside to do her business, which should give you enough time to finish your breakfast. Are you sure that'll be enough to tide you over until lunch?"

"Yeah, it should be, Dad," said Tyler, working on his second Pop Tart. "I'll meet you out front by the car."

Sadie ran into the kitchen from the living room when David called her. The dog jumped up into his arms, and he carried her outside. Once finished and back inside, she collected her treat and immediately climbed to her favorite spot on the sofa, curling up and facing the TV. She cocked her head as if reminding him to set the station to the Cartoon Network.

With the dog situated, he gathered his briefcase and coat. Before he set the security system, he glanced around the living room and peered into the dining room. Sadie seemed happy, and nothing seemed amiss. The previous night's odd experience seemed more and more unreal in the light of day. He shrugged sheepishly, believing it had everything to do with lack of sleep that weekend coupled with an overactive imagination. He stepped outside, locking the front door behind him.

"Are you ready to rock n' roll, son?" he asked, once he reached the black BMW Z4. Whoever took Tyler to school got to drive it for the day. "Today, with that jacket this ride definitely matches your look."

"Maybe… but please don't call me 'Studly' in front of my friends," he pleaded, as they climbed into the car.

"No problem… Johnny Bravo," teased David. Tyler shot him an irritated look. "Okay, I'll quit."

For the next several minutes they rode in silence. Tyler scanned the car's stereo until he found his favorite station, an alternative rock venue that brought a smile to David's face. While most men his age preferred nineties music, the rocker in him still liked the latest sounds.

"So, you and Mom had a great time, I take it," said Tyler.

"Yeah, we did," said David. "The next time we visit Tennessee, I'd like to take you kids with us."

"What's so special about Tennessee, other than the fact you were born there?" he asked, disdainfully. "Without the Titans, Grizzlies, and the Predators, what else is there? It's not like there's a Universal Studios, and there isn't a beach either."

"True," agreed David, seeing more and more of his own cynicism in his son. "I admit there wasn't a whole hell of a lot to do in Chattanooga when I was a kid, and things haven't changed much since then. But, Gatlinburg—now that's a place with plenty to do."

"Hmmm... the pictures on the web that Auntie Jan showed us were nice, but mostly of mountains that would only count as foothills here in Colorado. The 'Strip' looked pretty cool, though, and maybe a few rides at Dollywood might be worth checking out. Still, I dunno…."

Despite Tyler's smug smile, David could tell he was intrigued enough not to completely pan the idea of a family vacation trip to the Tennessee side of the Great Smokies.

"There are ghosts, too," said David, immediately wondering where in the hell the thought came from. Even more, why in the hell did he voice such an absurd notion? It didn't take long to regret it.

"Really?" Tyler perked up. The fact they arrived at Goddard Middle School was the only thing that saved David from a deeper explanation. "Tell me about the ghosts in Tennessee, Dad."

"It'll have to wait for another time, son. There's Jarrod and Smitty."

David pointed to Tyler's two best friends. He watched his son walk with them to the school's main entrance, so proud of the boy becoming a young man. And, as Miriam had prophesied, several girls came up to Tyler and admired his new jacket, while Jarrod and Smitty looked on with apparent envy.

* * * * *

Norm Sowell leaned over David's desk at Johnson, Simms & Perrault, the accounting firm they worked for. Deeply tanned and strikingly handsome with piercing blue eyes, thick dark hair, and a disarming smile, Norman Sowell III fit the perfect image of corporate success in an Armani suit. David's best friend outside of Miriam, he had built an impressive resume from his tireless drive as the firm's top attorney. Pals for nearly twenty years, shortly after they met as incoming freshmen football players at the University of Colorado, their mutual love of sports and the great outdoors attracted them to Boulder. Like David, Norm hailed from the southern part of the country, in his case, Tupelo, Mississippi.

"So, how was your trip, bro?"

"Great," said David. "Honestly, I'd have to say it was one of the best times Miriam and I've shared in the past ten years."

"Good for you, David," said Norm, sounding slightly surprised. "You seem happier than before you left, so if that's what adds the spice back into your love life, then more power to you." He nodded as if impressed. "How about we shoot for twelve-thirty for lunch?"

"Sounds good," said David. "I'll meet you out front. I brought the 'Z' today, so we can get back here before Ned sends out a posse looking for me."

He lowered his eyeglasses, which he only wore when working, grinning slyly in reference to Norm's penchant for long lunches to take care of personal business.

"That'll work," said Norm, chuckling as he started down the hall toward the legal department. "See you then!"

It was a very busy morning, and the lack of sleep on top of such an enjoyable, and yet strange, weekend made it hard for David to focus. Nonetheless, by noon he managed to make a serious dent in the mound of paperwork stacked upon his desk. His boss, Ned Badgett, came by just before he planned to meet Norm for lunch.

"It's good to have you back, David," he said, squeezing his shoulder. "Did you find the place we talked about?"

"Yeah, I did." David smiled, and for an instant thought about Allie Mae's Treasures and the lonely 'Allie +' carved into the oak. "The spot was as special as you said it'd be. Thanks again for the advice, Ned."

David was momentarily unaware his smile had faded, and consciously boosted it with happier thoughts.

"No problem at all." Ned studied David's face as if trying to define the subtle change in demeanor. Still, he seemed pleased by his report.

Significantly older than all of his subordinates, Ned did little to minimize the fact. His gray, thinning hair and drooping jowls clearly announced he had passed the short end of sixty. A driven perfectionist, he took an instant liking to David when he joined the firm after Norm successfully recruited him away from Blakely & Jones, a much smaller accounting firm, four years earlier. Ned planned to retire soon and groomed David to step into his role as manager of the mortgage services department. Like him, Ned grew up in rural Tennessee and went to college in Colorado, in his case the University of Denver. Their common heritage helped create a bond of mutual kinship.

"I'll take it easy on you today, and let you get through the rest of the King's Inc. reports Nancy brought up here earlier." Ned glanced at the shrinking pile on David's desk. "We've got the Applewood Associates audit coming up Thursday, so we'll want to go over the preliminaries on that tomorrow."

After Ned returned to his office, David locked his laptop. He glanced at his watch. *12:31 already…. Shit!* Grabbing his coat, David breezed through the row of cubicles, intent on catching Norm before his buddy harassed him for being late. Instead of the elevator, he took the stairs to the main floor of the historic building. The stately Victorian mansion located near the heart of downtown Denver had been renovated six years earlier, with ten offices on the main floor and another six upstairs.

The upper landing overlooked a grand foyer and was graced by an immense stained-glass window dominating the back wall of the building, next to the elevator. Featuring an angel blowing a trumpet, David often wondered if the mansion had originally been a church turned into a home as an afterthought. On either side of the landing stood a double oak staircase of exquisite workmanship from the late nineteenth century.

He ran past a marble fountain directly below the landing's balcony. At the reception desk, Nancy Geddings, the firm's chief admin, was busy reviewing invoices from a recently delivered supply shipment. He asked if she had seen Norm. She excused herself from her assistant and came to where he stood. A beautiful woman of Haitian descent, who preferred to dress conservatively with her hair in a severe bun, she often gave the firm's clientele the incorrect first impression of a stern, matronly woman.

"He was here a moment ago," she advised, her warm voice sweetened by a strong island accent. "There he is."

Peering around a large potted fig tree obstructing her view of the building's front section, she pointed to Norm standing just outside the main entrance. David's footsteps echoed across the parquet floor as he hurried over to him.

"I thought you might've forgotten," said Norm, as soon as David joined him on the patio. Norm took one last drag from his cigarette and mashed the butt on top of the stone lion closest to him, flicking it onto the front lawn. "How about Mario's today?"

"I can go for Italian, I guess," said David, leading the way to his car.

On the way to the restaurant, Norm brought David up to date on what he'd missed since last week, which consisted of several new clients and the two corporate audits in progress. He included the latest hot little thing that fell within range of his radar. A dedicated hedonist since college, Norm had just begun detailing his latest sexual conquest when they reached Mario's parking lot. In most other ways like brothers, David hated the continual reports on Norm's sex life.

"So, did you ever find the place Ned told you about?" Norm asked lightheartedly, once they were seated at a semi-private table in a corner, and had ordered lunch and a couple of Heinekens.

"Actually, we did," said David, which brought another surprised response from Norm. "I guess he's not as full of bullshit as you've thought, huh?"

"I guess not," he agreed, nodding before taking a long drink from his beer. "I suppose you're not going to tell me the finer points I'm just dying to hear about. Are you, now?" He grinned playfully.

"I never have before," David replied, smiling coyly. He paused to take a quick sip from his beer. "Let's just say ole Ned Badgett's Lover's Lane in Cades Cove, hidden away in the Great Smoky Mountain wilderness, was the best damned place to reignite the spark we've been missing lately."

He took a bigger drink while Norm nodded his head as if somewhat envious. David knew better. The matter would disappear from the landscape of Norm's sullied mind before they made it back to the office, replaced by a more lurid fantasy.

"Well, it's too bad the place is so goddamned far away," said Norm, allowing for sly grin wide enough to reveal the full line of expensive veneers. "I suppose the next lonely legal assistant I screw will have to settle for the spa in Glenwood Springs, or a little ole chalet in Aspen."

"I suppose so," David agreed, wishing for a moment Norm could relate to his monogamous orientation.

The conversation's focus shifted to business once their food arrived, and they returned to the office by two o'clock. David attacked the remaining stack of paperwork with a vengeance. Hoping to get through it all by six, he worked without a break and thought he might successfully reach that goal, when he received a call from Nancy just before five o'clock.

"Who is it, Nan'?" he said, tersely into the phone's receiver.

"It's Miriam," she replied, sounding worried. "I know you're swamped, but your wife says she needs to speak with you right away. It's an emergency."

* * * * *

"'See if you can transfer my appointments from three-thirty on up to four-thirty to Eileen and Jim, will you, Mary?"

Miriam hurriedly removed her white office coat, being mindful to grab her stethoscope and penlight before handing the coat to Mary Lavoi. She placed the tools inside her top desk drawer, and reached for her purse and jacket next to the chair.

"Is it that bad?" asked Mary.

Her light, gray eyes misted with concern. She pushed her glasses further up the bridge of her nose. Miriam's longtime assistant stood by the door to her boss's office holding Miriam's work coat. Tall and slender, with fragile bones from arthritis that belied her face and dark hair's youthful appearance, Mary seemed unsure of whether to hang up the coat and get busy making arrangements for Miriam's patients or give her a hug.

"I don't know yet," said Miriam, rushing to the doorway. "But it's been a long time since I've heard Jill cry like that!"

It had been a crazy day at Littleton Children's Clinic, the pediatric practice she shared with two other physicians. Most of her patients from the previous Thursday and Friday had insisted on seeing only her, crammed in between other appointments.

And now this to top it off!

"Go on home." Mary placed a hand gently on her shoulder. "I'll take care of everything, Miriam. It will all work out fine." She smiled and limped toward the clinic's reception area.

"Thanks, Mary, you're a life saver," Miriam said, and headed to the building's side exit that opened to the employee parking lot. "I'll call you as soon as I find out more about what's happening at our house."

Miriam nearly ran to where her Chrysler minivan waited. Meanwhile, Mary watched her boss carelessly speed out of the parking lot through a small window next to the clinic's fax machines. She frowned and shook her head until the minivan disappeared from view.

Chapter Seven

"It's your turn to take Sadie out, Chris," said Tyler, raising his head above the cushioned top of the sofa. His brother and sister had just arrived home from school.

"Why didn't you take her out when you got home, Ty?"

Christopher laid his backpack next to his sister's in the dining room before moving into the kitchen for a snack. The clock read 2:48 p.m. He peered into the living room and frowned at his older brother lying on the sofa with his eyes glued to the television.

"I did," said Tyler, his tone perturbed. "But she's over here whining like she needs to go out again."

Christopher grumbled an inaudible response and called Sadie. Rather than jump up and paw at his knees like she normally did, she curled up at his feet with her tail tucked between her legs.

"Did you make a mess in here, Sadie?" he asked sweetly.

As if his tone was serious, she looked up meekly. Worried, he began investigating the main floor, and the dog followed him until he reached the dining room. Sadie stopped and growled.

"It's all right, girl. What's wrong?" he asked. She whined in response before letting him pick her up. He carried her into the dining room, searching for a mess. But, he didn't see or smell any dog urine or feces. He shivered from a cold draft. "Let's go outside, Sadie."

He carried her to the back door, and once outside she climbed out of his arms. She seemed okay, so he let her roam the backyard while he turned to go inside. Jillian waited for him in the doorway.

"Mom said this morning that Auntie Jan will be by to check on us between four-thirty and five," she advised. "She wants us to have our homework done before she gets here."

"What about Ty?" Christopher asked, brushing past her on his way inside. "He has to do his homework, too."

"Already done." Tyler raised his head above the sofa's cushions again, so they could both see him from the kitchen. "All that's left for me is to study for a history quiz on Wednesday."

"Why are you always *so* lucky?" Jillian glanced at the load of books visible within the mesh sides of her backpack, as it leaned against the dining room doorframe. Life as a sixth grader was so unfair. "I can't wait until I'm in the eighth grade!"

"Yeah, well it'll probably be a lot harder for you then, too, since I'm the one with all the brains in this family."

"That's *not* true and you know it!" she fumed. She grabbed a Gatorade from the refrigerator and picked up her backpack, slinging it over her shoulder before walking into the living room. She paused next to the TV. "When Mom gets home, I'm telling her what you said. Come on, Chris!"

She motioned for Christopher to follow and stepped toward the foyer and stairway. He remained in the living room, mesmerized by the same cartoon that engrossed Tyler.

"Chris!"

"Huh?... Oh, I'll do my homework here in the living room, Jill," he said, and went to the dining room to get his backpack.

"Suit yourself!" she called to him disdainfully, as she climbed the stairs. "If you're not done with your homework by the time Auntie Jan's here, I'll let her know you've been goofing off watching that stupid show!"

She reached the landing and limped down the hallway to her bedroom. The stairs always made it hard on her hip, but she insisted on her bedroom being on the second floor with everyone else—despite her dad's offer to make the den the very best room in the house for her. Once inside, she closed the door and laid out the books on the bed by subject matter. She planned to systematically attack her studies in hopes of enough time leftover to visit her closest friend, Marianne Stevens, who lived directly across the street. She set the Gatorade down on the nightstand and picked up her iPod, pulling the headphones over her ears. Then she sat on the bed in front of her books.

Knock... knock... knock.

"Who's there?"

No response. She got up from the bed and went to her door. There wasn't anyone there.

"Chris? Ty?" She peered down the hall in either direction.

The hallway was empty. She heard her brothers downstairs commenting on the coolness of a wicked battle scene in a "Naruto" re-run on TV. She shrugged and closed the door. As she got comfortable on the bed, another three knocks resounded.

"Who keeps doing that?" Irritated, she remained seated on the bed. She pictured her brothers snickering quietly on either side of her doorway, waiting for her to open the door and step into the hallway, so they could give her a good scare. "I'm not at all amused or afraid, so why don't you go back downstairs!"

Jillian stared at the door when she received no response, debating whether to open it again. Her leg muscles were tensed in preparation to leap from the bed and hobble to the door once her annoying siblings knocked again.

Knock... Knock... KNOCK!

The force of the last knock shook the door and caused her to shrink back. More angry than afraid, she jumped off the bed and stomped to the door, where she swung it open. Again, no one was there.

You guys think you're so-o-o smart!

She stormed out of her room and quickly invaded Tyler and Christopher's bedrooms. Jillian checked the closets and under their beds, thinking she'd find them hiding there. When she couldn't find either one, she boldly moved through the bathroom and guestrooms. She even checked her parents' bedroom and master bath.

As she passed by the top of the stairs, she heard her brothers' boisterous laughter erupt from the living room. *How'd they get back down there so fast?* She paused to listen, until her anger got the better of her.

"You both had better stop messing with me!" she yelled down the stairway. "*You hear me?*"

"What in the hell?" Tyler replied from the living room.

She heard him get off the couch and soon saw his tousled hair as he peered up the stairs.

"What are you talking about?" he asked. Christopher's face appeared in the stairway beneath Tyler's chin. "We've been down here watching TV, which is a heck of lot more interesting than bothering you!"

"Yeah, right!" She folded her arms across her chest like their mom would do when agitated. "I'm supposed to believe it was the boogey-man up here knocking on my door, huh?"

"We don't know what you're talking about, Jill," said Tyler, smugly. "Sounds like a personal problem to me."

"Oh, yeah? Well, jerk, if you mess with me again, then *you* get to be the one to tell Auntie Jan why I didn't have enough peace and quiet to get my homework *done!"*

Tyler rolled his eyes as he and Christopher returned to the living room.

Jillian stormed to her bedroom and slammed the door. She angrily climbed onto the bed, where it took a moment to regain her composure. When ready to resume her homework, she slipped on the headphones to the iPod. She paged through the math book, a pencil in her mouth and the latest Justin Timberlake tune playing in her ears, when something heavy slammed against her door.

It shook the wall on either side of the door. She had been looking at her book, but peripherally saw the door buckle inward for an instant, to the point it might splinter.

That's pretty weird.... What would make it do that?

Her anger quickly evaporated, giving way to instinctive fear. Something was terribly wrong here. She removed the headphones and slowly got off the bed, holding her pencil in front of her as a weapon for protection from whatever lurked on the door's other side.

"Is that you, Ty? Chris?"

Her mouth felt dry as sandpaper, and she prayed they were the pranksters. When no one responded, she forced herself to move forward, her legs acting as if they had become lead weights. She opened the door cautiously.

Craning her neck into the deserted hall, she looked both ways. Meanwhile, she heard her brothers laughing downstairs in the living room. It seemed unlikely they had done this.

More like impossible.

She stepped into the hall and almost called to them. But she would never hear the end of it if either one saw her this frightened. She returned to her bedroom, looking over her shoulder as she stepped inside.

After closing the door, the hair on the back of her neck began to rise and tingle. An incredible chill crossed her left side near where her dresser sat, creating two waves of gooseflesh along her left arm and leg. The feel of her bedroom had changed. Always the coziest room in the house during winter, and a problem in summer when the sun's heat pelted the back windows mercilessly, now frigid unfriendliness embraced every inch.

While deciding whether to flee or stay, three more evenly spaced knocks resounded. This time they came from *inside* the Queen Anne styled dresser, an heirloom from her mother's side of the family.

She let out a frightened yelp and dropped the pencil on the floor, where it rolled under her bed. The dresser began to shake, growing steadily more violent until the legs lifted into the air. It slammed heavily upon the floor with a deafening crash. Unable to move at first, Jillian stumbled past the possessed antique and back into the hallway. Screaming.

Chapter Eight

David arrived home shortly after six o'clock. The autumn sun had dipped below the foothills, and darkness shrouded the metropolitan sprawl that included Littleton. The porch and security lights were on, and the fact Tyler had already taken the past week's bagged garbage out to the curb brought a smile to his face. The large trash container barely held the extra Chinese take-out and pizza boxes his kids had subsisted on since the past Thursday, when he and Miriam flew to Tennessee.

He thought about the latest conversation with Miriam, over the phone, and his smile faded. His daughter's pleas in the background for him to come home right away were what compelled him to leave work early. Jillian preferred her mom when it came to seeking comfort. But she always came to him when she wanted protection, and that worried him. After promising Ned his work would be caught up by the next night at the latest, he grabbed his coat, laptop, and briefcase, and then left the office.

"I'm glad you're here," said Miriam, right after he stepped through the front door. "Sorry about this."

Jillian's head rested on her mom's lap as they sat together on the sofa, her eyes red from tears. Tyler sat in the recliner, his attention entirely absorbed by the game device he held. Christopher was drawn to the same diversion, and stood next to the chair as he looked over his brother's shoulder. Only Janice seemed as upset as Miriam and Jillian, seated in the loveseat.

"It's okay, babe," said David.

He hung his coat on the hall tree and joined everyone in the living room.

"Everything's going to be fine, sweetie," he assured Jillian, pausing to kiss Miriam and massage his daughter's shoulder. "Your mom told me that you heard something in your room. Would you like to tell me about it?"

Jillian sniffed and nodded.

"Nothing happened, Dad," said Tyler, without looking up from the game he played. Christopher nodded an emphatic agreement to his brother's assessment.

"You weren't there!" Outraged, Jillian sat up, pointing at them accusingly. Miriam restrained her from going after them.

"That'll be enough, Ty!" scolded David. "I asked Jillian what happened—*not* you. As soon as I get her story, you and Chris can fill me in on other details."

"Yes, sir," said Tyler, sullenly. He paused to cast a mournful look toward his dad.

"All right, Jill," said David. "Tell me what happened."

"Someone was in my room today." She cleared her throat. "They knocked on my door and then got mad. They slammed something against it, and whatever it was shook the entire wall!"

She looked into his face, imploring him with glistening green eyes to believe her.

"I couldn't see who it was…. It was like they were invisible!"

First the dog, then me last night, now my baby girl? Dismayed, he wondered again about the taunting voice he heard while everyone else slept. Maybe he didn't imagine it after all. He nodded and gazed up at the ceiling while picturing what happened upstairs that afternoon.

"Are you done, Jill?" Tyler turned off his game player and retracted the recliner in one fluid movement. He glared at his sister. "If you are, I'd like to give Dad some valuable information before he wastes most of tonight looking for someone he'll never find!"

Jillian's face flushed with anger, and she seemed ready to lash out again.

"It'll be all right, Jill," Miriam whispered in her ear. "Daddy will take care of this. Trust him."

"Go ahead, Ty," said David, evenly. "Let's hear what you've got to add to this."

"Well, Dad, first let me point out that me and Chris spent the *entire* afternoon down here in the living room. And, yet, Jill accused us of knocking on her door." He paused to look over at Jillian again. "She accused us of doing it *twice!* We stayed downstairs, like I said. We never heard any knocks, and we certainly didn't hear the big bang she claims shook her wall. God knows we would've heard it, or at least felt something in the living room if that really happened."

Jillian began to weep again, and Miriam pulled her closer.

"All right, son," said David, unsure what to believe. What Tyler said made sense. "How about you, Chris? Is that also your version of what happened this afternoon?"

"Yeah." His uneasy glance flitted from Tyler to Jillian. He was obviously torn by allegiance to both.

"Are you sure?" David persisted.

"Yes, Daddy." He looked down at his feet and wouldn't raise his eyes.

David nodded thoughtfully before turning his attention to Janice.

"Did you see or hear anything unusual, Jan?"

"No, I didn't," she said. "The excitement was over by the time I got here, other than Jill being so upset. Miriam was already home, checking every room in the house with Ty.

Maybe, it's just a plumbing problem or the house settling. I've read where that can happen out of the blue sometimes."

She added an optimistic smile, although her eyes looked worried. Miriam nodded to confirm she agreed with Janice's suggestion.

"Tell you what, Jill," he said, returning his attention to her. "Why don't we eat dinner, and then Daddy will go upstairs and take a look. I *promise* to get rid of whatever's up there, sweetie. What do you say to that?"

Her face immediately brightened. David knew she firmly believed in his ability to fix everything. She smiled and stood up, hugging him tightly.

Smiling, he wished he could enjoy the moment as her hero. He now had a tall order to fulfill, since fixing the problem meant truly understanding it first, which he didn't. David confidently looked around the living room while holding her close. But he was unable to push aside the nagging worry things could soon get worse.

* * * * *

Once dinner ended, he picked up a flashlight and rubber hammer from the garage. As an afterthought, he added a handful of small mousetraps left over from last spring, when Christopher stumbled onto a mouse nest in one corner of the garage. He strolled past his family on the way upstairs. He wanted his younger kids to notice what he carried, so they'd sleep well that night. Hell, he couldn't afford another sleepless night himself. If the kids or Miriam couldn't sleep that night, he'd be screwed the next day.

Everything upstairs seemed to be in good working order. That's what he expected to find. He hoped the charade of setting up mousetraps in each bedroom would ease his daughter's worries until he could come up with a better plan. He added a few traps in the guestrooms and master bedroom for good measure.

As he stepped into his and Miriam's darkened bedroom, he heard a rustling sound on the far side of the bed, near the headboard next to his nightstand. He turned on the overhead light and the noise ceased. He lifted the bedspread and peered beneath the bed, shining his flashlight toward the deepest corners. Except for a few loose papers and one of his socks, the area was clear. A quick search by his nightstand revealed nothing amiss.

Thinking there might be a field mice problem after all, he set the last mousetrap behind the television set. Unlike the other traps, he added a small cheese bit from the bait container he brought along. Once the trap was armed and ready, he checked the faucet and commode in the master bathroom, to ensure nothing else could explain Jillian's experience.

When he moved back into the bedroom, a noticeable chill had invaded the air in his brief absence. The room's windows were closed and locked, and when he checked the thermostat, the heater was on. Thinking some other upstairs window had been left open, he moved to the doorway and turned the light off as he went out. Behind him, the rustling resumed. It sounded from near the dresser. Hoping to catch a rodent in the act, he whirled around and flicked on the overhead light again.

He hadn't thought about Allie Mae's Treasures since his conversation with Ned that morning. However, when he saw the dresser drawer where it lay hidden ajar, he wondered if the little bag had anything to do with the recent strange events.

That's frigging lunacy, David. Just a totally ridiculous idea.

As utterly ridiculous as the notion seemed at first, he couldn't easily dismiss it. Yes, it was the kind of superstitious nonsense religious fanatics and some conspiracy theorists might believe. However, Ockham's Razor espoused the simplest answer, no matter how absurd, should be looked at seriously if everything else failed to provide a satisfactory answer. So, what else could explain the crazy shit that had happened since Saturday afternoon?

David stepped to the dresser and fully opened the drawer. The bag was still concealed beneath a pile of neckties, right where he had left it yesterday afternoon. He dug it out, stuffed it inside his slacks' pocket, and gathered his tools before heading downstairs.

"Well, did you find anything, Dad?" Tyler asked with a smirk, when David returned to the kitchen. Everyone was sitting around the kitchen table.

"Other than it being a little nippy upstairs, everything's okay."

He disappeared momentarily into the garage with his hammer and flashlight. Upon his return, Jillian looked worried. He remembered Miriam said something about their daughter's room feeling like an icebox earlier. *Shit!*

"Hey, sweetie, don't you worry. The temperature's warming up now, and we're in good shape."

Jillian was enjoying a slice of devil's food chocolate cake Janice baked that afternoon. She gave him a hopeful nod.

"Whatever it was must be afraid of your big bad dad," David assured her, adding a fatherly wink that always made her grin. She didn't disappoint, as she responded with a gorgeous smile. "Now, that's my girl!"

"Thanks, Daddy!"

She rose from the table and ran up to him, wrapping her arms around his neck.

"Anytime."

Miriam also rose, grabbing a few plates from the table, and seemed more at ease. She mouthed a silent thank you for his efforts.

"I think I left an amortization report Ned needs me to look over tonight in the car," he said, pleased overall by everyone's reaction. "I'll be right back." He left the kitchen.

"Don't you think you should grab your coat?" Miriam called, when he opened the front door. "It's supposed to get down into the thirties tonight, and the temperature has already dropped quite a bit since you got home."

"Nah, it'll just take me a sec!"

He stepped outside and jogged to the end of the curved driveway where the trash container sat. He pulled the bag from his pocket and lifted the container's lid, checking first to make sure no one watched him.

"Goodbye Allie Mae," he whispered gleefully, and prepared to drop it in a crevice between mashed garbage sacks. The bag began to vibrate. Startled, he let it slip from his hand. Under the glow from a nearby streetlamp, he watched in amazement as it jiggled and squirmed before disappearing inside a crumpled pizza carton.

Determined to make sure the bag stayed put, David slammed the container's lid shut and secured it tightly. Shivering in the cold night air, he waited, expecting something else crazy to happen. The trash container remained quiet.

"Honey, are you all right?" Miriam stood on the front porch.

Damn it!

"I'm fine!" he called, praying she hadn't seen what just happened. He jogged to where she waited, thinking of what he should tell her, and fearing it would be the truth if she asked the right question.

"I couldn't find the report," he told her when he reached the porch. "But I took the opportunity to throw away some trash I left in the car."

"I told you it was cold out here."

She sounded suspicious, shivering from the night's briskness. *Probably telling herself 'he never leaves trash in his prized sports car'*, he thought. He followed her and closed the door, pausing to take another look toward the curb through the front door's peephole. For now, the trash container remained as he had left it, as a motionless sentry at the edge of the curb.

He locked the door and walked upstairs to the master bedroom. The room's temperature was almost back to normal, and the rest of the second floor carried blissful warmth once again. Pleased by his apparent success, he returned downstairs.

At bedtime, despite his repeated assurances, Jillian insisted on keeping Sadie with her. Janice left at nine-thirty, and Miriam retired upstairs. Once ten o'clock came, Tyler went to bed, leaving David as the only one downstairs. He watched the news and a sitcom re-run until eleven.

Unlike the previous night, he didn't sense anything unusual while moving up the staircase. No voices, strange noises, or anything else to make him look over his shoulder. Relieved, he climbed into bed with Miriam, snuggling close to her as he pulled up the covers. Sleep came easily, and he didn't stir at all until she woke him at daybreak.

Chapter Nine

"Sadie? Where are you, girl?"

Tuesday afternoon. Tyler disarmed the security system and closed the front door behind him, laying his backpack and leather jacket on the sofa. He whistled for the dog, and while he waited for her to respond, he changed the television station from the Cartoon Network to the G-4 Network. After watching the latest advertisement for a new Xbox accessory, he called Sadie again. There was no answer. Not even a hint of the soft jingle from her collar that sometimes announced her approach.

"'Here, Sadie! Come here, girl!"

He checked the den, and walked into the kitchen, continuing to call her on his way through the dining room back to the foyer. There wasn't any sign of her on the main floor. He looked up toward the upstairs landing.

"Sadie, are you up there?"

He climbed the stairs and stood in the hallway. It was too quiet and unusually cold, as if someone had left a window wide open.

Didn't Dad notice something similar last night?

Maybe the dog was sleeping in the master bedroom, since she often liked to take her naps under Mom and Dad's bed. But Tyler remembered watching his dad close the bedroom door, when the two of them were the last ones to head downstairs that morning. The door remained closed.

"Sadie?"

He moved down the hallway in the other direction, toward his room. His door was also shut. The only open doorways were to Christopher and Jillian's bedrooms. Since Sadie had slept with Jillian the past two nights, he checked her room first. The dog wasn't there, but his little sister's bedroom seemed very creepy and colder than the hallway.

He moved to Christopher's bedroom. Not finding the dog there either, Tyler stepped into the hallway. He heard Sadie whimper in the corner of Christopher's room. Burrowed underneath a large stuffed tiger on the floor, below his brother's window, her labored breaths reminded him of what happened Sunday night.

"Hey, girl, are you all right?"

He walked over and stooped down, petting her head while looking over his shoulder. Nothing seemed out of place, although it was difficult to say for sure. His younger brother did little to organize his room. Despite Mom and Auntie Jan's efforts, Christopher somehow managed to make his bedroom look like he hadn't a dresser or closet to his name.

"Let's go downstairs." Tyler made sure his tone was soothing. He scooped Sadie into his arms, where she shook terribly. "What's up with you, anyway?"

Heavy panting with eyes half-open was the dog's only response. He carried her out of the room and to the stairway. Just as he reached the stairs, the front door creaked open. Her ears perked up, and she began to whimper.

"Jill? Chris? Is that you?"

No verbal response, but the floor creaked in the living room. Tyler's carefree footfalls announced his return downstairs. Once he reached the front door and closed it, he encountered a similar uneasy stillness like upstairs. The temperature had dropped here, too, and very recently. It was *much* cooler than the temperature outside. He didn't see anyone in the living room or dining room. However, something about the air seemed kind of weird, as if charged with energy.

Worried the sudden jumpiness might get the better of him, he shifted his focus to the logical and explainable. Maybe the wind caused the door to open, and the house settling was what made the floor creak—the same things Dad mentioned yesterday when Jillian lost her damned mind over nothing.

"Hello, Zachariah-h-h-h!"

"What the… *who's* here?"

Surprised, he almost dropped Sadie while he jumped toward the front door. The dog curled even tighter against his chest, digging her front claws into his shirt to ensure her own safety. With his heart thumping madly, he peered into the living room where the voice came from. He didn't see anyone. The voice sounded like it belonged to a young woman with a strong Southern accent. Her tone, however, seemed unnatural, cold, and quite unfriendly.

"Come out and show yourself!" he demanded.

Not as tough sounding as he would've liked, he thought about Jillian. Maybe she was trying to get him back after yesterday. That would sort of make sense. But, where in the hell did she learn to talk like that?

He moved into the kitchen, and Sadie lifted her head to let out a low, menacing growl.

If Jill's messing with me, then why is the dog acting like this?

Sadie should be wagging her tail. Other than his mom, the dog favored his sister over everyone else.

There was no one in the kitchen. The curtains above the sink swayed, like a slight breeze grazed them. Thinking whoever was in the house with him might have stepped into the dining room, he quietly set Sadie down on a kitchen chair, despite her repeated attempts to jump back into his arms. She continued to whine, but once he got her to remain on the chair, he took a few steps toward the dining room and then reversed his path. He ran through the living room and didn't stop until he passed the foyer and reached the stairs near the dining room's other entrance.

As before, he didn't find anyone.

"Okay, Jill. I get it now," he said, snickering nervously. "You're trying to freak me out after what happened yesterday. Right? Well, it won't work because—"

"Guilty… both you and yer brother-r-r!"

An icy breeze embraced his back, from where the voice came. He tried to turn around, to take a look at whoever was there. But he couldn't. He couldn't move, which amazed and frightened him even more. The only thing he knew for certain was that it wasn't Jillian. No frigging way.

"Yer blood for mine," the hollow voice whispered, sultrily.

The coldness intensified... the mysterious presence drawing ever closer. Out of the corner of his right eye he saw wisps of reddish blonde hair. He finally managed to turn his head, but her image blurred and disappeared. Taunting laughter caused him to throw up his arms to protect himself.

The laughter grew steadily louder and more derisive. Trembling in fear, he thought he might faint. But the laughter faded, replaced by the sound of running footsteps on the driveway. The doorknob began to jiggle as other voices resounded on the front porch. Relieved it was Jillian and Christopher, they were already arguing over whose turn it was to take Sadie outside to do her personal business.

"Hi, Ty," said Christopher, the first one inside. He sounded cheerful, but frowned when Tyler stared at him without a reply.

"Hey," said Jillian, her tone casual until she turned to look at him. Like her younger brother, she frowned. "What's up with you? You look like you've seen a ghost."

He shook harder. Jillian and Christopher dropped their backpacks and came to him. Although frightened, he wasn't about to talk about what had just happened. Empowered by the urge to protect them, he stated the tremors came from hunger. He followed them into the kitchen, looking warily over his shoulder toward the foyer. Jillian had been right after all, and everyone else was wrong. There *was* someone in the house with them… someone hard to see, and definitely not nice.

Chapter Ten

David pulled in the driveway just before 7:00 p.m., parking the minivan behind the BMW. It had been a very long day. It started with the long line of parents in their vehicles waiting to drop off kids at Chester Elementary School. As a result, Jillian and Christopher were late to class. He should've known that's how the rest of the day would go.

When he arrived at work, several amortization reports from last week needed to be completely redone. Shortly after 9:00 a.m., a representative from Kings Inc. brought in another box of investment documents left out from the original files his department received in September. To get everything fixed by six o'clock, it meant skipping both breaks and taking lunch at his desk. The mound of paperwork grew another few inches in height, and the meeting to go over the prelims for Applewood Associates was now postponed until Wednesday morning, set for eight o'clock sharp.

He gathered his briefcase and laptop and stepped out of the minivan. Rather than going inside the house, he walked over to the empty trash container sitting next to the garage. He opened the lid, using the garage's floodlight to see inside the container. A small amount of liquid rolled around the bottom. Other than that, it was empty.

He closed the lid, smiling at the prospect of Allie Mae's Treasures and the rest of their garbage lying someplace in the Morrison dump, where it would be crushed and buried within the next day or so. His mood considerably brightened, he whistled a happy melody to the front door and stepped inside. Miriam and the kids waited for him in the living room.

"I take it you all have eaten," he said, after he hung up his coat and joined them.

"Not yet," said Miriam, her tone serious. "We need to discuss something with you first."

The kids sat with her on the sofa. Miriam said something that morning about Janice having a date tonight. As he surveyed his family eyeing him solemnly, he wished for a buffer like her, at least long enough for him to figure out what this was all about. Something wasn't right, and he could tell Miriam had a bone to pick with him.

"So, what's up?"

He sat on the loveseat instead of his preferred Lazy-Boy, hoping a different vantage point provided an edge. While waiting for a response, he noticed the deep worry on his younger children's faces. Miriam seemed worried, as well, just beneath her simmering anger. Tyler's expression surprised him most. His normal upbeat and brash demeanor was absent, and he sat there quiet and sullen.

"There's something in the house," said Miriam.

"What do you mean?" he replied, his mouth dry as he considered what she meant.

"*Sh-h-h!*" she whispered, forcefully. "It's starting again. Be quiet, and you'll hear what we've been listening to for the past hour."

She and the kids glanced in different directions, but all had their heads upturned toward the ceiling as they waited for something to happen. At first, he heard nothing beyond the ceiling fan's soft whirr. Then, a series of gentle taps resounded from the corner of the living room to the right of the fireplace, a few feet behind him. It sounded as if a handful of tiny marbles had been dropped onto a hardwood floor upstairs. However, no such floor existed on the upper level. The only exceptions to the wall-to-wall plush carpets were the tiled bathrooms located a good distance from where the taps originated.

What in the hell is that?

More ceiling taps emerged from near the kitchen.

"I guess we've got a really big rodent problem." He stood to get a closer look.

A tough sell, although he could picture a small army of field mice networking beneath the plywood, and along the wooden beams separating the two floors. He remembered the fine-fillet job these little creatures did to the fiberglass insulation in the garage, spreading small, pink tufts along an intricate maze they created near the hot water heater.

"Sit down, David, and listen!" said Miriam, sternly. She motioned for him to return to his seat. "It'll change in a moment, and you'll see we're not talking about mice, rabbits or any other four-legged creatures from around here!"

She returned her gaze upward, this time to the fan/light fixture in the center of the living room. Tyler, Jillian, and Christopher's eyes were already locked onto the spot.

David brought his gaze to the same location. A loud scratching noise erupted from above the fixture. Strong enough to shake the fan's blades, the closest thing he could compare it to was thick tree branches being dragged across the ceiling toward each corner of the room. Meanwhile, strange whispers reverberated around the room.

It sounded like several voices at first, but he soon realized it was all one voice echoing eerily upon itself. The effect chilled him and made it hard to hear what was said. Like the hollow voice he heard two nights ago, it sounded female in gender. But unlike that voice's clear diction with a southern drawl, the words were much more hushed and difficult to decipher. David glanced at his family perched on the edge of the sofa, ready to flee at a moment's notice.

"What do you hear?" Miriam asked, the earlier harshness in her voice softened by uncertainty.

Relieved her anger had cooled, he could tell she expected him to somehow make it go away; to forever banish the mysterious pestilence. It brought little comfort, however, since he seriously underestimated the scope of the problem.

"I can't make out the words," he said, after straining to hear the whispered message again.

"But, you hear the girl's voice, right?" She sounded hopeful, that she and the kids hadn't suffered a hallucination.

"Yes…I do."

David rose to his feet and moved to the ceiling fan, standing beneath it. The voice's diction was easier to hear. Almost chant-like above the barely audible clicks caused by the fan's on/off chain brushing steadily against the light fixture.

"He's coming… the moth to the spider… while the butterflies watch!"

"What do you hear now?" Miriam tentatively arose from the couch.

"Well—"

His reply was interrupted by an immense thud shaking the entire ceiling. It caused him to duck while Miriam scurried back to the couch. She and the kids huddled close together. Several more thumps followed from upstairs, as if the furniture was being pushed across the carpet and slammed against a wall.

David ran upstairs. The ruckus continued until he reached the landing, and then it ceased. The chilled air reminded him of their unheated garage in the dead of winter, and it felt much colder than the previous night in the master bedroom.

"David, are you all right?"

"Yeah, I'm fine!"

He heard Miriam's footsteps along with the children moving toward the stairs from the living room.

"Don't come up here until I say it's okay!"

The master bedroom and a guestroom sat above the living room. He stepped toward the guestroom, motioning again for his family to stay put where they gathered at the foot of the stairs.

He pushed the door open, which creaked tiredly, and stepped inside the room. Nothing was out of place, except it felt a lot warmer than the hallway. He shut the door behind him and moved to his and Miriam's bedroom. He heard movement behind the closed door and leaned in to listen. Someone approached from the other side, as if sensing his presence. He turned the knob and threw the door open, flicking on the light.

The room was empty. He checked the closets and under the bed before moving into the bathroom. In addition to being cold as hell, a maddening sensation of being watched stayed with him as he moved about the bedroom and bath. When he returned to the bedroom's doorway, he paused to survey the room, listening intently.

"David? Are you all right?"

Miriam's voice startled hm. She and the kids were huddled on the stairway.

"I'm okay." He backed out of the bedroom, turning off the light before pulling the door shut.

"What did you find in our bedroom?" She met him in the middle of the landing, before he guided her to the stairs.

"Nothing," he replied, and let out a low sigh. "Other than feeling like Siberia up here, I didn't find anything that explains the noises we heard."

She shivered, folding her arms tightly across her chest. Near the top of the stairs, the kids waited anxiously. Looking at them all, David had no idea what to do next. How could anyone effectively deal with an unseen menace they knew virtually nothing about? He urged everyone downstairs, where they grabbed their coats. After he coaxed Sadie from her latest hiding place beneath the sofa, the family fled their infested home.

Chapter Eleven

"How do we make it go away?"

Miriam took a sip from her strawberry shake after posing the question to her husband, who finished his second burger. They sat in the minivan's front seats, parked beneath a streetlamp at a local family-owned burger drive-in called 'Pops', in Littleton's older business district.

"I don't know," said David, quietly. He paused to sip his chocolate shake and turned to face her. "We're not going to be driven out of our house by whatever this thing is."

"Maybe we should call somebody," she suggested, her tone apprehensive. "Don't they have people in the yellow pages who deal with stuff like this? I remember watching a program on the Travel Channel last week before we went to Tennessee, where this family brought in some researchers and psychics to investigate why their home was haunted."

"Ghostbusters?" David chuckled. Seeing his joke wasn't appreciated, he added, "So, you think we really have a ghost?"

She nodded.

"Well, I'm not so sure," he said, determined to keep his personal experiences out of the discussion. "I imagine there are folks like that available. But I doubt they're in the phone book. Besides, how would we know if they were crackpots or not? I watched a rerun of that show with you, remember? As I recall, the house was still haunted when the camera crews and everybody else were done. I'll bet that family's now the butt of every joke in their neighborhood—just as we'd be."

She frowned.

"Like I said, I'm not letting this thing take over our house," he said gently. "If worse comes to worst, I guess we can contact a priest or whoever else to come over and bless the place."

"We're not catholic, and neither of us have been to church in years. So, how's *that* supposed to happen?"

Her anxiety worsening, it was obvious she'd already made up her mind a malicious entity had taken over their home. Of course, he thought the same thing. He glanced in the rearview mirror where all three kids watched, and then back at his wife's troubled expression. Sadie sat perched on her lap with a near identical look.

"All right, you've got a point," he conceded. "But let's be careful to not overreact to any of this."

"Do you think something followed us home from Tennessee?" Miriam asked, as if she considered the idea for the first time. "I mean, the strange experience we had in Cades Cove.... Maybe we weren't supposed to go to that ravine, David. Don't you remember the weird look the park ranger gave us when you asked him if he heard of the place?"

"I think his reaction was based more on his unfamiliarity with the spot," he countered. "Ned told me not many folks knew about the place, and it sure as hell looked like it when we got there."

"Yeah, it did." She glanced at the kids.

They all leaned forward in their seats, eager to learn what went on during their parents' anniversary excursion. She smiled and assured them everything would be fine, and not to worry. She returned her gaze to David.

From the look on her face, he could tell what she thought about now: Allie Mae. Even so, he knew she wouldn't mention the girl from Cades Cove tonight. Not if it meant further frightening their children by giving a possible identity to the unseen menace in their house.

"Let's not make any assumptions just yet," he advised, intending to move her thoughts as far as possible from what happened in Cades Cove.

"Maybe it's not from the park itself," she wondered aloud, and eyed him suspiciously. "Do you recall hearing a loud ringing sound in the chalet during the last night we were there?"

Shit! He assumed only he'd heard the ringing noises.

"I don't know… maybe it's what woke me up," he said, trying to be evasive while his mind sought a new distraction to bring her mind back to Littleton, Colorado and their present situation only. "Remember when I broke the glass in the kitchen? You know I don't often wake up in the middle of the night, a noise like that might've been what did it."

Her expression changed. It was subtle and barely detectable, and he knew she restrained herself for the kids' benefit rather than his. A small fire ignited in her eyes, and she straightened in her seat while she held him in her gaze. It was if she could somehow see his mental images of the strange nocturnal events from the last two nights. If only he'd possessed the foresight to dispose of the little cloth bag before they left Gatlinburg. Or better yet, never lifted the damned thing out of the ravine's cool grass in the first place.

"No, it was earlier than that, David," she said. "It happened just after you first fell asleep, and the ringing happened twice. I thought about waking you, but the second ring was weaker and sounded further away than the first ring, as if it came from outside the chalet."

She continued to eye him intently, and the fact he was unaware of the earlier ringing that night made him feel vulnerable. He realized he had to be extremely careful with what he said, as well as what he chose to omit. To escape her stare he turned his attention to the kids.

"Did anything unusual happen while your mother and I were gone?"

They all shook their heads.

"Let me rephrase that," said David, as his first question was too vague. "Did anything we should know about happen while we were in Tennessee, from Thursday night until we came back Sunday afternoon?"

They glanced at one another. He noticed Tyler's stern look to his younger siblings, who appeared to debate silently whether or not to divulge a secret.

"What is it?" David moved his gaze from oldest to youngest, settling on Christopher, who seemed the most nervous. "Tell me what happened, Chris."

"Ty broke a window," he said, his voice barely above a whisper. He looked down at his feet.

"What?" It caught David off guard. "In our house? Which one?"

"The one in his bedroom." Christopher glanced at his older brother, who let out an exasperated sigh.

"It was an accident, Dad," Jillian piped in. "Any of us could've done it, because we were playing football too close to the house."

"I'm sorry," added Tyler, for the moment refusing to look up, shaking his head.

Normally quick to berate the kids for being careless, David refrained, having found a perfect detour from the world of shit he was headed towards. As for Tyler's window, he recalled noticing something odd about it the other night when he investigated the mysterious voice. He smiled a little at the ingenious effort to conceal the window's damage under the guise of a Halloween decoration.

"What's so funny?" Miriam eyed him curiously.

"I take it that you knew about this?" he said, his smile turning into a wry smirk.

"Jan told me when we got home, while you and the boys were taking the luggage upstairs," she admitted. "Only one pane was actually broken, and two others are cracked. I already called a glass company, and they're supposed to send someone to replace it on Friday. Jan and the kids did a great job covering the hole in the window after it happened. As long as the blinds are down, it should keep the outside cold air from getting inside the house."

She glanced back at the kids while patting Tyler's knee, who continued to look at his lap.

"Something *else* is making the house so cold!" added Jillian.

"Well, can I count on you three to be more careful next time?" David's smiled widened. "If so, I'm willing to let it count as a learning experience. What do you all say to that?"

Tyler raised his head, as if surprised. He looked over at his mom and then at his younger brother and sister before returning his gaze to David.

"Sure, Dad," he said, his smile hopeful. "I promise to think before I act next time."

"Me, too!" said Jillian, and Christopher echoed her enthusiasm.

"All right, that's settled."

Pleased by the response, David shifted in his seat so he could face everyone. Miriam seemed grateful for how he handled the situation. He now understood its importance to everyone, until the more recent unsettling events took precedence.

"Did anything else happen from the time of the football incident to when your mom and I came home Sunday afternoon?"

"Nothing happened until Sunday night with Sadie, Dad," said Jillian. "Remember when we couldn't find her, and she hid under the bed? And, she wouldn't come to anyone but Mom? Then, Mom said something scared the 'H' out of Sadie, and you asked her if she thought we should take Sadie to a vet?"

"Yes, sweetie, we all remember."

David smiled at how his daughter turned into a motor mouth when she got excited. Tyler had once been like that, and Christopher would go through the same stage someday. His eldest son's voice snapped him out of the moment of nostalgia.

"Sadie's been acting pretty weird ever since," added Tyler.

He seemed less upset. David hoped after going easy on the window incident, it would help Tyler confide in him more.

"Anything else from Sunday?"

They all said no.

"How about you, babe?"

"Nothing I can think of," said Miriam. "The next thing, I believe, was yesterday afternoon when Jill heard the knocking upstairs."

David felt relieved nobody else heard the eerie voice and laughter Sunday night. He finished writing Miriam's observations on the pad when Jillian spoke up.

"Do you remember how my room got really cold, and all of a sudden Grandma's dresser started shaking?" she reminded her mom. "It rose into the air and then slammed back down on the floor."

David frowned and looked at Miriam, momentarily forgetting his own white lies while ready to admonish her for the omission.

"I should've told you about it," she confessed. "But after neither of the boys could confirm the knocks and the loud slam against Jill's door, I honestly didn't know what to think. Sorry about that, sweetheart."

She reached to Jillian and gently clasped her hand. Jillian squeezed her mother's hand tightly.

"Are you boys sure you didn't hear or see anything unusual yesterday afternoon?"

"No, Dad, we didn't," said Tyler, after a brief glance at Christopher, who confirmed it by mouthing no again. "Just a typical Monday afternoon for the two of us."

"So, there's nothing else from yesterday or last night."

"Oops, Daddy, I just remembered something," said Christopher. "Sadie was acting really strange when Jill and I came home from school yesterday. It was my turn to take her outside, but she acted like she might've had an accident somewhere in the house. I never found any dog poop or pee, but she whined a lot when I checked the dining room."

"Sadie's not been herself since we got back from Tennessee," added Miriam, stroking Sadie's neck while she sat contented in her lap. "You know, they say animals can see and sense things we can't. Isn't that right, baby girl?"

The dog looked up at her face in response to the coddling. Sadie licked Miriam's hand and cast a brief glance toward David, making him wonder if the dog had any idea what they discussed. Miriam looked up in time to see his smirk.

"Don't be surprised if she's the only one who really knows what's going on," she chided.

"Hopefully it won't come to that," he said, the smirk fading. "I guess that's it for Monday. What about earlier today?"

"Something happened to Ty that really upset him." Miriam patted Tyler's knee lightly again. "But he has yet to tell anyone about it."

"He was shaking when Chris and I got home!" added Jillian, surely not realizing her tone was closer to exuberance than concern. Tyler scowled in response.

David turned to face him, and he immediately looked out the side window. He was likely embarrassed from being so scared earlier.

"Tell me what happened, son."

Tyler shook his head defiantly, and continued to stare out the window. Under the glow from a streetlamp nearby, his eyes welled up and his chin quivered.

"I suppose it can wait until another time."

David reached back to grasp Tyler's shoulder as a show of his affection and support. Tyler nodded but didn't remove his gaze from the window.

"Jill called me soon after she and Chris got home," said Miriam. "I rushed home after getting Eileen to take my last two appointments. I owe her lunch twice in the next week, since she did it for me yesterday, too."

"That's when the noises in the ceiling started," said Jillian, taking advantage of her mom's sidetrack and obviously enjoying the attention.

"Actually, it didn't really get going until about twenty minutes after I got home," said Miriam, shooting a wry look at Jillian. "Everyone was sitting on the sofa. I could tell from the look on Ty's face that he was really upset about something, and Jill and Chris were trying to get him to talk about it. Maybe if I had enough time, I could've gotten him to tell me what happened. But, no sooner had I made a cup of hot cocoa for him and brought it into the living room, the noises started. They were subtle at first."

She paused to look out the passenger window, as if afraid the unseen menace now lurked somewhere nearby.

"That was the calm before the storm," she resumed, turning to look at David. "Loud crashes followed, like somebody picked up our bed and dresser and slammed them onto the floor upstairs. You should've seen us then. We were all huddled on the couch, crying like babies."

Her mouth began to quiver, and she folded her arms tight across her chest. David sought to comfort her, along with Jillian and Christopher.

"Tell you what," said David, while everyone except him and his oldest son wept. "I've got an idea on what might help everyone feel a little better, to take our minds off all of this."

"Like what?" Miriam asked between sniffles. She glanced at the dashboard clock, which read 9:04 p.m.

"Something fun."

* * * * *

In response to his first idea, to take them to see the latest Disney flick, Miriam reminded him Christopher and Jillian's usual bedtime had already passed, and Tyler's wasn't too long after theirs. His second idea of visiting a local arcade to let the kids wind down met with more disdain, since it seemed he hadn't listened to her objection to the first idea. Besides, video games didn't exactly chill the kids out.

His last idea of checking into a hotel for the night was one she'd considered, and wanted. She called Janice first before giving the final okay. As it turned out, Janice was on her way back to her townhouse after the dinner date when Miriam called her mobile phone. She offered for them to stay with her. Miriam and David would share a guestroom while the kids slept on the sofa bed in her living room. She also reminded Miriam that she had plenty of dog food from Sadie's most recent stay.

They took Janice's offer, and dropped the kids and Sadie off at the townhouse, located on the other side of their subdivision. They returned to the house to get some things. From the outside, their home appeared as they left it. The lights they kept on brightly illuminated the main floor. David and Miriam stepped inside, their senses heightened.

The chill had receded noticeably. David led the way upstairs, Miriam clinging to the back of his coat. The hall and bedrooms no longer seemed a haven of hostility, while the heater steadily brought the temperature on the second floor back to 70 degrees. They found very little out of place. The only thing of note was their bed pulled out slightly from the wall.

Hoping the menacing presence had truly vanished, David told Miriam he intended to remain in the house. He encouraged her to stay with Janice if she preferred, helping her pack clothes and toothbrushes for the kids. Reluctant to leave him alone, she said she'd come back to stay with him.

Alone in the house, David waited in the living room for her return. As soon as Miriam pulled the minivan out of the driveway, he began to hear creaks in the floorboards upstairs. Perhaps it was just the house settling. But, the noises continued, as if someone moved back and forth near the front windows in the master bedroom.

He moved below the area where the creaks originated and listened, feeling his heart pound heavily. A sudden noise came from the kitchen, and he whirled in that direction, only to realize it was the refrigerator's icemaker.

Feeling foolish, he wondered if every noise in the house would make him skittish. Then, definite footsteps resounded from the landing upstairs. He steadied his breathing while stepping quietly into the foyer. Unlike the other night, he didn't want to rush toward the noises like a crazed bull. He moved upstairs methodically.

The landing lay fully exposed by the hall light left on earlier, and was empty. He couldn't remember if he left the master bedroom light on, or not. A soft glow emanated through the small space between the closed door and the carpet. Cautiously, he approached the door and heard footsteps inside the room. It sounded as if some type of heavy broom was being dragged across the carpet.

David placed his hand on the doorknob and turned it.

Shit... this sucker's really cold!

The noises continued. He counted silently to three and pushed the door open.

As he expected, no one was visibly there. However, a trail of small twigs and dried yellow leaves were spread across the carpet in the shape of an arc around the bed from nightstand to nightstand. The twigs and leaves lay intertwined in a deliberate pattern.

Beyond the initial surprise, his first thought was it must be part of some symbolic ritual. His next thought? No way in hell it could remain there, even though he wished Miriam could view it first to help decipher the meaning. But, he couldn't let her see it, and for only one reason. The little cloth bag with Allie Mae's Treasures stitched upon it, which now bore smeared pizza stains from when it fell into the trash container the night before, rested on the bed. The obvious centerpiece, it sat between two decorative pillows and another below it.

The minivan's headlights flashed though the bedroom windows, announcing Miriam's return. Surprised nearly half an hour had passed since she left to go to Janice's place, he hurriedly gathered up the twigs, leaves, and bag, stuffing them inside the same dresser drawer he used Sunday night.

She entered the house just as he scooped up the last few twigs and leaf fragments. He noticed his hands smelled funny, as the leaves carried a peculiar odor. He ran into the bathroom and washed them thoroughly with the antibacterial soap Miriam preferred. She stepped into the bathroom, startling him.

"I'm feeling a little jumpy too," she admitted, after he stifled a gasp. "The kids have settled in for the night, and I gave Jan money for breakfast and a snack at school tomorrow. Even Sadie seems calmer now that she knows she won't be here tonight."

She let out a long sigh, laying her coat and purse on the bed.

"Are you sure you're okay staying here tonight?" David asked, as he joined her in the bedroom. He wrapped his arms around her waist.

"Yeah, I think so." She sniffed the air. "Do you smell that?"

"Smell what?" He was now aware of the leaves' acrid aroma.

"It smells like mice or something," she said, bending down to lift the bedspread. She positioned her nose a few inches above the carpet. "It reminds me of the lovely mouse shit you found in the garage last summer," she advised, once she stood. "That smell wasn't here earlier."

"It's hard to say." He shrugged. "We could sleep someplace else tonight. In one of the guestrooms, maybe?"

"No," she replied, hands on her hips while she looked around the room. "If I'm spending the night in this house—our *home*—then I'm staying here in this bedroom. It will take more than just the smell of mouse turds to get me to leave."

She moved past fear toward anger. Figuring out what to do about the little bag that refused to go away might be harder with her more pissed off than afraid. But at least she wouldn't overreact to every creak and bump she heard, which meant the actual prospect of her sleeping would be better. As for David, he no longer expected a restful night's sleep.

"I guess it's settled," he said, forcing a smile that lasted long enough to sell the illusion he wasn't worried.

By the time they were ready for bed, the strange odor had mostly disappeared. But, a feeling of uneasiness pervaded the bedroom. Lying in bed, huddled close together, they turned off the TV after watching part of an HBO special. Eleven-thirty approached, and the bedroom's only illumination came from a lone nightlight near the bathroom. Tired, anxious, and not knowing what to expect, they continued to hold each other close until they both drifted off to sleep around midnight.

Chapter Twelve

David fell from a dizzying height, moving at incredible speed through an immense chasm. Cold wind whipped around him, and he thought for sure that he would pass out from stark terror. Suddenly, he quit falling, and instead drifted in pitch darkness. The frigid air steadily became warm and humid, while the distant remnants from his screams echoed eerily above. As the echoes died, other sounds replaced them…. Birds and insects sang nearby.

Light peered under his eyelids, and he slowly opened his eyes. Everything was blurred. When his vision cleared, he found himself lying on his back, sheltered by an oak tree's shade. Cool blades of grass pressed against his skin through his pajamas. The sound of water trickling nearby drew his attention to a small stream coursing through rows of oaks, elms, maples, and a horde of white pines.

An array of beautiful, wild flowers in brilliant shades of yellow, blue, and orange covered the banks of the stream. Sitting up, he noticed a group of closely clumped oak tree saplings across the streambed.

"My God!" he whispered.

The trees were familiar, although much younger than when he and Miriam had seen them a few days earlier. Somehow, he had returned to the secluded Lover's Lane of Cades Cove.

At first, he assumed it was only a dream. When he crossed the ravine to get a closer look at the saplings, however, the stream's cold water splashing up against his bare feet and ankles obliterated the idea. The shock alone almost caused him to retreat, especially once the water level reached his knees. He persisted, scrambling up the opposite bank while shivering from the stream's coldness. The sun's warmth trickling in through the upper branches of the taller trees brought goose bumps to his exposed flesh.

This can't be real... but it sure as hell feels like it!

The rock ledge at the top of the ravine seemed identical to the one he and Miriam had stood upon. And, across the stream, the oak he had found himself lying under a moment ago marked the identical spot where he and his wife ate lunch the past weekend, and later made love. Incredulous, David turned his attention to the names on the trees, noticing the carvings seemed fresher. The obvious signs of aging he recalled were absent. Walter

Smith, Marylee Oliver, and the date of June 13, 1908 looked fairly new, and there was no sign of the later carving from the 1930s.

He ran his fingers across the carved letters, comparing the way they felt under his touch against the other time he did it. They lacked the smoother, eroded feel of something old, and a splinter pricked the skin of his index finger. David stepped back from the trees and gazed toward the deeper woods further downstream. Even the etched names on those trees seemed sparse compared to what he recalled.

A pair of excited voices drew his attention to the top of the ravine. He crouched behind a thick maple and peered toward the ledge. The voices belonged to a couple of kids.

"I win!" shouted a boy from atop the ledge.

"Ya cheated, Zachariah!" accused the girl. "Ya started runnin' first, but I almost caught yer sorry behind, anyways!"

"Nah, you couldn't catch me if ya's ridin' old man Olsen's best horse!" retorted the boy.

David stood. Being careful to remain out of sight, he saw each child clearly. They faced each other on the rock ledge. Dressed in a loose-fitting, white shirt and brown trousers rolled up at the bottom, the boy's dark hair and features reminded him of Tyler, when he was a bit younger, maybe around the age of ten or eleven.

The pretty girl seemed about the same age, with shining strawberry blonde hair that hung just below her shoulders. She wore a plain gray dress in a style David remembered seeing once in an old photograph, like what one might find in an antique store. Her feet were bare, and she held one hand on her hip while the other pointed meanly at Zachariah.

"That's not true and you know it!" she scolded, her deep green eyes burning in anger. "If we started at the same time, I'd have beaten ya *draggin'* old man Olsen's *slowest* mule behind me!"

The boy stepped back and smiled. But he looked perplexed.

"Ya expect me to believe you'd do that?" He sounded skeptical. "Allie Mae, yer the biggest exaggerator the world's ever seen—that's fer sure!"

David gasped, as he learned the little girl's name.

"Sh-h-h!" she whispered. "Did ya hear that just now?"

She looked toward the ravine until her eyes settled on his hideout.

"Over there!"

She pointed right at him, just before he slid away from her view. It seemed wisest to stay hidden, and only covertly observe them. The kids weren't a threat, but an adult could be. He thought of the horrible tales he heard growing up in Chattanooga about what happened to unwanted strangers in the backwoods of Appalachia.

"Don't try 'n change the subject, Allie," said Zachariah. "Ya know, I've a right mind to tell yer daddy about all yer exaggerations. I'll bet he'd be more 'n pleased to give ya one hell of a whippin'!"

"Ya don't dare!" she said with playful arrogance. "And, if ya did, you'd soon be pullin' one of the longest reeds from behind y'all's place for yer pa to whip yer butt for swearin' just now, once I tell 'em all 'bout it!"

"I's just playin'," said Zachariah, still smiling, although the seriousness in the boy's voice let David know he feared his pa's anger. "So, ya think someone's over yonder?"

"I surely do," said Allie. "Let's go find out who's hidin' behind them trees!"

David frantically looked for another hideout. A large, moss-covered boulder surrounded by heavy brush sat nearby. He scurried over and crouched behind it, praying the pair didn't see him as they climbed down into the ravine.

"What exactly did ya hear, Allie?" asked Zachariah, once they reached the maple.

He peered at the tree's exposed roots and frowned.

"'Looks like someone was here," he said. "The grass's all pressed down."

"Could be an animal... but I believe I heard a man's voice," she said. She bent down and touched the grass. "He was whisperin' somethin'. The grass's wet, too."

They both scanned the area to determine where the ravine's mysterious visitor had moved. David peered at them through the brush, his heart racing.

"Ah-ha! I think I found the critter makin' all the commotion!" Zachariah announced proudly. He stepped toward the stream and picked up something. A large bullfrog squirmed in his grasp. "Here's yer whisperin' man!"

The frog croaked deeply while it tried to free itself. Zachariah thrust the frog into her face, but she didn't flinch. Instead, she took the frightened creature from him and it stopped squirming. It croaked softly in her hands.

"That's a present from me to you, Allie Mae," said Zachariah, his hands fidgeting as he held them together. His face flushed.

Allie smiled at him while she stroked the frog. She then looked around and let her gaze settle upon the boulder where David hid. Squinting her eyes, he thought somehow, she could see him through the dense brush surrounding the rock.

"Come with me," she said.

Zachariah followed her to a small patch of yellow and purple wildflowers nestled in front of the boulder. Meanwhile, David tried to push himself into a slight crevice in the boulder's base. Looking at her through the brush, he was amazed by Allie's striking beauty. He watched her gently pick a handful of columbines and turn to face Zachariah.

"I've got a present for ya, too, Zach."

She handed him the flowers, blushing.

"Gosh… thanks, Allie!"

Zachariah stood silent for a moment while his face grew darker. It looked as if he had something important to tell her.

"What's wrong?" she asked.

"Nothin'," he told her, and took a deep breath. "I-I… I'll always be true to ya!" He blurted it out.

"I know ya will," she said, her voice soothing.

The bullfrog let out a deep-throated croak, and they giggled. Allie Mae pulled the frog close to her chest and grasped Zachariah's hand.

"'Friends for life?" She smiled at him.

"Yep, friends for life," he replied, his own smile very broad, with several teeth missing.

David smiled, watching their interaction until they disappeared from view. He raised himself to get a better look as they walked to the top of the ravine, hand in hand. She suddenly turned her head toward him, forcing him to drop prostrate on the ground while he silently cursed his hasty indiscretion.

What's wrong, now?" asked Zachariah.

The two stopped walking, and although he couldn't see them, David knew they both looked in his direction. He heard soft footsteps approach. After an agonizing few minutes spent wondering what would come next, the footsteps moved away.

"'Prob'ly nothin'," said Allie Mae, once she returned to where Zachariah waited by the oak trees. "Just a snake or some other vermin."

He heard the boy say, "Let's get on home." Their voices faded once they climbed out of the ravine.

David couldn't resist getting one last look at her, leaving the safety of his hideout for a better view. As he reached the clump of oak saplings, the pair had climbed back onto the ledge. Allie turned her head toward him again, and despite his quickness to duck from her line of vision, he knew she saw him. Not merely on account of the fact she smiled knowingly. Rather, the seductive wink that followed. It surprised him, so much that he stepped back carelessly. He tripped over a fallen tree limb near the bank and fell backward into the stream below. Embraced by sudden coldness penetrating his body far more than the cold Smoky Mountain water could've done on its own, he screamed.

He woke with a start in his bed, panting heavily from the nightmare. The air in the bedroom frigid, he saw his breath in the room's dimness. With his teeth chattering, he pulled back the blanket to reveal his drenched pajamas. He hoped it was only perspiration, but then he felt a small, muddy leaf stuck to the bottom of his right foot.

I was really there!

He looked over at Miriam. She slept soundly, her bed covers pulled tightly around her neck to keep warm. He quietly slid from underneath his covers and stood next to his nightstand, removing his soaked pajamas and dropping them in a pile by the bed. He checked his side of the bed, relieved to find the blanket, sheet and mattress pad slightly damp. The stream's water hadn't touched anything until the very instant he woke.

Shivering, and with gooseflesh popping up everywhere on his naked body, he quietly lifted another blanket from the cedar chest at the foot of the bed, and climbed in. Pulling the blanket all the way to his nose, he tried to ignore the bed's cold clamminess pressed against his back. Once the terrible chill left his body, he began to drift off to sleep. Just before he did, a loud crack ripped through the air from behind the television set, causing Miriam to stir briefly. She readjusted her body on her side of the bed, and pulled the covers up even tighter.

As for him, falling asleep again wouldn't be so easy. He knew the source of the sound. It came from the mousetrap he set the other night, the small metal hinge slamming down on the bait nugget carefully placed on the trap's wooden base. He knew without checking it lay empty.

The cable box on a shelf beneath the TV showed the time as 12:40 a.m., and he thought again about the similar times for what happened in Gatlinburg and the incident Sunday night. A definite pattern had emerged. His nervous gaze shifted from one end of the room to the other while he worried what would happen next.

Sleep did come, but only intermittently, and it brought little rest. He awakened several times each hour, while blurred images and shadowy silhouettes flitted between the bedroom and the various dreamscapes he visited. He found eventual peace, but not before the early light of dawn drifted into the room, announcing the promise of a bright, but weary, Wednesday morning.

Chapter Thirteen

"You look like you could use a few more of these," said Ned Badgett, offering David a cup of steaming black coffee. It was just after 10:30 a.m., Wednesday morning, and the Applewood Associates meeting ended a short while earlier.

"Thanks."

David took the cup from his boss while balancing a manila folder against his chest. The folder was overflowing with report copies from the meeting.

"I'm really sorry I dozed off in there," said David, frowning from embarrassment. "You know it's not like me to do that."

"I know," said Ned, his smile compassionate as they headed to the mortgage department. "I'm thinking you had a much better time last weekend than you've let on. You could probably use another vacation to recover."

"I'll be all right." David tried not to think about the past weekend and everything that had transpired since. "Lord knows I can't afford to fall any further behind."

They soon reached his desk. The paperwork pile from yesterday stood taller than his desk lamp and a second pile had recently risen next to it.

"I intend to have all of this cleared away by Friday night at the latest." He set the file next to his briefcase on his desk. Before he sat down, Ned leaned toward him from across the desk.

"Stephen noticed you dozed off, too," he said.

"He did?"

David grimaced at the thought of Stephen Perrault, one of two chief executives running the firm, having less than a positive impression of him. Rarely in town, Mr. Perrault often traveled across the country with his sales staff, and preferred his team of managers to handle the firm's day-to-day operations.

"David, it's okay," Ned assured him. "He knows you're our department's ace, and he's quite comfortable knowing someday you'll be running things for us. It's not just my idea you could use some more time away from the office. He's the one who first suggested it. Hell, you've still got more than six weeks left in your vacation accrual. But getting you to use any of it's like pulling teeth!"

He chuckled and moved toward the aisle.

"Maybe you're right," said David. "When we have some downtime, say in mid-November, I'll take a few more days."

"How about a couple weeks off for Thanksgiving?" Ned suggested. "That's if you survive until then. If I see any more signs you need time off before November, you won't be allowed back in this place until you've taken at least one more week off. You got that?"

"Then who would get this stuff done?"

"Tracy and Dan should be ready for some additional work. Just keep it in mind. I'll check up on you later this afternoon, and perhaps bring you a refill."

Ned tapped his own coffee cup before moving to his office.

"It's going to take a helluva lot more than two newbies and some coffee, my friend," David mumbled, turning his attention to the mountain of work.

* * * * *

Anxious to check on the kids, Miriam listened to the phone ring on the other end of the line. Finally, an answer.

"Hello?"

"Hey, it's me." Seated at her desk with her Blackberry pressed close, she glanced toward the open doorway of her office. Almost noon, it had taken nearly four hours to find a moment to call Janice. "Did the kids get off to school okay?"

"The morning went without a hitch, although Ty mentioned something about a missing book report," said Janice. "He thinks he might've left it at school yesterday, but he's not sure."

"Did Jill remember her field trip money and the permission slip?"

Miriam rose from her chair and moved toward the doorway. She closed the door, muting the latch's click as much as possible.

"Yeah, she remembered to put the envelope in her backpack," said Janice. "All in all it was a smooth go today. Is that the only reason you called?"

"No… it's not," she confessed, and then grew silent while deliberating on how to approach what was foremost on her mind.

"So, what's up?"

"It's David," she said.

"Is he being an insensitive ass again? Surely, the changed man you told me about on Sunday would last longer than a few days."

"No, that's not it," said Miriam. "It's more like he's hiding something from me. I'm sure of it."

"About what's going on at your house right now, or do you think it's something else?" Janice sounded worried. "He's not having an affair, is he?"

"Oh, no," laughed Miriam. "I'm surprised you'd say that! But I believe it does have something to do with what's going on in our home."

"What do you mean?"

"Well, for one thing, his reaction to what took place last night seemed odd," she explained. "It's like he wasn't at all surprised to hear the pounding on the ceiling and the strange whispers. I mean, the kids and I were huddled on the couch about to pee our pants because we were so scared, and he acted as if he was searching for a water leak!"

"Maybe he was trying to appear brave," countered Janice. "How would you have felt if he had jumped onto the couch with you and the kids?"

"You've got a point, but still…."

"I know you so well, Mir," she said. "It's not just what happened last night that's got you thinking like this."

Miriam thought about the past Saturday in Cades Cove, and the strange feeling that embraced her when she gazed deeper into the woods beyond the ravine. It was an incredibly sad and lonely feeling, and it made her think of what it had been like when her mother passed away a few years ago.

"I think it's more the way he's looked at me since Monday morning," she said, pushing the unpleasant thought from her awareness. "It's as if he has something he wants desperately to keep from me. In a way, it reminds me of when I busted him for visiting those porn sites on the Internet a few years ago, after he first denied doing it."

"I remember how pissed off he got about that."

Janice chuckled. Miriam chuckled, too.

"Well, the trip to Gatlinburg was so good.... I just wish I knew what he's hiding and why," said Miriam. "I'll talk to him about it tonight, if you don't mind the kids hanging out with you for another day or so."

"You know they can stay with me for as long as you need. Whether Ty can survive that long without his XBox is my only concern." Janice laughed.

"I appreciate everything, Jan. Oh, and I plan on telling David about your spiritualist friend's offer to come over and cleanse the house. I've got a nagging gut feeling that if we wait too long to take care of this, something terrible will happen."

"I agree, Mir. I feel the same way."

"Hey, do you mind if I call you back later? Mary's at my door, and she's trying to get my attention. It must be important."

"That's fine. I'll talk to you then.

Mary Lavoi stood on the other side of her office door window, waving three large tan envelopes containing x-rays Miriam waited on. She motioned for Mary to come inside her office. Following a busy morning, the afternoon promised to be even more hectic.

* * * * *

Norm Sowell came over to David's desk at noon. "Did you forget about lunch today?"

"Huh?" David sat up with a start. His laptop lay open with the screen blank. He had dozed off again, and this time for nearly half an hour.

"Man, are you all right?" Norm looked more amused than worried. His furrowed brow and eyes that were a pair of narrow blue slits shining out from his tanned face belied his sly grin. "I do believe you've been sleeping on the job, my friend. Or, maybe having a little too much fun at night, and I don't necessarily mean at home with the wife."

"Sh-h-h!" David whispered sternly. "Keep your voice down! Do you want everyone around here to think I'm some slacker? And, to answer your other comment, no way, not ever. That's your style, my friend, and not mine."

Norm stepped back with a look of feigned offense. He moved into the aisle, arching his back as he scanned the area. Satisfied they were alone, he stepped inside the cubicle and propped his arms on either side of the entrance to David's home away from home.

"I hate to tell you this, bro, but your pals over here are probably aware you've been snoozing, seeing they've all left for lunch already," he said, chuckling. "I suggest we head out before they come back with a pillow and a blanky for you!"

"Very funny," David replied, irritated but finding it hard not to smile. He closed his laptop and took off his glasses, setting them next to the PC. "I think you should drive this time, buddy, because I'm not feeling myself today."

He grabbed his coat and joined Norm in the aisle.

"No problem." Norm patted him on the back as they headed for the elevator. "But you're going to have to fill me in on the wild escapades that are obviously keeping you up late these past few nights." David cut him a look. "With the wife I know, I know!"

The two left the building and headed to Norm's Jaguar in the parking lot. Since both had busy afternoons awaiting them when they got back, they opted for an O'Charleys a few blocks away. David ordered iced tea instead of his usual beer. Once it arrived, along with Norm's preferred Heineken, David asked a question he thought he'd never consider prior to Sunday night.

"Do you believe in ghosts?"

"You mean the kind that say 'boo!' and go bump in the night, like Casper?"

Hating Norm's contemptuous smirk, David regretted bringing up the subject and the likelihood of being mercilessly teased for the next several months. He glanced around in hopes none of the restaurant's other patrons were listening in on their conversation, and thankful they shared a booth instead of a table.

"I'm serious."

Norm's smirk faded as he studied David's face. He tapped his fingers against the label on his Heineken, obviously buying time to think.

"I can see you are serious," he said. "I've got to admit I'm going to be real disappointed if that's the reason for your lack of sleep, rather than some intense sex with your lovely wife."

"Well, do you or don't you?" David was unable to mask his growing irritation.

"It's hard to say," Norm replied, relaxing against the back of his seat. "I haven't even thought about anything like that since I was a young boy with an overactive imagination. Now, my imagination's only active if we're talking about pussy." He flashed an impish smile. "Why do you ask?"

"There's something in our house."

"You're not yanking my chain, are you?"

He sipped his beer while his smirk returned, bigger.

"I wish I was," said David, loathing Norm's look. He pushed ahead. "More than that, I wish it was something on a small scale, like most of the haunted house shit you see on TV late at night."

"So, what are you talking about here? If it's more than some nighttime phantom, is it a screaming banshee, like my auntie used to talk about when I was a youngster?"

"What's a screaming banshee?"

Norm shook his head and took another drink from the Heineken, glancing at his wristwatch before answering David.

"According to Estella, my aunt, a screaming banshee is a restless spirit who's often given to spells of violence—like shattering glasses or throwing candlesticks and shit like that across a room," he said. "You know, your basic poltergeist activity. Also, legend says they fly shrieking into forests late at night. It's Old Irish folklore."

"How in the hell do you know so much about this stuff?"

Norm's knowledge of the supernatural impressed David, suspecting it far exceeded his own, to his surprise.

"How in the hell do you not?" Norm replied. "You grew up in the south. Don't tell me that you never heard any ghost stories growing up in Chattanooga."

Their food arrived. They moved their plates and utensils aside to allow enough room for the large platter of ribs set before them. As soon as the waiter moved to his next table, David picked up where they left off.

"To be honest, I don't remember hearing any stories like that," he said. "I vaguely recall a few times when ghosts were mentioned. But, my childhood was such that I avoided my folks' discussions, since they usually led to fights anyway."

He grew sad while reminiscing on his early youth.

"Hey, we don't have to talk about the past if you'd rather not." Norm placed a small pile of ribs on his plate. His latest smirk had disappeared, which made David feel less self-conscious. "We'll keep it to the here and now."

"Okay," David said, exhaling deeply.

He told Norm what happened Sunday night when he heard the mysterious female calling from downstairs. He paused to put some ribs on his plate and study Norm's expression. For the moment, Norm seemed interested, so he shared everything else that had taken place.

"You've got some pretty weird shit going on, my friend," observed Norm, between rib bites. "I take it something else happened later last night for you to be as tired as you are today."

"Yeah, something did," said David. "Miriam and I dropped the kids off at Janice's townhouse, where they'll be staying until we figure out how to get rid of this thing. While we were gone, the ghost, or whatever it is, set up some kind of strange symbol or message in our bedroom. It did it while I waited downstairs for Miriam to return, after she took some clothes for the kids and other stuff to Janice's."

Norm stopped eating for a moment, and David could almost see the spinning wheels in his warped mind.

"Not that kind of message," he said. "It was made of twigs and leaves arranged in a half-circle around our bed. I cleaned it up before Miriam got back, so she wouldn't panic, and everything seemed okay when we went to bed. Oh, one other thing. Since Monday night, our house has felt like a frigging icebox."

"Cold spots, huh?" said Norm. "That's common when a house is haunted. Jesus, I'm surprised I remember so much from what Auntie used to talk about."

"Well, last night I also had the strangest dream," said David. "I was taken back to the very spot Miriam and I visited last Saturday in Cades Cove. It seemed so real, man, but like I was visiting the place a hundred years ago. There were two young kids, a girl and a boy, and they were dressed like people living in the early 1900s. The girl could hear me, and I think she saw me, too. I fell into a stream and woke up, soaked to the bone in our bed."

"Wow," said Norm, after taking a moment to reflect. "So, how do you plan to take care of it?"

"I'm not sure." He paused to drink his tea. "You don't think I'm crazy, do you?"

"Yeah, you're crazy all right," said Norm, grinning. "I'd have to see things for myself before I could tell you what I really think. That's not to say what y'all have gone through lately doesn't have its own merit."

"It's just you're a very practical, pragmatic kind of guy." David raised his half-empty glass in a weak salute.

"Exactly!" said Norm, tipping his beer bottle.

He appeared relieved, having learned the extent of David's troubles with very little personal expense to himself.

If only I could be like you, my friend, thought David, wistfully.

Chapter Fourteen

A strong breeze moved through the treetops, rustling golden aspen leaves and the fiery red foliage from several mature maples gracing the Hobbs's front yard. Mid-afternoon, crisp and cool, the sun glimmered brightly in a cloudless sky. Janice pulled her Subaru up the driveway and parked directly in front of the steps leading to the front door.

"You're sure you want to go in there?" she asked Tyler, who sat next to her in the front passenger seat.

"I don't have a choice." He studied the front of his house, his gaze intense as he surveyed each window, trying to see past the drawn curtains and plantation blinds. "My book report's got to be in there. I'm pretty sure I left it in the living room after I finished working on it this past weekend."

"Would you like for me to come with you?"

She sounded nervous, and from the look on her face, he could tell she would've been just as happy to forget about his homework assignment and get the hell away from there. Even from the safety of the car, the atmosphere felt charged and uneasy, even worse than it had inside the house yesterday. She began to open her mouth, perhaps to offer to rewrite the damned thing herself.

"No. It should just take me a minute. Well, five minutes tops," he assured her.

After yesterday's meltdown, he didn't want her thinking of him as weak and in need of someone to hold his hand. He tossed his backpack into the backseat and got out of the car, shoving the sleeves of his new jacket up over his elbows to make him feel tougher.

"Are you sure?" she asked again, disengaging her seat belt.

"Yeah, I'm sure," he said, forcing a smile. "I'll be right back."

He patted the Subaru's hood as he went by. When he reached the front steps, a chill much cooler than the usual October air greeted him. He took out his key and drew a deep breath, and unlocked the front door. The door creaked as he pushed it open, adding extra creepiness to a moment that didn't need it. Dad insisted on leaving all of the doors leading to the outside untouched by WD-40, since he liked knowing when someone went in or out.

Tyler left the door ajar, stepping inside the foyer and over to the security alarm box. Once he disabled the alarm, he moved into the living room. He noticed the room felt colder than outside. It seemed surreal hearing the heater hard at work while the air remained frigid. He searched in earnest for his book report, trying not to think about his weird house.

The report wasn't on the coffee table. He checked the shelves and storage area beneath the tabletop, but didn't find it there either. Thinking he might've stashed his homework assignment in the end table between the sofa and recliner, he checked there next. While sifting through a pile of scratch sheets he used for math assignments, he glimpsed a shadow moving across the far side of the living room and into the kitchen.

He looked up, gasping slightly, and glad Auntie Jan wasn't there to see his reaction. Telling himself it was just the heightened wariness getting the better of him, he finished sorting the papers in his hand and set them on the end table, heading next to the entertainment center. A soft rustling noise emerged from the kitchen.

Tyler stepped back from the entertainment center, holding his breath while listening. When the rustling continued, he tiptoed toward the kitchen. The noise stopped as he came around the corner. It sounded as if it came from near the kitchen island. Even now the row of copper pots and pans hanging from the rack above the island swayed, as if someone had brushed against them on their way out. The hairs on his neck sprang to life, as it reminded him of what happened yesterday with the kitchen curtains.

Just let me find the stupid report, and I'll get the hell out of here!

He moved to the counter near the oven where his dad often left the mail. The report wasn't there either. He checked the dining room before returning to the foyer, where he glanced at the Subaru through the open front door. The car idled softly less than twenty feet away. For the moment, Janice had her head down, reading a book of folk tales his parents bought for her in Gatlinburg.

He shifted his gaze to the staircase and back to the car's safe haven. Tyler debated whether or not to forget the report and take a hit on his history grade. But the nagging thought of hard work thrown away urged him on. The only logical place left to check was his bedroom.

He took a deep breath and walked up the staircase, determined to ignore the tingling sensation along his back and arms. When he reached the landing, he heard more noises coming from inside his parents' bedroom, behind their closed door. No longer tempted to investigate hidden mysteries, he hurried to his bedroom.

Tyler opened his bedroom door and slid inside. It made little sense that the room with the broken windowpanes seemed much more comfortable than anywhere else in the house. But it was. Wasting no time, he searched his desk and nightstand for the report.

The search proved fruitless. Having confirmed the report as officially lost, he decided to bolt. His grade would suffer, but he figured his parents would go easy, considering. As he reached his doorway, the front door creaked and swung open.

"Auntie Jan?" he called, ashamed by the edge in his voice.

There was no response, and then the door slammed shut. Maybe the wind did it. He recalled a pretty fierce gust when he got out of the car. But, when he looked down the hallway, his parents' bedroom door stood wide open.

Oh, shit!

Something rustled downstairs. Janice rang the doorbell and pounded on the front door frantically.

Auntie Jan can't get in? She must be locked out of the house!

The rustling grew louder, as if the back door had opened and the wind flowed freely inside. The wind moved from the living room into the foyer and rose up the stairs, lifting the row of family portraits hung on the stairway's wall. Terrified, he listened to the progress of the draft, the wooden picture frames tapping against the wall as they settled into their original spaces.

It was too late to run downstairs and get out. He stepped inside the safety of his bedroom. As he did, the weird voice from yesterday called to him from atop the stairs.

"For so-o-o long I've waited, my love. My dearest Zachariah-h-h-h!"

The floorboards on his side of the hallway began to creak. Nobody was there.

"Now I'll have my vengeance."

The menacing voice drew nearer. The closer proximity of the last phrase accompanied more creaking floorboards next to Christopher's bedroom. Tyler slammed his door shut and locked it. He picked up his prized baseball bat that bore the signatures of his favorite Rockies' players from the trophy shelf above his nightstand. He wielded the bat in front of him, ready if needed.

The footsteps stopped outside his door. An unnerving silence followed, seizing the entire second floor, while Janice's muted cries for him grew frantic. The wait for what would come next was excruciating. Without warning, something heavy crashed into the door. The force was strong enough to bend the door's hinges inward. He backed up, bumping into his desk while desperately searching for anything else that could serve as a better weapon. Finding nothing, he became aware of a light tapping sound against the glass panes of his window behind him.

Tyler almost lost his balance as he whirled around, glancing warily over his shoulder at the bedroom door. With his heart pounding like a sledgehammer, he looked over at the Halloween spider he'd created to hide the football accident. For a moment, he half expected the orange-eyed arachnid to come to life and leap at him from its cardboard patch. The tape had separated on one end and the wind now whistled in from outside, pushing and pulling this portion of the patch against the window frame. At least the tapping sound had a logical explanation. What happened next did not.

A blue plastic folder arose from the small space between his desk and the window. At first, he could only see the corner of the folder. As it brushed noisily against the back of the desk, he realized no wind could thrust it through the cramped space. The folder soon appeared in its entirety, and it was the one that held his report.

"Impossible," he whispered. He reached down and picked it up. It was empty. Whoever was messing with him wasn't finished.

"'Lookin' for this?"

Just like the day before, he couldn't move. It was as if every nerve had frozen. But, the voice sounded softer, almost husky. Fine wisps of reddish blonde hair appeared in his periphery. Unlike his previous experience, he had no idea how this peculiar female crept up behind him with the door shut. She held his report in her right hand, outstretched from behind him just above his waist. Her arm and hand were bare, porcelain white except for the bluish ends of her fingertips.

Unsure of what else to do he reached for the report, hoping her gesture was friendly. But, as soon as he touched the papers, brushing his hand against the pale, cold wrist of the girl, she tightened her grip on the report. He turned to look at her. Before he saw her face, he felt a powerful push against his back, launching him across the desk and sending him crashing through his bedroom window.

"Time to die-e-e!" she shrieked.

Glass shards and splintered pieces of the window frame sliced through his skin, and he tumbled down the steep gabled roof beneath his window. A fifteen-foot drop awaited him before he would slam into the concrete walkway that surrounded the backyard's sprinkler system. In panic, Janice ran as fast as she could to the backyard, screaming Tyler's name while his cries filled the air.

Chapter Fifteen

"Come on…*come on!"* David hissed at the pickup truck in front of him.

Like him, the slow-moving vehicle seemed headed to Littleton Adventist Hospital. When he reached the parking lot, David swerved around the truck, glaring at the old man driving the pickup who returned his irritated gaze with a similar facial expression. He pulled into the first available spot and parked his car, feeling a tad guilty when he saw the aged gentleman help a crippled elderly woman get out from the truck's passenger side.

"Sorry about that," he said in haste, as he ran past the couple on his way to the automatic door leading to the Emergency Room's reception desk. Janice met him when he approached the waiting area, her eyes red from crying.

"How is he?"

His voice was thick from worry. The only thing he knew at that point was Tyler had a serious accident at the house. Janice called his office, speaking with Nancy and Ned before they tracked him down in a meeting with his support staff.

"We spoke to the doctor a short while ago, and Ty is going to be all right," said Janice. She pointed to where Miriam sat next to Jillian and Christopher. "Mir is a mess over this, as you can imagine."

Miriam sat huddled in one corner of the room with a child on either side. They hugged their mom and lovingly stroked her shoulders as she wept. It touched him, seeing how mature his youngest kids seemed as they comforted her.

"Everything's going to be all right, babe," said David, once he reached her. He reached down and took her in his arms.

"It tried to kill him, David!" she cried in anger. "It pushed him through his bedroom window!"

She pulled away and narrowed her puffy eyes.

"Or, should I say *she?!"*

"What? Who's 'she'?" His mind reeled. He knew exactly whom Miriam meant. At the same time, he pictured his son being shoved through the upstairs window. *How in the hell can a ghost do something like that?*

"Don't play coy with me, David!" She took hold of his face in her hands to where she could look directly into his eyes, and he couldn't avoid it. "You know *exactly* who I'm talking about!"

Guilt forced him to close his eyes. He didn't know what to tell her. He often found it maddening to try and gauge how much she knew about an issue, as opposed to what she didn't. She obviously had guessed the gender of the presence in their home from the whispers the afternoon before. Did that also mean she had made the same connection as he, that it was the ghost of Allie Mae?

Until she actually said so, past experience taught him not to jump to such conclusions. Lord knew he'd be in a deeper world of shit if he asked her if she meant the young girl from Cades Cove, and it turned out she didn't—despite this being the most likely verdict.

"Ty went into the house looking for his history report, since it wasn't in his desk or locker at school," said Janice, bringing them back to the more important issue of their son. "I should've insisted on going into the house with him. He left the front door open while I waited in my car, and he promised to be out in five minutes. When six minutes passed, I got out of the car. Immediately, the front door slammed shut. I ran up the walkway and tried to open it, but it wouldn't budge. My house key wouldn't even turn the lock. After that, I heard a girl's voice giggling. It was a really strange laugh, like it came from everywhere on the main floor."

She paused, after noticing the fascinated but frightened looks on Jillian and Christopher's faces.

"Maybe I should wait to finish this later, when we can talk alone."

"No, it's all right, Jan," Miriam assured her, while standing. She pulled up Jillian and Christopher from their seats. "I'll take the kids to get something from the vending machines in the hallway. That should give you enough time to tell David the rest of what you told me earlier."

She dabbed at her eyes and walked toward the reception desk, her head bowed low while the children kept up, clinging tightly to her arms on either side. Just before reaching the desk, she turned to the left where a small row of vending machines stood. One of the receptionists glanced at her as she walked by, and then cast a suspicious scowl in David's direction.

"Tell me the rest of what happened," he said to Janice, sliding into the chair next to hers.

"Okay, David." She took a deep breath and released it, briefly looking at her feet as if collecting her thoughts. "When I heard the crash and the glass breaking upstairs, I panicked. I was about to break the dining room window and climb in, when I heard Ty's screams from the back of the house. I had to climb over the fence, since I couldn't remember the combination to the gate's lock. I found him hanging from the floodlight pole, where his leather jacket had snagged. It caught him just beneath his shoulder, and kept him from falling headfirst onto the sprinkler system."

David shook his head sadly, forced to visualize what might've happened if the jacket hadn't prevented Tyler's fall.

"He broke his collarbone…." Janice began to cry again. "When the ambulance arrived, he finally started telling me what happened. Until the paramedics got him down from the roof, he was in far too much pain to speak clearly. He told me that he caught a glimpse of a girl in a light blue dress with reddish-blonde hair. Then, he told me that she spoke to him, and that she had said something to him yesterday, as well. 'She calls me Zachariah, Auntie Jan' he said. 'Why does she call me that?'"

Her shoulders shook, and David tentatively reached over his seat to hug her, finding it hard to prevent his own tears. He looked up when Miriam returned, noticing the kids had moved to a nearby play area.

"So, Jan's told you about Ty's injuries?"

"Injuries? She told me about his collarbone, but what else happened?"

David prepared for the worst, pulling away from Janice to face his wife.

"His neck and hands were cut pretty badly. One of the doctors said there's a really bad scrape along his back...."

Miriam started to lose it again, looking for somewhere to sit before she collapsed. David stood up and rushed to catch her, but she waved him off, taking the chair across from where Janice sat. Her anger still hovered near the surface.

"You need to be honest with me, David," she said, glancing briefly at Janice. "It's the girl, isn't it? The girl named Allie. She followed us home for some reason. I know it and *you* know it."

What else could he say? The mention of the name Zachariah by Janice especially chilled him. The boy in his dream had so reminded him of Tyler, when his son was a few years younger. If Allie Mae's ghost invaded their home, could she confuse the two boys as being one and the same? Could it also be the case for the name Billy Ray he heard Sunday night, that she confused him with some other man?

"Well?"

"Maybe it is her... her ghost."

Like when he first mentioned the idea to Norm earlier that day, it made him uncomfortable admitting it might be true.

"How long have you known?" Greater fury simmered within her reddened blue eyes.

"Since Sunday," he confessed, releasing a deep sigh. "In the middle of the night I heard a girl's voice call out to some guy named Billy Ray from downstairs. I got up to investigate, and I never found anyone in our house. But, before I came back to bed, I heard the same ringing sound you and I heard the night before in Gatlinburg. This time, it originated from the crystal bowl on the dining room table."

"The antique your Aunt Ruth gave us for last year's anniversary?"

"Yeah, that one," he confirmed. He sat in the chair next to hers.

"Why didn't you tell me about this earlier?" she demanded, the wrath in her eyes gaining strength. "If you had told me Monday night, Jill's experience that afternoon wouldn't have been taken so lightly. Christ, David, if you'd mentioned this last night when you grilled everyone like Sherlock Holmes, Ty would've never gone inside our house alone!"

She shook with rage while he tried to move closer to her, bringing his arms around her while whispering his regret, over and over until she allowed him to hold her tight. She buried her head against his shoulder and wept. His eyes filled with tears, preventing him from noticing the doctor who brought the latest news on Tyler's condition.

"Mr. Hobbs? I'm Dr. Chadwick."

A comely man, tall and slender, he had blue eyes almost as bright as Miriam's, and kept his graying hair trimmed close to the scalp. David stood to shake his hand.

"Your son is going to be fine. But, he'll be wearing a sling and a collarbone brace for a few weeks," the doctor advised. "Fortunately, the fracture is slight. He's a strong boy."

"What about the cuts and the scrape along his back?" asked Miriam.

Dr. Chadwick hesitated, as if considering her present condition.

"The one on his back required the most attention, since sliding down the roof left him with a pretty good gash," he advised. "It will heal up fine, but will likely leave a scar. As for the other cuts across his hands, his neck, and beneath his chin, they should heal completely, leaving slight scars if any."

"When will he be ready to go home?" David asked.

"Within the hour, I believe," said Dr. Chadwick. "We're finishing the stitches on his back and left hand. Once those are in place, he'll be free to go. I have already arranged for a follow-up next week with Dr. Pierce, the bone specialist your wife prefers, to make sure the collarbone is healing correctly. You folks have a good night."

"Thanks, you, too." David watched him leave the waiting area and turned his attention to Janice. "Did you contact the police about this?"

"When I called 911, at the time I didn't know for sure what happened, as I told you earlier," she said. "I told them that he fell out of his upstairs bedroom window, and was hanging from the roof. For all I knew at the time, he might've jumped through the window from fright. I sure would have."

"Me, too," he agreed.

"I didn't think you would want me contacting the police directly without talking to either of you first," added Janice. "One of the guys who got him down mentioned the torn-up window frame to the other paramedics. If Ty hadn't told them that he got careless standing on his desk, and fell through the window by accident, you both could expect a call from Child Services."

David nodded, thoughtfully, hoping neither DCS nor the police dropped by. If they did, it would be better if that happened after he had a chance to examine the damage to the window frame, and knew what to say to them. He also needed to get rid of Allie Mae's cursed bag, and the leaves that smelled like mouse shit, before they were discovered. The items wouldn't land him in jail, but they would most certainly get him a permanent transfer to Miriam's doghouse.

Nearly an hour passed before Tyler's official release from the emergency room. The sun had dipped below the foothills. Jillian and Christopher voiced new complaints about being hungry, which two more candy bars from the vending machines did little to appease. Once the family and Janice left the hospital, the inherent grogginess from the painkilling shot Tyler received for his fractured collarbone, and the lingering soreness in his back, made stopping at a restaurant impractical.

They ordered pizzas upon their return to Janice's place. After David picked up Tyler's prescriptions at a local pharmacy, he and Janice helped Miriam get the kids settled in for the night. It was time for him and Miriam to pick up more clothes and other supplies from their beleaguered house. David brought along a few trash bags and some thumbtacks to cover the broken window in Tyler's bedroom.

Driving the BMW through their upscale neighborhood almost seemed like any other autumn evening, until they reached the curved driveway to their home. The once warm and cozy Cape Cod seemed foreboding next to its neighbors. Both floors were immersed in darkness, including the front floodlights that normally came on automatically each evening. It was as if the house wished to be left alone.

"Why don't you wait here, and I'll go get whatever we need," he suggested, and started to get out of the car.

"What, so I can possibly lose you, too?" she replied. "I'm coming inside."

Before he could stop her, she stepped out of the car. She led the way up the steps to the front porch. The security lights immediately came on. David paused to study the lights before joining her on the porch, since they hadn't worked earlier. Miriam inserted her key into the front door, and they stepped inside the house together.

Moving upstairs right away, Miriam straightened several tilted portraits lining the wall opposite the banister. The chilled air on the second floor enhanced the house's creepiness, prompting David to turn on both hall lights on the second floor. Miriam entered Jillian's bedroom to grab a few things, which gave him the opportunity to view the damage in Tyler's room. She reminded him to grab some clothes from his dresser and closet.

Tyler's door nearly fell off its hinges when David opened it. He couldn't believe the deep cracks and fissures that lined the door's length on either side. It made him worry more about the volatile nature and strength of the thing that crashed into it.

He turned on the light. Jagged glass shards from the window along with broken plantation blind slats covered the desk. Splintered wood protruded out of the hole where the window used to be. He tried to ignore smeared bloodstains along the edge of the windowsill, where his son had obviously sought to grab onto something as he fell out of the window. Finding it difficult to concentrate on the task at hand, David hurriedly split the seams of the trash bags, and tacked the bags around the hole.

Miriam screamed while he gathered some jeans and sweatshirts for Tyler.

"Where are you?!"

In a panic, he ran to Jillian's bedroom, since he last saw her there.

"I'm in here, David!" she shrieked from their bedroom. "Get in here right *now,* damn it!"

He dropped Tyler's clothes in a pile by Jillian's door, and ran to the master bedroom. The door was slightly ajar when he pushed it open. Miriam huddled over something on the floor near the dresser. His heart pounded heavily once he saw his empty necktie drawer. He moved over to where she knelt, tentatively peering over her shoulder.

"What in the hell is *this* doing here?"

She turned her head, snarling the words while she pointed to a circle made of leaves, twigs, cufflinks, handkerchiefs, and the most colorful of his horrid neckties. Roughly three feet in diameter, the circle's items were interwoven in an intricate pattern. But the vilest item lay in the center.

"You never gave it to the ranger that night, did you?!" she accused him, snatching the little bag with "Allie Mae's Treasures" stitched upon it from the bedroom carpet. She shook it hard enough in his face for the bag's musty smell to fill his nostrils. Repulsed, he drew back.

"I tried to give it back—God *knows* I did!" he replied, indignantly. "I couldn't do it! Something stopped me!!"

"What? That's the craziest thing I've *ever* heard you tell me!" She stood, still clutching the bag. "I can't believe you did this, David! Do you mean to tell me that you had absolutely *no* control of giving it back to the lady at the visitors' center in Cades Cove?"

She trembled, and David knew he had just seconds before she really lost it.

"Yes, that's exactly what I'm saying." He took a step closer, intent on gathering her in his arms.

"*Don't* even think about it—stay right where you are!" she warned, pointing the bag at him.

He stopped, unsure what to do next.

"Even if that were true, what about everything else that's happened since? You didn't think it might help matters by letting me know this damned thing was in the house? Hmmm?"

Again, he could muster no reply, knowing it was futile to defend the logic behind his actions since Saturday afternoon. Regret washed over him while he relived every moment, seeing the folly in each decision. Everything that went wrong since wouldn't have happened… or would it have?

"I can tell what you're thinking, David. You can forget about coming up with some bullshit excuse!" The blueness of her eyes deepened as her rage bubbled over. "You could've prevented *all* that has happened!"

She moved up to him with the bag still in her trembling hands, the bell clinking softly against the torn locket and broken tooth.

"And to play us all like fools last night in the van…. God I could frigging *strangle* you right now, I'm so *angry!*"

"Miriam, please—"

"Please, *what!*" she shouted, and brushed past him, carelessly tossing the bag onto the top of the dresser.

She picked up two suitcases that were fully packed with the kids' and her things. Without looking back, she walked out into the hallway and moved to the stairs.

"Come get Ty's stuff and I'll meet you in the car!"

David looked at the bag, picturing a number of ways to destroy it. He preferred the image of it burning in the fireplace downstairs, the pale blue "Allie Mae's Treasures" smoldering before turning black. Flicking the light switch off angrily, he walked to his son's pile of clothes. The sound of a girl giggling came from the master bedroom's darkness. He almost responded with the most vicious tirade he could muster, but heard Miriam slam the sport car's passenger door. He picked up Tyler's belongings and headed downstairs, ignoring the prickly feeling along the back of his neck that didn't stop until he joined her in the car.

Things remained tense between them on the way to Janice's place. Once they reached the townhouse, Miriam left everything in the car for him to haul inside. When Janice asked what happened, Miriam shook her head and motioned for her to go back inside.

"I suppose it might be best if I get a hotel room, or stay with Norm tonight," David offered, when all other attempts to get her to speak to him failed.

"Whatever you wish to do," she replied tersely. "I need time to think."

"You know I love you and the kids very much!" he called as she disappeared inside the townhouse with the last of Tyler's clothes.

She didn't turn around to acknowledge what he said. But, he thought he heard her say 'I love you too' before closing the front door. He remained parked in the driveway for nearly fifteen minutes, hoping she would emerge one last time. When she didn't, he pulled onto the street and drove away, intent on leaving the neighborhood until he could come up with a remedy to repair the damage he'd brought upon his family.

Heading north on I-25, he placed several calls to Norm, frustrated but not surprised to hear his voicemail message each time. He drove to Norm's upscale condo near downtown Denver, and waited almost two hours. Around eleven o'clock, he realized Norm might not be coming home tonight.

Getting a hotel room didn't appeal to David. Instead, something compelled him to return to Littleton. He traveled near-deserted streets and watched laughing people tumble out of the bars and clubs Norm frequented along the way. For the first time ever, he envied them and their seemingly uncomplicated lives.

Near midnight, he pulled into the driveway of his deserted house. When he and Miriam had left in haste, the house was completely dark. All of the lights had since been turned on. It seemed his unwanted guest knew he'd return, and wanted him to feel more welcome this time.

David parked the car. Rather than get out immediately, he kept the stereo on and stared at the dashboard while again reliving the events that brought him to this lonely place. The easiest way to sort through his thoughts had always been to write them down. He picked up a small steno pad and pen from the glove box, intent on making his own chronological list from Saturday until the present moment. That's when he heard a noise coming from the porch. The front door's handle jiggled, and the door creaked open. Without removing his gaze from the doorway, he quietly closed the pen and returned it with the pad to the glove box. He turned off the car stereo. Whether an invitation or a dare, he accepted.

Chapter Sixteen

Miriam peered in the driver's side of the BMW. The sky had grown lighter on the eastern horizon, and a glance at the dashboard's clock confirmed the time as 5:56 a.m., Thursday morning. David awoke with a start after her panicked knocks upon the glass.

"What are you doing out here, hon?"

She sounded worried, and it might've brought badly needed comfort if he didn't feel as disoriented. *How in the hell did I end up in here?*

"I guess I fell asleep," he replied, groggily, after rolling down the window. He didn't wish to alarm her more than she looked, but initially he couldn't recall much of anything since they parted ways the night before. His throbbing neck confirmed he had likely slept for at least several hours in the cramped car. "Why are you here?"

"Looking for you, obviously. Norm tried to call you, after he got your messages around midnight. When he couldn't get a hold of you, he called me. I immediately tried to call you, and couldn't reach you either. I've been worried sick!"

The glow from the nearby floodlights revealed circles under her eyes. She looked her age for the first time in years. It upset him to cause her such worry. At the same time he felt reassured, since worry meant caring. He still had an opportunity to fix the damage. It wasn't too late to salvage his place in her heart.

"Well… are you going to tell me what's going on, or not?"

As surprised to find himself out here as she, David tried to remember what took place after he came back to the house. The images were fleeting and difficult to focus on, but he did recall images of being chased through the house by a dark phantom brandishing a long, sharp scepter of gold with a white tip dripping blood. It was like some sort of crazy nightmare, but somehow felt real…. The cloaked apparition's size and shape constantly changed, like a misshapen shadow that grew taller or shorter, depending on a light source's proximity. He especially remembered how the shadow absorbed everything it touched while pursuing him.

He pushed aside the images and stepped out of the car, his cramped legs painfully objecting. Disheveled, his dress shirt was ripped near the neck with the top two buttons missing.

What in the hell did happen last night?

He caught a glimpse of his roughed-up reflection in the windshield, before limping to the front of the car where Miriam waited. It appeared there was a bruise above his right eye, but maybe it was just the distorted view of his face in the windshield's curve.

"I'm starting to remember… I came back here after I couldn't get in touch with Norm," he said. "I didn't know if I'd stay here or not, but obviously I did. The front door opened on its own… it was almost midnight. But after that, I'm not sure. The next thing I know, you're pounding on the car window to wake me."

"Someone smacked you pretty hard," she said, studying his face. She took his arm to help him navigate the steps. "Are you sure you're all right?"

"Yeah, I'll live." *So, it is a bruise!* He forced a wry smile.

"Let's get you cleaned up. Then I'll tell you about the project you have this morning."

"Project? What about the kids?"

"Jan is taking Jill and Chris to school, and then she's staying home with Ty today," said Miriam. "She finished her latest editing assignment last night, a few days ahead of schedule. Her next one doesn't begin until after she meets with her boss next week."

David nodded, deciding not to push her about what she had in mind for him to do. She unlocked the front door, and they stepped inside. The recliner was lying on its side, and the coffee table had been kicked over. Loose papers and magazines were scattered across the living room floor. *Jesus, what did happen last night?*

"It looks like a small war zone in here," she whispered, sounding more worried than before.

The kitchen table was shoved up against the bay window facing the backyard. One chair was broken, and two others leaned against the dishwasher and oven. Several copper pans were missing from the rack above the kitchen island.

The dining room's table, chairs, and hutch had been spared. Only one of the chairs had been pushed aside. The crystal bowl hung precariously over one end of the table. A slight breeze would send Aunt Ruth's anniversary gift crashing to the floor. Miriam pushed it to the table's center.

"You don't recall any of this?" She asked incredulously, upon reaching the stairs. Two of the portraits from the stairway wall had fallen. She gasped, and ran up the stairs to retrieve the prized oil paintings of their youngest children from three summers ago. Fortunately, only the frames were damaged.

David suddenly recalled running down the stairs, knocking the portraits down as he swung at his undefined pursuer. "Something chased me, but I only caught a glimpse of who or what it was," he said, joining her on the staircase.

The images in his mind remained sparse, and he hoped to get a clearer picture. However, no clarity came, only an apprehensive feeling. He looked nervously toward the landing, and she followed his gaze.

"Come with me, hon," she said, gently.

She took his hand. He returned her forgiving smile with a weak grimace, and squeezed her hand tightly. Together, they moved to the second floor.

Rather than search for additional damage, she led him to their bedroom. Nothing in the room had been disturbed since the previous night. The strange circle remained intact upon the floor, next to the dresser. The leaves' pungent odor filled the air. The little bag sat on top of the dresser where Miriam carelessly threw it, the leather strap dangling over the dresser's front edge.

Until that moment, he hadn't noticed the padded white envelope she carried under her arm. She set it next to the bag on the dresser. *My project?*

"Go ahead and get ready for work, so we can talk about what you'll need to take care of this morning on the way to your office."

Miriam took a pair of plastic sandwich bags from her coat pocket and moved to the circle. She bent down, and carefully lifted some of the leaves and twigs from the shrine, placing them inside the bags. She stood, grimacing, while rubbing her fingers together. She sniffed the leaves' residue.

"God, this shit stinks!"

David gingerly gathered his wardrobe and moved into the master bathroom. Once naked, he stepped to the sink to brush his teeth. The bruise above his eye drew his immediate attention. The skin around it was tender to the touch, and there would be no way to hide it. He noticed four other bruises above his right shoulder.

Each bruise was roughly four inches long and an inch wide, and they formed a slight arc beneath the right side of his neck. He leaned toward the mirror to get a better look. The arc resembled the fingertips of an unusually large hand grabbing him from behind.

He couldn't picture the ghost of some girl doing this kind of damage, until he thought about what had happened to Tyler. He'd gotten off much easier by comparison.

"David, are you all right?" Miriam called from the bedroom. "There's a lot that needs to be done before either of us go on to work, so if you need help with something, I'm here."

"I'm okay… just about to step in the shower."

He stepped under the jets before the water warmed up. Gasping from the initial cold spray, he regretted not having time for the eventual heat to soothe his wounded flesh. He hurriedly dressed, and rejoined her in the bedroom, his hair still damp.

"So, what's this project about?"

Sitting on the bed, she opened the envelope and pulled out a typed letter from inside. "This is our apology to the tourist department of the Great Smoky Mountains National Park," she explained.

He quickly scanned its contents, noting it omitted the paranormal experiences they endured. Instead, it positioned the bag as something that inexplicably ended up with their belongings. He handed the letter back, and she slid it inside the envelope, along with the bag and the kids' arrowhead and pyrite souvenirs. She sealed the mailer, and stood up from the bed.

"Why are we sending the other stuff back, too?"

"It's actually Jan's idea, but I think it makes sense. We don't know for sure what's causing the problems around here. Sending everything we picked up from the park back to Tennessee will hopefully do the trick."

David's brow furrowed, and he started to say something cynical. She stopped him, pressing her index fingers against his lips.

"You've got a few minutes to grab a bite downstairs, and then it's off to the post office for you, Mister."

Her smile demure, she brushed her hand down his bearded chin and neck, allowing it to rest upon his chest. He reached up and gathered her hand in his, kissing it sweetly. He squeezed her hand again, and led her out of the bedroom. David glanced behind him a couple of times on the way downstairs, but didn't notice anything unusual. Like Monday night, when he threw the bag in the trash, there were no feelings of being watched or followed. He silently prayed sending Allie Mae's Treasures back to its rightful home in Tennessee would bring peace.

"How did you find out where to send it?" He had noticed the Gatlinburg address on the mailer.

"Jan helped me locate it online last night." She paused to straighten the portraits nearest the bottom of the staircase. "Once you mail it, we can hope and pray Allie finally finds peace. In the meantime, Jan is going to find out what plant or tree these leaves come from, and what they might represent. I told her about the circle upstairs. She immediately called that friend of hers, who's supposed to be good at dealing with this sort of thing. Jan says she's willing to help."

More open-minded than before, David assured her that he'd do whatever she asked, regardless of who or what was involved.

"Well, this woman told Jan whatever it is that followed us home from Tennessee might not be your everyday kind of ghost," said Miriam. "There could be something else involved, as well."

They moved through the dining room on the way to the kitchen, and his stomach growled noticeably.

"Why don't you eat something, and I'll tell you more about what Jan learned later on... maybe tonight."

"All right," he agreed, grabbing a bowl from a cupboard and a box of cereal from the pantry. "I'll mail the package first thing."

"I want you to send it by Priority Mail, with a delivery confirmation to ensure it actually gets there, David."

She poured him a glass of orange juice from the refrigerator and brought a jug of milk over to the kitchen table. He picked up two chairs for them to sit on.

"I'll make sure I do that." He motioned for her to join him at the table.

"If we had more time, I'd make you a cup of coffee. I know how much you hate anything instant," she said, moving her chair to face him. She watched him while he ate quickly. "I hope to God this works. If you *ever* pull a stunt like that again…."

She didn't need to finish for him to know there would be no more clemency. Divorce had never been mentioned between them, not even during the most trying times of their marriage a few years back. But, it would be a foregone certainty should the malevolent spirit visit further harm on his family because of him.

"I swear upon my very soul that I'll *never* be dishonest to you again, Miriam." He reached across the table and offered his hand. She clasped it, and squeezed tightly once more. "The package will be on its way back to Gatlinburg this morning."

He finished breakfast just before seven o'clock. His briefcase and laptop were already in the car. David grabbed his coat and took the sealed mailer. After resetting the alarm system, they exited the house.

"Please call me when you're done," she said, after he walked her to the minivan, where they kissed and embraced. "Okay?"

Her eyes were misty. It seemed to him that she had something else to say, but wouldn't.

"I'm on my way to the post office," he assured her. "I'll pick up some hot coffee from 'Micky-D's', and be the first one in line."

"Be careful not to spill anything on the envelope," she said, worriedly.

"So, I guess it's okay if I spill it on my lap, huh? Thanks!" He laughed, hoping to cheer her up. "I guess we could sue them for a million bucks if that happened!"

"Just protect the mailer." Miriam grinned weakly, and climbed into the minivan. She started the engine, letting it idle. "As long as it reaches the park service in Gatlinburg, I'll be happy."

"Me, too," he agreed, leaning in the doorway to kiss her one last time. "I'll call you once the deed is done. That reminds me, I better call Ned and let him know I might be a little late."

"Okay. I better get going so you can get all of this taken care of. I love you."

"I love you, too, babe."

He stepped away from the Chrysler, watching her pull the vehicle out of the driveway. He got in the BMW, letting it warm up while he placed a call to Ned, who reminded him about a staff meeting he needed to attend at nine o'clock sharp. David prayed he didn't encounter unforeseen traffic on his way to the local post office in Littleton.

* * * * *

"So, how did it go this morning?" Janice was on the other end of the line.

"All in all, it went fine," Miriam had just reached the parking lot of Littleton Children's Clinic. "Hang on a sec while I park the van."

She pulled around the building to the employee section, pleased to find that her partner Dr. James Phillips hadn't double-parked his prized Viper in her space. He had done it twice during the past week.

"Okay, I can talk now."

"I know you've only got a moment, Mir. Is David all right?"

"Yeah, he's fine," said Miriam. "But, something attacked him last night. I found him sleeping in the car, and he was completely disoriented when I woke him. You should have seen him, Jan. He's got one hell of a bruise above his right eye, and his shirt was torn."

"Really? I truly think what Sara told me on the phone last night fits the stuff that's going on in your home. Was it still freezing inside?"

"No, it wasn't," said Miriam, her tone solemn. The excitement in Jan's voice bothered her a little. "The house felt a lot like it used to feel, before all of this shit started happening. The place is a wreck, though, with knocked-over furniture everywhere. One of the kitchen chairs is broken. I don't know if the ghost or David did it. He said something chased him last night…." She started to cry.

"Mir, I know this is hard for you." Janice's tone was compassionate, tempering her enthusiasm from a moment ago. "Did you remember to pick up the leaves and twigs you told me about last night?"

"I did," she said between sobs.

"Did David see you do this?"

"I'm sure he did, but he never asked about it. I did my best not to let him know how upset I am. I should've gone back there after midnight, when I couldn't get a hold of him!"

"Don't be so hard on yourself, Mir. None of what happened last night was your fault," Janice assured her. "You had no idea he'd be there. Didn't David tell you that he'd get a hotel room if he couldn't stay with Norm?"

"Yeah, he did. But, if anything worse had happened to him last night, I don't think I could ever forgive myself for it. I'm still so scared!" Miriam cried harder.

"Mir, everything's going to be all right, I'm sure of it. Sara will be coming over this afternoon to meet with us. Is four o'clock still be okay?"

"It should be." Miriam's tears slowed, buoyed by the hope Janice's friend might end the torment. "I'll call you if I'm going to be later than that."

"All right, I'll see you then. You will get through this, Mir, and I'll be there with you, every step of the way."

"I know. Thanks, Jan," she said, sounding more like a doctor as she continued to pull herself together before going inside the clinic. She gathered her purse and attaché case and stepped out of the van. "I'll see you later on today."

Miriam took a deep breath outside the employee entrance to the clinic. She knew her eyes were red, which would be remedied as soon as she retrieved the eye drops from her desk. In the meantime, she pulled her sunglasses over her eyes, and forced the warmest smile she could muster. She stepped inside the entrance, uttering a silent prayer the day would go by quickly.

Chapter Seventeen

David hurried to his desk, throwing his notepad and briefcase next to his laptop. The staff meeting had ended at eleven. If he'd known the meeting would take so long, he would've taken whatever flack from Ned for being late, and remained in the line that stretched from the postal counter out through the glass double-doors of the Littleton post office. Everyone, it seemed, wished to get their postal business done before the weekend.

Thinking he could sneak out of the meeting and mail the package from the main post office in downtown Denver before ten o'clock, he decided not to wait in line. The mere thought he might've arrived at work on time anyway made him feel more remorseful. Worse, Miriam had tried to call him a couple of times.

"I got here as quick as I could, man." Norm peered over the cubicle's wall while David hastily organized his workload for the afternoon.

"Are you okay with going to lunch early, so I can run a very important errand?" asked David, looking over the top of his eyeglasses that had slid to the end of his nose.

Norm shrugged and walked around the corner into David's work area.

"Sure."

"Do we need to stop at your office, so you can get your coat?" David reached inside the bottom drawer of his desk, pulled out the mailer, and grabbed his jacket.

"It's in my car, bro," said Norm, stepping aside to let him lead the way to the landing. "The forecast said it's going to be in the low sixties by afternoon."

"Well, if you don't think you'll need it, let's get going!"

David trotted down the stairs to the lobby with Norm right behind him, nearly knocking over one of the newest interns carrying a stack of folders up the stairs. Norm apologized after David scolded the guy for not using the elevator. From there, they cut across the lobby to the main entrance, drizzled with light water spray from the fountain as they passed by. David sent a halfhearted wave to Nancy and her assistants on his way out.

"Hey, wait up, man!" Norm called, after he stopped to briefly flirt with a new girl manning the switchboard. "Why are you in such a big friggin' hurry?"

David's only response was to point at the mailer. He waited impatiently, while Norm hurried to catch up.

"I've never known you to be in such a hurry to mail a package before," said Norm, frowning. "Not even at Christmas. For that matter, I've never seen you in such a hurry for anything! It must be pretty important."

"It is," David confirmed. "I was supposed to mail the damned thing this morning for Miriam, and I didn't get it done after I promised I would."

He jogged to his car parked less than thirty feet away, taking his coat off since it felt like sixty already. Norm didn't need any more prodding to keep up. He jumped into the passenger seat once David unlocked the doors.

"Here, hold this." David handed the envelope to him.

Unlike his normal habit of babying the prized automobile, David raced through the parking lot to the alley behind their office. He continued the frenetic pace as they pulled onto Pearl Street.

"It's been awhile since I've seen the wild side of Mr. Hobbs," observed Norm. He smiled wryly as David maneuvered through traffic, taking a couple of side streets to get closer to Sixteenth Avenue, where the post office sat. "If you would've asked me for directions, I know a shortcut better than this one."

"Yeah, I bet you do," David agreed, tersely, for the moment focused on the road. "I promised Miriam I'd get it in the mail first thing this morning, and she's left me messages trying to find out if I've done it yet."

"What did you tell her?"

"I haven't returned her calls." He sighed. "That's why I've got to get the package mailed ASAP, so I can let her know it's done."

"The Great Smoky Mountains National Park... 107 Park Headquarters Road, Gatlinburg, Tennessee, 37738. Hmmm," mused Norm. He shook the package, which jingled when the bag's contents and the other items clinked together. "Sounds like coins and some rocks."

"Be careful with that, man!"

"Ooh, you're quite touchy today." Norm grimaced, but the glint in his eyes revealed amusement. "Where did you spend last night anyway?"

"In my car." David shook his head disgustedly. "Miriam found me parked in front of the house. I don't remember much, after I quit trying to call you last night."

He looked at Norm, who studied the bruise on his forehead.

"So, I take it that's where the shiner above your right eye came from?"

"Yeah, I think so."

David sped through the last intersection, and veered to a lone parking spot near the post office's main entrance. He was thankful he didn't have to park further away in one of the garages.

"Is it safe to assume what's inside this package is related somehow to your bruise, the calls to me last night, and the strange conversation we had yesterday?" Norm turned to face him as he cut the ignition. "Maybe it's related to what happened to Ty, too, huh? Sorry to hear about his broken collarbone and all. Miriam told me last night he's going to be okay."

"Yeah, it's all related. I appreciate your concern about Ty." David removed his seatbelt and reached for the mailer.

"Not so fast, hot shot!" Norm pulled it out of reach, grinning playfully. "First, I want to know what's inside, and why you think it's going to help matters by sending it to Gatlinburg, Tennessee." He shook it again, bringing it close to his ear while he listened to the jingling.

"We don't have time to discuss this right now," said David, in irritation, worried Miriam could call again at any moment. She'd likely be super pissed he hadn't kept his promise to mail it first thing. But, when Norm kept the package away from him, he realized he wouldn't get it back until he answered his question. "The stuff inside that envelope belongs to a girl, along with a couple of arrowheads and some fool's gold I found along the path to the ravine I told you about."

"A girl, huh?" Norm examined the width of the package. "Is it something she'd wear?"

"It's more like keepsakes," David explained. "Stuff that mattered to a teenager growing up in Cades Cove."

"So, it's not something like panties with bells attached to them?"

David glared at him.

"I'm just kidding, man. You've got to allow me my sordid fantasies."

"The items in question are around a hundred years old, Norm," David explained, hoping it provided the mental image of a once lovely young female now either dead and rotting, or existing as a century-old woman in a nursing home. Judging by the grimace on Norm's face, it worked. "We're hoping the park service will know what to do with the stuff, and maybe find a way to get the bag to the girl's family."

"Man, I must confess there are times I wish I was a young man growing up in Appalachia, say a hundred to a hundred and fifty years ago," said Norm, handing the package to him.

"How so?"

Norm's statement surprised David. He wondered what in old Appalachia would be interesting to a man who seemed to possess everything in the modern age. Norm had money, a sense of prestige, and a steady supply of willing females to help satisfy his unquenchable thirst for sexual conquest.

"Did you ever see the movie *Cold Mountain*?"

"No, I can't say I have," said David, unlocking his door and prepared to get out of the car.

"It came out a few years back. There's this one scene where Jude Law's character and another guy are staying the night with a hillbilly family during the Civil War." Norm shifted in his seat to better regard him. "Everyone got drunk and then they left Jude Law's character and the most attractive female in the house by themselves. He gets up to leave, and she pulls out her leg to stop him from walking by, ripping open her blouse to offer herself. He doesn't go for it, but then she lifts up her dress and bends over, shoving her naked ass high in the air and begging him to screw her. He almost goes for it, but his character's noble—sort of like you, and so he doesn't do it. But, if it were me.... Let's just say I've purchased long, Victorian dresses reminding me of the scene, and had a woman or two wear them—sans panties, of course. Just stockings or nothin' at all."

Norm grabbed a slim, silver box from his breast pocket and tapped out a cigarette. He wore another amused grin in response to David's look of pained tolerance.

"Please don't smoke in here until we're on the road again," said David, as he stepped out of the car.

"For your information, I planned on waiting for you on that bench over there by the steps," he advised, obviously perturbed by David's lack of affinity for either of his addictions. He stepped out of the car, and David locked the doors. "Might as well enjoy a day like this while it lasts."

"There could be a line inside, but I'll try to be quick." David deposited enough quarters in the parking meter to cover a lengthy wait inside the post office.

"Lighten up, bro." Norm placed an arm on his shoulder as they walked toward the post office's entrance. "It's been years since I've seen you this uptight. Go in there, mail your package, and then forget about it, man. I'm expecting my good ole buddy to be the guy that comes out of there when you're done."

He smiled, nodding before sitting on the bench.

"Lunch is on me today," said David. He turned and ran up the steps to the post office entrance.

"That'll work for me!" Norm called after him, taking a long drag from his cigarette and exhaling a string of smoke rings into the air. "See you in a few!"

Chapter Eighteen

Janice's Subaru pulled up to the Hobbs' house just before 5:00 p.m. The Colorado sun already leaned into the lower peaks of the Rocky Mountains, signaling darkness would soon follow. She finished parking the sedan near the steps. Along with Miriam and Janice's friend, Sara Palmer, she got out of the car and all three stood in the driveway, surveying the front of the house.

"I'm ready to go inside," Sara announced, after she gathered a duffel bag from the car.

A stoutly built blonde in her early forties, she wore a colorful smock beneath a brown leather coat that hung just below her knees. An amethyst crystal necklace adorned her neck, and it matched a pair of long earrings. Possessing an easy smile and soft voice, Miriam liked her the moment they met, less than an hour ago at Janice's townhouse. At first glance, she wouldn't have guessed Sara's vocation as a certified Wicca witch.

"Are you girls going to join me, or would you prefer to wait outside?" Sara's emerald eyes flashed with amusement. She pushed aside her shoulder length hair, and adjusted the strap on the duffel.

"I'd like to join you," said Miriam. "But, I want to stay out of your way while you perform the rituals we discussed earlier."

"I'll hang out with Mir downstairs," Janice advised. "From what she's told me, it needs to be cleaned up after what happened last night. Once you're done with the main floor, she and I can work on that while you're upstairs."

"All right, then. I prefer to follow both of you inside, a step behind the normal energy flow here at the house."

Sara waited for Miriam and Janice to move up to the front door before joining them on the porch. Miriam unlocked the door and pushed it open, and all three women stepped inside the foyer. The hinges squeaked loudly as she closed the door behind them. The rest of the house seemed uncomfortably quiet, as if holding its breath in anticipation of the witch's visit.

"I'll start in the living room," said Sara.

After Miriam and Janice restored the coffee table to its original position, Sara set her duffel bag on it. She removed two wooden dusters from inside the bag. One was made of peacock feathers, and the other from completely white feathers. She also took out an ornate brass incense container, a glass vial filled with blessed water, and a small leather-bound book.

Sara lit the incense through an opening in the container's side, and connected it to a long leather strap. She pulled the strap over her head, so the container rested against her waist. She picked up the other items and began moving through the living room, pausing to close her eyes every few steps while she whispered phrases difficult for Miriam to discern. To her, it seemed as if Sara had immediately forgot hers and Janice's presence, chanting and brushing past them as they stood next to the sofa.

When she swept the furniture and the fireplace with the white feather duster, Miriam decided to wait to do anything else until after Sara had moved through the den, kitchen, and dining room. Continuing to ignore them, the 'witch' slowly moved upstairs. Miriam peered around the corner to watch her until she reached the landing, noticing she had opened the little book and read from it while moving toward Tyler's bedroom.

"Sara brought that with her especially for Ty's room," Janice whispered.

"Is that where she plans to use the holy water she brought?"

"That's for your bedroom. Like she stated earlier, it's tough to break a spell sealed by hemlock leaves."

"I can't believe David and I were foolish enough to handle the leaves as we did."

Miriam thought of how she rubbed the leaves' residue on her fingers, and brought it dangerously close to her nostrils last night and this morning. Certainly, David did the same thing when he piled the leaves and twigs in his dresser drawer two nights ago.

"It's a blessing neither of you are in the hospital right now," Janice agreed. "Let's go ahead and finish cleaning, so we can leave once Sara is done."

"That sounds like a great idea," said Miriam, noticing the worry in Janice's eyes.

She followed her into the dining room where they straightened the chairs and centered the crystal bowl on the table.

"David did mail the package, didn't he?" Janice asked, once they moved into the kitchen to clean up the mess there.

"He did," said Miriam. "He finally returned my calls to him around noon, when he left a message. He gave me the tracking number when I called him back. He said he wasn't able to mail it in Littleton due to a long line this morning. At least the package is on its way back to Tennessee now."

"So he mailed it from downtown? A long line would be a certainty there, I'd think."

"Yeah." Miriam chuckled. "But, he made sure to get it done before he ate lunch, and it's verified by the 11:28 a.m. receipt time on the tracking report. I confirmed it online. He also paid extra to have it delivered overnight."

"That's impressive." Janice smiled as if surprised David would spend the additional cash for what might normally be considered an unnecessary extravagance.

"I thought so, too. He's working hard to make up for all of this." Miriam returned Janice's smile with her own, although she couldn't hide her anxiety.

They finished hanging the copper pots before moving on to the den and garage, which looked undisturbed. When they returned to the living room, Sara came down the stairs.

"Everything is all right for now," she announced upon reaching the living room, her tone serious. "As a precaution, I'd like to come back tomorrow."

"What did you find up there?" asked Janice.

"Aside from the damage done to Tyler's room and the binding circle in the master bedroom? Nothing," she advised. "And that presents a problem."

She moved to the coffee table, where she began putting the dusters, book, and empty vial inside the duffel bag.

"What do you mean?" asked Miriam, alarmed. "Does this mean that sending the stuff back to Gatlinburg won't be enough to fix everything?"

"It still might work," said Sara, her tone compassionate. "If I were to make a prediction, I'd say it should take care of everything that has befallen your family."

She removed the incense container's strap from around her neck, and extinguished the burner, closing it and setting it down on the coffee table to let it cool.

"Normally, when a cursed item is removed from a home besieged with problems like you have experienced, there's still a trace which those of us able to see the other side can still sense," she explained. "It's usually very faint, but can be detected for quite awhile. Have you ever spent the night in a hotel room that's supposed to be non-smoking, but you know someone has smoked there in the not-too-distant past?"

Miriam nodded, recalling the family's trip to Hawaii the past summer, and the cheap motel they stayed at near Waikiki for one night before their reservation at a nicer resort began. Even though the room was designated as a non-smoking room, it stunk of cigarette smoke severe enough to trigger asthma attacks for David and Christopher.

"Imagine if every non-smoking room you ever visited was like that," said Sara. "That's normally what it's like for me to visit *any* haunted place, even if the source for the disturbance is long gone."

She returned the incense container to the duffel bag.

"As we discussed last night, hauntings usually start out very subtle. A creaking floor, and maybe a knock or two on the walls, are eventually followed by something like a chair moved out of place or a light turning on or off," she continued. "But, that takes weeks and often months to manifest. The major disturbances and voices you told me about only happen in the most severe hauntings, and I've never heard of anything happening within the span of a few days…."

Sara's words trailed off and her brow furrowed. She cocked her head to the side as if listening, but then shook her head as she looked around the living room.

"What is it?" asked Miriam.

"Nothing important," she assured her. "Anyway, despite the destruction to your son's bedroom door and window, as well as the circle in your bedroom, there should be plenty of psychic residue. There isn't any, at least nothing I can sense. It's as if everything was staged, like what you or I might find on a Hollywood film set. That's why I need to come back tomorrow, in order to be sure."

"You don't think *we* staged it?"

"No, not at all." Sara stepped over to Miriam and clasped her hands in hers. "I *do* believe everything you've told me. It's just odd for something that has wreaked such havoc in one location to suddenly disappear as if it was never there in the first place."

Sara patted Miriam's hands before letting go. Then she turned to leave, heading for the front door with Miriam and Janice behind her. The last one outside, Miriam paused to make sure the security floodlights came on with the onset of dusk. She set the alarm and closed the door, joining Sara and Janice inside the Subaru. They pulled out of the driveway, and all three looked back at the house. Sara commented on how it seemed like any other home on the block, and would be a nice advertisement for the good life in suburban America. The contradiction to what she had expected to find dominated their discussion the rest of the way back to Janice's townhouse.

Chapter Nineteen

"I've got two tickets to paradise, ba-be-e-e... two tickets to paradise!"

Norm leaned over David's cubicle, waving a pair of tickets to the Broncos' next home game set for Sunday afternoon. David barely acknowledged his presence, and Norm wondered if it was because of his terrible effort to carry the old Eddie Money tune.

"Didn't you hear me, David? It's the Oakland Raiders, man, and I've got two tickets, mid-level on the forty-yard line!"

"Sounds good," said David, his tone curt while he hurriedly backtracked through a report. To Norm, it appeared to be the last of the preliminary Applewood Associates paperwork.

"It should sound frigging great!" he said, irritated.

"What?" David glanced briefly at him, and held up his index finger for Norm to give him a moment. Once he traced the last of the numbers in the list, he slapped the pencil on his desk. "Yes!" he shouted, glancing at his laptop's clock. 5:58 p.m.

"Hang on for another minute, Norm. Let me get this over to Ned before he leaves. I'll be right back."

David stood, grabbing the report and brushing past Norm, who weakly waved the tickets as David went by.

"Whatever you say, bro."

Fidgety and always curious, Norm shuffled some of the papers on the desk; careful not to mess with anything David was actively working on. He moved a small pile of manila folders, when something jingled and fell to the floor. He peered under the desk, and at first didn't see anything. But, then he noticed a leather strap to whatever had fallen as it lay near the bundled electrical cords from David's docking station and printer. He pulled on the strap, hearing the jingle again, and the little cloth bag came into view.

"Allie Mae's Treasures," he whispered, picking it up. He smiled as he studied the pale blue stitching. "Well, well, David. What have you been up to lately?"

He craned his neck to peer down the aisle. David stood inside Ned's office. Norm shook the bag gently, hearing the items clink and brush against each other. They were identical to the sounds he heard when he shook the mailer earlier. Curious, he opened the bag and peered into it, seeing the glint of the bell and what looked like a gold necklace, a shiny blue ribbon, and a letter of some sort. An odor also arose from inside… a mixture of lilac, honeysuckle, and female pheromones.

"Huh? Why you little devil. After years of playing the perfect husband, it appears Mr. David Hobbs takes a little action on the side after all!" He chuckled and allowed himself to laugh more heartily until David returned.

"Sorry it took me so long."

Norm closed the bag and shoved it inside his pocket, undetected, while David moved over to his desk to shut down his laptop.

"Now what were you asking me earlier—something about the Broncos?"

"I've got great seats for us this Sunday, if you're interested? That is, if you don't have anything else to keep you from witnessing a good fight between the Broncs and the Raidahs?"

Norm eyed him knowingly, and David responded with a perplexed look.

"I'm definitely interested," said David. "I don't foresee any problems getting free for the game, but I'll have to check with Miriam."

"Is she the *only* one you need to check with?" Norm grinned like the Cheshire Cat.

David studied him curiously. "Does the bruise look *that* bad?"

Norm's only response was a shit-eating grin.

"Of course, Miriam is the only one I need to check with!" said David, indignantly. "What kind of question is that, anyway?"

"Let's just say you and I need to have a serious talk about the secret life of David Hobbs and the things, how should I put this, the things he covertly treasures?" Norm moved toward the aisle, pausing in the cubicle's doorway. "Meet me at my place at noon on Sunday and we'll ride to the game together. Just be ready to tell me what you *know* I'd love to hear about, you ole player, you!"

"All right, I'll see you then." David shook his head as if puzzled.

Norm watched him fill his briefcase with other reports from an upcoming client's file. He decided to leave his buddy in peace, while looking forward to grilling David Sunday afternoon.

"You're not planning to stay late tonight, are you?" David called after him.

"Afraid so, David!" Norm responded over his shoulder. "Stephen wants the final revised contracts between us and Applewood on his desk first thing tomorrow, since he won't be back in the office until late next week. He's taking the wife on a cruise."

"Well, see if you can get out of here before too late tonight," said David, sounding relieved.

I wonder how relieved he'll be when he discovers his little naughty bag is missing?

"I'm looking forward to the game. Talk to you tomorrow!"

"See you then!" said Norm.

When out of David's view, he chuckled, patting his pocket on account of a sudden worry the bag might not still be there. It was. Norm smiled while closing the door to his office, intent on taking time a little later on that evening, in hopes of learning more about what David had been up to lately.

* * * * *

David hurried downstairs, pausing to say goodnight to Nancy, who was also ready to leave for the evening. Other than Norm, only the night watchman, Troy Stewart, would remain in the building.

David glanced over his shoulder at the upstairs windows more than once while walking to his car, but at the time didn't think much of it. Once on the road, he reflected on the events from earlier. He pictured the mailer traveling in some speedy USPS airplane on its way for delivery in Gatlinburg, Tennessee tomorrow. His thoughts turned next to his family. Miriam had forgiven him, and he could hardly wait to be with them again after one night away from his wife and two from the kids.

The last thing he thought about once he reached Littleton was the strange exchange he shared with Norm before leaving. *What in the hell did Norm mean by his allusions to 'secret treasures' and 'you ole player'? And what about his silly smile that reeked of knowing arrogance?*

"It'll have to wait until tomorrow, I guess," he mused quietly, pulling into Janice's driveway. Jillian and Christopher were waiting by the front porch to greet him. Each grabbed an arm once he got out of the car, and led him inside the townhouse.

Chapter Twenty

Troy Stewart came by Norm Sowell's office just before midnight. It wasn't the first time that Norm had stayed this late during the past week, and the night watchman tapped the tip of his flashlight on his door, halfway open.

"'You planning to call it quits and go home sometime soon?" he asked, poking his head through the doorway.

"Hey, there, Troy!" Norm looked up from his laptop and the contract drafts he had spread across his desk. Unlike the more austere offices on the second floor, his furnishings included a handsome cherry bookcase that covered most of the wall next to his matching executive desk. "I take it you're about to leave for the evening?"

He leaned back in his plush, high-backed leather chair that squeaked slightly as he turned to face the doorway.

"Evening? In about three minutes, it'll be morning!" Troy's brilliant smile flashed, and his deep brown eyes twinkled playfully from within his flawless ebony skin. "Since it doesn't look like you're quite ready to leave yet, I'll let you set the alarm on the side entrance downstairs like we did on Monday night. Just remember not to step outside for a smoke until you're actually leaving the building for good. Otherwise, you won't be able to get back inside until Johnny gets here around five-thirty."

"Gotcha. Thanks man." Norm stood up to stretch his back. "I should be out of here by one o'clock at the latest. It just depends on how long I can go without another cigarette!"

"All right, Mr. Sowell," said Troy. "I'll be leaving you, then." He headed to the elevator across the landing.

"'Have a good night, Troy, and I'll see you tomorrow afternoon!" Norm called after him as Troy stepped inside the elevator.

"All right, see you then, Mr. Sowell!"

Norm moved over to his doorway, listening to the elevator's chimes and the soft purr of its motor as it carried Troy down to the first floor. He left his door cracked open to keep his office from getting stuffy.

For a moment, he absently tapped his fingers across the silver cigarette case in his breast pocket. The temptation for further distraction before he finished tonight's work grew strong. But, the reality of not being able to get back inside the building before Johnny Townsend or Nancy Geddings arrived in the morning deterred him.

He moved back to his desk and sat down. As he did, a slight jingle emerged from inside the little bag in his pants' pocket. He pulled the bag out, recalling his experience from earlier at David's desk. He eagerly loosened the leather strap and opened it, inhaling a deep whiff of its aroma.

"Ah-h-h, something young and *sweet!*" he enthused. "What I wouldn't give for a piece of where this came from!"

He took another whiff, smiling dreamily while he let the odor fill his nostrils. Satisfied from the fix that successfully replaced the nagging urge to smoke, he began to close the bag, then peered inside it and stopped. He thought he saw a broken tooth, which he hadn't seen earlier. Norm cleared a space on his desktop and opened the bag fully, spilling its contents in front of him.

"Well, what have we here?"

He sifted through the items, pushing the sleigh bell aside as he picked up the letter. Once he realized that a male had written it, he tossed it aside. Next, he ran his fingers across the shiny blue ribbon, admiring its fine texture. He set the ribbon next to the letter and moved on to the torn locket attached to the gold chain. Turning it over in his hands, he determined that an inscription had been engraved on its back. The inscription was too faint to read, so he set the locket down next to the other items, and curled the chain on top of it.

That left the tooth. As he brought it closer to his face, the aroma he so admired wafted toward him, coming from *inside* the chipped bicuspid.

"Well, I'll be goddamned!"

Astonished, he noticed that there was encrusted blood on the tooth's side, and wondered how the thing could smell like that. He leaned back in his chair, holding it between his thumb and index finger while he continued to study and sniff it. He remained mesmerized until the elevator's motor started up again.

Norm sat up straight and gathered the items, hastily stuffing them all back inside the bag. He then closed it, pulling the leather strap tight before placing it inside the top left-side drawer of his desk, beneath his laptop. The handsome digital desk clock next to his darkened PC read 12:33 a.m.

Who in the hell could that be?

He stood up and moved toward his doorway, his lips pursed and brow furrowed as he tried to figure out how more than twenty minutes had slipped away. He could've sworn only five minutes had passed since he opened the bag. As a result, he'd have to stay longer than he wanted.

The whir of the elevator's engine began to slow, and the chimes announced its passenger had reached the second floor. He pushed his door open and stepped into the hall.

"What did you forget, Troy?" he called out into the landing's dimness. "You might as well stick around and leave with me…."

His words trailed off when the elevator's door finished opening. Nobody was there. The fluorescent light's glow inside the empty compartment poured out into the deserted landing, until the door slowly closed.

"Troy?"

He moved out into the landing, peering toward the shadows in the far corners on either side of the majestic stained-glass window. For the moment, the only illumination came from the gold-tinted security lights downstairs and the streetlights in the rear parking lot that shined through the window's angelic imagery, creating a colorful array of hues and odd shapes upon the landing's gray carpet.

He paused to listen…. Other than the soothing sound of water moving through the fountain on the main floor, he heard nothing. He moved over to the banister and looked out toward the security post. It was closed, and the main reception area sat empty.

"Are you down there, Troy?"

The echo from his voice reverberated against the walls of the deserted first floor.

"I guess not," he said, feeling foolish for his nervousness. He shook his head and grinned sheepishly, then moved back to the lighted hallway next to his office.

Just before Norm reached his office, the landing's nineteenth century floorboards creaked. He stopped in the hall, listening for the noise to repeat itself. All he heard was the splashing water downstairs. Then, the floorboards creaked again.

"Who's there?" he called out, after taking a cautious step toward the landing.

There was no reply, but the soft creaking continued. The slender hairs on the nape of his neck tingled once he realized the creaks resounded from the middle of the landing's floor, where the streetlight's glow revealed it to be empty. The floor less than twenty feet away creaked, and he heard something brush lightly across the carpet. Whatever made the noises was headed toward him.

"Who the hell's up here?" he demanded, his tone slightly alarmed. The creaking and brushing sounds stopped. "Come out and show yourself!"

Again, there was no response. Norm remained in the hallway for nearly a minute, peering out into the landing. After hearing nothing else above the fountain's continual flow, he walked over to the light switch. He pushed the lever up, and an immense brass chandelier above the landing sprang to life, brightly illuminating the entire floor. He was definitely alone.

"I've got to quit spending so many hours here at night," he mumbled, silently chiding himself for being so jumpy. He started to reach for the light switch to turn it off, but decided to leave it on for now.

"I owe this to you, David," he muttered, before stepping back inside his office. "Your good buddy's imagination is now getting the best of him, too, no thanks to you."

Leaving his office door wide open, he moved back to his desk and sat down. He awakened his PC and began sorting through the most important contract documents. Hoping to complete the most pressing work quickly, he intended to come back early in the morning to finish the rest. He had just picked up from where he left off earlier in the revised Applewood service contract details, when the chandelier above the landing turned off.

Seeing the landing plunged into instant darkness left him more unnerved. He gathered the loosely strewn pages on his desk, ready to leave immediately. Something very weird was happening in the old Victorian mansion. Having heard tales of ghostly presences from the girls at the reception desk, he intended to ask Troy if he ever witnessed strange events like this when he saw him the next afternoon.

Norm cleared his desktop and placed the contracts inside the top drawer. That's when he heard a whisper, just outside his doorway. He paused to listen. He couldn't be sure, but it sounded as if the owner of the hushed voice stepped away, toward the landing. *The goddamned floor is creaking again!*

He grabbed his briefcase and sport coat and headed for the door.

"No-o-or-r-r-ma-a-a-n!"

The voice emanated from the landing and belonged to a young woman. Her unmistakable Southern style was soft and sultry. But, the voice also seemed empty and lonely, as if it resided someplace far away. Unnatural sounding… it made him pause in his doorway. Before he could muster a reply, she called to him again.

"Come to me, No-o-o-r-r-r-ma-a-a-n-n-n! I'm ready to give ya what ya desi-i-ir-r-re!"

"Who's out there??" he called to the landing, surprised by the weakness in his legs. Tentatively, he crept over to the light switch, his unsteady hand reaching to turn the light back on.

"Don't turn it on, darlin'!"

The voice sounded closer now, warmer and even more seductive. Despite the weirdness of the situation, his sexual curiosity was now fully aroused. It sounded more like an adolescent than an adult…. *Who is she?* Peering into the landing's shadowed corner nearest him, he detected the silhouette of someone standing there.

"Step out to where I can see you!" he ordered, keeping his hand on the switch, ready to turn the light on if she didn't comply.

"Whatever ya say, Nor-r-m-m-a-a-n-n!"

The girl had her back to him, and as she stepped to the side away from the shadows he saw her long blue dress that hung down below her ankles. The likely source for the brushing sounds he heard across the carpet earlier, it no longer mattered to him. His eyes moved up and down her shapely form. Her strawberry-blonde hair flowed past her shoulders and shimmered under the window's colorful glow. She continued to move over until she stood near the center of the window, and then she turned her head to where he could see the right profile of her face.

A slight gasp escaped his throat. From her delicate nose, cheekbones, and lips along with long eyelashes that surely adorned a pair of gorgeous eyes, he knew the girl was stunning. Powerfully aroused, he could already tell where this encounter would likely lead. Her smile naughty, she turned her head to where she held him in the gaze of one eye. A few strands from her hair fell over her face, making her even more alluring.

"Do ya want me?" she asked.

What in the hell?

He couldn't believe his ears. His heart began to beat harder, while his mind sifted through sordid images and the possible legal implications of having sex with an underage female.

"No one'll ever know, 'cept us," she assured him. She winked and motioned for him to join her by the window.

Did she just frigging read my mind?

It didn't matter. Driven by his strongest addiction far more than his God-given cunning intelligence, he set his briefcase down and took off his coat, dropping it on the floor. He moved up behind her. When within a few feet, she placed one hand upon the window, sliding it down the glass as she bent over, thrusting her hips high in the air. With her other hand, she pulled her dress up to her waist.

The fragrance of lilac, honeysuckle, and a distinct female scent wafted toward him. Under the streetlight's illumination that cast colorful rays upon her naked backside, he saw her sex was ready, positioned as the fulfillment of his favorite fantasy. From her nymph-like feet and long slender legs to the gentle curves of her nubile butt, he knew it could be a very long time before he had an opportunity like this again. He smiled lecherously, his arousal coming to full strength.

"What are ya waitin' for?" she asked, her voice muffled by her hair covering her face "Don't ya want to fuck a hillbilly like me?"

Her words took him aback, and he thought about what he told David when they drove to the post office. If not for the delectable gift positioned less than a foot away, he might've come to his senses and ran downstairs to get away.

"What's your name, sweetheart?" He leaned down to get a better look at her nakedness. The aroma of lilac and honeysuckle grew stronger.

Just like the goddamned tooth!

"Does knowin' my name truly matter?" she replied. "Wouldn't ya just rather enjoy yer fantasy of who I am, and leave it at that?"

He reached out and touched her, caressing curves and her readiness. But the flesh was cold.... He assumed she had waited somewhere outside for much of the evening. Maybe, she had been hiding in the parking lot, and then sneaked inside when Troy left for the night. Perhaps, also, she was some under-aged whore that David picked up off East Colfax as a joke, and then paid to come up here and mess with him after their earlier discussion. He had always pictured his buddy as an uptight goody-goody, but David must've found out he took the peculiar little bag from him and decided on a clever plan to pay him back for stealing it. Hell, David was probably waiting in the parking lot right then. Thinking along these lines, he wondered if he should put on some protection before taking advantage of the 'gift'.

"You'd best seize the moment, Norman, before what's offered to ya's pulled away," she advised, huskily. She tilted her head to where he could see her gazing up at him through thicker locks of hair hanging down over her face. "It's not like you've felt the need to protect yerself before. Why don't ya pull it out and show me? Maybe after we're done, I'll slap another kind of wet one on ya!"

The way she addressed him, so sexy and full of heat, was driving him nuts. And the accent, which sounded as if it truly came from the hills of the old South, made him believe his ultimate fantasy would soon be fulfilled. Though a little weird in the set up, David had come through in a way he never imagined possible. He planned a handsome payback for him, beginning with a nice steak dinner after the Broncos' game on Sunday.

Norm hastily unzipped his pants, almost tearing his slacks and boxers when he pulled them down below his knees. Then he entered her.

"Yeah, that's right, you hillbilly wench!" he told her as the unusual coolness gripped him. "I'm going to give you what you're begging for!"

But as he penetrated it felt as if he had reached an icy reservoir. The freezing embrace sent a surge of incredible exhilaration through his entire being. His body began to shake, moving toward an orgasm unlike anything he'd ever experienced before.

He couldn't control his furious thrusts in a desperate attempt to get even closer to the strange rawness within her and hang on as long as possible. Her soft moans became more impassioned, and she raised her voice to where he could hear what she said. If he hadn't been so enraptured by his own desires, he might've asked her what she meant by the weird phrases she chanted.

"Moonlight from the shadows hide…feed the solace of the night...."

"Oh-h-h, this feels so goddamned *good!*"

"Dust to life when death is nigh…warm flesh and blood whither and die...."

"What in the *hell* does that mean?" He uttered between gasps, knowing he couldn't hold back his release much longer. "Tell me that nothing satisfies your hunger like Norm can!"

"The soulless one will soon arrive…let us feed him, to not deny...."

"Goddamn it girl, tell me what I want to hear!" he shouted, but too late. His release came suddenly, as a surge of violent chills raced through his entire being. *"All right, bitch! Well, I'm gonna deliver what you deserve, you sleazy whore!!"*

"What'd ya just call me?"

She stood up, reaching behind to pull him out. Her dress dropped back down to her ankles, immediately concealing her nakedness. She held his member tight, and her grip's strength both surprised and frightened him.

"Huh? What in the hell's wrong with you?"

Norm couldn't remember exactly what he said to piss her off, as often in the throes of passion he spit out the first thing that popped into his head. But he knew the words 'bitch', 'sleazy', and 'whore' came pouring out of his mouth at some point. Her sudden mood change wasn't the first time he elicited such a response. However, this particular female had a vise-like hold on the favorite part of his body, and the deepening coldness in her hand frightened him.

"How 'bout I fulfill my other offer to ya, Norman?"

Her tone was menacing, completely void of the sultry sweetness she addressed him with earlier. She turned to face him from the right, her profile as beautiful as before. But, she frowned, and the eye peering at him through her hair narrowed.

"I really should be getting on home now, Miss." He placed his hand on her icy wrist to try and pry it off his aching erection. "I-I'm sorry if I offended you.... Maybe we can try this again sometime, and I promise not to be such an asshole."

But she didn't let go. He fought desperately to pry her fingers, but couldn't budge them. They were clamped onto him like the jaws of a pit bull. Fear escalated into sheer panic, and he began to whimper, begging her to please release him.

"No, I'll *not* let go, Norman!"

"Please! I'll do whatever you want!" He hated the way she drawled his name, and was angry at himself for finding it alluring earlier. Something was terribly wrong… something *so dangerous* about her. He couldn't believe he let himself fall prey like this, grimly certain that some psychopath had slipped into the building when Troy left, and that it had nothing at all to do with David Hobbs.

"Oh, but yer wrong about that!" she said, surprising him more by letting him know his thoughts were open to her. She brought her face closer to him, as she did the aroma of death wafted in his nostrils. "I've got a pendin' appointment with Billy Ray, and he's goin' to learn firsthand all about what yer set to go through, darlin'."

She began to push him backward, further tightening her grip to where the pain between his legs was excruciating. Norm shrieked.

She giggled meanly. "Norman, are ya ready for somethin' else that's cold and wet?"

He continued to fight as she effortlessly pushed him, his boxers and slacks tangled around his ankles while his shoes slid across the floor. At first, the form of a lovely girl remained, her beautiful hair shimmering like a halo in the colorful rays created by the streetlamp's glow through the ornate window. Her face hidden in shadow continued to feed the illusion of unspoiled beauty… but that changed as she pushed him closer toward the banister. For a mere instant, he saw her face clearly.

"What in the hell are you?" With both hands, he desperately tore at her fingers that grew increasingly colder. *"Let me go—PLEASE!"*

She pushed him until his naked backside touched the coolness of the handcrafted banister behind him, and then she stopped. Mercifully, her face disappeared in shadow once more. He glanced over the edge, listening to the water splash in the fountain twenty feet below. Meanwhile, a gurgling noise erupted from where her neck should be, and as he turned back to look at her, a stream of blood poured down the left side of her dress.

"Would ya like to truly become one with me, Norman?" she asked, her voice a mixture of sarcasm and amusement, punctuated by the gurgling noise coming from her open throat. "Or, how 'bout we settle for a lil' ole kiss instead, to send ya off right proper-r-r-r?"

He pushed himself as hard as he could against the banister. When he looked up he saw her face again, eerily aglow from the security lamps' soft illumination. His shrieks were continual as terror gripped him completely. She drew ever closer, embracing his torso with her free hand. Her other hand still held him fast, where the tissue had turned purple from blood not being allowed to flow back through his body.

She raised him off the floor, his pants and belt dangling below his ankles as his knees cleared the banister. He scarcely believed her effortless strength, although by now he understood she wasn't anything human.

"No, no…*No, don't do it! I beg you…PLEASE DON'T!"*

Norm began to lose control of his bladder and bowels. His eyes blurred as tears flowed down his face. The girl who only moments ago fulfilled his fantasy like no other woman could, chuckled merrily. His tears obscured much of her hideousness, but not enough to hide her dreadful smile.

"Good bye, Nor-r-r-m-a-a-a-n-n!" she told him sweetly, and then launched him off the landing.

Screaming as he flailed his arms to try and turn over, as he headed for the ground floor, Norm's bound ankles kept him from being able to control his descent. An incredible sharp pain ripped through his torso when he landed on top of the fountain. The decorative spire pierced him, slicing through his liver while crushing other vital organs in his midsection. Impaled upon the fountain covered with his blood, he glimpsed the water around him turning dark.

Norm tried to reach for his pants so that whoever found his body wouldn't see him like this. But, he couldn't move without incurring far greater pain. Waiting for the end to come, he turned his gaze up toward the landing.

The girl's form had changed. The gorgeous hair that captured his fancy when he first saw her billowed around the silhouette of her face. An immense shadow drifted over the edge of the banister, absorbing the rest of her body. Her gurgled voice echoed around him as the shadow descended toward the fountain.

Norm gulped once and closed his eyes. Death couldn't come soon enough.

Chapter Twenty-one

"Honey… Ned's on the phone," said Miriam.

David had just finished taking a shower in the guest bathroom of Janice's townhouse. He quickly toweled himself dry and stepped into his bathrobe, tying it at his waist while he opened the door. She held the phone out to him, covering the receiver until he could take it.

"How did he get this number?" he asked. David glanced at his watch on the bathroom counter, which read 6:40 a.m. "I wonder what couldn't wait until eight o'clock."

He smiled, until he saw tears welling in her eyes. Her bottom lip quivered as she handed him the phone. He started to pursue her out of the bathroom, but she motioned for him to first take the call. Janice stood nearby, and looked equally upset.

"Hey, Ned." He stepped back inside the bathroom and closed the door most of the way.

"Hello, David," said Ned. Often serious, he sounded unusually somber. "Sorry to bother you so early and calling you at this number. It's the one left on the voicemail at your home."

"Is something wrong?" David immediately worried he had miscalculated the final figures on the Applewood report he gave Ned last night.

"Yeah, there is."

The line went quiet for almost a full minute, leaving David to wonder if Ned had set the phone down. He could tell his boss had arrived at the office already, and other voices made it sound like the normal Friday morning bustle started a few hours earlier than normal. He thought he heard Ned gasp and struggle to breathe.

"Ned, are you okay?"

"I'm here…. I wish to God I wasn't the one to have to tell you."

"Tell me what?" David's worry turned to alarm as Ned wept. "Did I really screw something up on the reports?"

"Oh, no," he assured him. "If only that were it."

"Are Martha and your boys okay?"

Maybe that was it, given Miriam and Janice's upset behavior.

"They're fine. Thanks for asking."

"Well, whatever you've got to tell me can't be *that* bad, can it?"

"David… Norm is dead."

"What?" He almost dropped the phone. His knees buckled before he could close the toilet lid for a place to sit. "What did you just say?"

He knew full well what he heard, but wanted desperately for it not to be true.

"Norm was killed sometime last night after Troy left. I'm so sorry."

"How can this be?" sobbed David. Miriam pushed open the door and rushed into the bathroom, throwing her arms around him, crying just as hard. *"I just spoke to him last night! Oh my God, he can't be gone!"*

"I wish more than anything it wasn't true. Nancy gave a positive ID to the police once Johnny discovered his body. They're both having such a hard time dealing with this too…." Ned began to cry. "We all loved Norm, David. He and I've known each other for more than ten years. I know it's so much worse for you. I'm so, so very sorry."

Ned cried harder, and as Miriam shared David's pain, Janice and the kids soon crowded their way into the bathroom, trying to console their father and finding it impossible not to cry themselves. David wasn't able to talk again until almost 7:30 a.m. Ned remained on the line and Miriam at his side. Janice finished getting the kids ready for school.

"How did it happen?" David hated asking, but needed to know.

"The police aren't sure, yet," said Ned.

"What, are you saying he was murdered?"

David couldn't picture anyone bearing a grudge against Norm, other than a miffed boyfriend of one of the many females he'd bedded over the years.

"All they're saying right now is it looks like a homicide," Ned advised. "Two detectives from the Denver Police will be here this morning to interview everyone employed by us. Knowing how especially close you were to Norm, I've asked the Captain I spoke with earlier to have them make a special trip this afternoon to speak with you at your house, unless you'd rather meet with them at Ms. Andrew's home."

"I'd rather not trouble Jan," said David, thinking it would also be best without the kids present. "Why don't I come to the office and speak with them there along with everyone else?"

"No, David," said Ned. "I'm placing you on mandatory bereavement leave from today until next week, after Norm's funeral arrangements have been finalized. The days will be comp'd for you, since Stephen and everyone else around here knows you two were like brothers."

"But, what about the amortization details and the other unfinished reports for Applewood you mentioned before I left last night?" asked David, annoyed. How in the hell would he survive? Not by spending idle time at home, where the loss of Norm would bring a constant assault upon his psyche and soul. "What if I come in for awhile today and take everything with me to work on over the weekend?"

"Not happening," said Ned. "After the police interviews are finished this morning, we're closing the office until Monday. Stephen has already decided to call the Applewood folks and make them aware of what's happened, and that it will take a few days for us all to recover. He's confident John Meier, their chairman, will understand. We're slightly ahead of our original completion schedule anyway."

"What time will the detectives come by?" David resigned himself to the fact he had no choice but to go along numbly with his boss's decision.

"I told them two o'clock, but if you'd rather change it to another time either earlier or later, I can do that."

"Two will be fine."

"All right. Again, I'm so, *so* sorry, David."

"Me, too."

He started to weep again, and Miriam pulled him closer. For the next half hour, he cried in her arms. Reluctant to leave him, she needed to take care of her patients who couldn't be rescheduled for the following week. She left just before eight-thirty, mentioning on her way out the door that the glass company would come by their house sometime in the afternoon to repair Tyler's window. David offered to let the repair crew inside the house, since he'd be there anyway to talk with the detectives.

He finished getting dressed, and shared a few cups of coffee with Janice while they talked about Norm, whom she once dated in college and remained on good terms with since. When ten o'clock arrived, David left the townhouse and headed for the Park Meadows Mall. He hoped to kill some time and distract his thoughts by visiting the various stores. It didn't take long to recognize it wouldn't help. Instead, he stopped by the closest liquor store and purchased a twelve-pack of beer.

Just before eleven, he arrived at the house. He sifted through the mail while opening his first Heineken, confident whatever supernatural presence had besieged his residence had left. Feeling good to be home again, he hoped it would lessen the terrible grief that would come for him in the coming days and weeks. In the meantime, he flipped through the latest National Geographic until noon, when he made himself a sandwich. He straightened up the main floor and grabbed another beer while he awaited the detectives' arrival.

* * * * *

"David Hobbs?"

The two DPD detectives mentioned by Ned stood at the front door, and the one who spoke held his badge up near his face.

"Yes." David opened the front door wide enough for them to step inside. They arrived ten minutes early, right before his fifth beer. The lightheaded effect from the first four made him glad he hadn't opened another bottle.

"I'm Detective Daniel Colby, and this is my partner, Detective Mike Kenyon," said the first detective, motioning to the other as they stepped into the foyer.

A slender man in his early forties, Daniel Colby's sandy hair hung in short bangs on his forehead. His face flushed slightly, and the prescription eyeglasses he wore magnified his light blue eyes. The detective sported a curved moustache, almost Fu-Manchu, and his voice seemed unusually raspy, as if he'd spent many a long night on the short end of a whiskey bottle.

Mike Kenyon was much younger and more handsome, and stood almost a foot taller than his partner. Mike's hazel eyes shined bright within a dark face. His generous smile, chiseled features, and sharp hairline made him look like a TV star instead of an actual policeman.

David closed the front door, and they followed him into the living room, where he invited them to sit on the sofa.

"Can I get you guys anything to drink?"

"At the moment we're okay," said Daniel, nodding to Mike, who indicated he didn't need anything either. "We appreciate your willingness to discuss Norman Sowell. We understand you were quite close. You might want to take a seat and get comfortable, Mr. Hobbs. We have several questions."

He motioned for David to sit across from them in the loveseat. Detective Kenyon pulled out a smart phone, while Detective Colby produced a small steno pad and a small recorder. For the next half hour, both detectives asked him questions... many more than the several they indicated at the interrogation's outset. All of the questions had to do with Norm, his various habits and vices, and David's close relationship with him. Near the end of the conversation, David became antsy, wondering why neither detective had shared anything about Norm's murder with him.

"You think he was murdered, right?" he finally asked. "Can you tell me what happened?"

"We're still gathering evidence, but at this point his death is being treated as a homicide," said Daniel.

"What have you been told so far, Mr. Hobbs?" asked Mike.

"Nothing, other than the fact Johnny Townsend and Nancy Geddings found Norm this morning when they came in," said David. "That's all Ned told me when we spoke earlier."

"Did he tell you where Mr. Sowell's body was discovered?" Daniel glanced at his partner.

David shook his head.

"Certain aspects of the investigation must remain secret for now, but it appears Mr. Sowell fell from the upstairs landing to his death," said Daniel.

"At this point, we're trying to get a lead on finger prints and blood samples we found at the scene, as well as other evidence from Mr. Sowell's office," added Mike. "It could take a few weeks to get the final analysis from our labs downtown. Did Norman ever prefer sex partners other than female?"

"Huh?" Surprised, David couldn't picture what the question implied. "Norm was a strict heterosexual, as far as I know. Why do you ask?"

Both detectives declined to answer, leaving David with a plethora of unpleasant musings about Norm, as well as many more questions. But neither man offered David anything to go on. While Daniel collected his recorder from the coffee table, Mike asked to use the bathroom before they left. As he moved past the living room, one of the bedroom doors upstairs slammed shut.

"Is anyone here with you?" asked Daniel, stepping into the foyer and glancing up the stairway.

"No." David followed close behind. "One of my kids must've left a window open."

It sounded as if Tyler's door was the one that had shut, since a door rattled against a splintered doorframe. David pictured the plastic trash bags being torn loose from the window frame, allowing the wind to enter Tyler's bedroom.

"Do you mind if we take a look?" Mike rejoined them and turned his attention up the stairway, as well.

"Is that really necessary?"

It irritated David the detectives cared about the noise upstairs, and yet had told him virtually nothing about what had happened to Norm. He suddenly worried what the detectives might think if they discovered the damage inside Tyler's bedroom.

"It will be a quick look."

Before David could react, Detective Kenyon had already moved passed him and climbed the stairs. Detective Colby and David followed. The detectives walked down the hall toward Tyler's bedroom. After examining the fractured doorframe together, Mike opened the door and they stepped inside. David noticed their scowls had deepened as they looked around the room, their gazes settling on the hole in the wall and the bloodstained windowsill. David's patch job remained intact.

"My son had an accident the other day when he came home from school, and he fell through the window," offered David, thinking how lame that sounded as the words left his mouth. They merely nodded while moving about the room. "I should've mentioned this downstairs, but with what happened to Norm and all, I forgot about it. Does your need to look around up here have anything to do with him?"

"As I said earlier, we're in the early stage of our investigation." Daniel regarded him evenly. "Are you sure there's no one else in the house with us now?"

""As far as I know, there's no one else here. My wife's at work and the kids are at school." David looked at the sealed window patch again, wondering briefly if the ghost had done it.

The bag's been sent back to Gatlinburg… it must be some other open window up here.

"I'd like to have a look at the other rooms up here, if you don't mind, Mr. Hobbs."

Daniel didn't wait for David's response, moving into the hallway with his partner. What could he say or do anyway? They could probably get a warrant, if necessary, and it wasn't like he had something to hide… or did he?

Oh shit!

He suddenly remembered the strange circle made from leaves and his personal items, which was still on the floor in front of his dresser in the master bedroom. The circle would probably mean nothing to them, but he didn't want to get caught up in a discussion on how it got there. He cursed the fact he didn't clean it up earlier when he returned to the house.

The detectives had already moved to the other side of the hall, apparently satisfied with what they'd seen in Jillian and Christopher's bedrooms. David caught up with them just as they reached the first guestroom. Since nothing resembled Tyler's bedroom, he hoped to get them to return downstairs. He tried to focus on what to say, regretting the beer buzz, when the phone rang. The only landline handset upstairs sat on Miriam's nightstand.

"We can wait for you to get that if you'd like," said Mike, after the phone rang for the third time.

David moved past them to the master bedroom, closing the door behind him after stating he'd be just a moment. By the time he reached the phone, it ceased ringing. The caller ID showed the call came from Miriam's office, and he intended to call her back as soon as the detectives left. He moved quietly over to the cedar chest at the foot of the bed, where he pulled out a blanket from inside. Three firm knocks resounded from the other side of the bedroom door.

"Mr. Hobbs?"

"I'll be right there!"

David hoped his voice sounded relaxed enough. Unsure what it would take to make things look less suspicious, he laid the plaid blanket upon the floor, careful to fully cover the circle. He closed the lid to the chest and tiptoed toward the doorway, opening it just as Daniel prepared to knock again.

"Sorry about that. My wife called."

The detectives looked annoyed, and David hoped it hadn't sounded as if he scurried about from outside his door. They stepped into the bedroom, and after scanning the room, Mike moved to the bathroom while his partner checked the closet. Finding nothing out of the ordinary, the detectives prepared to leave. Detective Kenyon noticed a small, curled yellow leaf sticking out from under the blanket on the floor. He quickly moved to it, while David's throat constricted.

"Check this out, Danny," he told his partner, lifting the blanket and revealing the circle beneath it. He pulled out a pair of latex gloves from his jacket's inside pocket.

"Well I'll be damned," whispered Daniel, who pulled out a similar latex glove and placed it on his right hand. "Would you mind telling us what happened here, Mr. Hobbs?"

The detective pulled out a compact camera from his front coat pocket and took several pictures of the circle. He and Mike stooped down and removed a few leaves and twigs, and placed them inside small plastic evidence bags.

"I don't know for sure," said David, sighing deeply and shaking his head, angry with himself for not getting rid of the circle earlier.

"But, you didn't want us to find it, did you?" accused Mike. He sealed the first bag and placed it inside the same pocket he withdrew his gloves. "'Are you sure you don't want to tell us anything?"

Both he and Daniel eyed him seriously, and David doubted either man would believe what actually happened. Without knowing what else to tell them, and realizing any further deception on his part would be ill advised, he told them the truth. A summarized version, anyway, that focused on him and his eldest son hearing or catching glimpses of a mysterious female in the house.

"Tyler told us that she pushed him through the window, and is also responsible for the damage to his door frame," he said. "No one else in my family has actually seen her, although everyone has experienced some pretty strange stuff since Sunday. My wife will tell you that she believes the girl is the one who left that circle on the floor."

He braced himself for contempt and ridicule, surprised when neither detective so much as cracked a smile. Instead, they nodded knowingly to each other.

"Can we talk with Tyler and the rest of the family this evening, say around five o'clock?" asked Daniel. "I'd also like for our techs to come out here to look at this."

"Sure," said David, wondering why there was so much interest in the circle. "Will you at least tell me if this has something to do with Norm?"

"Sorry, we're not at liberty to discuss anything until we've had time to go over everything we've collected so far," said Detective Colby. "Just make sure nothing's disturbed up here, Mr. Hobbs."

"All right." David shrugged. "There's a crew coming by to fix the window, but other than them, I'll make sure everyone else steers clear of upstairs."

"Can you postpone the repair on the window, at least until our guys finish looking around up here?" asked Detective Kenyon. "Frankly, it would be better if nothing in the house is disturbed at all until the techs are done. They might not be able to come out here until tomorrow, but will you please do that for us?"

David agreed, although wishing they'd extend the same courtesy and shed a little light on what had happened to Norm. Meanwhile, the detectives prepared to leave the bedroom. Just before they reached the hallway, Daniel had one more question.

"How did you get that bruise above your eye, Mr. Hobbs?"

"I don't know."

Neither detective masked their growing suspicion. David felt the blood rush to his face, but fought hard to quell his indignation.

They think I'm involved in Norm's death? How could they?

Without saying another word, the detectives headed downstairs. When he caught up with them in the foyer, Daniel handed David a business card with his contact information.

"We'll be back this evening," he advised. "If you think of anything else you'd like to share before then, call me."

* * * * *

Once a couple of blocks away, Daniel picked up the radio handset beneath the dash and dialed the dispatcher.

"This is Colby," he said into the receiver, glancing at Detective Kenyon in the passenger seat. "I'm requesting a background check on one David Hobbs, 1737 LeClair Drive in Littleton."

The female dispatcher repeated the information in code, chiding him playfully for not using the proper protocol. He laughed and thanked her for the advice before hanging up the handset.

"Do you think he did it?" asked Mike, for the moment staring ahead as they prepared to leave the neighborhood.

"You're asking me if I think he killed Norman Sowell?"

"The twigs and leaves look like they're the same ones spread around the fountain," noted Mike. "That would definitely link him to the crime scene. And, the bruise on his forehead looks like it came from a fight."

"Yeah, I suppose it does," sighed Daniel. "But, the girl he mentioned… that would also be consistent with the evidence we've seen so far."

"There's no frigging way any normal female could subdue a two-hundred and twenty-pound man like Norman Sowell and lift his frame above that banister and throw him down to the first floor—much less get him to land on the top of the fountain like what happened," countered Mike. "But, another two-hundred and some-odd pound man like David Hobbs could."

"Not really." Daniel glanced at his partner, who turned to meet his gaze. "Granted, he looks like a strong guy, and my thinking could change if it turns out there is trace evidence on Norman Sowell's hands or anywhere else at the crime scene that's linked to Mr. Hobbs's DNA and the injury on his face. But, I'm not sure even a world-class body builder could lift someone that heavy above a four-foot railing and thrust him another fifteen feet to where his torso landed on the fountain's spire. Remember, the only bruises we found were on the guy's pecker. Whoever lifted him and threw his body did so with ease. My original thought about it being some kind of sexual-masochistic suicide leap would still be the best fit for the facts so far, if not for the bloody fingerprints in his office."

"And the leaves, man…. It's too big for a coincidence to find the same shit upstairs in Hobbs' bedroom," said Mike. "Do you think maybe he has a partner, like the girl he mentioned? There's evidence to support that idea."

They were nearing the business district of Littleton, and Daniel maneuvered the cruiser toward I-25's entrance, the preferred thoroughfare back to the police station.

"Maybe. What did you think of the window frame in the boy's bedroom?"

"It looked as if a mini-MAC truck slammed into it." Mike chuckled nervously, obviously considering the absurdity of what he witnessed.

"Well, we both know the likelihood of a girl or David Hobbs doing that kind of damage without a stick or two of dynamite is remote," reasoned Daniel. "There's still something important missing… a piece to the puzzle not yet revealed. Let's wait until we speak to the rest of the Hobbs' family before drawing any conclusions. I'm looking forward to visiting with the oldest boy. Tyler?"

"Yeah, that's the kid's name." Mike pulled out his phone again. "I'll make a few notes for when we return later today."

"'Sounds good." Daniel veered into the turn lane to get onto I-25 heading north. "Let's get the necessary permissions from the Littleton PD, and call Judy so she and her forensic team can stop by the house later today."

"I'm on it." Mike made the calls while the cruiser sped toward downtown Denver.

Chapter Twenty-two

"Hey, babe, it's me.... Sorry I missed your call." David spoke to Miriam from the kitchen phone. "I just finished talking to the police. Do you happen to have the number for the guys coming out here to repair the window?"

"Don't you remember they gave us a four-hour window between one and five today to be there?" she said, sounding a little irritated by his apparent impatience.

"It's not what you think," he assured her. "The cops don't want anything done to the window until their forensic specialists look at it first."

"Did they say why?"

"Well, the detectives examined the window and the damage to Ty's door, and they took samples of the leaves and twigs from our bedroom," he said. "They didn't come right out and say so, but they indicated what they found upstairs is somehow related to what they found at the office when Norm's body was discovered.... They asked me about the bruise on my forehead, and I told them I didn't know how I got it. They seem to think I'm somehow connected to Norm's death."

"Oh, David, I'm so sorry," she said, gently. "Let me call the window company and see if we can reschedule for next week. You just try to relax until I get there. I'll be out of here in about an hour. Okay?"

"Yeah. I'll see you then, babe."

He bit his lower lip to keep from crying. He hung up and moved to the kitchen table, looking out the bay window into the backyard. The leaves covering the ground seemed to have grown tenfold since Sunday night, when he walked around the house looking for a prowler. At least he had a distraction to pull his thoughts from Norm and what just transpired with the detectives. But he needed to check on something else first.

He retrieved his coat from the foyer, and after fishing through several pockets he found a small slip of paper. David headed for the den and his laptop. The USPS database confirmed the drop-off transaction for the parcel he mailed at 12:03 p.m. the previous afternoon. The package arrived at the Knoxville airport's post office at 5:38 a.m. this morning, and then it was delivered in Gatlinburg less than four hours later, at 9:27 a.m.

Relieved, he closed his laptop. After grabbing his coat, he retrieved his work gloves and a rake he hadn't used in years from the garage. Then he set out for the backyard where the leaves were thickest, hoping to break a sweat and push back the pain and sorrow continuing to close in on him.

Under an overcast sky, the latest forecast called for snow by evening. The leaves in the middle of the backyard rose above his ankles, and as David surveyed the backyard, he glanced back at the house. Most of the drapes and plantation blinds were closed on both floors. The splintered wood around Tyler's window, and the bent post that held the security flood lamp on the gabled roof below the window, caught his eye before he turned away. An icy shiver coursed up and down his spine, forcing him to again consider the entity's violent tendencies.

He set out in earnest to clear as much of the yard as possible, and soon had filled nearly a dozen bags. David decided to rake one last pile before calling it quits. As he finished, an unusual noise emanating from the treetops in the yard of a large residence several acres away, to the north of his home, drew his attention.

The treetops swayed noticeably, as if an invisible massive hand pushed its way through them. To his amazement, the phenomenon moved into the next neighbor's yard, as the tall pines and maples began to sway back and forth. All the while, the noise grew from a heavy rustling to where it sounded like a massive swarm of angry hornets. By the time it entered his next-door neighbor's backyard, he had the eerie impression that the invisible force was moving toward him specifically.

He held out his rake in front of him, scarcely believing what was happening. The treetops at the edge of his property began to shake as the unseen swarm approached. Suddenly, someone tapped his shoulder from behind.

"David, it's me!" Miriam shielded her face as she stepped back. She held his prized camera, falling to the ground as he barely missed hitting her with the rake.

"Damn it, you scared the shit out of me!" David dropped the rake to help her to her feet. "I'm sorry, babe.... Are you okay?"

"Yeah, I'm fine. I didn't mean to scare you, hon."

Miriam reached up and kissed him, which softened the scowl on his face. Meanwhile, her attention was drawn to the far end of the backyard. David followed her gaze, thankful that only a light breeze moved through the trees.

"What's with the camera?" he asked, anxious to think about something else.

"Just following up on an idea Jan and Sara gave me," she said. "Since there were almost a dozen exposures left from our trip last weekend, I decided to finish the roll with a few pictures taken around the house."

"As in the bedrooms upstairs?" He closed the last bag and slapped his gloves on top. "You were careful not to mess with anything. Right?"

"Yes, don't worry. I was careful not to disturb anything. I won't start cleaning things up until after the detectives and the lab techs are done."

"So, have you finished the roll?"

"Not yet," she said, smiling impishly. "After I took a few shots from both upstairs and downstairs, I saw how hard you were working out here and decided to save the last one just for you, hon."

"It probably will suck. If I were you, I'd aim the camera at something else." He began stacking the bags in a row.

"Not so fast, silly." She gently pulled his arm to make him face her. "Come on… stand over here."

She directed him to the largest maple in the yard, coaxing him to lean against it like Paul Bunyan, holding the rake out proudly to one side. She backed up and knelt on the grass, aiming the camera's lens toward him.

"Now, smile for me, David. Smile for me as if I'm the naked dessert you might get tonight… *if* you play your cards right!"

That brought a smile, brighter than he presumed possible, enticed by her offer and grateful for her presence.

"Gotcha!" She stood and rejoined him. "I want to get these developed tonight, once the police have finished their work. Jan's picking the kids up and will bring them here."

"I guess we'll be having pizza again, huh? The detectives asked me to leave everything untouched, including the kitchen. How do you propose we keep the kids occupied in the meantime?"

"They'd love to hang out with you, if that's okay."

"Sure, I'd like that." The sorrow lifted slightly at the mere prospect of being around his kids. "I'd like to be with them and you."

"Are you sure?" She looked up, her sad eyes hopeful.

"Yeah. *Yes*, I am," he assured her. "Now, go on inside. I'll join you as soon as I'm done taking these bags to the garage."

"Yes, sir!" She saluted him, adding a seductive smile before moving back to the porch. "The yard looks great, by the way."

He looked around, pleased that he'd accomplished quite a bit in a short amount of time, while pushing the heaviness in his heart as far away as he could manage.

"It's a start, babe!" he called after her, just as she stepped inside the house.

After she closed the patio door behind her, he glanced toward the corner of the yard once more. Everything seemed at peace. He grabbed the rake and a pair of full bags in each hand, and headed for the garage.

* * * * *

The detectives returned just after five o'clock as promised. By then, the temperature outside had dropped to near freezing. David and the kids joined Miriam and Janice in the living room around four-thirty, where they awaited the detective's arrival. As he had with his parents, Tyler offered very little information to Daniel Colby and Mike Kenyon, and only confirmed what David had told them. Unable to mask their growing frustration, the only thing that kept them from pushing Tyler harder was Jillian's antics. She desperately wanted to tell them all about her experience on Monday.

Soon, Judith Krantz and her team of three forensic specialists arrived. The team spent twenty minutes on the main floor before moving upstairs. Meanwhile, Daniel and Mike interviewed Miriam and Janice, focusing on their relationship to Norman Sowell and what they knew about the girl Tyler sketchily described. For the most part, they ignored David after their cordial greeting, but glanced at him several times during their interviews with Janice and the family.

He sensed the weight of their suspicion. Yet, it seemed inappropriate to say anything, despite the seething indignation he kept in check. He hoped to ease their distrust once they got around to interviewing him again. However, they avoided speaking to him directly. Instead, they revisited several questions with Tyler and Janice. Once the forensic team finished their work around seven o'clock, the detectives followed them out of the house.

"I appreciate your family's time and cooperation, Mrs. Hobbs," Daniel told Miriam. "We'll be in touch if we have any more questions."

He smiled at her before stepping onto the porch, zipping his coat to avoid the night's chill. Tiny snowflakes filled the air.

David noted both detectives' gentle treatment of his wife, amused at how her charm enamored them. If nothing else, her presence made the second round of questions less accusatory and intrusive.

"Well he seems nice," she said, after closing the door.

"I doubt he or Detective Kenyon care much for me," said David, as they moved into the living room. "Thank God you don't look anything like Broomhilda, or this might've been unpleasant."

She giggled at his wry smile, punching him lightly on his arm. Janice chuckled, and stated she noticed the same thing. Meanwhile, Miriam looked into her husband's eyes, as if gauging his present emotional state.

"I think we should leave everything alone in here for now," she said, once he stepped toward his cherished La-Z-Boy. "Just in case the police need anything else from us."

"They lifted that little shrine from our bedroom, including all of my hideous neckties. What more could they possibly want, unless they're planning to take the doorframe from Ty's room?" He inched closer to his recliner.

"Just the same, we should stay with Jan," she advised. "At least for tonight. Besides, Sara will be there around eight, and she's looking forward to meeting you."

"The fortune teller lady you mentioned last night?" He knew he sounded annoyed, but that's the last thing he needed right then. Hell, the lady couldn't even sense the ghost's presence in their home, according to Miriam.

"She's not a fortune teller, David," said Janice, sounding defensive. "She's a psychic who also happens to be a paranormal investigator, one that's *very* good at what she does. But, if you want me to cancel our plans to meet with her tonight, I'll call her right now."

"No, Jan," Miriam cut in before David could tell Janice to do it. "We planned it with her last night, and as booked as you said she usually is, I'd hate to cancel on her at the last minute. If David doesn't want to meet her, you and I can visit with her for awhile." She moved to him and placed her arm around his waist.

"I guess I can hang out with the kids while you do that," he said, responding to her loving smile with a sheepish grin. He welcomed any distraction to keep his mind off Norm, and he looked forward to intimate time with Miriam later. "Jan, are you sure you don't mind having us all crammed into your townhouse?"

"Not at all," said Janice. "You guys can stay as long as you like."

Christopher chased Jillian through the kitchen and into the dining room, nearly knocking a ceramic serving bowl from the antique hutch to the floor. While David got after them, Janice and Miriam gathered more clothes. Miriam helped Tyler with his coat, and Janice rounded up the younger kids.

Jillian picked up Sadie and David set the alarm. After the rumble of the Chrysler, BMW, and Janice's Subaru faded into the chilly night, a gust of wind swept a flurry of snowflakes across the backyard to the deck. The backdoor's brass handle rattled, and the slightly parted curtains lifted into the air as something colder than the wintry weather, and much more unfriendly, drifted inside the house.

Chapter Twenty-three

A few minutes before eight o'clock, Sara Palmer arrived at Janice Andrew's townhouse. Unlike the colorful smock she wore when Miriam met her yesterday, Sara dressed more conservatively this time. Clad in a thick wool sweater, blue jeans, and boots, no one would have any inkling she had a connection to the paranormal, other than the crystal necklace and amulet she wore around her neck.

After Miriam introduced her to David and the children, Sara sat down near the end of the sofa, setting the duffel bag and coat at her feet. Sadie jumped into her lap, which surprised David, since the dog had never taken so readily to a stranger.

Janice had prepared a marvelous chocolate torte, and when he got up for a second slice, Sara stopped him as he went by. She took his hands in hers while telling him how sorry she was for the recent loss of Norm. He thanked her, and moved into the kitchen, where Miriam caught up with him.

"What was that all about just now?" he asked. "She wasn't just offering me sympathy for losing Norm, was she?"

"No, she wasn't, hon," she said. "Please don't freak out about it. This is how she becomes familiar with your energy. She did it to me, too, yesterday afternoon. She said it helps her better define the scope and cause of a haunting."

Despite her optimism, it still sounded like a load of new age bullshit to him. Yet he kept the latest misgivings to himself, for Miriam's sake, since she believed in Sara.

When they returned to the living room, it surprised him that Tyler had struck up a lively conversation with their guest. The two discussed her son's present pursuits as a software consultant to noteworthy computer companies like Apple and Microsoft. Tyler seemed to soak up every bit of advice Sara gave him, as to what courses to choose in high school and the best colleges and universities in the Rocky Mountain region for computer programming and graphic design.

Satisfied for the moment she wasn't a complete flake, David relaxed a little, observing from a distance this woman who seemed full of energy and life. By the time nine o'clock arrived, the kids finally left the adults alone. Tyler and Jillian did so reluctantly, perhaps drawn as much by the mysterious contents inside Sara's duffel bag as her vibrant personality.

Sara looked at David once the children were out of earshot. Her stare made him uncomfortable. The vivacious smile faded from her face.

"You're the one," she said. "The bond is to you."

"What do you mean?" he replied, guardedly.

Sara looked away, as if studying the various features of the living room. Her gaze settled upon the large dream catcher Janice had hung on the wall next to her front door. She stood up and set Sadie on the floor, before walking up to David.

"She chose you when she saw you and Miriam in Tennessee," she said. "There's some deep connection between the spirit and you. It could be she has mistaken you for someone else she was well acquainted with in her lifetime. Miriam told me that you said the spirit whispered the name Billy Ray. Does that name mean anything to you?"

He shook his head, as the first thing that popped into his mind was Billy Ray Cyrus, the country singer. Pretty damn sure that wasn't the right connection, he waited for another clue.

"I can see why you'd think that." Sara sounded amused, and as if she discerned his thoughts. "Well, it's not so important why the spirit thinks it, as well as her reasons for thinking Ty is another boy named Zachariah. What is important is that we find a way to stop her before she becomes violent again."

"I thought sending all that stuff back to Gatlinburg would take care of everything," said David, echoing Miriam's fears from the previous afternoon.

Sara picked up her coat from the sofa and put it on.

"It should still work," she said. "But I can say this for certain. When I first met Miriam yesterday, I didn't feel the entity's presence. Only your wife's overwhelming sadness about what has befallen your family. When I visited your home, I didn't feel anything unusual, despite the physical evidence that clearly indicated something supernatural had visited the house. But now it's no longer the case. I feel the entity's presence, and it's strong."

"You're talking about the girl, Allie Mae, right?" asked Janice from her reading chair, next to the fireplace. "How's that still possible, since whatever belonged to her is no longer here?"

"It is Allie Mae," confirmed Sara. "Honestly, I don't know why her presence is stronger. I do know she isn't here with us right now. She's somewhere else, maybe even far away, watching… watching and waiting."

"Waiting for what?" David wondered aloud.

"Get your coats and come with me," said Sara. "I'd like to visit your house once more."

Janice volunteered to stay behind with the kids, who eagerly agreed to accompany her to Walgreen's, to pick up the ingredients for some s'mores and the pictures she and

Miriam dropped off earlier. Sara joined David and Miriam in the minivan, and they pulled into the driveway of their home. At first glance, everything appeared as they left it.

Sara followed Miriam and David onto the porch, looking warily around and breathing deeply, as if trying to absorb the essence of their home. She motioned for David to lead the way, with Miriam following. After another cautious glance over her shoulder, she followed. David closed the front door and together they moved into the living room. Sara set her duffel bag on the coffee table, and pulled out an analog Nikon camera equipped with a flash, an EMF detector, and a small digital recorder with an external microphone.

"I'm not here to bless the place," she said, perhaps noting Miriam's perplexed look. "This is more of a fact gathering mission, so we can work toward ensuring the entity's presence doesn't remain in your lives."

Sara handed the EMF detector to Miriam, explaining how she wanted her to watch for energy spikes in the device's digital readout. She gave the recorder to David, after turning it on and making sure it worked. She advised him to be careful, and not allow the slim vinyl strap or anything else brush up against either the external or internal microphones of the recorder while they moved through both floors.

"Are you sure you want us to help you with this?" asked Miriam.

"Absolutely," she said. "This is different from what I hoped to accomplish yesterday. Having your and David's senses and observations to go along with my own should only prove helpful."

She motioned for them to follow, and they explored the darkened den, kitchen, and dining room on the first floor. Every now and then she'd stop and snap a picture or two, which prompted David to ask if having the lights on would be helpful. She replied it wouldn't, since anomalies often appear in photographs taken in darkness. After checking the garage, the group moved upstairs.

Another portrait had fallen on the stairway. Careful in setting it aside, they continued to the second floor, moving through each bedroom and bathroom. Sara snapped more pictures while Miriam and David followed close behind. The exercise proved uneventful, since the house felt as normal as it had earlier. There were no noticeable cold pockets or creaking floors, or anything else to draw attention.

But, while moving down the stairway, the reading on the EMF detector jumped. Sara instructed Miriam to let her know if she saw a spike larger than point five on the readout. This one jumped nearly three full points and happened twice in rapid succession. They all stopped, and Sara snapped pictures around them from the second roll of film. As she did, the master bedroom's door clicked shut, indicating something caused it to close when just moments ago it stood wide open.

In the dimness, Sara frowned and shook her head. She led them back up the stairs and down the hallway to the bedroom. She allowed David to turn on the hall light. She moved to the door and tried to open it. It was locked. Miriam tried to open it as well, but it wouldn't budge. Using the small universal key that worked when the kids locked themselves out of their rooms didn't help either.

"Well, it looks like we'll have another door to replace," said David, wryly, ready to ram it with his shoulder. Before he touched the door, the latch unlocked and the door slowly opened. He took a step to move inside, but Sara stopped him.

"Don't do it!" she warned, moving in front of him. She took a step inside the doorway, but retracted her foot. "Very strange," she whispered. "I'm not allowed inside the room."

David tried to go into the bedroom and she prevented him again, much more forceful this time.

"No, David! I don't know what we're dealing with here. It feels too dangerous to venture beyond the door's threshold!"

She closed her eyes and began to chant, and the temperature around them began to drop. Miriam clung tightly to David's arm as they looked on. Sara's chants became more fervent, and as they did, a rustling noise emerged from the master bedroom's darkness. The noise grew louder in response to Sara's efforts to match it with her words, until finally the floor in the hallway shook, causing everyone to fall backward. The hall light above them flickered and went out, leaving partial illumination from its partner on the other side of the hallway. Rather than test the entity's resolve any further, they ran downstairs, hearing the bedroom door slam loudly as they hurried out of the house.

*****

Janice and the kids returned from their trip to Walgreens, just after ten. David and Miriam were sitting with Sara at the kitchen table. No one smiled, and for the moment, everyone's collective attention was focused on Sara's recorder.

"I guess it's safe to say tonight's visit didn't go so good, huh?" Janice started a fresh pot of coffee. "There's still nearly half a torte if anyone wants some."

"I believe we'll all pass on that, dear," said Sara, echoing less than enthusiastic responses from David and Miriam, who sat on either side. "Coffee sounds good, though."

"Are you sure?" Janice asked Miriam. "I noticed you passed on it earlier, Mir. It's double Dutch chocolate, the world's best mood lifter."

"I should've had some then, Jan," she said. "I guess getting the hell scared out of me is an effective appetite suppressant. If I gain a few pounds around the holidays this year, at least I'll know how to quickly take them off again." She smiled weakly.

"So, what happened?" Janice joined them at the table, where she handed the photo packets to Miriam.

"Well, she's back, and pretty much chased us out of our home." Miriam's eyes were still red from the experience.

"Allie Mae's spirit?" Janice sounded surprised. "Did the equipment Sara brought pick up anything?"

"I plan on getting the pictures I took tonight developed tomorrow," Sara advised. "But, we also got one of the highest EMF spikes I've seen in quite awhile. Here's the thing that really gets me."

She pressed play on the recorder sitting in front of her. At first they heard only light conversation among the three of them, along with David's comments about checking the thermostat again before they left. It marked the point where they headed downstairs, preparing to leave. Then, Miriam excitedly mentioned the EMF spikes. At the same time, the recorder captured what sounded like a chorus of dissonant whispers.

"This was right when things got hairy for us," commented Sara. "Keep in mind, we didn't hear any of the whispers you're listening to now."

"It sounds like there's more than one voice. Can you tell what's being said?" Janice leaned toward the recorder.

"Hardly," said Miriam. "We've been sitting here listening for the past twenty minutes. We can only make out bits and pieces. It's a lot like what happened the other day, when the kids and I heard the whispering in our living room."

"Listen, as it gets noisier and stranger," added Sara. "Right about now we're on our way upstairs, because the master bedroom door closed on its own."

A crackling sound punctuated the undecipherable whispers, followed by the discussion between Sara and David about entering the bedroom. Janice's eyes grew wide as she listened to Sara's alarmed tone on the recorder and the ensuing rustling noise that steadily grew to a windy roar. The recorder caught the powerful tremor moving through the floor, as well as the panicked trio scrambling down the staircase, gathering Sara's duffel and exiting the house without bothering to lock the front door. Before Janice could comment on what she heard, Sara stopped her.

"Sh-h-h!" she said, waiting for another section she wanted her to hear. "This is the most important thing, right here."

Everyone leaned in closer. At first, they only heard the excited chatter. But, as Miriam and Sara climbed into the minivan, and David came around to the driver's side, a voice spoke clearly into the recorder he still carried.

"Watch yer back, Billy Ray-y-y! Yer time of reckonin's comin' soon-n-n-n!"

The threat was followed by a girlish giggle that echoed and died away.

"After doing this for nearly thirty years, this is the strangest haunting I've ever dealt with." Sara stopped the recorder and looked over at Miriam. "Normally, EVPs only contain fragmented phrases from an entity, and are difficult to define. I've only witnessed a handful of lucid statements, and none of those were as clear as this one. The only thing I can compare it to is the Bell Witch of Tennessee. That spirit reportedly conversed for hours at a time with the local ministers who tried in vain to get it to leave the Bell family alone. Maybe there's something in that Tennessee water."

"So, what do you suggest next?" Janice seemed reticent after hearing the taunt from Allie Mae and Sara's advisement.

"I plan to speak with a friend of mine tomorrow, after I drop off the film. He's a parapsychology professor at the University of Denver," said Sara, placing the recorder in her duffel. "I've already spoken with him about what I found in your house yesterday. He's especially curious about the hemlock leaves, since aside from being long renowned for their mystic and murderous properties, hemlock isn't native to this part of the country. But it thrives in the southeastern portion of North America, in the very region you visited a week ago. I'm also hopeful he can hook me up with some of the sound engineering graduates at the University. Maybe they can gain better clarity from the whispers we captured."

"I want you to know I appreciate everything you've done for us, Sara," said Miriam, echoed by David and Janice.

"I know." Sara patted the back of Miriam's hand. "Let's take a look at those pictures."

Miriam opened each pack, passing the individual shots around the table after taking a look. The first roll of film, taken entirely in Gatlinburg, revealed nothing unusual. David's keen photographic eye produced several shots everyone agreed would be excellent candidates to be enlarged and framed. The first few shots from the next roll were much the same. But all of the other photographs taken from the time Miriam and David ventured past John Oliver's homestead, and on through that afternoon's final shot in their backyard, revealed a variety of anomalies.

Miriam noticed a few streams of reddish light and solid yellow orbs in some of the photographs. Not knowing specifically what to look for, she passed them to Sara, who examined them more closely. Sara set the majority of the photographs from the second roll aside in a pile, stating they contained significant paranormal evidence.

Dismayed to see the shot he took of Miriam in the ravine marred by a bright orange streak, David thought he messed it up, and all the trouble he went through in getting the picture was for naught. However, Sara told him the hazy streak could signify something noteworthy took place when the photo was snapped. She brought the image close to her eyes for a better view, squinting as if trying to decipher something else she noticed.

While they sat at the table reviewing the pictures, Janice's phone rang. Ned Badgett called for David, and Janice apologized for not delivering an earlier message from him. David excused himself, taking the call in Janice's office.

"Sorry to call you so late," said Ned. "I know this has been a terrible day, especially for you. How are you holding up?"

"It hasn't fully hit me yet," David confessed. "The true test will come after things get back to normal again, and Norm's not there every day as he has been for nearly twenty years."

"I imagine it'll take some time to heal, David. If there's ever anything I can do, please don't hesitate to ask."

"I'll do that."

An awkward moment of silence passed before Ned spoke again.

"Maybe your idea of taking a few things home to work on might do some good after all," he said. "It's really to help keep your mind occupied, since we've got everything covered this coming week in your absence."

"I'd like that," David agreed. "Can I stop by the office tomorrow and pick up a few reports?"

"Either that, or I can bring them to you if you'd rather," said Ned. "The police are finished with most of what they need, though some areas are still taped off and will remain that way until next week. I have to take care of a few things at the office tomorrow morning. No one else will be there since it's Saturday, and I thought it'd be a good opportunity for you to stop by. Or, like I said, I can bring the files you want by your house in the afternoon. The weather forecast calls for heavy snow tomorrow evening, so I'd like to come by there no later than three o'clock, if that's all right."

"Why don't I meet you at the office around eleven, tomorrow morning?"

"Eleven will be fine. See you then, David."

After he hung up, David remained in Janice's desk chair for a few minutes, admiring the award plaques on her wall for the outstanding editorial work she had done on several bestselling novels. While he read the presentation comments on the largest plaque, Tyler and Jillian pushed the office door open.

"Dad, you've got to check out some pictures of you from last weekend and today!" said Tyler, excitedly.

"There's a ghost's face in them!" added Jillian.

He followed the kids into the kitchen, where Christopher leaned against his mother's shoulder while she examined six photographs spread before her.

"Come look at these, hon," she said, pushing the pictures toward him.

He joined her at the table, looking at the photos while everyone else waited. In each one, either solo or with Miriam, strange white mist-like forms appeared near his right shoulder. The two most prominent images showed up on the pictures taken by Miriam as they exited the trail to the ravine in Cades Cove, and the one where she got him to pose like Paul Bunyan in the backyard less than eight hours earlier.

"Here, David, use this," said Sara, handing a magnifying glass to him.

He held it over the photo from Cades Cove, placing the magnifier above the picture of him holding the rake Paul Bunyan-style. In disbelief he leaned in closer, comparing the two images.

"This is incredible," he said softly, studying the hazy images and examining the other four pictures.

He couldn't believe what he saw in all of the photos, caught by the fast shutter speed of his preferred analog camera. He started to look at other pictures in a pile next to Miriam, but she stopped him.

"None of the others look like these," she advised. "So, no, it's not a problem with the camera or the film. The only pictures that look like this are ones with you in them. There are a few other shots containing orbs and colored streaks, but none look like these."

He looked at the pictures again, noting the figure next to him in each one appeared identical. Each hazy image consisted of a partial face, with the portion closest to him too faint to discern. Only the right side, from the bridge of the nose to the wispy ethereal hair, was clear and cast a shadow behind it. The eye's details and prominent cheekbones determined the face might belong to a gorgeous young woman, whose paleness resembled a film negative. She seemed to be looking directly at him, and one might think she favored him. But the shape of her mouth said she didn't. Her mouth was opened wide into a terrible scream.

Chapter Twenty-four

"I'll be back by one o'clock at the latest," Miriam told Janice, grabbing her coat and attaché case. "Maybe if David feels up to it, I'd like to take him and the kids to a movie this afternoon once he gets back from the meeting with Ned."

Getting an early start, she planned to use Saturday morning to catch up on the pile of paperwork that had accumulated during the past week at the clinic in her absence.

"What time do you want me to wake the kids up?"

Janice followed Miriam to the front door. Not yet 7:30 a.m., she tightened the sash on her bathrobe when the cool morning air rushed into her home.

"Let them sleep as long as they need, provided it's not after twelve," said Miriam, closing the door halfway. "David should be up by nine, or ten at the latest, and then he'll be going into the office shortly after that."

"I know he mentioned something last night about going into work, but I thought he was supposed to take the next week off." Janice frowned. "I can only imagine what it will be like for him to go in there after what happened."

Miriam nodded sadly.

"He promised he'd only be there for about an hour," she said. "Just long enough to meet with Ned, and pick up some reports to work on at home. Then, he won't be back there for at least a week."

"Let's see… David Hobbs, noted workaholic and the compulsive creator of home projects to keep him and his family occupied, is going to be content to sit around here working on a few reports while watching daytime game shows and soaps for a week. Ri-i-ight!"

Janice stifled a chuckle, grimacing as if she regretted the joke at a time like this. Miriam said she wondered the same thing, but added she'd do everything she could to keep him occupied... so long as they didn't have to also deal with Allie Mae's ghost. Janice patted the feathers from the dream catcher next to the doorway for good luck. After she watched Miriam drive away, she closed the door and played with Sadie for a while, before straightening the living room and kitchen in preparation for when the kids and their dad woke up.

* * * * *

Christopher and Jillian arose first, just before nine o'clock, followed by David around nine-thirty. Tyler didn't stir until his dad woke him, just before he left to meet Ned at the office. Tyler stumbled into the kitchen, his hair in his face and the strap on his sling twisted. Janice and David adjusted the sling and helped him with the brace.

Without the usual heavy traffic, the drive to downtown Denver might've been pleasant, if not for the deep sorrow gripping David's heart. When he reached the rear parking lot of Johnson, Simms & Perrault, he parked the Chrysler next to Ned's Mercedes. A cement bench sat empty nearby, where Norm and other smokers took many of their cigarette breaks. David's chest tightened. Somehow, he managed to subdue the powerful urge to turn around and go home. He forced a smile and stepped out of the minivan. Ned waited for him at the side entrance.

"Are you sure you're okay with this?" asked Ned.

He seemed to notice his pallor and the dark circles around his eyes. David didn't have to say he slept horribly.

"I should be."

For a moment, Ned looked as if he wanted to give him a hug, which David feared would bring on an uncontrollable deluge of emotion. Thankfully, Ned seemed to sense it, and instead led him to the building's main entrance in front. The curtains in the lobby were closed. Once they stepped beyond the foyer, the only illumination came from the security lights and a faint glow from Ned's office upstairs.

"Is that where they found him?" David pointed to the marble fountain, where the water had been shut off.

Yellow police tape extended from the bottom of the staircases to both sides of the fountain, and was wrapped around a matching pair of marble cherubs. In the dimness, a few twigs and leaves remained from the ring that had enclosed the fountain when Norm's impaled body was found. It chilled David, and he clearly understood the detectives' interest in the strange circle left on his bedroom floor.

Allie Mae's spirit was here. Did she kill Norm?

"Yeah, it is," Ned quietly confirmed, continuing toward the staircase next to the vacant reception desk. "They should have all of this cleared away before Monday morning. Oh, and by the way, Norm's mother, brother, and sister will be in Denver later tonight. The funeral won't be for at least another couple of weeks, pending the coroner's report. It will likely be held in Tupelo, Mississippi, where he'll be buried. In the meantime, Nancy arranged another service to be held for Norm's friends and co-workers tomorrow afternoon. Norm's family has graciously decided to join us. Nancy told me this morning the service is scheduled for two o'clock."

"Where will it be held?" David's mouth suddenly felt dry. Still wondering about the hemlock leaves and twigs, he glanced repeatedly at the fountain while he and Ned climbed the stairs to the second level. "I'd like to visit with Norm's family when they get settled, if I can. It's been a couple of years since I last saw Jonas, when he came up here with his fiancée to ski."

"I'll give you the number to the Holiday Inn they're staying at in Aurora," Ned said, as they reached the top of the stairs. "The service will be held at a Methodist chapel not far from here, but I forget the name of it. I'll get you the name and address before you leave. Nancy's calling everyone else this afternoon from her home to give them the details and directions on how to get there."

The two men walked into the mortgage services area. David stopped to look across the landing to the hallway where Norm's office sat. More yellow tape blocked access to the office.

Are there more leaves and twigs in there? The detectives said something about other evidence.

"I probably shouldn't be telling you this, but the police told me this morning they're moving closer to finding Norm's killer, or killers, I should say," said Ned, following David's gaze toward Norm's darkened office.

"They are?" He turned to look at Ned, hoping his disbelief wasn't apparent.

"They confided in me that one is definitely a female. The bloody fingerprints they found on Norm's desk match other fingerprints recovered from someplace else," he said, moving to the wall to flick on the row of fluorescent lights above the cubicles. "They're hoping to make a positive ID on her, which should lead to a break in the case."

"So, was it Norm's blood on the fingerprints?" David wondered why such important information had been withheld from him.

"I'm sorry, David. I thought you knew," said Ned, worried he had caused him further pain. "Since the detectives spoke to you yesterday, I assumed… I guess I shouldn't have assumed anything. To answer your question, yes, it's Norm's blood."

"That's okay," said David. "I just hope they find her soon and have the ability to bring someone like this to justice quickly."

He feigned complete seriousness, thinking the police had zero chance of catching a ghost. The main thing now? Finding out more about the matching fingerprints, since they likely came from inside his home. The fact Ned knew about them, and he didn't, provided further proof the police considered him a strong suspect.

"I agree." Ned turned to face him when they reached David's cubicle, and again looked like he wanted to offer a hug. "Well, I'll leave you alone for a few minutes while you pick up the reports you'd like to work on. I'll meet you on the landing when you're ready to leave." He moved down the aisle to his office.

Everything was still a mess, piled next to his PC station from when he left in a hurry Thursday evening. David took a moment to straighten his desk. He took several manila folders full of reports not yet completed and placed them inside his briefcase. Looking to add a few pencils and pens to take with him, he opened his desk's top drawer.

The little cloth bag from Tennessee rested loosely on top of a pair of half-used note pads and an unopened pack of post-it notes. He collapsed in his chair while his chest tightened. The side with Allie Mae's Treasures stitched in light blue thread faced him. David picked up the bag, his hand shaking while he drew it closer to examine new stains. A different crimson from the encrusted pizza stains, the patterned striations came from slender fingerprints dipped in blood. Norm's blood.

Terrible images filled his weary mind, along with answers to questions tormenting him since the day before. The fingerprints had to belong to Allie Mae—a ghost's, as impossible as it seemed. He fell deeper into despair, knowing his efforts to mail the bag back to Gatlinburg proved futile.

So, she killed Norm... but why?

Curious, he opened the bag and peered inside, preparing himself for the musty smell he loathed. The odor surprised him, diluted by a floral fragrance that wasn't there before… along with another scent.

"Huh?"

He understood, grimly, what likely happened. Norm couldn't have tampered with the package he mailed. The metallic jingle in the mailer, when David handed it to the postal worker to be weighed and processed, confirmed that much. But somehow, Allie Mae removed her bag of treasures from the mailer and brought it to the office. She used the bag to seduce Norm and lure him to his death.

It made perfect sense. The honeysuckle-lilac and feminine odor wafting from the bag would've nailed Norm's insatiable lust. If nothing else, he knew Norm probably thought the item was a novelty, and had no idea about the danger awaiting him.

"I thought you'd be waiting in the landing by now. Are you okay?" Ned stood next to his cubicle. "Your face is ghostly pale. Can I get you something to drink, David?"

"I'm all right, really." He closed his hand around the bag and threw it into his brief case, along with some pens and pencils.

Ned glanced toward the landing, as if he heard something.

"I'm ready to go now," said David, closing the drawer to his desk.

"Are you sure you're okay?" Ned asked again, glancing at David's empty hand.

"Yeah, I'm sure." David stood. He silently prayed his boss only caught a slight glimpse of the bag, and hadn't noticed the bloody fingerprints. "I'm ready to go."

"Here's the phone number to where the Sowell's will be staying." He handed a note to David once he joined him in the aisle. "They should be there around seven tonight. And, here's the address and directions to the chapel for tomorrow's service."

David placed the note inside his wallet. They left the department together, and Ned shut the lights off. Before exiting the building, David thought he heard the landing's floorboards creak behind them. Forcing himself to smile while Ned told a funny story involving his newest grandchild, he followed him outside and waited for him to lock the entrance's double doors. Not once did he raise his eyes toward the dim figure he sensed glowering at them from behind the landing's banister.

* * * * *

He debated all the way back to Janice's townhouse on how he should break the news to Miriam that the bag never made it back to Tennessee. The haunting had grown so much worse, they might never be free of it or its owner.

Christopher and Jillian chased each other through the main floor, while Tyler stretched comfortably on the sofa, reading his latest anime magazine. Janice greeted David warmly, asking how everything went. Not ready to tell her what he found waiting in his desk, he forced another smile. He told her that he got through his first visit back to the office with Ned's help, and that he brought home enough reports to keep him plenty busy for the next week. She returned to the kitchen to put finishing touches on a peach cobbler she recently baked. His smile brightened, and he told her that he wondered what smelled so delicious. He joined Tyler in the living room.

He shared some laughs with his son while they watched a reality-dating program on TV. Just before the program ended at one o'clock, Miriam arrived. She hugged each of her three children and delivered an especially warm hug and kiss to him.

After she chatted a moment with Janice in the kitchen, David quietly accosted her, stating he had something urgent to discuss. Since their two youngest children had just gone upstairs, and Tyler and Janice remained occupied in the living room and kitchen, he suggested they talk in Janice's office.

"All right," she agreed.

She looked worried, and he knew the façade of hiding his own angst must be crumbling. He hurried her into the office and closed the door.

"What's with the briefcase?" she asked.

"I found something at work that I had hoped to God I'd never see again," he began. His tone bore a mixture of sorrow and anger as he set his briefcase on Janice's desk. "Allie Mae's Treasures never made it to Tennessee."

"What?" Her response came out much louder than he hoped, although he knew this wouldn't be pleasant. "What do you mean, David?"

He rushed to open the locks on the briefcase. Rather than answer her, he turned the case around to where she could see the little cloth bag bearing new crimson stains.

"Why in the hell didn't you mail it back to Gatlinburg?!" she shrieked.

"I did mail it!" he told her, trying hard not to get any more upset. "I even checked the confirmation yesterday, and the mailer was delivered to the park's office in Gatlinburg around nine-thirty that morning!"

"Then... *how* did it get back *here*?" She slid down into the desk chair, bringing her closer to the bag. She noticed the additional stains. "Is that what I think it is?"

Tears streamed down her face.

"It's Norm's blood, I'm sure." His voice fell to a whisper. "I wish I knew what to do."

"Call the police, *that's* what you should do!" she said angrily, and for a moment he thought she might accuse him again of this being entirely his fault. She didn't. Instead, she picked up the bag and held it tightly, as if determined to either hold onto it forever or crush its contents into dust. "Will we never be free of this shit?"

Her shoulders heaved. Clinging to the bag, at first she resisted his efforts to comfort her. But she allowed him to gather her into his arms. She hugged him tightly, and as she did the bag fell from her grasp, its contents jingling when it landed on the floor.

"We'll figure something out, Miriam, I promise," he told her, burying his face in her neck while he fought his own tears.

"Did you hear that?" She pulled away and leaned her head toward the office door.

"Hear what?"

"Sh-h-h... *that!"*

She didn't wait for his reply. She jumped up from the chair and ran to the door, throwing it open. As she did, Christopher and Jillian's screams resounded shrilly from upstairs. Miriam caught Janice on the way to the second floor, with David and Tyler right behind them.

While fear inspired Jillian's tears, Christopher's came from physical pain. Miriam examined Christopher's outstretched arms while Janice consoled Jillian. Neither child could stop crying. Miriam and Janice soon cried with them. Tyler looked bewildered, unable to remove his eyes from his brother's arms. David followed his gaze and watched a pair of handprint bruises emerge on each arm.

"Oh, my baby, I'm so sorry... *so* sorry!" Miriam drew Christopher close and kissed his cheeks. She dropped to her knees, still clinging to him. "My poor baby!"

"She hurt me, Mommy!" sobbed Christopher, looking over at his dad and brother. "She hurt me because I'm *next!* She's going to *kill the seed*—that's what she said!"

He cried harder, and David came over and dropped to his knees as well, not caring whether Miriam tried to push him away or not. He reached around her and pulled them both toward him. They wept together.

"Did you see anything?" Janice asked Jillian, gently, to which she shook her head.

"How about you, darling?" Miriam asked Christopher. "Did you see her?"

He nodded warily.

"What did she look like?"

"I could only see her up to here," he said, pointing to his chest between sobs. "She was barefoot in a long blue dress... and her arms were really white. I couldn't see the rest of her because... *nothing was there!"* He cried harder.

Tyler looked around anxiously. Up until then, he had said little about the ghost's appearance. David had no doubt it matched what Christopher described. He wondered if Allie Mae appeared similarly when she attacked Norm. No one could ever confirm that. Hostile toward the males in the family and his closest male friend, he took her threat seriously. Recalling Sara's pronouncement from the night before, he realized the only way for his family to be free of the spirit's powerful hold came through him. Everyone he loved would remain in grave danger, including the females at some point. If a cure to free them all existed, he had to find it alone. He rose to his feet.

"I love you so much, Miriam, and I love each of you kids with all of my heart—and I love you, too, Jan."

"Where are you going?" asked Miriam, as he left the room.

"For a ride!" he called back to her, as he ran downstairs. "And I'm taking Allie Mae's shitty little bag with me!"

Before she or anyone else could stop him, he gathered up the bag, his briefcase, and left the townhouse. He returned to their beleaguered home on LeClair Drive, where he ran upstairs to the master bedroom. Ignoring the knocks and creaks resounding throughout the second floor, he hurriedly packed a suitcase with enough clothes to last a week.

Miriam tried to reach his cell phone several times, but he waited to call her back until he was headed north on I-25. Despite her pleas for him to return to Janice's, he refused to endanger anyone further, promising to call her once he found a suitable place to stay. Soon after he hung up the phone, he veered onto 6th Avenue west to Golden, which seemed like a fitting destination. Located halfway between Boulder and Littleton, where his life in Colorado began and where he stood on the verge of losing everything, he needed an answer… a miracle. Quickly.

Chapter Twenty-five

It was almost midnight that Saturday, and David had shared intimate tears with Jonas and Margaret Sowell over the phone. He promised to meet them for brunch Sunday morning, at a restaurant not far from the chapel where the service would be held. As he prepared for bed, the phone in his suite at the Residence Inn in Golden rang.

"Hi, hon." Miriam sounded tired.

"Hey, babe," he said, sitting down on the edge of his bed. "So, are the kids finally asleep?"

"Tyler was the last one up, until about an hour ago," she said. "I miss you."

"I miss you, too." He looked up toward the ceiling, fighting the urge to cry.

"Did you already take care of everything we discussed earlier?"

"You mean the flight, rent-a-car, and reservations for a couple of nights in Gatlinburg?"

"Yes."

"I decided you were right, that I should spend tomorrow night visiting Auntie in Chattanooga," he said, referring to his dad's sister, the only living relative he had. "I'm flying there instead of Knoxville, and then driving to Gatlinburg. I found a Comfort Inn that will allow me to check in late tomorrow night in Pigeon Forge, which is next to Gatlinburg."

"Good, that should work out fine." She sounded pleased.

"The only drawback is I can only stay two nights in the room, because it's still peak season—even during the week," he advised. "So, if this takes longer than a day or two to resolve, I guess I'll have to stay in one of the seedier places in the area."

"I know how busy the nicer hotels and chalets stay out there," said Miriam. "Remember how we had to have our reservations for our anniversary trip booked last spring? I guess we should consider it fortunate that you're getting a room at all."

"Yeah, I guess so."

"What time is your flight?"

"It departs at five, so that means I'll need to be at DIA around three-thirty. I'm glad that you'll be with me at the service tomorrow. I'm meeting Jonas and Margaret at noon for brunch. We'll be at the IHOP downtown. Can you get away early and meet us there?"

"I'll be there," she promised. "This has got to be incredibly hard for Jonas and Margaret. How are they holding up?"

"Not so good." He fought to keep from crying, knowing he couldn't win the battle much longer. "I'm sure they'll be glad to see you. Talking with them made me realize how lucky I am to have such a wonderful family and a woman like you in my life to… to help get through this."

"Count on me, David," Miriam assured him. "I'm always there for you. Always."

They both grew silent, weeping and unsure what to say. Finally, David spoke.

"Has anything else happened since I left this afternoon?"

"No, nothing has," she told him, still sniffling.

"So, she's been quiet." Afraid to mention the ghost by name, Allie Mae remained foremost on his mind.

"Yes, she has. That's the only reason I'm not fighting you, even though I'm scared shitless about what might happen. I wish I was coming along!"

"Then who'd protect the kids if it turns out I'm wrong, and the ghost isn't after me, but everyone else in our family?" He hoped she bought the flawed logic. "Besides, you're destined to worry regardless if you're with me or if you're at home. I know I'll worry less if you're with Janice and the kids."

"I suppose you're right." She sighed. "Promise me that you'll be extremely careful!"

"I promise."

"I better go…. I'll see you in the morning downtown," she said. "I love you."

"I love you, too."

He finished getting ready for bed, clad only in his briefs and a t-shirt. Once comfortable under the sheets and thick blanket the Inn provided, he watched the end of a Turner Classic movie. Since he didn't have to get up before 10 a.m. to make his breakfast date with the Sowell's, he stayed awake until one o'clock. He hoped this would thwart the spirit who seemed to favor that hour, should she actually pursue him in the hotel room. So far it had been relatively quiet, with the only disturbance coming from a drunken couple in the next suite. After leaving the light on in the bathroom with the door ajar, he waited for sleep to come.

"David. Da-vid…. Hey, wake up!"

"Huh?" He glanced at the alarm clock on his nightstand. The red digital numbers showed the time as 1:55 a.m.

"Goddamn, bro, you're hard to rouse!"

"Norm? Is that *you?"*

A slight chill embraced David, sending a surge of shivers across his body. He sat up in bed, peering toward the chair and table next to the air conditioner/heater unit. The curtained window behind the table was shut tight, and he recalled leaving the curtains cracked enough to allow a sliver of light from a nearby street lamp into the room. He discerned the outline of someone sitting in the chair.

"Yeah, it's me." The shadowed figure sounded like Norm, though the voice seemed forlorn. "I've come to give you a message."

David reached for the lamp next to his bedside and started to turn it on.

"Don't do it!" Norm warned. "Not yet."

"And why the hell not?" demanded David, reaching for his jeans.

"Please, stay where you are!"

Now that sounded just like Norm, the irritated tone familiar.

"All right." David leaned against the bed's headboard.

"She knows what you're up to, and I think it just might work," said Norm. "That is, if you play your cards right. I wish I could tell you exactly what to do, man, but I'm unable to do that. She's got me stuck here until her anger's satisfied."

"Allie Mae?"

"Yes."

"She's the one who killed you?" David wanted it confirmed.

"Yes, and if you're not careful, you'll be joining me soon." Norm's tone became more sorrowful as he spoke.

"So, going back to Cades Cove is a key part to working this out, huh?" David leaned slightly toward the figure to try and make out any features. Even though the voice sounded like his best friend, he wondered if it was his tormenter in disguise.

"I have neither the talent nor anywhere near the power she has to pull something like that off, but I understand why you'd think I'm her pretending to be me," he said, alluding to David's thoughts. "As to your question, going back to Tennessee is the right thing to do. But, what needs to happen from that point, I can't honestly say. All I can tell you is I sensed her surprise when you decided to go back, like she had you pegged as a selfish bastard like myself. The fact you're willing to try and make amends, and face her head-on to protect your family… well it's something she didn't expect."

"Any suggestions, like what you'd try in order to fix this shit?"

"I honestly don't know," Norm replied. "It's a good idea to follow your instincts. Make sure that's what you pay attention to and not your fear. It's exactly what you did this past afternoon at Jan's place, when you realized what needed to be done. You'll need to do the same thing once you return to Allie Mae's stomping grounds."

"What's her last name, or do you know?"

Having a full name certainly could help him track down Allie Mae's family history, as well as where she lived and was buried—all pertinent information in finding the right resolution to appease the angry spirit.

"All I know is what you know, bro," said Norm. "I didn't even know her first name until I heard you and Miriam call her 'Allie Mae' in your recent discussions. Of course, it's the name on the little bag that now bears my blood."

"Can you at least tell me what she looks like?"

All David had to go by were fragments from his dream, and the recent photographs' phantom images. What Chris saw only confirmed the dress color Tyler told Janice about. David feared he might not recognize the spirit if he saw her. Certainly, Norm had seen her up close, given the sexual nature of the detectives' questions on Friday.

"You don't really want to know, bro." Norm sighed deeply.

David became aware the apparition had stood up. As his eyes continued to adjust to the dimness, he saw Norm's shadowed head blocking the faint outline of the lamp above the table. Brushing sounds on the carpet foretold Norm's shuffled progress toward him.

"It might be better to simply show you how she left me, since I have to stay like this forever… unless you're successful," he advised, continuing to approach the bed. "Go ahead and turn on the light."

David hesitated, suddenly fearing what he might see. He preferred the mental picture of Norm as a vivacious and stunningly handsome man, whose smile was worth far more than the monetary wealth he'd accumulated since graduating from law school thirteen years ago. To allow anything other than that image to become permanent in his mind wasn't an acceptable option for David to even consider.

"Go ahead and do it!" urged Norm. "Do it before I lose my nerve to go through with this!"

He stood before the bed. In the sparse illumination provided by the bathroom's light, David could see part of a bare leg and the tails of the lavender dress shirt Norm wore the last time he saw him alive. He reached over and flicked on his bedside lamp. The darkness vanished in a wash of soft light.

"Oh my God!" David murmured in horror.

Norm appeared just as Allie Mae left him, impaled upon the fountain's ornamental tip. His dress slacks and boxers were still around his ankles, although not visible to David at the moment. Norm's swollen phallus pulsed unnaturally, throbbing as if Allie Mae's fingers that caused the blackish bruises still had a firm grip. But, that wasn't the worst. Norm's midsection had a gaping hole where blood seeped, trickling down his dress shirt and legs.

"Look at me, David, and remember what you see!" cried Norm, his pearly white teeth stained from the blood thrust of his mortal injury. His face ghastly white, his brilliant blue eyes had turned pale gray. "Think of what you see standing here the next time you're curious about what *she* looks like!"

He moved around the bed and shuffled ever closer to David, who instinctively pushed himself away.

"Can she be gorgeous? Hell, yeah! But, know this, too, David. Allie Mae is the most hideous creature you or me will ever lay eyes on. Something happened long ago to change her beauty, and whatever that thing is, it still lurks within her. When it's active, you don't want an up-close view of her face. You'd be better off gazing at the face of Medusa instead!"

Aghast, David pushed himself all the way to the other side of the bed.

"Take a good *long* look!" Norm leaned over the bed. The trickling blood from his midsection became a gushing rush that poured out onto the covers, splashing up against David as he futilely tried to escape. *"Don't you dare forget what you see now and everything we discussed tonight!"*

Norm leaned in ever closer. David began to whimper, trying to curl up and away from the encroaching corpse of his dearest friend aside from Miriam. Norm reached out and grabbed David's leg with his hand, sending an painful chill that radiated up through his entire body.

David screamed.

He woke with a start, panicked by the darkness in his suite at the Residence Inn. Fumbling for the lamp's switch, he nearly toppled the digital alarm clock to the floor. The clock read 2:01 a.m.

Relieved to find he was alone, the soft glow from the lamp illuminated the entire room. There was no blood on the bed, or anywhere else. No sign of Norm either. The only things different from when he retired an hour earlier were his bedspread, which now hung mostly off the bed, and the curtain behind the table. The curtain was drawn shut.

Chapter Twenty-six

David's flight on Delta didn't actually leave the ground until 5:13 p.m. Sunday evening. Happy to get a window seat near the front of the aircraft, "Allie Mae's Treasures" lay safely hidden from view inside his briefcase. Worried it might disappear again, he checked several times. Once the plane cleared the rough turbulent winds DIA was known for, he tried to relax, staring absently out the window while he reflected on the day so far. Breakfast was a somber affair, although Norm's kin from Mississippi were glad to see him and Miriam. They spent much of the time reminiscing about Norm's antics as a younger man, since his family didn't see much of him after he became a busy and successful corporate lawyer.

Grateful for his wife's presence at the service, it gave David the strength to walk to the podium where he spoke of the special bond he had with Norm. There wasn't a dry eye in the cathedral by the time he finished. Miriam grasped his hand once he returned to his seat, squeezing it tightly.

Afterward, she drove him to the airport. They held each other tightly for almost ten minutes at the security checkpoint, and David got in line. He waved to her one last time before she walked away with her head lowered, her long dark hair covering her face as she cried.

The plane landed in Chattanooga at 9:25 p.m. After collecting his luggage and rent-a-car, he drove to the eastern outskirts of Chattanooga where his aunt resided. He regretted not calling ahead of time, after he remembered she often retired early.

He parked the rented Buick in her short driveway, and headed up the steps to her craftsman cottage built in the early 1930s. A scraggly pussy willow tree to his left brought back memories of painful whippings he received as a child, courtesy of the tree's wands. He peered through the window closest to the front door before ringing the doorbell. Sitting in an overstuffed chair next to the television set, his Aunt Ruth knitted an afghan. She rose from her chair once the doorbell rang, with her cocker spaniel named Max barking at her side.

"Why David, what a surprise!" Her face lit up once she saw him standing on her front porch. Max continued to bark, unfamiliar with his scent. He hadn't seen the dog since Max was a puppy, roughly twelve years ago. "Come on inside!"

She opened the door and let him in, pushing Max behind her with her leg while scolding the dog to behave.

"Have you eaten dinner yet? I can throw together some soup and cornbread for you, if you're interested in having any?"

"Actually, I've already eaten, Auntie," he lied, hoping his growling stomach didn't give him away. "I'm sorry to stop by so late. I just flew into town on business, and thought I'd come and see you since it's been awhile."

"Why, I believe it's been almost four years since my trip to see you and Miriam in Denver," she agreed, shaking her head. "We shouldn't go so long between visits, don't you know!"

"I agree, Auntie," he said, thinking *she's right* but also grateful for the reprieve.

He looked around, noticing she changed the wallpaper in the dining room, besides adding the new plasma TV in the living room. Still, to him the house reeked from being the source for most of his unpleasant childhood memories. His aunt had lived in the house for most of her life. Much of the past twenty years were spent alone. Her husband died six months before David graduated from college. Before then, the house belonged to his grandfather, for whom he harbored deep resentment.

"Let me take your coat, David, and you can join me in the living room."

She hung his coat next to the front door, and he followed her into the living room, where she motioned for him to sit on the couch. She returned to her armchair, setting the needlework aside. Although some new pieces had been added in recent years, the room carried the same early American style he remembered.

"It's so *good* to see you, David! How long are you here in Chattanooga?"

"I won't be staying here. My business meetings are in Gatlinburg. But, since I hadn't visited down here with you in awhile, I decided to fly to Chattanooga and then drive up to my hotel room in Pigeon Forge tonight."

It was a mixture of truth and lie he thought he could live with. Telling her anything about his true purpose and intentions would only lead to unending questions, and opinions he could live without. Besides, if she had any inkling he and Miriam vacationed in Tennessee just over a week ago, it would crush her.

"Well, this is *so* nice!" she said, obviously touched by his thoughtful gesture. The dagger piercing his guilty heart twisted in further. "But, that's a long drive. Are you sure you wouldn't like to stay here with me tonight, and then make the trip up to Gatlinburg first thing in the morning, when you've got the benefit of daylight? I've got a spare bedroom upstairs, as you'll remember."

She looked so frail and vulnerable, and for a moment he seriously considered the offer. Ruth Guarnier was a slender, handsome woman, even as she rapidly approached seventy, with kind, deep brown eyes. If not for the multitude of fine lines on her forehead, and the long silvery hair pulled tightly behind her head, she could've passed for someone twenty years younger. But, he could tell the onset of rheumatoid arthritis made it difficult for her to get about these days. Having Max certainly made things less lonely, yet David knew she relished the opportunity to visit with another human being—especially her own flesh and blood.

"I can stay for half an hour or so, Auntie," he said, hating himself for the disappointment he saw in her face. "My room's already guaranteed, so I'll have to show up there sometime tonight. At least by three in the morning."

"Well, if you feel tired, I want you to strongly consider staying here until tomorrow," she said, her countenance lighting up again. "You can count on the finest country breakfast at daybreak, too!"

"That's a mighty tempting proposition."

Unable to keep from smiling, he always loved that about her. Hell, if she had protected him from those who liked to hurt him as a boy, he knew they'd enjoy a much better relationship now. But, he couldn't help linking her to his painful past…. Maybe she should move. If she left the house filled with painful memories behind, he might see her differently.

"I have an eight o'clock meeting tomorrow morning, where I need to deliver a presentation." He pictured himself handing the bag to a park ranger or someone else behind a desk at the Great Smoky Mountains National Park headquarters.

"Well, all right." She adjusted herself in the chair, grimacing slightly. "Damned bones," she said, her tone a mixture of playfulness and irritation. "Gettin' old should be reserved for tax collectors and politicians!"

"I can see why you'd think that," he said, chuckling and feeling more at ease in her presence. He thought of some photographs Miriam wanted her to have. "I'll be right back, Auntie. Miriam sent something for you." He hurried outside to his car.

Max rose from her side to run after him, barking from the porch while he retrieved the pictures from his briefcase. Under the sedan's dome light, the bloodstained surface of the bag seemed bright and fresh. He shuddered, forcing his eyes to look away, and slammed the passenger door shut before racing up the steps to the bungalow's front door. He scurried inside, hoping Max's territorial moxie would ward off anything that tried to follow him inside his aunt's home.

"Well, what have you got there?" Ruth asked, when David returned to the living room.

"Miriam planned to mail these, but thought it would be better for me to bring them to you." He handed her the photographs, and sat down on the couch again.

"My, oh my, have the kids *grown!*" she enthused, after viewing the first few shots. "Chris looks more and more like you, David, and I think Jill's going to be as beautiful as her momma when she's all grown up—with lighter hair, of course!"

When she got to Tyler's picture, she paused to study it, seemingly surprised by what she saw.

"Boy, is that child a Hobbs or what!"

"You should see how the girls his age react around him." He smiled proudly.

"His age? Honey, I think you'd better keep a good eye out for a teacher or two who might stray where they shouldn't!" Ruth lingered on the photo, examining it more closely. She started to say something else, but didn't. Instead, she placed the pictures on a small drum table near her chair. "Well, you be sure to tell Miriam just how much I appreciate her thinking of me like this."

"I definitely will, Auntie."

"You did say you're heading to Pigeon Forge tonight, didn't you?" She wore the same look she had a moment before, when she studied Tyler's most recent school photo.

"Yeah, I did," he confirmed. "I'll be staying at the Comfort Inn for the next two nights at least."

"Grandpa's people used to own a farm out that way," Ruth told him. "They raised hogs and had roughly two hundred and forty acres of corn and tobacco. When it fell on hard times during the early 1960's, they packed up and moved everything to the other farm they kept near Ringgold. They couldn't sell the first farm on account of Grandpa's asking price, until long after he died. It sold for quite a penny in 1982, and is now part of some fancy gaming strip up there from what I understand. The bulk of that money remains in a trust fund."

"I had no idea." It surprised David that his family actually once owned a second farm near Gatlinburg. He wondered if his aunt had any access to the trust fund, noting that her living arrangements seemed as unpretentious as ever. During his last visit to Chattanooga, eight years ago, he learned the other farm in Ringgold sold for a modest amount that was split up between several heirs, including Ruth. It left her just enough to pay off the final mortgage on her house and purchase a brand-new Ford Taurus, still parked in the driveway.

"The money's there in case Medicare fails to take care of me like our current administration promised." She chuckled, adjusting her back-support cushion. "But I don't ever intend to touch it. When my time on planet earth's up in the next ten to fifteen years, you can be sure that a nice nest egg awaits you and the kids. The proceeds from the sale belonged solely to Grandpa's direct heirs, which aside from me include just y'all, since everyone else is gone. After I leave, the money's yours to do with as you please."

He didn't know what to say, other than he really needed to revisit the reasons for his animosity toward her. After all, deep inside he had always loved her. The bitterness that kept him from acting on his true feelings would surely bring a day of immense regret.

She seemed to sense the revelation made him feel uncomfortable.

"Can I at least get you some tea?" She stood before he answered, grimacing, and hobbled toward the kitchen. "Better yet, I've got a pineapple upside-down cake I made just yesterday. Half the time I end up throwing most of what I cook away, since it's too much trouble to put up leftovers, and Max has to watch his weight. Don't we, Maxie?"

The dog followed her to the kitchen, and David could hear the soft jingle from his collar, picturing Max smiling and wagging his tail as if next in line for some dessert.

"Did you make it the old-fashioned way, with an iron skillet?" he called to her from the living room.

"Now, how else would a true southern gal bake an upside-down cake, David?" she scolded, playfully. She peered around the corner of the kitchen.

"Sorry, Auntie," he said. "You don't see much true southern cooking in Denver."

She laughed and returned with a big slice of cake, along with a steaming hot cup of orange pekoe tea. For the next hour, they talked about everything from the kids and how they did in school to the football fortunes of the Volunteers and Golden Buffalos, as well as those of the Titans and Broncos. Since Ruth had interacted with Norm on several occasions over the past nineteen years, he worried she might ask about him. Luckily, she didn't. When it was time for him to leave, he walked with her to the front door, telling her that he'd like to meet her for lunch at the airport before he flew back to Denver, tentatively set for Wednesday afternoon.

He stepped into the night's coolness, and Max growled.

"Oh, stop it now!" Ruth chastised her companion, and then looked at David with an amused expression. "He never even growls at the mail carriers anymore, but he growled twice tonight, once right before you got here and again as you're leaving. I'd say Max is trying to warn you to be careful, because he's not worried about taking good care of his momma, don't you know!"

They hugged and told each other goodbye, and he headed to his car. By the time he reached the driver's side, his aunt had already shut the door and closed her curtains. The air around the car felt much colder than it had when he first arrived. He climbed in quickly and started up the Buick's engine. He didn't need another reminder to get going.

* * * * *

He arrived in Pigeon Forge just after 2:00 a.m. Pleased by the Comfort Inn's accommodations, the night manager gave him a corporate upgrade. After getting settled, he called Miriam one last time to let her know he arrived safely at the hotel. They had already discussed his visit with Ruth once he left Chattanooga, and it pleased her that Ruth liked the pictures.

She made him promise to call her in the afternoon, after he returned Allie Mae's Treasures to its rightful place. Still unsure if that meant simply handing the bag over to the park headquarters, or actually taking it to the ravine, it became the last thing he thought about while pulling the bedcovers up to his neck. Soon after, he fell asleep.

Chapter Twenty-seven

David slept soundly, and didn't awaken on Monday morning until almost eleven. Since his agenda for the day consisted of just one thing, he took his time getting ready, allowing the luxury of a nice long shower. The bruises on his forehead and shoulder were healing, and the yellow halos had greatly faded. It amazed him that Miriam never learned of the handprint bruises. The subject never came up in their conversations, and she hadn't seen him without a shirt since the previous Monday night. It provided a cold reminder of how their revived physical passion hit a dead end once the spirit's wrath invaded their lives.

His leisurely pace cost him breakfast, unless he wanted to drive around Pigeon Forge or Gatlinburg looking for one of the restaurants specializing in breakfast throughout the day. He ate lunch at a coffee shop near the hotel. Afterward, he got directions on how to find 107 Park Headquarters Road in Gatlinburg from the hotel's desk staff.

Cloudy with a steady drizzle for much of the morning, the sun appeared by the time David pulled his car onto the main drive, US Highway 441, to Gatlinburg. When he reached the Great Smoky Mountains National Park office, he parked near the door. About to step out of the car, he hesitated. Something told him it wasn't the right place to drop off the bag, making him think of the admonishment from Norm's ghost.

He decided to drive into the park, and soon reached Cades Cove. The debate became whether he should go to the ravine or to the visitors' center next to the old cable mill. He found himself parked in front of the gristmill's outbuildings. He got out of the car with the bag gripped securely, like a slippery fish he didn't dare lose hold of, and made his way to the visitors' center. He patiently waited for an attendant helping another tourist to finish, so he could embarrass himself with his absurd story.

No matter how he phrased it in his mind, it sounded ridiculous.

'Hi, my name's David Hobbs and I've come all the way from Colorado to give back this little bag covered in bloody fingerprints and pizza stains. Yeah, I know there's a broken tooth in it, too. But, I can assure you the blood that's on the tooth and the bag is not from the same person. I believe the bag is a hundred years old. No, ma'am, not the bloodstains... just the bag. The bloodstains are from my best friend, who was murdered by the spirit to whom the bag belongs.'

While fidgeting, a ranger walked up and offered assistance. David hesitated, fearing a worse reaction than from the other park employee. Already too late, the ranger noticed the bag held tight in his hand.

"You look like someone who holds a secret he can barely keep quiet about," said the ranger.

David could only stare in response, both at the audacity and accuracy of the ranger's words. He recognized the older man from a tour he and Miriam had taken, nine days earlier. His salt and pepper hair worn in long braids, along with his strong facial features, revealed the ranger's Native American heritage even before David confirmed it from the name on his badge, *John Running Deer*. His warm brown eyes twinkled with keen interest as he awaited David's response.

"I'm looking to return this," David said, holding his hand out and loosening his fierce grip so the ranger could see the bag clearly.

He picked it out of David's hand and examined the name and stains on it. He turned the bag over in his hands and almost opened it, but instead shook it while listening to its contents jingle.

"The bag somehow got mixed up with our stuff when my wife and I visited here a couple of weekends ago," explained David. "Once we found out about it, we wanted to bring it back here at the first opportunity to do so."

"Are you from Littleton, Colorado?" the ranger asked, lifting his eyes from the bag.

"As a matter of fact, I am," he confirmed, feeling uncomfortable from the scrutinizing gaze of John Running Deer. It seemed as if the man could see through him, and David feared he might be more formidable to hide the truth from than even Miriam.

"What's your name?"

"David. David Hobbs."

"Nice to meet you, David Hobbs," said the ranger, extending his hand. "John Running Deer."

"It's a pleasure, Mr. Running Deer," said David, impressed by the powerful grip. Ruggedly handsome, the ranger stood an inch shorter than he.

"Please… feel free to address me as either John or Mr. Ranger," he said, revealing a generous smile. "Follow me."

The two moved inside the gift shop and past other tourists, who paused to watch them weave through the circular post card and novelty displays on the way to a long counter located in the back. John stepped around the counter and opened a drawer beneath it, producing the mailer David had sent last Thursday.

"This was forwarded to us by our main office in Gatlinburg on Saturday, since it contained a letter dealing with several items being returned to the cove," he said, showing the empty mailer to David. "The letter mentioned the little bag you've brought with you today. Did you forget to put it inside the envelope?"

He handed the mailer to David, who examined it along with Miriam's letter inside. The arrowheads and pyrite piece were also present. The mailer bore no tears or damage, other than when it was officially opened. Avoiding any details about how Allie Mae's Treasures ended up missing from the padded envelope, David shrugged and handed the package to John.

"In your wife's letter, she stated the items in question were picked up while you were visiting the old ravine which used to serve as Cades Cove's Lover's Lane. How'd you learn about that place?"

"My boss back in Denver, Ned Badgett, told me about it before we came here," said David. "I thought it would be a great place to visit for our fifteenth anniversary."

"Well, congratulations on making it to your fifteenth anniversary. You do mean you've been married to your wife that long, correct?"

David nodded.

"That's interesting. The Badgett clan was one of the last to leave, back in 1934, when Congress first created the Great Smoky Mountains National Park," said John. "Not many folks visit that particular ravine anymore, although my people once revered it above all other places in the cove. I doubt someone just recently lost this out there, don't you?"

John eyed him, and David feared the man stole a peek into his most hidden thoughts.

"I've been debating whether to return the bag here, or if I should return it to the ravine," said David, glancing over his shoulder to make sure no one else listened. "I set up a picnic blanket with my wife beneath one of the larger oaks near the top of the ravine, and that particular oak has the name Allie carved inside a heart engraved on the tree's trunk."

John nodded thoughtfully, and returned his attention to the bag, picking it up and shaking it.

"It might not make a difference either way," he said. "If you'd like, I can take it back there today or tomorrow, along with a few other odds and ends sent to us since last week."

"So, something like this has happened before?"

Startled to learn of other items, David wondered if the same kind of events precipitated similar notes and objects mailed to the park service in haste.

"Afraid so," he confirmed, opening another drawer a few feet away from the one that had contained the mailer. "It happens all of the time. I'd say we get anywhere from fifty to a hundred items returned each year taken from various areas throughout the park. But the largest concentration comes from Cades Cove. At least that's where we get items with the longer letters." His eyes twinkled, as if he found the whole business amusing.

"What kind of things do you normally get back?"

"Usually arrowheads and rocks, like the ones you sent. Or, other items that could've once been used as tools, either by the Cherokee who once lived here or from the first white settlers in the early 1800's," he said. "Now and then we get something like a rusted door hinge or a ceramic whiskey jug—odd things like that. I've never seen a little bag like what you've brought in here today."

He studied the bag again, feeling its texture and gently squeezing the items inside. David wanted to reach over and open the damn thing, so John could look inside, and grew irritated watching him.

"Like I said, I'll be happy to take this back to the ravine for you by tomorrow." John looked up as if aware of David's annoyance. "Unless, you're in a bigger hurry to take the bag back there yourself. You'd at least have the satisfaction of leaving it exactly where you found it."

A feeling of dread descended upon David, and he realized why he brought the bag in here after his debate in the car. He didn't want to take it to the ravine. He feared the spirit would be waiting for him, maybe lurking behind the oak bearing her name. Confident no one heard Miriam's orgasmic cries two Saturdays ago, certainly no one would hear him scream either.

"I'd truly appreciate you taking care of this for me, John," said David, hoping the ranger didn't sense just how grateful he would be. He looked forward to the end of their conversation, so he could get the hell out of there and head back to Pigeon Forge.

"All right." John picked up Allie's bag of treasures and tossed it into the drawer and closed it. "It's been nice meeting you, David Hobbs."

He extended his hand, and David responded with a grip almost as strong as the ranger's.

"Thanks for your help."

John watched him go, and then stepped onto the floor of the gift shop. He confirmed the start time of the next Cable Mill tour that afternoon for a group of senior citizens browsing through the circular post card displays. When he glanced out a nearby window facing the parking lot, David's rented Buick was already gone.

* * * * *

He hurried back to the hotel. For the rest of the afternoon and evening he remained in his room, reading most of a John Grisham novel he purchased in Chattanooga's airport. The only interruption was the steak dinner he ordered through a local takeout restaurant. Every so often he got up and stretched, walking around the room and checking the bathroom and balcony. As far as he could tell, nothing had followed him from the visitors' center.

Miriam called him at ten o'clock. He had left her a voice message earlier. Like him, she worried whether or not John Running Deer would actually take the bag to the ravine.

David told her that he'd like to move his return flight to Denver from Wednesday afternoon to Tuesday evening. It just depended on whether his auntie could meet him for lunch then instead of Wednesday. Otherwise, he'd stay in Chattanooga Tuesday night, and would fly out Wednesday as originally planned.

They finished their conversation, and David got ready for bed. He grew tired enough to retire around eleven-thirty, and decided not to leave any lights on. He thought it might bring good luck if he refused to give in to paranoia. Peering at the shadows of his room once his eyes adjusted, he listened to the steady hum of the heater sending warm air into the room. He fell asleep around midnight.

Chapter Twenty-eight

When the clock's alarm went off at 7:00 a.m. Tuesday morning, David didn't awaken right away. Instead, the steady pulse of the annoying beep merged into his dream. The slick weight of a heavy hoe in his sweaty hands slammed into the unforgiving earth over and over again, in perfect rhythm with the beep. Hot sun in a cloudless summer sky beat down upon his bare neck, and burning pain told him the sun's anger would be with him long after his present chore ended at nightfall. He continued to churn the dry earth, as sweat poured down his dust covered face and body.

Clad in torn boots, trousers, and a low-neck t-shirt, the hard, torturing work provided a balm to his bitter mind. Overflowing with rage, he wanted revenge against the community that wouldn't accept him as an equal, as one of their own.

But damned straight the earth would obey his command to produce... even if it killed him making it happen. He grinned maliciously, pausing to look out over the several-acre spread of crusted land. Like he'd tame a young harlot refusing to cooperate, he'd teach the land a lesson. Then everyone would see that he and his kin ain't idiots for trying to save the god-forsaken hell-hole, where the soil had long suffered from drought and neglect. Once he proved 'em wrong, he'd shove this very hoe all the way up their pompous asses, until it smashed their teeth on the way out from their smirking faces.

"Screw em' all!" he hissed, and returned to slamming the hoe into the earth. Over and over, deeper and deeper, in line with the steady pulse of blood flowing hotly through his veins, until the alarm's steady beep grew louder and replaced the images of the dream.

David sat up, fumbling in the room's dimness to turn off the alarm. Light from daybreak crept through cracks along the edges of the window's curtain. He wiped his eyes to regain his orientation. Images from the dream faded. The intense malice and anger was difficult to believe, and he wondered what it meant. He didn't recognize anything from the dreamscape... a mule pulling a cart nearby, and the view of a modest shack sitting at the edge of the barren field he furiously tilled by hand.

Chalking it up to the mashed potatoes and gravy that hadn't set well the previous evening, he let the matter go and started getting ready. He finished brushing his teeth, and was about to trim his beard when he noticed his wristwatch was missing. Thinking he might've laid it on the dresser next to the TV, he checked there first, pushing aside the television pay-per-view advertisements and a Ripley's brochure as he searched. Not finding it, he turned his attention to the nightstand.

His watch sat on the far side of the alarm clock, the gold band forming a perfect circle. In the circle's midst sat the little cloth bag, its leather strap hanging over the band as if someone casually deposited the bag there during the night.

No friggin' way!

David slowly approached the nightstand, glancing nervously around. He wondered for a moment if John Running Deer decided to have some fun with the foolish man from Colorado, who traveled fifteen hundred miles to deliver an item that should've been easy to mail. Then he noticed footprints next to the bed.

The light gray carpet looked fairly new, and the fibers appeared resilient enough to bounce back from foot traffic to keep the carpet looking neat and even. It should make the carpet resistant to footprints. He looked around, seeing no other footprints in the room, not even his own. The only ones were these, left next to the nightstand and bed. Much smaller than his shoe size, two identical sets of barefoot indentations had been left on the carpet's surface. One pair faced the nightstand and the other faced the head of the bed. The depth of the imprints told him whoever made them stood in each spot for quite a while.

He shuddered at the thought of Allie Mae watching him sleep. Perhaps she laughed to herself at his naivety, thinking he could dispatch such an ominous opponent by leaving the dirty work for someone else. He stared numbly at the scene for several minutes, until he finally picked up his watch and set the bag on the bed. Fearful the spirit might return at any moment, he showered quickly. Once dressed, he threw the bag in his briefcase and vacated the room.

He stopped for breakfast at a nearby pancake house after he checked out of the hotel, and drove into the national park. When he arrived at nine o'clock, the Cades Cove visitors' center was far more crowded than the previous day. He waited for John Running Deer to finish a tour, perusing postcards inside the gift shop.

"Mr. Hobbs, I understand you've been waiting for me," said John. "What can I do for you this morning? I don't suppose you came back for the little bag you left here yesterday." He smiled impishly.

"As a matter of fact, I did come back here because of it," said David. He looked around, uneasily. The gift shop had quite a few patrons. "Can we talk someplace private?"

"Sure." John glanced at the counter where they had talked previously. Another employee assisted a tourist wearing a backpack. "We can talk in my office."

He led David out of the gift shop, and past the main information counter to a door near the east corner of the building. A storage room, it also served as a workspace.

"Micky, Cheryl, and I share the office, so please excuse the mess," he advised, turning on an overhead light and pointing to a metal folding chair on one side of a mahogany desk.

He moved to another chair, gathering several loose papers strewn across the desktop. "Our main office is in the park station on the other side of the cove."

A little cluttered due to lack of space, rows of boxes were stacked neatly around the desk. An old meridian phone sat next to a flat-screen computer monitor.

"I found this waiting for me on my nightstand this morning." David set his briefcase on top of the desk, and opened it to let the ranger see the same item he'd left with John the previous afternoon.

"Wait here, please. I'll be right back."

Frowning, John rose from his chair and left the room.

David was drawn to a row of photographs on the right side of the desk. He studied the ones that appeared to belong to John. The first was a group photo with several other rangers taken next to Abrams Falls in Cades Cove. The second featured John on a boat in Mexico, where he and another Native American man held a trophy swordfish. In the next photo, he stood arm and arm with an attractive blonde woman, taken twenty to thirty years ago. The last one, and the most recent, featured him with his arm around the waist of a beautiful, dark-haired girl in her early twenties.

"That's my granddaughter, Evelyn," John commented as he stepped back into the office and closed the door. "One of her boyfriends took the picture last summer down in Charleston."

"She's quite beautiful."

"Why, thank you." He returned to his chair. "I thought I should check the drawer where I put the bag yesterday before jumping to any conclusions. But, it's not there, and none of the other employees working here yesterday got into that drawer after you left. Won't you sit down?"

He motioned for David to take his seat.

"Can I get you some coffee, or tea?"

"Coffee sounds good."

John poured a cup from a portable machine and handed it to him, along with two small containers of cream and a sugar packet, at David's request. He pulled out a pencil and tablet from the top drawer, and set the tablet on the desk near the open briefcase.

"You've got a hell of a problem, I'd say," John observed, solemnly. "Hand-delivering the bag hasn't worked out any better than sending it through the mail." He wrote a few notes on the tablet's page.

"What if I'm supposed to take it back to the exact location where I first saw it, in the Lover's Lane ravine?" said David, thinking of what Miriam had told him. "It could be the key to the whole thing."

"Maybe." John looked up from the tablet. "I thought the same thing yesterday, even though you said it somehow got mixed up with your things. Since you now say you actually saw the bag while in the ravine, I must also assume you took it home willingly."

David realized he had slipped up, and evasiveness about any other details would be much harder.

"Okay," he sighed. "I did know it was there when we left the ravine. Miriam wanted me to turn it in here before we left Cades Cove, and my intent was to do just that… but, I couldn't do it."

John didn't reply right away, continuing to jot down his notes. When finished, he laid the pencil down.

"May I?"

David encouraged him to remove the bag from inside the open briefcase. Holding it carefully, John loosened the leather strap. The powerful mixture of mustiness and the alluring floral fragrance wafted toward him, causing him to draw back. He squinted and pulled the bag closer to his nostrils.

"It didn't start out smelling like that," said David. "It used to just smell like something old, like when I was a kid playing in my grandmother's closet."

"That odor is still there beneath the other ones," noted John, sniffing the bag. He turned it over in his hands, rubbing fingers across the stitched name as if reading some sort of psychic Braille. But, unlike yesterday, where he did this without going further, he went ahead and emptied the items onto the desk.

After sifting through them, he paused to unfold the note and study it. But he soon set it aside, commenting the handwriting was too faint for his older eyes. Turning his attention to the tooth, he examined its blood-encrusted enamel.

"I'm going to go out on a limb here," said John, his voice quiet and serious. "I see the bruise above your eye and the tiredness in your face. You've brought these things to us, which can transport themselves several miles on their own. I also recall the urgency in your wife's note, when I first read it Saturday and again yesterday."

He stood and leaned across the desk.

"I've seen many strange and wonderful things during my lifetime," he continued. "I'm willing to bet you've seen strange and maybe not quite so wonderful things recently. I might be able to help you, but you must trust me. It appears a powerful asgina, or spirit, followed you home to Colorado from the ravine and isn't ready to let go of you just yet."

"What do you suggest I do?" David clung to the thin hope John Running Deer might free him from the ghost's tenacious grip.

"The first thing I need is for you to tell me everything that's happened, from the time of your picnic in the ravine until today," he said, sitting down. "The more details you remember, the better our chances will be in coming up with a cure for you and your family."

David agreed, feeling desperate. To his surprise, telling his story to a relative stranger came out a hell of a lot easier than it did with Miriam and Norm. He told John almost everything, sparing only the lurid details from his dream of Norm. When he finished, the ranger sat back, his expression somber.

"I'm not sure returning Allie Mae's Treasures to the ravine is the answer," he said. "As I told you, we get items all of the time. Some of the letters we've received over the years tell of runs of bad luck and occasional poltergeist activity that suddenly visited the lives of those who've taken something from the park. We try to take the things back to the exact spot they were removed from, but it hasn't always worked. We've rarely heard from the people again, unless they return to thank us."

He paused to pick through the objects on his desk.

"Your situation is different. My feeling is we should try to find Allie Mae's relatives, since what's here should be of value to her descendants. It might be the very thing that brings her peace in the spirit world."

"How do we accomplish that?" The idea of returning the bag to the ravine alone seemed more attractive to David than trying to find the owner of a partial name from a century ago.

"It sounds like a difficult task, I know," agreed John. "But, I've got a contact who works for the census bureau in Knoxville."

"How long do you think it would take them to find Allie's relatives?"

"If I call Diane today, she might have an answer for us tomorrow. Definitely, by the weekend at the latest," he said. "Keep in mind that we're talking about a small community which never grew beyond six hundred souls."

"I was planning on going home tomorrow," said David. "If worse comes to worst, I can wait here longer, I suppose. I'm not so sure Allie Mae will be as patient."

He thought of Norm's injuries and those administered to him and Tyler. Hell, tonight might be too late. John eyed him as if he could see the images in David's mind.

"I've been running the names I remember through my memory since we met yesterday, but I can't recall an Allie or Allie Mae in any of the cove records I've ever seen from the end of World War I through 1934, or even among the last stragglers who finally came back to gather the belongings they left behind in the early 1950s." He got up to get another cup of coffee. "Would you like a refill, David?"

"I'm okay at the moment, but thanks," he said, taking another sip.

John returned to the desk with a steaming cup and a less serious look on his face.

"You know, another idea just occurred to me," he said. "I still intend to call my friend in Knoxville before lunch, but there's one other place we can check."

"Really?" David sat up straight, hopeful he could resolve everything without having to wait until Friday.

"One of the churches in the cove needed an extensive termite treatment a few years back, and several boxes of old church meetings and other notes were found in a forgotten storage area beneath the pulpit," John told him. "I remember going through the boxes out of curiosity, and I was surprised to find guest books and other attendance ledgers. I recall seeing a few birth and death announcements, too."

"Where are the boxes now?"

"Just a few miles away from where we're sitting," said John. "They're stored in the supply shed behind the park station I told you about. We've been waiting on the go ahead to ship them to Nashville for permanent storage. I wonder sometimes if the state's archives forgot about them. If you'd like to take a look through these boxes, I can take you this afternoon, once I've finished my one-thirty tour."

"I'd like that," said David. It could mean looking for a needle in a haystack. However, his years of experience doing client audits taught him the importance of never overlooking a possible resource, since often a missing figure or answer he needed came from the most unlikely places.

"Well then, give me a few minutes to make sure we're staffed through one o'clock, and I'll place the call to Knoxville," said John. "Would you be opposed to joining me for lunch?"

"Not at all."

Sensing John could use the next few minutes without an extra distraction, David excused himself from John's office. David told him that he'd wait by his car in the parking lot, and offered to drive to wherever John had in mind for lunch.

Almost eleven-thirty, they arrived at a park restaurant located just outside of Cades Cove. They talked about subjects that had nothing to do with Allie Mae, such as each other's careers and families. John's wife, the blonde lady in the photograph, had passed away six years earlier from breast cancer. Her death hit their only daughter and two granddaughters extremely hard. John Running Deer's passions in life were his family and the preservation of the wilderness his forefathers cherished.

John's last tour ended at two o'clock, leaving the rest of the afternoon free. The two men drove in John's cruiser to the park station. Once there, they cleared a table inside an office and brought in the boxes.

For the next two hours, they didn't find anything helpful, although the first boxes produced a fascinating assortment of documents that shed valuable light on life in Cades Cove during the two decades following World War I. John explained how the community had always been unusually close knit, and he learned to admire the people and their unique history, despite his Cherokee forefathers being forced to leave the area. "They were, for the most part, a very caring community," he commented, while helping David sift through church ledgers from 1919 through 1924.

They brought in the last boxes around five o'clock, when the security floodlights surrounding the station turned on. Not wanting to take a break, David started in on the first of these boxes while John took a moment to relax at the desk. While absently sifting through the contents of "Allie Mae's Treasures" spread out again on the desktop, John noticed the faint inscription on the torn locket.

He retrieved a magnifying glass and held up the locket. In the elaborate cursive style of the late nineteenth century Victorian period that pervaded into the early twentieth century, the inscription read: *To my darling granddaughter, Allie, on her 16th Christmas, 1915.*

"What year are we down to?" John asked.

"I'm just about finished looking through the ledger for 1918," said David. "It looks like there's several more like it still inside the box from earlier years. I can see the ones for 1916 and 1917 below what looks like a string-tied bunch of letters."

"Have you ever taken a close look at the locket?" John held it up by the golden chain.

"No, I haven't."

David paused to look where John sat. Even with the aid of his reading glasses, his eyes had grown tired from the time already spent studying the penned lines on the ledgers and other documents that had faded over the years. If John hadn't told him, he wouldn't have known he held the locket in his hand. He stood to get a closer look.

"I guess if we get any earlier than 1899 we'll be in deep shit," David observed dryly, after John showed him the inscription. "Miriam said something about it, or maybe it was about the young man who wrote the letter to Allie. Some kid named Seth, I think, who had gone off to fight in World War I."

John immediately took an interest in the information, carefully setting the locket down and unfolding the letter. Using the magnifier, the faded penmanship became decipherable to his older eyes. He read the contents while David stood by listening. Miriam had been right. The boy, Seth Sullivan, promised to marry Allie as soon as his enlistment ended.

Knowing the two items spanned a four-year period from 1914 to 1918, they had a smaller window to focus on. Reinvigorated by the hope they drew nearer to learning Allie's full identity, John joined David back at the table. He opened the last box while David finished scouring through the 1918 ledger.

"Ah, hell," sighed David, once he reached the November 1918 entries. He read a little bit more and looked sourly over at John sitting across from him. "There's a note here about a community service being held at the Missionary Baptist church, which I take is not the same church these documents came from, because it mentions another Sunday evening service to follow *in this building* after the other one had finished."

John nodded.

"Anyway, the service was to *honor the soldiers lost in the fight to keep Europe free from tyranny*, and attached to the page is an announcement listing nearly thirty names of the men who died overseas," David continued. "In the middle of the list is the name Thomas Seth Sullivan. It might not be the same kid, but I doubt it. You said the community never grew beyond six hundred people."

John asked to see the ledger and the announcement, and soon after David handed it to him, he agreed it had to be the same young man.

"Well, I guess it explains why only her name is carved on the oak tree where Miriam and I had our picnic."

"A broken heart can be a terrible burden," agreed John. "Especially for a female growing up back then, when women were considered old maids by their early twenties."

David looked up, surprised and unaware of that fact. Since John had already set the journal down, busy rummaging through a box, he moved to 1917's ledger. After another fruitless search, David picked up the ledger from 1916. From January through April, there were no significant entries. In May, however, he found something. Beneath an ornate Mother's Day announcement, which took place on May 14th, were two loose pages stuck together by glue or some other adhesive. From the look of how the pages mashed onto each other, it looked as if it might've happened by accident, perhaps when something spilled on the ledger and seeped onto the pages.

The adhesive had hardened to where one couldn't open the pages without tearing them. Not wanting to damage something which had value based on its age alone, David asked John to see if he could separate them. At first, John didn't have much success. When the pages began to tear, David suggested they move on to something else. Suddenly, the pages pulled apart, one falling to the floor while John held the other.

John looked astonished as he read the page he held while David picked up the other from the floor. Since John hadn't finished, David looked at the other page. It was a memo that detailed a meeting held the day after Mother's Day, May 15th, 1916. His mouth dropped open as he read it. A girl disappeared the night before, and the girl's parents and pastor had called the meeting in order to organize an extensive search for her. The girl's name was Allie McCormick.

"I think I found her!" he announced excitedly, while reading other details.

The memo further described Allie as the eldest daughter of Samuel and Esther McCormick, age seventeen. Members from all three churches in the area had gathered, with the intent to search throughout Cades Cove until they found her. He held out the page to John, feeling as if there might be light at the end of the hellish tunnel after all. Meanwhile, John finished reading the page he held in his hand. Unlike David, he wasn't smiling anymore.

"I think you're definitely correct about finding Allie's identity," said John, evenly. "But, before you get too excited, you need to read this."

David stepped to where John stood. David's smile faded. The page dealt with the same incident, but from another meeting several days later on Friday, May 19th 1916. It was a call to arms to find two local young men at any cost, that hadn't been seen since the disappearance of Allie McCormick. Their names were Zachariah and Billy Ray Hobson, and a sub note listed the older Hobson, Billy Ray, as a convicted felon.

"Shit!" Not believing his eyes, David carefully scanned the details a second time.

"They definitely are the same first names you mentioned," said John, having finished his review of both pages.

"Yeah, they are," whispered David.

"And the brothers' last name is similar to yours. Although, I doubt a spirit would use that as a reason to connect with the living."

David wasn't so sure. After all, the ghost seemed quite confident in addressing him and Tyler as Billy Ray and Zachariah. Hoping to learn more, he read through the rest of the 1916 ledger, disappointed to find no other mention of either Allie McCormick's disappearance or the Hobson brothers' fate.

"Well, I believe we now have enough information to work with," said John, glancing at his watch once David finished examining the 1916 ledger. It was just after six o'clock. "Diane should have the preliminary work done sometime tomorrow morning. I'll call her first thing and give her the names of Allie's parents as well as the Hobson brothers. I think it might be interesting to find out what became of them, too."

David felt reluctant to stop searching, but realized the likelihood of finding more gems was remote. After John secured the ledger holding the 1916 Mother's Day documents in a small safe located in the back of the building, they sealed the boxes, and returned them to the storage shed. David thanked him again, and they agreed to touch base Wednesday morning.

On the way to Gatlinburg, David changed his return flight home to the following Sunday afternoon. He hoped it gave John Running Deer's census contact in Knoxville enough time to get him the names of Allie's relatives.

Next, he called his aunt in Chattanooga. After explaining his business trip had been extended through the weekend, they made plans for lunch on Sunday before his flight to Denver. That left Miriam and the search for another place to stay through Saturday night. Since he was already near Gatlinburg, he grabbed a bite to eat while looking for a vacant hotel room on the strip. He planned to call her once he settled in for the night, and would give her an update on what happened that day.

* * * * *

The Whitestone Motel had the only vacancy on Gatlinburg's strip. Since it sat on the side closest to Pigeon Forge and furthest from the park, David reserved it for only three nights, hoping to get something closer on Friday afternoon.

Built in the early 1960s and named for its stone façade, the motel looked as if it hadn't been remodeled since. David checked into the room on the first floor shortly after eight o'clock, near the far end of the building where the parking lot bore numerous potholes. Greeted by the smell of stale cigarette smoke and mildew when he stepped inside his room, at least the bed linens and towels appeared clean. Mold encroached along the edges of the bathtub and sink. The room's overall condition affirmed why the innkeeper seemed eager to reserve it for three nights. He wondered how a motel like this survived when it wasn't peak season.

"Hey, babe, it's me." He held an old rotary telephone receiver pressed tightly against his ear. The room had two double beds, and his luggage lay open on the bed closest to the door while he stretched out on the bed next to the bathroom.

"I'm still in Gatlinburg, so let me give you the number where I'll be the next few nights."

"What's wrong?" Miriam sounded alarmed. "I thought you were going to Chattanooga tonight and would be flying home tomorrow!"

"I know… me too," he replied. "But, Allie Mae had other ideas. I found her bag waiting on my nightstand when I woke up."

"What?"

"I know, darlin', I know… that's how I felt this morning," he said, his tone soothing. "But, John Running Deer, the ranger I told you about last night, helped me find out who she was today. Her name was Allie McCormick, and he has a friend who can hopefully help us track down her relatives. John thinks it could help her find peace."

"I don't know if that will work." It sounded as if she tried to cover the receiver, so he wouldn't hear her sniff. "I think you need to take the damned thing back where we first saw it, to that tree in the ravine!"

"John told me yesterday they get a lot of stuff taken from the park each year," he said. "Returning an item to the original spot it was taken from doesn't have much effect one way or another on the hauntings people experience. He even offered to take the bag there for me when I left it with him yesterday, and you'd think the spirit knew that too. Obviously, there's something else she's after, and it makes sense she'd want me to find the rightful heir to the bag."

"I'm still not convinced."

"There were a couple of other things we learned today," added David, hoping to get her to agree. "The locket has a faint inscription that says it was given to Allie Mae on her sixteenth Christmas back in 1915. And the boy named in the letter, Seth Sullivan, showed up on a list of young men in a church ledger who died in World War I back in 1918."

"That poor girl."

"Yeah." The image that popped into his mind definitely wasn't the one in hers. He pictured Norm's violated corpse pleading for David not to forget what she did to him. "So, is everything okay at home?"

"Jan and I went over to the house today," she said. "It might be safe to move back this weekend, but I want Sara to visit first to make sure."

"Nothing's happened in the townhouse or anyplace else, I take it?"

"No, nothing has." A moment of awkward silence followed. "So, when are you coming home?"

"I changed my return flight to Sunday, and I've already set a lunch date that afternoon with Auntie," he said. "John thinks it might take until the weekend to find Allie's relatives. Hopefully, it'll all be finished by the time I check out of here on Friday. Maybe I'll drive down to Chattanooga and spend a day or two there."

"I miss you so much, David." She sounded hushed and lonely.

Miriam took down the address and phone number of the Whitestone Motel before she hung up, leaving him to listen to a crackling dial tone indicative of the motel's aged phone lines.

To keep distracted, for the next few hours he worked on the Applewood reports, finishing half of them. By then it was almost midnight. After the unexpected visitation from Allie Mae the previous night, he decided to leave the TV on low and faced it toward the door, providing just enough light for him to see the room entirely. With the covers pulled up to his chin, he stared at the clock on the nightstand. An aqua-colored monster from when the motel first opened, the minute hand crept slowly, tracking the time from 12:10 to 12:37 a.m. when he dozed off.

Chapter Twenty-nine

"M-u-r-r-r-der-r-r-er-r-r!"

David opened his eyes, awakened by the whisper. The room was completely dark, and not even the parking lot lamps' glow penetrated the murkiness. He noticed the curtains' unusual thickness when he turned up the heater before retiring, assuming it was the motel's way of compensating its guests for the sparse insulation. At least one couldn't be bothered by any car or truck lights coming in late, as most of the motel's patrons seemed to be in the long-haul transportation business.

The television was blank and silent, and David couldn't make out its outline. The heater's comforting hum was also absent. It left the room in a hostile stillness. The sound of a deep sigh filled the air above the space between the two beds. Something floated there.

He raised himself, fully aware of his distinct disadvantage. Peering into the darkness where the sigh came from, he reached for the lamp switch.

"Don't do it!"

The feminine voice surreal, the accent and the fact it sounded both near and far was familiar.

"Allie Mae?"

The air around him was already chilled from the lack of heat, but it grew colder. The presence was drawing close. A brilliant blue eye appeared, aglow in the darkness less than a foot away. The eye was especially beautiful, and it squinted. Perhaps it scrutinized him, or more likely, its owner was seriously pissed.

"What do you want from me?" David tried to remain calm despite his terror, but found it impossible to control the unsteadiness in his voice.

The eye moved closer, and as it did he became aware of a soft gurgling sound. It reminded him of the tiny streams he used to find in the mountain valleys of Colorado. Cold drafts of air brushed against his face, and the eye came within a few inches of his own eyes, as if the head shrouded by darkness positioned itself to kiss him. The smell of raw meat filled his nostrils. He pushed himself against the bed's headboard.

"To take back what you've stolen," the voice replied. It was softer and almost normal, erupting from the gurgling noise and sending an icy spray upon him. "And kill the wicked seed once and for all!"

"I didn't steal your bag of treasures, and I'll happily give it back!" He clutched the bedspread tightly, and shrunk away from the eye, the smell, and the gurgling. "I'll do whatever it takes to make things right!"

"It's too late to give it back," replied the garbled voice, sending forth another spray of chilled droplets onto his face. David cringed in response and closed his eyes. "It's too late to give back *my* life, Billy Ray-y-y-y!"

A splash of frigid liquid that landed against his throat and t-shirt emphasized the fervency of this last statement. Ever fearful, he opened his eyes. Another eye as grotesque as the first eye was lovely had since joined it. Its mutilated cornea and iris glowed as a ruptured mass of fire and blood within the torn edges of the socket the eye illuminated.

"I'm *not* Billy Ray! My name's *David!"* he shouted.

"Ya are what ya are and always will be, Billy Ray-y-y-y!" the voice hissed. "Y'all and yer seed have killed and taken whatever ya've pleased! But, no more…. There ain't no more hidin' from yer sins!"

"No, you've got the wrong guy! I've *never* done *anything* to you—"

"M-u-r-r-r-der-r-r-er-r-r!"

He threw his hands up to protect himself as she shrieked her condemnation over and over, the echo resounding loudly throughout the room before returning to where he lay huddled against the headboard. The frozen hostility gripped the base of the bed and steadily moved toward him, seizing the bones in his feet, legs, and thighs with painful surges that lingered as the bitter chill continued to crawl forward. Out of the darkness the two eyes suddenly looked up from just above his waist, as if the entity intended to caress his body like a famished lover. He whimpered in horror as something cold, wet and slimy crept inside his shirt toward his throat.

Screaming in terror, he slapped at himself, falling out of bed. He grabbed the nightstand, pulling the top drawer out while groping for the lamp's pole. A pair of frigid arms embraced him from behind, and icy fingers pinched his nipples. Coldness beyond anything he'd ever known flowed through him from behind, freezing his lungs. He began to pass out. Turning on the light switch was the last thing he remembered.

David awoke lying on the floor between the two beds. The nightstand lamp was on, and his head throbbed worse than any migraine he could remember. He groggily stood and moved to the clock, which faced his bed. It read 3:38 a.m.

After replacing the nightstand's drawer in its slot, and checking to make sure the heater still worked, he set the thermostat and blower on high and went into the bathroom. He intended to splash water in his face and take something for his pounding headache. But, when he looked in the mirror, he could only stare at his reflection.

His face and t-shirt were covered with blood.

Chapter Thirty

Tired and feverish, David headed to the park Wednesday afternoon. Finding it hard to keep his eyes open while navigating a highway slick from steady rain, the previous night's events remained fresh. He found himself reliving his first verifiable physical contact with the spirit of Allie Mae McCormick.

His first shower was an act of squeamish determination, and he forced himself to withstand scalding water for almost fifteen minutes. After thoroughly cleansing himself of the blood and other yellowish fluid he tried not to think about, he placed his bedclothes in a dry-cleaning bag he found inside the dresser. As for the bed linens, they weren't nearly as soiled as he expected. It made his later explanation of a sudden and severe nosebleed in the middle of the night to the innkeeper's assistant somewhat believable.

Propped up in a chair between the door and window, he wrapped himself tightly in a spare blanket he took from the closet. By then, the room's temperature had become comfortable. He kept the curtains pushed open and all of the lights on, waking every twenty to thirty minutes from the unsettling sensation of falling into a dark abyss.

By noon, he had dressed and taken the soiled bed linens to the front office, after tossing the dry-cleaning bag into a dumpster. He drove to the local Shoney's, sticking to the hottest items on the buffet bar. With three cups of coffee and another to go, he returned to the visitors' center in Cades Cove.

When David passed the wooden "Welcome to the Great Smoky Mountains National Park" sign, he opened the briefcase next to him to check on the bag. It was still there. He closed the briefcase and turned up the stereo, thankful for the clear signal from a classic rock station in nearby Knoxville.

John Running Deer finished his last tour of the day when David arrived at his small office inside the visitors' center. He motioned for David to join him at his desk, eyeing him curiously.

"Rough night?" John smiled, playfully.

"Rough isn't the right word for it," David replied. "I'll tell you about it later."

He smiled weakly as he sat across from John, sipping a cup of coffee purchased from a lobby vending machine.

"Well, I have some very good news," said John, pulling out a three-page fax from a manila folder. "Here's a report I received this morning from Diane Sellers, my contact at the census bureau."

David pulled his chair around to see it. Formatted as a summarized genealogy, the report began in 1901, when Samuel and Esther McCormick first took ownership of a small parcel of land, east of John Oliver's spread in Cades Cove. A blacksmith by trade, Samuel brought his wife and two daughters, two-year old Allie Mae and three-month old Emma Sue, from Asheville, North Carolina. Samuel also brought his mother, Virginia McCormick, to Tennessee.

Samuel prospered as a reliable smith, and soon purchased additional acreage along with adding horses, hogs, and other livestock. The family continued to prosper until Samuel died in April 1918 from influenza. The Oliver clan purchased the McCormick property in February 1923, after Esther died of tuberculosis. Virginia McCormick died of unknown causes in 1917.

The report contained no additional mention of Allie Mae or her eventual fate. As for her sister Emma Sue, she married a local farmer named Lester Crockett, who also migrated from North Carolina. His family purchased a homestead on the eastern side of the cove, near where the visitors' center stood today. They married in October 1921, and she gave birth to a daughter named Allie Esther Crockett almost two years later, in September of 1923. Emma died from the same disease that killed her mother, tuberculosis, in August 1926, leaving her husband to care for their only child.

In June 1934, Lester Crockett moved out of Cades Cove. He took ten-year-old Allie Esther, along with his new wife, Loretta, and their three-year-old son, Joshua, to a small town fifteen miles north called Rocky Grove. Allie Esther married a local man from Rocky Grove named Milton Edder, in May 1941. She bore two sons. The first son was named Ezra, and he was born in November 1946, after Milton returned home from Germany, after World War II. The second, Jacob, was born in August 1951. Ezra died in a car accident in 1962, and Milton passed away from a heart attack on Christmas Day in 1975. Ezra never married and had no known descendants.

Jacob Edder married Leslie Holmes from Knoxville in October 1984, and they moved to Johnson City, Tennessee in 1987. They had two sons: Michael, born in May 1990, and Vernon, who followed in July 1994.

"Here's the important thing," said John, pointing to the bottom of the second page. "According to the latest documents Diane found, Allie Esther is still alive."

"She would be a rarity, it seems, based on everybody else's lifespan listed here," observed David. "She'd be almost ninety by now, right?"

"Yes, she is," said John, and pointed to the next line. "Here's her current address, and the phone number should be correct. According to Diane, Mrs. Edder still lives in Rocky Grove, in the very same house her husband Milton purchased back in 1941."

They both looked at each other in silence, afraid to make the next move. They had successfully tracked down Allie Mae's closest living relative, but hesitated to make contact.

"Let me call her," said David, after staring at the desk phone for nearly a minute. "I'm not sure exactly what to say, but I'm pretty good at speaking with strangers on the phone. Unless you'd rather handle this." He looked at John.

"It would be best if you handled it yourself," he agreed, standing. He motioned for David to take his seat next to the telephone. "I'll give you a few minutes alone to talk with her, which will give me an opportunity to check on everything else around here. We've been unusually busy this week."

He left him with Allie Esther Edder's information. David took a moment to think about what he wanted to say to Allie Mae's niece. Then, he picked up the handset and dialed her number.

His mouth went dry, and his eagerness dimmed once the phone reached its fourth ring without an answer. He assumed he'd reach the number's voicemail, but the phone kept ringing. Just before he hung up after the eighth ring, someone answered.

"Hello?" The voice was soft and frail, and obviously belonged to an elderly woman.

"Is this Mrs. Allie Esther Edder?" David hoped he achieved the warmth of a neighbor, and not some cheesy telemarketer.

"It is," drawled the voice, in the accent once indigenous to the hills of eastern Tennessee and Kentucky, as well as western Virginia and North Carolina.

"Hi, ma'am, my name is David Hobbs. My family and I have come into possession of a keepsake we believe belongs to your family, and would like to return it to you."

David smiled, hopeful he might actually be near the end of his plight. It came out much smoother than he envisioned, and he was pleased she hadn't hung up.

"Oh? What kind of keepsake are ya talkin' 'bout?" She seemed curious, clearing her throat.

"It's a little bag made from cloth with a leather strap, and it contains a sleigh bell, a blue ribbon, a gold chain with part of a locket attached to the chain, and a letter," explained David. "It has 'Allie Mae's Treasures' stitched on the front of it in blue thread."

He waited patiently for a reply that didn't come. He thought he heard sniffling, and worried she might be crying. Something fell loudly on the floor, like a cane or maybe the phone itself, and he heard the anxious voice of a young man shouting something inaudible, accompanied by heavy steps running toward the phone across a hardwood floor.

"Granny? …Granny, what in the hell happened?"

David heard the old woman groan as the young man, obviously her grandson, helped her up. The noise from a chair sliding on the hardwood floor, along with the light strain of the two struggling to get her back into the chair echoed from somewhere near the fallen handset. Allie Esther said something about a man on the phone between sobs, and her grandson picked up the phone.

"Hello?"

"Hello," David replied, swallowing hard, not knowing how to continue.

"What the fuck do you want?" her grandson demanded, his tone menacing.

"My name is David Hobbs, and I—."

"I don't give a flyin' fuck who you are, you goddamned cock sucker!" said the young man.

"I have something that belongs to you!" David hoped the kid would pause long enough for him to explain.

"Ain't you listenin', asshole?" her grandson snarled. "I don't care why you called, just don't do it again!"

"It belonged to your grandmother's aunt!" Desperation took hold of David, and he looked anxiously over his shoulder when John returned, who appeared worried.

"I don't fuckin' care!" A moment of silence followed before Allie Esther's grandson resumed his uninvited malice, his voice hushed but shaking. "If… you ever call us again, mister, I swear to Christ I'll find you and tear your heart out and feed it to you while you lay dyin'. You got that? And, don't even think about comin' to see us, or I'll shoot your ass dead where you stand!"

Before David could say anything else, the line went dead. He stared absently at the cursed bag resting inside his briefcase on the desktop while he listened to the dial tone. It wasn't until the operator recording broke in that he looked at John again, who stood beside him.

"Was that someone in the household?" asked John, his tone compassionate. "I heard you from the lobby."

"Sorry about that," whispered David, descending rapidly into despair. The spirit's recent words rang true. It was too late to give the bag back, indeed. "I spoke to Allie Esther, and I think she collapsed once I told her about the bag. Her grandson threatened to kill me if I ever try to contact her again."

John nodded while he moved to the other chair, and prepared to sit down.

"I'm sorry to have bothered you with this," said David, getting to his feet and closing his briefcase. John stopped him.

"I've got an idea," he said. "The people who lived here before the park was created were an honest, hardworking lot. A handshake meant far more than a paper contract ever did, and important personal business was always best when face to face."

"What are you suggesting?"

The grandson's threats repeated in David's head.

"I don't think it'll be hard to find her address in Rocky Grove, although there are quite a few older dirt roads and hidden hollows up that way," said John. "If you and I went there together in my park cruiser, they might see that we're coming to them on official business, and not as a pair of panderers. Besides, seeing an old man like me might make the grandson hesitant to shoot… at least the old man." He cracked a wry smile.

"Yeah," said David, smiling weakly. "It would probably be better to wait until tomorrow, I imagine."

"Definitely tomorrow," John agreed. "I have two tours in the morning and another at one-forty-five in the afternoon. We can plan to leave around three if you'd like."

"All right," said David. "Did you want to meet here?"

"It would work better if we could meet at the park station, since it will be less of a drive from there," advised John. "We could be in Rocky Grove by three-thirty at the latest. It would be best if we found her place before sundown."

He didn't have to explain. If the young man was as violently disposed as he seemed on the phone, two strangers creeping around in the dark would be asking to get shot.

David gave John the phone extension at the Whitestone. He also gave his mobile number, and John gave David his office numbers and his home listing. John explained how his granddaughters had repeatedly tried to purchase a cell phone for him, but since he was never far from either his radio or office, he couldn't justify one.

David returned to Gatlinburg, and after stopping for dinner at the same steakhouse he and Miriam visited, he returned to the Whitestone. The room still reeked of mildew and stale cigarette smoke, but at least the maid service had put forth a better effort to cover these odors with a cinnamon-scented deodorizer. Even so, the unmistakable blood scent from the previous night's misadventure hung in the air above the bed he slept in.

David set his coat and briefcase on the table, and turned on the heater. He left the TV turned on to CNN, with the sound barely audible, and moved to the phone on the nightstand, where he sat down on the opposite bed. With his back against the headboard, David stared at his reflection in the dresser mirror across the room while waiting for Miriam to pick up.

"Hello, baby." Her voice sounded softer than usual.

"Hi, darlin'," he replied, aroused by how she addressed him.

"How did everything go today?"

"Well, Allie's niece seemed upset once I told her about the bag, and then her grandson threatened my life," said David. "But the beef vegetable soup from the lunch bar at Shoney's was delicious." He chuckled sadly.

"I told you the idea of contacting her family wasn't a good one!" Her sexy tone descended toward alarm. "Why don't you just take the bag back where we originally found it, and be done with this whole mess?"

"I need to try one other idea first," he said. "John and I are planning to visit Allie's niece's home tomorrow afternoon, and we're taking his official park cruiser. It should make her and her grandson more receptive."

"And, if the grandson tries to kill you, then what? Is John bringing Chuck Norris along, too?"

"That's not a bad idea!" He laughed. "Don't worry. If it gets too hairy, I promise we'll leave immediately. I'll take that damned bag straight to the ravine and head down to Chattanooga."

"You promise?"

"Yes, I promise," he assured her. "So, is anything new on the home front?"

The line grew silent, and for a moment, he wondered if she set the phone down. He could hear Janice playing with Jillian and Christopher in the background.

"Miriam?"

"I'm here," she said. "David, those detectives stopped by this afternoon. Sara and Janice were present when they came."

"What did the cops want this time?" He had hoped the detectives would wait long enough for him to return to Denver before showing up again. Dismayed, it also brought his grief to the forefront.

"I think before we spoke today, they considered you a likely suspect in Norm's death. I told them everything… including Allie Mae's ghost and what our family went through last week."

"Oh… what did they think?"

To her credit, sharing such a tale with two detectives from a well-respected police department took a lot of courage.

"You should've seen them, hon," she said. "At first, they grilled me about your whereabouts the night Norm died, as well as questions about your character. They really pissed me off, but I answered their questions patiently. I tried to get them to answer a few of my own, which they skirted around. They were about to leave, and I don't know what prompted me to tell them about everything else that's happened in our house. Maybe it was the looks on Janice's and Sara's faces, since I could tell they were dying to say something."

"So, by everything, did you also include the stuff that happened to us in Gatlinburg?" He hoped she summarized things succinctly, knowing every instance reported to the detectives could generate dozens more future questions for him to look forward to answering when he returned to Denver.

"Yes."

"Oh, God." He sighed, massaging his brow while he pictured the detectives' reaction. "What did they say, then?"

"They didn't laugh, if that's what you're getting at," she replied, sounding irritated. "They listened to everything I had to say. The smirks on their faces when I first started talking disappeared before I was halfway finished."

David sat in silence, staring at his reflection.

"I know what you're thinking," she continued. "But I'm right about this much. They at least believe something very strange has happened to the Hobbs family and their friends. The questions they asked afterward confirm this. It's like they were no longer worried about your immediate whereabouts. Instead, they spent the rest of their time asking Janice, Sara, and me for detailed descriptions of what we've all heard and experienced. Why in the hell would they take time to do that if they didn't believe at least some of what I told them?"

"You've got a point," he said. "Are they sending their buddies out here to come pick me up?"

"No. Detective Colby told me that he wouldn't bother us again until you're back in town. I overheard him tell his partner, Detective Kenyon, what I said might be worth looking into deeper, since they haven't been able to trace the fingerprints they've found to any known felons or other suspects. I'm sure neither one realized I was in earshot when he said that."

"You handled the situation better than I would have," he said, hoping she wouldn't stay irritated. "What did Sara have to say?"

"Well, after today's visit to our house, she said the place is ghost free," said Miriam. "She's convinced more than ever that you are the sole focus. It scares the hell out of me for your welfare." She seemed on the verge of tears.

"I'll be careful," he promised, knowing he might never share his experience from the previous night.

"You better call me immediately after you visit Allie's niece tomorrow afternoon!"

"I promise."

He hated telling her goodbye, especially not knowing how long he'd continue being away from home. After he hung up the phone, he gazed again at his reflection in the mirror until his eyes began to blur. Exhausted, he started to drift off where he sat. He awoke when the mirror stand rattled.

But, the room was quiet, with only the steady hum of the heater and the muted drone from the TV. He frowned at the thought his mind might play tricks on him going forward. It could only worsen the effect of anything new Allie Mae had in store. He decided to work on the reports again. However, the lack of rest had taken its toll, and he found himself nodding off and having to erase pencil lines.

Rather than fight it any longer, he closed up the reports and threw them inside his briefcase. He decided to take another hot shower, hoping to remove the last of the unseen nastiness clinging to his skin. When the water lost its heat he stepped out of the tub, and for a moment listened to his neighbors next door moving heavy furniture inside their room. It wasn't until he pulled on fresh underwear that he realized the commotion actually came from within his own room.

David hurriedly grabbed his bathrobe, tying it at the waist while he stepped into his slippers. With the towel still in hand, he opened the bathroom door and walked into the main room, steam from the bathroom following him. He moved past the washstand and closet, noticing the room had grown cold again despite the heater's steady hum. The lights were off.

The television's cord was nearly pulled out from the wall, brought over on its stand to where it faced the bed closest to him, the one he slept in the night before. The screen was aglow with distorted lines and images, and the set's single speaker hissed with static. It had been done to show him something, despite the room's dimness. A symbol similar to what was left in his and Miriam's bedroom in Littleton now encircled the bed at the Whitestone. Hemlock twigs and leaves extended from the wall on one end of the bed to the nightstand on the other.

Like the original arc in Colorado, Allie Mae's bag of treasures sat in the middle of the bedspread. White duck feathers formed a cross beneath it, and a number of white lily stems were intertwined. Together, they formed three perfect circles upon the cross. The bag sat in the center of the cross, and the three circles overlapped it and each other perfectly.

Splattered crimson crisscrossed the length of the bedspread in deliberate swirls. It would be pointless telling the night manager another nosebleed visited him. Without time to formulate a better plan, David relied solely on his instincts. He dropped the towel and quickly exchanged it for an extra pillow and blanket from the closet next to the bathroom. Then he bolted for the door, pausing long enough to grab his wallet, car keys, coat, and briefcase before lunging outside.

While slamming the door, out of the corner of his eye he saw a shadow descend from inside the doorway. The spirit had watched him from the ceiling, like a spider studying its prey. She would've blocked his escape had he waited any longer. An immense thud slammed against the door from the other side, shaking the wall and window of his room. A light came on in the room next to his, and he heard the muffled voices of a man and woman. They pulled their curtain back to give him an irritated look.

David ran to his rental car, his slippers scraping across the broken pavement. He climbed inside and started the engine, and by the time his neighbors came out, he had already left the premises of the Whitestone Motel. Unsure if they saw his exodus, without a doubt Allie Mae did.

With small streams of water dripping down his forehead, he glanced at his room when he reached the parking lot's exit. The heavy curtain had been drawn back, and only sheer draperies shrouded the room's contents. The lights were on, and a girl dressed in a long blue dress looked out the window. Even from the exit, he could tell her beautiful strawberry-blonde mane covered much of where her face should be. But where there was no hair, there wasn't a face either. Only a deep shadow.

He shuddered and looked away. Pulling onto Gatlinburg's main drive, he prayed fervently to find someplace safe. A place where she'd never find him.

Chapter Thirty-one

Thursday Morning. Sunlight trickled into the Buick's backseat. The clock on the dashboard read 7:06 a.m., and the parking lot of a popular pancake house on Gatlinburg's illustrious drive was already full. Awakened by the sound of a car door closing nearby, David peeked through the rear-passenger window. He watched a family exit their SUV and head toward the large cabin-styled restaurant, the youngest children skipping across the pavement.

Finding a place to hide and sleep last night proved arduous. After visiting more than a dozen area hotels and other restaurants, he finally happened upon the deserted back lot of this establishment. Even though it was impossible to find a comfortable position to sleep, there was no way in hell he would go back to the Whitestone while darkness presided.

David's stomach growled and he crawled into the front seat. Realizing he could do little about his hunger or anything else in his bathrobe and slippers, he grabbed the sunglasses from atop the driver's side visor and started the engine. He ignored the curious looks from the restaurant's patrons, and drove out of the parking lot.

Forced to return to the Whitestone to get his clothes, the motel's parking lot was mostly deserted. He parked the car in front of his room and cut the engine. The air felt crisp and cool, though it would change by mid-morning if the sky remained clear. He approached the room's door, noticing the heavy curtains in the window had been drawn shut. Cautiously, he inserted the key and pushed the door open.

The room was dark. He stepped inside and moved over to the light switch, flipping it on.

The spirit had left a terrible mess. The table and chairs were knocked over, and the mattress from the other bed had been thrown aside. The items obscured the TV and its overturned stand. Clothes from his suitcase covered the room, and the shirts and pants he hung from the clothes rack lay haphazardly on the floor next to the bathroom. The dresser's mirror leaned forward, as if sucked into the room by energy from the wraith's tantrum, and the dresser and nightstand drawers hung precariously on their hinges.

Even the phone book wasn't spared Allie Mae's wrath, having been torn into two uneven pieces. The bathroom lay in similar disarray, and it was soon apparent that only the Gideon Bible in the top drawer of the nightstand went untouched. He worried about the damages he would owe the motel. But, after lifting the mattress onto the bed and discovering the TV survived and still worked, he breathed a sigh of relief. The rest of the furniture was in no worse shape than when he rented the room two days earlier. The spirit had restrained her wrath mostly to his belongings.

Afraid the ghost might return at any moment, he sifted hurriedly through his torn clothing, finding a lone t-shirt and a pair of dress slacks that had escaped her attention. He grabbed his hiking boots, only slightly torn, and dressed while glancing warily around the room. Afterward, he set the Do Not Disturb sign so the maid service would ignore his room until he returned. David recalled seeing a Wal-Mart in Pigeon Forge, and he soon drove west on the main drive.

He picked up a few shirts and jeans, and other necessities to last the rest of his stay. At the checkout line, he added a disposable camera, thinking it would not only provide proof of Allie Mae's latest handiwork, but also protect him from getting sued in the event the Whitestone wanted more compensation than he intended to give.

David discreetly changed into the new clothes once he returned to the car, and drove to Gatlinburg. On a whim, he checked the first few hotels in the area and found a two-night vacancy at one of the Econo-Lodge hotels on the strip. After bringing the items he purchased into the new room, he grabbed the camera and returned to the car. When he arrived at the Whitestone, he accosted one of the maids cleaning a room near his, and handed her a ten-dollar bill for a handful of large trash bags. He returned to his room, armed and ready to clean everything quickly.

As he inserted the key, he noticed the curtains were open. The 'Do Not Disturb' sign remained on the doorknob, making it unlikely the maid staff visited his room. He peered through the window... it appeared that nothing had been disturbed in his absence. Quietly, he unlocked the door and pushed it open.

The room seemed colder, and the mist from his breaths floated toward the ceiling. He grabbed a chair to prop the door open, and took pictures of everything. The disposable camera's flash filled his vision with lingering bright dots while he moved through the room. When he tried to take a direct shot of the bloody shrine on the bed, however, the flash didn't work. He tried it again, and it still didn't go off. Fearing it would be unwise to stay much longer, he cleaned the mess.

He soon filled three bags with paper debris and his destroyed wardrobe. Next, he carefully lifted Allie Mae's little bag off the bed and placed it inside his coat pocket. He dumped the entire bedspread and bloodstained linens into two more bags. A plastic mattress cover kept the blood from seeping further. After wiping the cover off with a mangled towel from the bathroom, one last bag took care of everything else.

David had just carried the bags out of the room and into the car's open trunk, when the chair holding the door open flew into the room. The door slammed shut, and the curtains closed. A girlish, sardonic chuckle filled the air around him.

"Ya think yer *so-o-o* clever!" the voice taunted gleefully. "Run along and enjoy yer day, Billy Ray! We'll be meetin' up again *r-r-e-e-al-l-l* soon!"

The words swirled around him and the air's temperature rapidly dropped, where only a moment ago the late morning sunlight made him think he wouldn't need a coat after all. Her unseen, menacing presence moved closer, poised to do more harm. Rather than wait to find out what she had in mind next, he ran to the driver's side of the car and practically dove in. Her laughter filled the air in front of the windshield while he fumbled with the keys. The tires squealed when he pulled out of the parking space, which drew reproachful looks from the maid who had given him the trash bags, along with the housekeeper who stopped to watch from the second-floor breezeway.

The Buick screeched to a halt when he reached the front office. David ran inside the office, and agreed to pay that night's stay even though he had other accommodations. He tacked on another two hundred dollars to cover the bed linens and towels, and then scurried out of the office and jumped back in the car. He exited the Whitestone Motel's parking lot with the tire's squealing, offering a fervent prayer that he'd never see this God-forsaken hellhole ever again.

* * * * *

David regained most of his composure by the time he arrived at the park station, around two-thirty. Feeding his empty stomach helped, and he had thought it only right to offer his patronage to the pancake house where he loitered uninvited the night before. Afterward, he spent the next hour visiting the various arcades and gift shops on the strip while he waited for the morning's pictures to be developed. Worried about Allie Mae's determination to follow him, he half-expected her shadowed face and hideous ruptured eye to appear in his rearview mirror as he drove to the park.

He arrived at the station before John, and used the opportunity to examine the pictures. Most of the images turned out fuzzy, likely on account of the poor light and cheap camera. Yet, several shots contained solid white orbs Sara claimed could indicate a spirit's presence.

The picture of the bed hardly revealed Allie Mae's handiwork, which he feared since the flash failed. A reddish haze obscured the feather and lily cross. He noticed also the faint outline of what looked like a face behind the haze, and brought the picture closer. Shuddering, he sifted through the rest of the stack, curious if other pictures contained a similar image. Several other photographs revealed odd details he missed at first glance.

While studying one of the last pictures from the packet, a loud knock resounded against the driver's side window.

"Sorry I'm a few minutes late." John peered through the driver's side window, hands cupped to shield his eyes from the sun's brightness. "Are you ready to visit Allie Esther?"

"I am." David hoped John hadn't noticed him cower. He returned the pictures to the envelope while John grinned impishly. David stepped out of the car. "At least the weather's nice. Hopefully, it'll make for a much better experience this afternoon."

"Hopefully, indeed." John's attention was immediately drawn to the packet David held. "I take it those photographs were taken recently?"

"They're from this morning," David confirmed. "Allie Mae paid me another visit last night."

He handed the package to John.

"I'd like to take a good look at these later," John advised, after lingering a moment on the red-streaked photo of the bed. A sudden breeze moved through the towering evergreens behind the station, distracting him. When he brought his gaze back to David, he appeared worried. "We should be on our way."

The two climbed into the park cruiser, after John cleared a small stack of park brochures from the passenger seat. He handed David the manila folder from the previous day, and then drove down the graveled driveway.

"Did the symbols Allie Mae left in Colorado contain feathers and lilies?" John asked, once they were on the main thoroughfare leaving the park.

"No, they didn't," said David, looking at him. "Just hemlock leaves and twigs, along with the ugliest necktie collection known to mankind." He laughed sadly.

Gravely quiet since they drove away from the station, John nodded.

"So, there wasn't a cross?"

"No," David confirmed. "There wasn't any blood either."

John shot him a worried gaze before returning his attention to the road ahead.

"What is it?" asked David, when John said nothing. "I knew it was real bad when I first saw it last night, and I left the room and didn't return until this morning. She tore the place up while I was gone, including nearly every stitch of clothing I own. I've got it all in trash bags inside my trunk."

"Including the feathers?"

"Yes."

"I'd like to take a look inside the bags when we return from Rocky Grove," said John. "I now have a few questions of my own for Allie Esther today."

"What kind of questions?"

"You've described a form of witchcraft," said John. "It wasn't prevalent in the cove, but witchcraft was much more common among white settlers in Appalachia than folks today would like to believe."

"So, you think Allie Mae was a witch?"

David thought of Sara's observations, and the strange whispered phrases he heard during the previous week.

"Yes, I do," said John. "Over the years I've come across a few references to witchcraft, even though the community was very religious and close-knit. Such a thing wouldn't be taken lightly or even tolerated. If a person dabbled in anything outside of what the churches deemed as acceptable behavior, they'd be ostracized."

John turned north on a narrow highway leading to Rocky Grove. The hills on either side were dressed in a lush array of fall colors, and it gave the illusion of unspoiled beauty until they reached an area where a large section of land had been stripped bare. The once beautiful hillside had been butchered to make way for a brand new luxury subdivision, called Chestnut Landings.

"I guess it won't be long before there are a whole slew of restaurants, gas stations, and stores up this way," said David, as they passed the development. It made him think of a pristine area he and Miriam once loved in Colorado, where casinos and hotels sprung up near Cripple Creek.

"Everybody wants a piece of heaven on earth," observed John. "If only the earth's resources were infinite and able to handle the demands placed upon her by us all. There's a prophecy my grandfather told me when I was young, that a day will come when the Great Mother will shake herself like a flea-infested dog, freeing herself of us. Legends say it's happened before, and deep inside we know it'll happen again."

They exited the highway a few miles further up, where John had David read the directions to reach Allie Esther Edder's home. The first few side roads were paved, and led into dense wooded hills. They soon arrived at a graveled road called Bear Ridge Lane. Located at the very end of this road, the Edder cabin overlooked a bluff providing a gorgeous view of the blue hued mountains less than twenty miles away.

John pulled the cruiser to the front of the cabin and parked. A pack of large dogs, all German Shepherd mixes, barked loudly as they surrounded the vehicle. They snarled threateningly while John and David traded wary looks. A young man dressed in jeans and a white T-shirt appeared on the front porch. Clad in a John Deere cap pulled down to hide his eyes, and sporting an Amish beard, he stepped down from the porch aiming a double-barrel shotgun at the windshield.

"What the hell do y'all want?"

John rolled his window down just enough to be heard while keeping the dogs' snouts out of the cruiser.

"We're here on official business from the Smoky Mountains National Park!" he called. The young man stepped to the driver's side. "We've come to speak with Allie Esther Edder!"

"The hell you say!" retorted the man, moving closer and positioning the end of the shotgun just outside John's window. "I'll give y'all thirty seconds to get your goddamned asses out of here!"

"Our concerns with her will take fifteen minutes at most," said John bravely.

The gun's barrel tapped the glass.

"I don't give a fuck what you're here for, just get—"

"Vernon, put yer gun down, son!"

A pale elderly woman appeared atop the porch steps. Dressed in a long gray smock with matching slippers, she wore a knitted blue sweater pulled over her shoulders. With her long white hair pulled back in tight braids, she peered through thick prescription glasses while leaning on a walker. She shook an angry finger at the young man.

He looked back at the woman, whom David assumed must be Allie Esther. Her apparent grandson trembled with rage but respected her command, lowering the gun to his side. For the moment, he continued to glare at the cruiser's occupants.

"Call yer dogs and put 'em in the pen out back for now," she told him. "Then I want ya to grab two chairs from the kitchen, and bring 'em out here so we can visit with these men. Ya got that, son?"

"Yes, Granny." He sighed.

Vernon whistled shrilly and the dogs obeyed, following him away from the car. Once he and the dogs disappeared behind the cabin, John opened his door and stepped out. David joined him, carrying the bag, pictures, and manila folder.

"Come on up here, y'all," invited the woman. "We can visit for a 'lil while on my porch."

They climbed the steps and joined her. In the middle of the porch sat a circular oak table flanked by a pair of weathered pine rockers. The rocker closest to the front door contained two yellow seat cushions, and the other sat bare.

They introduced themselves and David apologized for upsetting her the previous afternoon, to which she thanked him. Admittedly caught off guard by the phone call, she was now ready to discuss her deceased aunt, Allie Mae McCormick.

She moved to the cushioned rocker, and by the time she sat down, her grandson arrived with two oak chairs from her kitchen. Vernon set the chairs next to her seat, and then brushed past the two visitors on his way to the other rocker, where he sat down. John sat in the chair closest to Allie Esther and David took the one next to him.

"So what do ya want to know about my momma's sister?" she asked, after David and John officially greeted Vernon, who barely nodded.

"As he told you yesterday, David recently came into possession of a small bag we are fairly certain belonged to her," said John, motioning for David to hand it to her.

"We'd also be grateful for anything you're willing to share about your aunt," added David.

His heart pounded, and he hoped his nervousness wasn't obvious. He stood at the door to salvation, and the old woman seated just a few feet away held the key.

She took the bag from him, bringing it close enough to examine through her thick eyeglasses. She seemed to study the stains, and momentarily closed her eyes as if meditating. She then loosened the strap to pour the items out onto her lap.

John and David braced themselves for possible embarrassment. But it didn't happen. Only the contents' original musty scent drifted and hung in the air. She sifted through the various items, lingering the longest on the torn locket and broken tooth. She turned the bag to where the cross-stitching faced her, running her fingertips across the faded blue letters.

"Vernon, go inside and fetch the box I showed ya this mornin'. It's sittin' next to the TV in the livin' room," she instructed without looking up. For the moment, she was focused on the objects laid on her lap.

He obeyed, and again brushed past David and John as if they were not there. He disappeared inside the cabin and soon returned with what she requested. Roughly the size of a small shoebox, the hand-crafted mahogany container with primitive designs appeared quite old. She took it from him and carefully set it on the table. Once open, she removed a small cloth bag almost identical to the one lying on her lap. The cloth was much cleaner than Allie Mae's, and the stitched title in green thread appeared worn and more faded. It read "Emma Sue's Treasures".

Allie Esther loosened the bag's leather strap and emptied the three items it contained on the table: a satin, green ribbon frayed at the ends; a sleigh bell like the one inside Allie Mae's bag; and, the front half of the torn locket. A gold chain attached to the locket appeared to be the original one, based on the etchings along the chain link's ridges, which were identical to the markings on the locket's outer rim and clasp.

She picked up the sleigh bell and shook it. A soft jingle resounded from the bell and she smiled sweetly, revealing a pair of yellowed teeth more than a couple of inches apart. The rest of her gums were barren.

"A Christmas bell," she told them, eyeing David as if aware he wondered why something mundane would be included in both bags. "Nice presents from elsewheres were scarce back then, or so my pa used to tell me when I's young."

John agreed, chuckling as he mentioned how his own father once told him the same thing, trying to impress how much better John had it than his father did when a child.

"May I?" he asked, reaching for the locket to get a better look.

"Go on ahead, if you'd like," she said, allowing him to reach over and pick it up. "I'm sure ya noticed it's the other half of the one y'all brought today."

"Yes, ma'am, I did," said John, examining it while David watched. It lacked an engraving since it was the front side of the locket. He gave it back, and she set it next to the bell and ribbon on the table.

"I dreamt of my momma last night," she said, after placing the items from Emma Sue's Treasures back inside the bag. "She looked just like I remember her before she took sick, sittin' on the swing we used to have in Cades Cove."

John and David nodded, very interested in what she had to say.

"Momma told me that I should try and help y'all, that yer in some real trouble." She eyed David seriously. "She kept sayin' 'remember the song, Esther. Sing em' the song yer great uncle Josiah taught ya when ya's young'...."

She grew silent and looked away, slowly rocking. They waited patiently for her to continue, while the shadowed eyes of her brooding grandson watched. Finally, she looked at Vernon and gave him a slight nod.

"Son, I want ya to get yer banjo out so I can sing em' the ode."

"For these two? Granny, they're friggin' strangers for Christ's sake!"

"Don't give me no lip, boy!"

"But, Granny, they ain't worthy! They're—."

"Damn it, Vernon, stop!" she warned him, rising up from her rocker to lean over the table. "It's what yer great grandma prefers, and I'm tellin' ya one last time to fetch yer banjo!"

He deferred to her authority, eyeing David and John coldly as he moved past. He again disappeared inside the cabin, the screened door cracking loudly against the doorframe. She watched him until out of earshot, and then returned her gaze to them.

"Y'all think we're a coven of witches, don't ya?"

"We have some questions concerning certain events David and his family have experienced recently. It doesn't mean we think you, Vernon, or most of your family have ever practiced witchcraft," said John, after exchanging surprised glances with David.

David started to pull out the pictures to show her, but John waved him off.

"But ya think my aunt was a witch," she said, leaning back in her rocker. "It's the reason folks in Cades Cove quit lookin' for her soon after she disappeared long ago. My pa told me a devil's circle was found deep in the woods behind my grandpa's house, and my momma and aunt were accused of conspirin' with Satan. It didn't matter none that grandpa and grandma were upstandin' members of the Methodist Church back then. My grandpa's ma, great grandma Ginny, had a reputation as a dabbler in the Indian's religion and it weighed heavier in folks' minds. Most church folk felt she and her two granddaughters gave therselves to the devil. It was all plum shameful!"

She began to rock again.

"What kind of circle was it, if you don't mind me asking?" John asked gently. He motioned for David to hand the packet of photographs to him.

She stopped rocking and studied the pair for a moment, a slight smile on her lined and weathered face.

"I believe ya both already know," she said. "We're not all witches, though Aunt Allie might've been. Momma definitely wasn't, but the fey runs strong in our blood, at least with the women in the McCormick line. That was Momma's maiden name before she married my pa. Before she died, she gave me the bag that's sittin' here on the table. She told me to hang onto it, and I could reach her through it."

"So, your mother has contacted you before from the other side?" David almost wished he hadn't asked, especially after she eyed him suspiciously.

"Yes, she has," she said. "But, until last night and earlier this mornin', I hadn't asked her much since the passin' of my boy Ezra and my husband Milton. Momma's bag will go to the next girl born in our family, probably through Vernon."

She craned her neck to the porch door. John and David followed her gaze. Vernon stood inside the doorway, frowning with the banjo strapped around his neck. He obviously heard the last part of their conversation, and John pulled the packet closer, as if fearful he'd destroy the photographs before Allie Esther ever saw them.

"Come on out here, son. We're ready for ya now."

Vernon stepped through the doorway, careful to keep the screened door from slamming against the doorframe this time. He moved sullenly to his seat, and adjusted the rocker to allow enough room to comfortably strum the instrument. Allie Esther sat up, coughing lightly as she prepared to perform the song.

"Son, would you mind gettin' me a glass of tea before we start?" She smiled sweetly at her grandson, and despite his irritation of having to set aside the banjo in order to respond to her latest request, he returned her smile. "I believe it only right if you'd also pour a glass for them, too."

He frowned, shaking his head as he went inside the cabin.

"He's really a good boy," she commented after he left. "He's more 'n able to take care of himself, but he prefers to keep an eye on his granny. I'm grateful for it."

They both smiled politely, although David couldn't picture where such a surly young man would find a place in today's society. Vernon returned with four iced teas, deciding to make one for him as well. After handing a glass to John and David, he placed his grandmother's glass next to her on the table and returned to his rocker. David hesitated before taking a sip, wondering if Vernon slipped something poisonous into his and John's drinks, or added some disgusting bodily fluid. After John took a hearty drink from his glass and commented how good it tasted, he took a small sip.

"This song's been played by our family for almost ninety years," said Allie Esther, after she sipped her tea and Vernon took a moment to tune his banjo. "We call it the Ode to Allie Mae."

Vernon began to strum the banjo and Allie Esther tapped her right foot on the porch. After getting in rhythm with the intro, she began to sing. She surprised David by the clarity, strength, and passion in her voice, revealing a strong will to live that belied her frailty.

"She's born in the spring of eighteen and ninety-nine.
Her ma and pa came from Carolina to the valley so fine.
In the meadows of Cades Cove with sister Emma she'd play.
'Til the night someone took darlin' Allie away.
Oh, where'd ya go, darlin' Allie Mae?
Why can't we find ya in the valley ya so loved?
Mama still cries and Papa won't rest,
'Til we find out what happened to their lost daughter, Allie Mae.
Some say she done run off and married her beau.
They went to the city a long time ago.
Mama and Papa never thought this was true.
To leave the valley she so loved, Allie'd never do.
Oh, where'd ya go, darlin' Allie Mae?
Why can't we find ya in the valley ya so loved?"

A breeze moved through the treetops near the cabin as Allie Esther moved through the second chorus of the song, drawing John and David's attention. They glanced at the front yard until she began the third verse.

"Rumors and hushed secrets said Allie'd been killed.
By her lover, Zachariah, or his brother named Will.
Though no one ever found her, no bones were unearthed.
We're sure she never left, 'cause the valley's been cursed."

They looked at each other as soon as they heard the line about Zachariah and his brother. Meanwhile, the wind picked up, sending gusts across the front yard. Yellow, orange, and pink leaves from a large maple fell to the ground in rapid swirls. Allie Esther and her grandson also noticed, but continued through the third chorus and soon began the ode's final verse.

"It was nineteen and sixteen when we lost Allie Mae.
'Til the day they died, ma and pa would wait
Down through the years we've heard whispers at night.
Is it the wind, or Allie's ghost stoppin' by?"

Allie Esther's foot stopped tapping as she finished the last line, closing her eyes while her grandson continued to play the rest of the song. When finished, he joined David and John in waiting for her to awaken. Nearly five minutes passed, and the wind blew dried leaves and other debris onto the porch steps. Vernon reached over and patted her arm. Immediately she stirred, frantic as she looked around. She began to cry.

"Granny, what's wrong?" he asked, alarmed.

Her only response was to shake her head while she hurried to return the items still spread out on her lap to the stained little bag that once belonged to her aunt. Once all five items were back inside, she pulled the leather strap to close it. With shaking hands, she motioned for David to take it. Of course, he was reluctant to do so, until John prodded him with a sharp elbow to his side.

"I can't accept it from ya!" she shouted. Tears streamed down her face, and her gray eyes seemed surreally red within the magnification of her thick lenses. She motioned for Vernon to help her stand up in her walker. "Allie Mae's here—she just spoke to me!"

"Her spirit?" asked John, rising to assist her grandson, who meanly waved him off.

"Yes, she's come to prevent me from takin' ownership of yer bag," she said, weeping. "I've got no quarrel with either of ya. But she does. She warned me not to get involved unless I want her anger rainin' down like a spring hail storm on me and my grandsons!"

"I don't understand," said David. "Why wouldn't she want her prized possessions in the hands of those who loved her enough to create a song dedicated to her memory?"

"Well, she doesn't, mister!"

After glancing at his grandmother, to which she nodded, Vernon pushed both David and John toward the porch steps.

"I'm so sorry," she said, and moved to the screened door after returning her mother's bag of treasures to the mahogany box on the table.

"Please—"

David hoped to convince her to take the cursed object. But, he couldn't entreat her further before being shoved down the steps by her menacing grandson, who had grabbed his shotgun from the corner of the porch next to the door. John didn't let David say anything else, pulling him to the cruiser and forcing him inside the vehicle while he ran to the driver's side and got in.

The dogs suddenly appeared as a furious pack that raced toward the car from behind the cabin. It seemed unlikely the elderly woman released them from their pen. Since Vernon hadn't left their presence, and now trotted down the porch steps armed with his shotgun, it meant someone else had set the dogs free to make sure the two visitors didn't entertain any thoughts of lingering.

Facing a shotgun-wielding lunatic flanked on either side by rabid canines, John handed the pictures to David and backed the cruiser down Bear Ridge Lane. Soon, only dim outlines were visible at the end of the road, and dusk absorbed the fading daylight. Safe enough to turn the cruiser around, John sped toward the main highway that would take them back to Gatlinburg.

"Did your friend in Knoxville ever find out anything about the Hobson brothers?" David asked, leafing through the pages inside the manila folder once they passed the Chestnut Landings development.

"There wasn't much," said John. "Diane confirmed two clans of Hobsons resided in Cades Cove from May 1898 until January 1919, and both were originally from Kentucky. The name of Zachariah Hobson was confirmed, but he disappeared from the area along with several other Hobsons by 1917. No other records from the state's archives show his name after that. She didn't find a record of a Will, William, or Billy Ray Hobson. I'm sure you're wondering if maybe their descendants would be interested in taking ownership of the bag."

"Yeah. It's pretty desperate, I guess," said David, his mood glum. "I'd better call Miriam. I honestly don't know what to do next, other than take the damned thing back to the ravine first thing tomorrow and get the hell out of here. Maybe I'll get lucky, and she won't follow me home this time."

"Maybe," echoed John, glancing briefly at David and then returning his attention to the road. It was 5:03 p.m., according to the dashboard's clock. The surrounding hillsides and woods grew darker. "I have one last idea that might help, if you're interested in hearing what it is."

"I'm game for anything at this point." David let out a low sigh.

"Maybe we should fight Allie Mae's magic with Cherokee medicine," John suggested. "It's too far to travel to meet the last surviving Shamans of my people, but I have someone in mind who knows enough of the ancient ways and can use them effectively. I believe this person can heal the spirit's anger."

David nodded in the dimness to show his interest.

"It's Evelyn, my granddaughter," said John. "Ever since she was young, she's been uniquely gifted. She learned from my father and also studied under a Sioux Shaman in

North Dakota one summer a few years back, who was willing to teach a woman since most young men from the tribes have turned their backs on the old ways." He sounded sorrowful as he mentioned the last part.

"'You think she'd be willing to help? I can make it worth her while financially if she were to try."

"I'm sure you would," said John. "But a home-cooked meal from her grandfather should suffice." He chuckled, and the sadness seemed to dissipate.

"Well, when were you thinking of doing this? I mean, does she live around here?"

"Tomorrow afternoon," said John. "I don't normally work on Fridays, even during the busy season. She's been after me to spend time with her and my other granddaughter, Hanna, for the past month." He looked over and smiled.

"That should work fine, provided Allie Mae doesn't kill me first," said David, returning the smile with a wan smirk.

John told David he would give him directions to his cabin, near Cades Cove and not far from the park station. Evelyn lived in Johnson City, less than an hour away. He planned to call her that night, and confirm the time with David.

Feeling slight hope, David called Miriam from his cell phone when John pulled the cruiser onto the main thoroughfare into the park. After telling her how the afternoon went, he told her about John's latest idea. Omitting what happened the past night and that morning, he told her the Whitestone's ancient amenities brought about the change to the EconoLodge.

Jillian picked up the second phone in Janice's townhouse.

"Daddy?"

"Hi sweetie!" Surprised to hear his daughter's voice, it immediately warmed his heart.

"Mom says you won't be back until Sunday," she said, sounding bummed. "Why can't you come home tomorrow? The fall play is in the afternoon, and I wish you'd be there!"

"Jill, I would if I could." David hated the disappointment in her voice. "But, the problem we had in the house last week—remember that?"

"Yeah, I do." She sounded nervous, like she didn't want to relive the memory.

"Well, Daddy needs to take care of a few things here in Tennessee, to make sure it doesn't happen again." He lifted his voice with fatherly confidence to sell the assurance. "I should be home on Sunday."

"I understand," she said, sighing deeply. "So, will you take us to the Halloween party at the Benson's Sunday night?" A glimmer of hope lifted her tone.

"If all goes well here, yeah, I'll be happy to do it, sweetie!"

He forgot about the annual Trick or Treat party the Benson's held for the neighborhood kids the weekend before Halloween. Tyler wasn't so keen about it, but Jillian and Christopher had marked the kitchen calendar once October 1st arrived.

"I'll see you Sunday, Daddy. But if you get everything taken care of by tomorrow morning, the play is at two-fifteen in the school auditorium!"

He chuckled as she hung up the phone, and then realized the line remained active.

"Miriam, are you still there?"

"Yeah, I am," she said, chuckling. "What a pistol, huh?"

"Yes, she is."

"So, John will contact his granddaughter tonight, and you'll meet with her tomorrow?"

"That's the plan."

"If it doesn't work, will you *please* just do what we agreed on and take the bag back to the ravine, and then hop on the next plane home?" She sounded especially worried.

"Yes, I promise this is the last thing I'll try."

John smiled while listening to him tell her how much he loved and missed her.

"You're a lucky man, David Hobbs," he said, after the call ended. "You have a family who cherishes you, which is the greatest treasure there is. I can tell how much you cherish them, too."

"I really do," said David, fearing he might never see his wife and kids again. He regretted more than ever his decision to bring the little bag to Littleton, Colorado.

"We'll find a way to free you from Allie Mae's spirit," John told him, patting his knee. "One way or another, we *will* find a way."

* * * * *

When they reached the park station, John drew David a map to his cabin and confirmed his home phone number. David promised to call once he got settled. In addition to the photos, he also gave John the trash bags from his trunk, since he asked again to examine their contents. David then returned to Gatlinburg, treating himself to dinner at a quiet Italian restaurant near the hotel.

It was almost eight-thirty when he arrived at his room on the third floor. Unlike the previous four nights, he left the little bag outside in the Buick's glove box. He unpacked the new clothes purchased that morning and got ready for bed. When he called John to let him know his new number, John told him Evelyn happily agreed to meet with them at his cabin the following afternoon at two o'clock. With the good news, David called Miriam. Following a chat that lasted the better part of an hour, he retired shortly after 10:00 p.m., leaving the television and every light on in the room. His determined effort to keep his tired eyes open became impossible, and before the night's news broadcast ended he fell fast asleep.

Chapter Thirty-two

It rained all morning Friday. David slept through most of it, after visiting the hotel's continental breakfast in the lobby around seven. He purchased two boxes of large bandages for his neck from the gift shop. Though the wounds stopped bleeding hours earlier, the four red streaks drew a number of curious looks from both the hotel staff and other guests. He didn't linger, grabbing a few Danish rolls and a large glass of orange juice before returning to his room.

The events of the past night, after he fell asleep, were blurred in his tired mind. Some images were clear, like his shock when he abruptly awoke at 12:20 a.m. and looked in the dresser mirror. Four tiny crimson rivers poured down his neck and onto his t-shirt.

What in the hell?

David asked the question over and over, especially once he determined the wounds were real. A squadron of deep scratches pulsed in anger along the right side of his neck.

Unlike his previous nocturnal experience at the Whitestone, wiping the blood off with a wet wash cloth did little good. Grimacing from the sting, he marveled as the wounds quickly refilled and oozed with a fresh army of red corpuscles. After an hour of losing blood, enough to make him consider calling the front desk for directions to the nearest hospital, the flow ebbed. It was two o'clock, and he couldn't go back to sleep… at least not yet.

Another dream, and as before, David recalled bits and pieces. In some ways, it reminded him of the one he had Monday morning, where his heart overflowed with rage, and he experienced a powerful urge to get even. But, this time, he attacked someone.

What did she look like? Think, David—damn it, think!

The images were blurred, and he had hurt more than one person. A woman and a man… the guy tried to interfere.

Interfere with what, for Christ's sake?

Reddish strands of hair filled his vision…. He sat on top of her, and the other man tried to pull him off. David punched him and he hurt the female. She retaliated by raking her hand across his neck.

The girl did this to me? How in the hell—

He returned to his bed to sit, and noticed his wristwatch sat next to the alarm clock. Like the previous times it disappeared from his wrist, Allie Mae's little bag rested neatly inside the watch's circumference.

Allie Mae did this? Why?

The questions stayed with him long after the dawn's light peered through the room's curtains, and gained strength after he returned with breakfast. Did all of this somehow relate to her death?

And if so, is this the beginning of her planned revenge, to butcher me with her bare hands?

When a satisfactory answer never came, he showered and dressed, using the remaining bandages to cover the wounds. By then it was nearing noon. With the bag in his coat pocket, he grabbed his briefcase and left the room.

Relieved the rain had tapered to a light mist, David grabbed a burger and coke before heading for the park. John's directions instructed him to take several detours not easily discernable once the rain picked up again. After a few wrong turns, and a near collision with a van hydroplaning across the park's two-lane highway, he finally arrived at John's log cabin shortly after one o'clock. An immense picture window dominated the front of the older A-frame structure.

"I'm a little early," said David, as he greeted John on the front porch. John's smile faded when he saw the bandages on David's neck.

"What happened to you?"

"Honestly, I'm not sure." He followed John inside. "I guess what seemed like a dream was, in fact, reality."

Much larger than it appeared from outside, the cabin included a spacious loft on the second floor that faced the window. A tall rock fireplace dominated the living room, where a crackling fire burned brightly. The place felt cozy. Furnished with leather chairs and a couch, all four walls were decorated with a variety of Native American artifacts. The living room sat next to a kitchen area that featured a grill enclosed by smaller stones similar to those used to create the fireplace. The rich aromas of grilled beef and baked cinnamon filled the air.

A beautiful young woman with long dark hair and large brown eyes sliced vegetables on a cutting block next to the oven. She looked up from her task when John led David into the living room; he recognized her from the photograph on the desk in the Cades Cove visitors' center.

"David, I'd like you to meet Evelyn Sherman, my granddaughter, known also as Two Doves Rising," John proudly announced.

She rinsed her hands and wiped them on the apron she wore, and stepped over to where they stood. Tall and shapely, she was dressed in jeans and a flannel shirt that almost matched the outfit her grandfather wore.

"It's nice to meet you, David." Evelyn extended her hand. "Grandpa's told me all about what you've been through lately."

"I'm glad you were able to come today," he said, squeezing her hand gently before releasing it. "Hopefully, we can find a way to finally put an end to this whole thing."

"That's my intent," she assured him, and returned to the kitchen. She resumed her task of cutting vegetables while her grandfather inspected her work. Evelyn shot him a look to leave her alone, and he chuckled playfully while peering at three large rib-eye steaks cooking on the grill.

"It may take more than just this afternoon's session to complete everything," she advised David, looking up from the cutting block after John left her alone.

David nodded in response, hoping it wasn't the case and that everything *did* get done that day. He offered to help in the kitchen, but she and John insisted he make himself comfortable by the fire. He moved to the chairs closest to the fireplace. The strong scent of hickory prevailed over the other aromas, and David watched the flames dance around several large logs on the hearth.

"I'll take your coat," said John, seemingly satisfied with dinner's progress. He disappeared with David's coat down a hallway to the right of the fireplace, where the bedrooms were located. When he returned, he carried a small first-aid kit. "Let's take a look at your neck."

Evelyn paused to watch her grandfather pull aside the bandages on David's neck. He grimaced while John cleansed the wounds and added a topical antibiotic before dressing them with a surgical bandage.

"That should last awhile," John advised. "Before you leave later today, we'll dress the wounds once more. It must've been quite a dream." He eyed David thoughtfully.

"I don't even know where to begin," said David.

Evelyn joined them in the living room.

"Dinner should be ready in the next twenty minutes." She seemed worried, and her gaze focused on his bandaged neck. "We'll get started soon enough on the other, after we've had a chance to enjoy our meal and chat for awhile."

"I thought you were supposed to be the chef today?" David chided John. He didn't wish to think long about Evelyn's troubled look. She was his last hope.

"It started out that way, but she's the boss."

"You're *so* funny, Grandpa," she said. Her raised eyebrow reminded David of Miriam, and he missed his beloved wife more than ever. "If I hadn't come to your rescue, we wouldn't be eating anything 'til late tonight."

She alternated her playful gaze between him and David, and then sauntered back to the kitchen area. "You could make it up to me by setting the table," she said over her shoulder.

"Yes, I suppose I could."

"I'll join you, John," said David, rising to his feet.

The two men moved into the kitchen, mindful to stay out of Evelyn's path as she hurried from the grill to the oven, and then to the counter where she placed a delectable apple pie. The dinner table sat flush against the cabin's rear wall. Soon after they finished setting the plates and utensils, the steaks were ready.

John and Evelyn sat across from each other while David took a seat in the middle facing the wall. An antique electric lantern, that long ago ran on gas or oil, hung on the wall above a portrait of John's late wife. The lantern radiated soft light upon the table now loaded with food.

They enjoyed light conversation during their meal. Evelyn talked about the Masters Degree in civil engineering she was presently pursuing at the University of Tennessee in nearby Knoxville, along with her recent engagement to the boyfriend John previously mentioned. David's eyes misted as he shared family pictures from his wallet. John seemed pleased by the conversation between his cherished granddaughter and their guest.

After dinner, with the dishwasher humming in the background, Evelyn asked David to rejoin her at the cleared table. John moved into the living room, where he relaxed in a recliner across from the television set.

Evelyn brought a deck of large cards and a leather bag to the table, along with a thick white candle. She sat in her chair, and motioned for David to pull a chair close to hers. Once comfortable, she lit the candle and closed her eyes, speaking a prayer in a language unfamiliar to him. When finished, she smiled and asked to see his hands. She brushed her fingers over the back of his hands and turned them over to examine his palms.

"I'm not a fortune teller." She chuckled.

Watching her fingers trace the lines in his palm, he looked up in surprise. Her words matched his silent musing exactly.

"Don't be alarmed, David. I've been able to read thoughts since I was young," she explained, continuing to examine his hands. "It comes from Grandpa's side of the family. I'd bet he has yet to tell you that his grandfather was once a powerful Cherokee medicine man."

"That's true… he hasn't told me about it yet." David glanced at John, who was seemingly engrossed by a movie.

"Don't let him fool you," Evelyn whispered, wearing a wry grin. "I'm sure he's well aware of what we're discussing. He was once next in line to be a shaman for our people, but didn't want the burden. My grandmother used to tell me when I was young that he hoped somehow the line would be broken, and that no one else would be saddled with the gift and the enormous responsibility that comes with it."

"It didn't happen, obviously," David observed, wondering if John could've handled the proper disposal of Allie Mae's Treasures without enlisting her help.

"Don't worry, David, you're in good hands with me," she assured him, revealing his thoughts were open to her. "I've spent many years practicing my gifts, and as such, am much better prepared to deal with the spirit and her powerful wiles. Grandpa would be no match for her when she brings her wrath full force, which could happen at any time."

She closed his palms and nudged his hands back to him. Next, she pulled out the deck of cards, closing her eyes and passing her hands over the deck. She asked him to shuffle the cards.

"Your lifeline is strong." Evelyn watched him struggle with the cards, larger and thicker than a standard poker deck. "Your destiny is not to die anytime soon, provided you take care of yourself. So say your hands."

He continued shuffling the cards, dropping a few on the table.

"Take your time, and be careful not to expose the card faces." She picked up the fallen cards, placing them in a neat stack to her left near the wall. "When you feel at peace, stop and cut the deck."

He nodded, focusing on the cards. Determined to shuffle the awkward deck evenly, he finally found a rhythm. After several more shuffles, he set the cards on the table and removed the top third. He placed the smaller portion next to the rest of the deck. She picked up the larger portion and took the first nine cards, setting them face down on the table, five vertical and the other four bisecting the middle to form a cross.

"I've been told by some very good readers how I do this incorrectly," she said, while laying the cards down. "But, these same readers have vouched for my accuracy. I've come to understand the cards are merely a guide for what my visions and intuitions already tell me. I'm also clairaudient, which means I often hear the information I'm given about a person or situation. That's actually my strongest gift, which is how I read thoughts. I hear what people think."

He nodded, feeling more self-conscious. Evelyn turned over the cards. The intricate artwork surprised him. Some images were beautiful, while others were disturbing in their rich, dark detail. True to her heritage, all of the cards followed a Native American theme. David had no idea what any of the images signified.

Her fingers lingered the most on three cards. The first two depicted a colorfully adorned Indian chief and a proud warrior. The other card depicted a skeleton obscured by a black cloak, the universal depiction of death.

"You're correct about this one." She tapped the face of the grimly decorated card. "It doesn't always mean something bad. It can mean the end of some process, like a resolution."

She pulled the card aside, studying it in silence before pushing it toward him. She moved on to the card depicting the chief.

"This one represents you," she advised. "It tells me that you hold the key to your own salvation in this matter."

Evelyn lifted the card and placed it on top of the one depicting Death. She moved next to the warrior card. For a moment, she hesitated before picking it up, as if unsure what to do with it. She cocked her head sideways while deciding its fate.

"This is the result you're after, David," she said, lifting the card and placing it on top of the other two. "I believe it signifies your eventual cure, your conquest over the force tormenting you these past two weeks. But, the other cards on the table point to a struggle for the victory, and I can see the difficult journey your soul has already taken."

She pointed to the other cards left from the cross, which included a dejected Native American male hanging from a tree, two lovers embracing, another male disheveled with a comical expression, and a beautiful Native American girl with a full moon behind her. The last card she pointed to depicted a demon of some sort, similar to the totem pole icons he once saw long ago in Washington, during his football days at the University of Colorado.

She picked up the extra cards from when he shuffled the deck earlier, and removed the middle one. The card depicted another Indian girl. The figure held a pair of scales, and appeared ready to add an item to the lighter scale in order to balance them.

"This is what she wants," said Evelyn, setting the card next to the other three. "She wants justice for a wrong she blames you for."

David studied the card, reliving the events of the past two weeks in his mind. It seemed ironic that a card painted so wonderfully, with a lovely female wearing a slight smile, should be defined as ominous. Evelyn didn't have to tell him what Allie Mae wanted in order for justice to be served.

"My guides are speaking to me," she said, interrupting his thoughts. He looked away from the card and into her face. Her eyes were half open, and she seemed on the verge of falling asleep. "They say there's a way to be saved, but you must listen well and follow their instruction."

He nodded eagerly.

"The spirit of the girl feels a connection to you," she continued. "They tell me the ravine that you and your wife visited is special to her. She spent a good deal of her lifetime there, and it's a sacred place. I say this for reasons I'll get to in a moment, but for now know that she considered the ravine her haven."

"Okay," he said, waiting.

"Her spirit is angry… thirsty for revenge." She opened her eyes fully. They seemed brighter.

"Allie Mae is like a child in some ways, and not in others. You remind her of someone, and I feel certain this is the man who took her life. But, there's something else with her… something that comforts her in the darkness, and is also part of the ravine. It's what drew her there in her early youth."

Evelyn asked to hold his hands again. David placed them in hers, while her eyes remained closed for a couple of minutes.

"Grandpa showed me what was inside the trash bags from your motel room," she said once she opened her eyes. "Now it makes more sense. This girl was indeed a witch during her brief lifetime. That's important for several reasons, and not just because it helps determine why she created the shrines."

She released his hands, and motioned for him to pull them back.

"The force that's with her makes her worse," said Evelyn. "It has merged with her own special telepathic abilities, and it is fed by the terrible anguish she died in. You'll need everything we can give you, in order to break her determination to take your soul. She's not just interested in your life, David. She would've found a way to kill you already if that was the case, like she did to your friend in Colorado. She wants *all* of you forever—to absorb the very essence of your core being!"

She paused to make sure he understood the gravity of what she said.

"Here's the strangest thing about all of this. My guides keep telling me, 'it's not just her—it's not just her'. It's the other thing with her that really wants you. It desires both your life and your soul. Think of a flashlight that contains a low beam and a high beam. Allie is the low beam, and she brings enough mischief on her own. She would be a terrible ghost to deal with, but one that could be subdued without the risk of life and limb. The other force is the high beam, and is much stronger and more malicious than she is."

"So, how in the hell do we defeat it? I mean, *can* we?" The situation had seemed hopeless, but now it felt as if he stood with one foot firmly planted inside his grave.

"Bring me the bag of her keepsakes."

He got up from the table and asked John where he placed his jacket. John directed him to the first bedroom down the hallway from the fireplace. His coat lay on the bed near the pillows. He retrieved the bag and returned to the table, handing it to her.

Evelyn opened the bag and peered inside. She inhaled the mixture of floral and musty odors that included the slight female scent. Rather than empty the contents, she studied them by jostling and shaking the bag until she could see all five items. She cleared a spot next to the candle, and placed the bag within an imperceptible circle she drew with her index finger on the table's surface. She chanted more unfamiliar words.

She took the leather bag and emptied nine onyx stones into her hand. Evelyn closed her hand into a fist. She instructed him to close his eyes and reach inside her hand, and remove three stones. David did as instructed. He placed the stones in a row on the table, with the gold symbols engraved on each stone facing up.

The symbol on the first stone resembled a slanted F. The one on the second stone looked like a diamond shape, where the widest portion had been attached to a vertical line. The last stone's symbol closely resembled a modern P, but primitive, with the rounded edges straightened and the letter's curve pointed.

"These are known as runes, and they predate the use of Tarot Cards, which are what I've used so far," she explained. "The Appalachian people have used runes since long before the Revolutionary War. They seem to help with my magic, since there's almost always a direct correlation between them and the cards. The ones I use are Norse in origin, and the names of the three you picked are 'Ansuz', 'Thurisaz', and 'Wunjo'."

She stopped to make sure he followed. He nodded, despite three more weird words and an unfamiliar divination tool.

"I'll make this as simple as possible, but try to stay with me," she said, her tone soft but serious. "All three runes you selected correspond to the cards I gave you. Ansuz has the same meaning as the Tarot's Death card. Thurisaz corresponds to the Chief card, and Wunjo is the same as the Warrior card."

"So, where does magic come into play here?" He struggled to understand the logic.

"The magic comes from the synergy created by these two methods," she said. "We will use the synergy to try and block Allie Mae's immediate schemes to destroy your life."

Evelyn instructed him to place the three runes around the cloth bag, setting the stones to where they formed a pyramid around it. She took four of the remaining six runes and set them outside the pyramid along its north, east, south, and west perimeter. She closed her eyes and whispered another prayer.

"This should hold her for now, and buy us enough time to put together a permanent spell to banish her from your life," she said, when she opened her eyes. "It's critical the bag and runes remain like this until the spell is complete."

"How long will it take?"

"I'd like to incorporate the moon's power, and the moon is now fading since its fullest power was this past Tuesday night. It'll definitely have to happen no later than tomorrow night, or you'll have to wait until the next moon cycle."

"I guess finishing tonight is out of the question. Can we make sure this gets done no later than tomorrow? I've got a plane to catch back to Denver on Sunday, and I sure as hell don't think Allie Mae will cut me a break for much longer."

She smiled compassionately, and placed her hand on the back of his.

"There's still enough time, so long as we prepare and follow through completely," she advised. "The moon should still be strong enough to enlist its power, and leave me enough time to put the prayers and root pastes together you'll need for protection. I have one errand to attend to tomorrow morning. Afterward, I'll pick up the necessary ingredients and meet you here in the afternoon. Until then, I'll need you to quietly reflect on all that's happened and what you wish to accomplish, both for you and her soul that suffers too."

"I'll do that," David assured her. "I appreciate you doing this for me. Let me at least pay you for your time and supplies." He pulled out his wallet and began to remove several twenties. She stopped him.

"I can't accept your money," said Evelyn. "It's customary for a shaman, even an amateur medicine woman like me, to be paid only in goods and services. What you've already brought to my grandfather is worth far more than my expenses, and my own intrigue compensates me for the readings."

"What have I done for John?" If anything, David felt indebted to him.

"I think you know," she said, smiling as she gathered her cards and the rest of the runes not in use. "Your friendship has lifted his heart."

She blew out the candle and stood, moving to a small tote bag near her grandfather's recliner. John pulled the lever to bring the chair straight once he noticed her presence.

David didn't know how to respond. In his mind, John had been a better friend to him—not the other way around. He watched him attend to his granddaughter, and hoped their friendship proved to be a lasting thing after the ordeal ended. He realized John's presence in his life the past few days had helped him cope with Norm's death, even though painful loneliness still awaited him once he returned to Colorado.

It was almost five o'clock. David stood and moved to retrieve his coat, as he planned to head back to Gatlinburg. Evelyn stopped him.

"You must stay here tonight," she said, her tone serious again. "I'm sure Grandpa won't mind your company. Regardless, it's too dangerous for you to leave right now, since it will be completely dark soon. When daylight returns tomorrow morning, you can take care of whatever business you still have in Gatlinburg. Until then, you need to stay here, indoors and preferably away from the windows."

"If John's okay with that arrangement, I don't mind staying. But what's so dangerous about tonight as compared to any other night this past week?" He trusted her admonishment, but wished he had his beard trimmer and toothbrush.

"As I told you earlier, and as you've already known in your heart, she's coming for you," said Evelyn, grabbing her coat and purse, and pausing to give John a kiss upon his cheek before leaving. She walked to where David stood. "Allie Mae likes the imagery of a spider seducing its prey. She's spun her web several times, which is what her shrines represent. She's already played with your body and mind, growing more intense with each visit. All that's left is to tear a hole in your being, and suck out your soul." She pushed on his chest for emphasis.

He understood. A mirror would suffice if he needed any further reminders, where the four scratches throbbed painfully beneath the protective gauze. Evelyn gave him a warm hug and exited the cabin. Before John could turn on the porch light to better illuminate the parking area in front of his home, she had already left. Her sporty Nissan raced down the long driveway toward the park's main thoroughfare.

Chapter Thirty-three

"She's right, you know," said John, peering through the window curtain beside the front door. The red glow from Evelyn's taillights faded from view. "You're safer staying here."

He closed the curtain and moved to the kitchen, grabbing a couple of Miller long necks from the refrigerator. He handed one to David.

"Your granddaughter is a lovely young lady" said David, as the two returned to the living room. "She could have her pick of any young man she wanted, I'd imagine."

"I wish she'd wait to get married," John replied, sadly. He reclaimed his recliner. "His family's nice, but she can do better."

David nodded thoughtfully, and sat on the couch across from him.

"Michael's handsome and wealthy, with a good sense of humor," John continued. "But, something's missing from his soul. He will hurt her."

He gazed into the waning fire with a grim expression. David recalled how John had been quiet during dinner, once Evelyn mentioned her beau and how much she loved him.

"I imagine it's tough for you," said David, compassionately. "I can picture how I'd feel if Jill hooks up with someone Miriam or I have doubts about when she grows up." He frowned, realizing in a year she'd be a teenager, and dating in a few years.

"They grow up fast," John agreed, looking at David. "Evelyn has a clear path to lasting happiness if she'll take it. But, as gifted and focused as she's been in regard to her career and spiritual talents, she lacks sound judgment when it comes to the men she chooses to love. She gives her heart easily, and I've seen it broken before by kinder men than this one…."

His voice trailed off and he looked toward the back door. David followed his gaze, and soon became aware of a soft scratching sound from outside the door's base. John stood and set his beer on the coffee table.

"Wait here."

He moved to the door, turning on the back-porch light as well as the security floodlights. The scratching at the door became more urgent, accompanied by a high-pitched whine. He opened the door. A beautiful white husky with light blue eyes jumped up and placed its paws on his chest, while dragging a chain attached to its neck inside the cabin.

"What's the matter, boy?" John patted the top of the dog's head and stroked the fur under its neck. "There, there… it's all right, Shawn. Good boy."

He removed the leash and threw it outside. Peering through the doorway, he cast a wary glance toward either side of the back porch. The dog stood next to him, whining again while pawing at John's leg.

"He's rarely skittish," John remarked after he closed and locked the back door, patting the dog's side as he turned to face David.

"I bet he's good company," said David.

John motioned for him to call the dog. When David did, Shawn came over to him, bending his head low to the ground and almost knocking himself over while wagging his tail.

"He's gorgeous."

"He's my buddy." John moved into the living room. "He'll be seven next month, and was a Christmas present as a pup from my other granddaughter, Hanna."

"I've always wanted a bigger dog," said David, massaging Shawn's neck and throat. He soon found the sensitive spot that every canine seems to have. "We have a small terrier named Sadie, and I've grown quite attached to her. Miriam and the kids love her even more. But it'd be nice to have a dog the kids and I could play Frisbee with."

He chuckled at the thought, but stopped once he saw John frowning. His attention was drawn to the back door again.

"What's up?"

"I'm not sure, yet."

Shawn left David's side to seek his owner's attention. John bent down to offer his own loving strokes, and the dog curled up on the floor next to him.

"Shawn rarely seeks to come inside, and prefers his doghouse," he said. "Only during the coldest spells in January and February does he stay inside the cabin. Did you feel him shaking?"

"Yeah, I did," said David. He thought the dog's excitement came from finding his owner had company. Sadie sometimes did that. But he thought about how she responded to the ghost's presence two Sundays ago in Littleton. "Do you think Allie Mae is here?"

"Yes." John's tone was solemn, and he returned his gaze to David. "I couldn't see anything out back, but it felt as if someone was watching. Shawn should've barked, as he usually does when either a stray bear or some other critter is on the premises. I was surprised he didn't bark earlier when you arrived, but that's happened before when other likeable folks stop by. For him to scratch at the door and whine like he did tells me that he feels threatened."

He got up and walked into the kitchen, calling Shawn. The dog didn't budge, curling up even tighter on the living room floor.

"Animals are much more perceptive of danger than we are, as I'm sure you know. It's the first time since I've had him that Shawn refused to come to me. I think it best we follow Evelyn's admonitions tonight…."

John's words trailed off again, and he looked up toward the upstairs loft. David followed John's gaze. For the moment, very little was visible beyond the illuminated A-shaped eve outside the enormous window. The varnished logs glistened in the security light's glow.

"Do you see her?"

"Not yet, but she's definitely near," said John. "I think it'd be wise to also close the curtains in here. I'll be right back and you can help me close the rest of them."

He went to a narrow staircase on the left side of the fireplace leading to the loft. As he climbed the stairs, the wind that had been gentle, and mostly imperceptible, picked up strength. He reached the loft and looked down at David, his expression puzzled.

"Do you hear that?"

"The wind outside?"

"No. Something else," said John, worriedly.

He moved to the side of the window where the curtains' cord hung, and began closing them. When more than halfway drawn, a dark shadow approached the glass, obscuring the security lights' glow and distracting John's focus to keep the cord straight so it wouldn't snag. A high-pitched screech filled the air as the darkness grew deeper, moving through the window's glass as if it didn't exist. A flowing mass of reddish-blonde hair appeared in the midst of the darkness creeping into the cabin, and the icy blue and hellish red eyes David had seen two nights earlier appeared within the mass of swirling strands.

John dropped the cord in surprise, stepping away from the window. A frigid draft moved through the living room, lifting the dream catchers and spirit chasers on the walls as it flowed toward David, who stumbled onto the couch in terror.

"Leave him alone!" John shouted, grabbing the cord and working furiously to close the curtains before the hostile shadow made it inside. "You're not welcome here—spirit be gone!"

Angered, the eyes turned toward him, the blue one narrowed with malice. John continued to rebuke the entity despite enduring a litany of garbled threats that didn't cease until the curtains were fully drawn shut.

"We'd better go through the cabin to make sure all of the windows are locked and the curtains completely shut!" he said, clambering down the stairs. "David, you check the bedrooms and the bathroom, and I'll make sure everything else is secure!"

David hurried down the hallway. After checking the bedrooms, he glimpsed the shadowed edge of the apparition descend toward the ground through an uncovered bathroom window. He ignored what sounded like fingernail taps on the window's glass while he hastily closed a pair of wooden shutters. He barricaded the bathroom door with a chair for good measure and went to look for John.

"Allie Mae might be inside the cabin!" he told John, who was rechecking the lock on the front door. "I heard her tap on the bathroom window when I was in there!"

"Did you close the shutters before you heard the noise?"

John moved toward the hallway.

"Yeah, I did. I barricaded the door just in case!"

David ran to catch up before John removed the chair shoved under the doorknob. When he threw open the bathroom door, the room sat empty, although the temperature had dipped noticeably. After peeking through the shutter blinds and glancing inside the shower, he shrugged and motioned for David to return with him to the main living area.

"I believe we got her out of here just in time," John advised, after taking a few short breaths and closing his eyes to meditate for a moment. "But she's still near… somewhere outside."

"Sweet Jesus!" whispered David. His heart pounded furiously while he gazed anxiously around the room. The sudden attack had caught him off guard, even though he expected something to happen. "So, what do you suggest we do next?"

"Well, I think we should stay calm and try not to put ourselves in harm's way... at least until morning." John grabbed another hickory log from beside the fireplace and threw it on top of the dying embers on the hearth. David noticed only four more logs, and he worried there might not be enough to get them through the night. "I expect her to try again to get in here, but the protection already in place should thwart her efforts now that the windows are blocked." John motioned to the items covering the walls around them, no longer swaying from the earlier breeze.

David started to say something, but the ceiling creaked as if someone walked on the roof above them, stepping across the shingles. Several knocks erupted from the northeast corner of the ceiling.

"Unfortunately, we'll probably be entertained like this for the duration of the evening."

John shook his head and returned to his chair. Shawn buried his head in John's lap. The knocks continued, moving to the other corners of the ceiling while becoming louder and more fervent.

"It's almost like dealing with one of my kids when they don't get their way about something," observed David, forcing a smile that poorly camouflaged his unease.

"It would be best to ignore the ghost, as if she were indeed a spoiled little girl."

John turned up the television, and David tried to ignore the spirit's antics—difficult to do when loud scraping sounds joined the knocks, spreading across the ceiling from all corners, similar to what he experienced at home in Littleton.

"You'll survive this," said John, almost nonchalantly flipping through the cable stations while David's eyes remained fixed on the ceiling. "You were destined at sometime in your life to encounter the spirit, and she has waited long for this. The Great Spirit has allowed it so. It doesn't mean she'll win. Not if your spirit remains strong."

John offered an assuring smile that was immediately followed by an even louder thud upon the roof, causing the overhead brass light fixture to sway. David half-expected a splintered hole to appear in the ceiling. For the moment, the logs and split-beams held up.

"We need a better distraction, in order to ignore her," said John.

He soon settled on an HBO movie David said was a decent flick, having seen it the year before with Miriam at a theatre. It seemed to do the trick, as the spirit's mischief soon waned. By eight o'clock, the noises had completely ceased. Shawn lay asleep at John's feet, and David stood up to stretch. He thought about Miriam, and realized she didn't have John's number. She'd likely try to contact him at the hotel.

He removed his cell phone from his belt clip. The 'no service' symbol lit up on the phone's display. He recalled having two bars of signal strength when he drove up the gravel road to John's cabin earlier, but he sure as hell wasn't about to step outside to see if the reception was better.

"Call Miriam on my phone," offered John, after David disgustedly shoved his phone back on its clip. "I've got free nationwide long distance, or so says the bill insert I get every month." He pointed to his landline phone, in a small cove next to the refrigerator.

"Thanks, John."

As David stepped into the kitchen, he recalled that Miriam said something about her and the kids moving back into the house that day. He tried that number first. The line crackled and hummed as it rang, and after four rings he got the voicemail. He tried it again and got the same thing. Since it was just after six o'clock in Littleton, he wondered if they had gone out for dinner. But when he got the same noise and Miriam's voicemail each time he tried her cell phone, he started to worry. He chided himself for overreacting, until he tried Janice's townhouse and cell numbers.

After two more attempts on each line, David urged John to come to him. His hand was shaking as he held the phone's receiver. John took it, and his solemn expression told David he heard the same thing. The shrill garbled noise grew loud enough to force him to pull the receiver away from his ear, and they both heard a high-pitched cackle resounding from the receiver followed by a dial tone.

David grabbed the phone from John. Frantically redialing the numbers over and over again he got the same response, forcing the two men to share the same conclusion.... Miriam and the kids were in terrible danger.

Allie Mae had returned to Colorado.

Chapter Thirty-four

"Mom says dinner will be ready in five minutes!" Jillian peered inside Tyler's bedroom to make her announcement.

"Tell her I'll be right down after I wash this stuff off my face," said Tyler, shooing his sister out of the haven he had reclaimed less than thirty minutes earlier.

Jillian frowned, but heeded her brother's wishes, disappearing into the hallway. He listened as she limped down the stairs to the main floor, feeling a tad bit guilty for being so harsh. He lingered a moment in his room, rubbing his fingers over the smooth plaster that filled the holes around his once-torn window frame. The new window still bore the sales sticker, which he chose to leave on until Dad returned home from Tennessee. Mom told him earlier today he could paint his room in any color he wanted, and she'd help him do it sometime next week.

"Why don't you wait until after dinner to wash your face, son, so I can help you with the sling?" Miriam called to him from the bottom of the stairs. She wore an apron and carried a spatula. "Besides, cabbage rolls are better while they're hot!"

"It'll just take a few minutes, Mom—I'll be fine!" he called from the hallway, grabbing a face towel from the linen closet next to the main bathroom. "This stuff's really starting to itch!"

Going on six o'clock, Miriam told him if it took longer than fifteen minutes they would start eating without him. Tyler flipped on the bathroom light and stepped inside. When he caught his reflection in the mirror, he smiled. Christopher and Jillian had been right. He did look like the real thing, *The Hulk*. Even though the green makeup had begun to crack, and the black circles around his eyes now smeared, he looked frightful. The sling on his right shoulder made a weird contrast to the costume covering his left shoulder and arm. He flexed his fake Hulk arm muscles and roared at his reflection, forcing as much malice as he could muster. It felt incredibly good to be frightful instead of fearful. He did it again and again, until Jillian called from downstairs to remind him the clock was ticking.

"All right, all right—I'm hurrying!"

He looked at himself again, unhappy at the thought he'd have to go through the process of getting dressed up in costume two more times, once on Sunday for the Benson's

Halloween Party and again on Halloween night. It meant he had to be careful with the costume and wig, and getting either item wet probably wasn't a good idea.

Tyler sighed as he trudged back to his bedroom, where he removed the wig and gingerly slipped out of the arm and shoulder cover Miriam altered from the original full torso Hulk suit. He returned to the bathroom.

As he stepped inside, he noticed the tiled floor seemed cold under his socked feet and the air much cooler than a moment ago. Since it made him think about what happened the previous week, he hurried to loosen the sling and set it on the counter next to the sink. Doing things one-handed had gotten easier for him. He grabbed his foaming face wash from the toiletry bag he had yet to unpack, and turned on the faucet, letting hot water run in the sink until misty heat rose into the air. When warm enough to wash his face, he glanced into the mirror.

Tyler gasped. He desperately wanted to run out of the bathroom, but couldn't move. The bathroom door closed slowly. As it did, he saw the highlights from a beautiful head of strawberry-blonde hair, hanging down in soft ringlets on a Victorian-style blue dress similar to what he once saw on display in a Central City boutique.

"Hello, again, Zachariah-h-h!"

The hollow voice was thick and sultry.

He tried to speak, but a low guttural sound was all that came out. His legs felt as if they might give way, and he watched in terror as the form moved closer in the mirror's reflection. The voice was the same one he heard three days earlier. However, where it emanated from was hard to say. It couldn't have come from the girl's face, because there wasn't one. A dark shadow floated where her head should've been, eerily surrounded by her shimmering hair. Like a china doll, the skin on her arms and hands was ashen, as well as her exposed neckline.

"I see you've missed me." She moved closer. The cold air dampened the rising steam from the sink's basin.

He whimpered, hyperventilating in panic. Clad only in jeans and a t-shirt, he shivered as the icy presence pressed against his back. His visible shallow breaths lightly touched the mirror's glass.

"Please… just go *away!*" he pleaded, his lips quivering. "Go *AWAY!*"

"Not without ya, my love," she replied, her words a frigid whisper. She crept nearer until her shadowed face came within an inch of his right ear.

Painful shivers raced down his spine, and gooseflesh covered every exposed area on his body. Frightened worse than before, he could've given in, hopelessly trapped in the upstairs' bathroom with this thing. This malevolent entity had shown she was not only capable of inflicting serious injury, but could also take life if she desired. No one had to tell him that she'd killed his dad's best friend, Norm Sowell. He knew it. He knew it if for no other reason than the police coming by twice since the past Friday to ask questions about Norm and her.

Was he next on her list? On the verge of succumbing to dire terror, something stirred within Tyler. It rose rapidly, until it raged as a violent eruption from his throat.

"DAMN IT, BITCH, GO AWAY, I SAID!"

He forced himself to turn and face her, flailing his available arm violently in her direction. His fist sliced through air icier than the breath on the back of his neck had been, but connected with nothing. He lost his balance and crashed into the bathroom doorknob, reopening one of the stitched cuts on his hand before he collapsed. His collarbone throbbed angrily while some of the stitches along his back broke open.

"Go away! Just go away… please!" he sobbed. *"Go away and leave me the hell alone!"*

Curled up on the floor, Tyler buried his face into his healthy shoulder, refusing to look at her. The bathroom door creaked open and someone grabbed him from behind.

"No-o-o!" he shrieked.

"Ty, it's okay!" Miriam gathered her son in her arms while looking warily around her. "I've got you, baby! It's me, your mom!"

Tyler turned his face toward her, looking anxiously around the bathroom.

"It was *her*, Mom! She was in *here!"*

His entire body trembled, and Miriam held him protectively. Meanwhile, the condensation near the top of the bathroom mirror began to freeze, forming an icy film that progressively descended toward the sink.

Janice arrived as Miriam stood and moved to the sink to shut the faucet off. She grabbed a washcloth and dabbed it in the warm water. She cleaned the blood from Tyler's torn stitches, and helped him to his feet.

"Get your clothes on, son," Miriam gently told him. She handed him the sweatshirt he wore earlier, while casting another distrustful glance around her. Janice stood in the doorway. "Go get Jill and Chris, Jan. We're leaving!"

Miriam helped Tyler walk out of the bathroom. Suddenly, the bathtub curtain began to sway, and the plastic rings rattled loudly. She let out a startled yelp, pulling the door shut behind her to keep whatever was there inside the bathroom. She urged Tyler to move quickly to the stairs. But before they reached the stairway, the bathroom door violently swung open. The doorknob slammed loudly into the bathroom wall.

"Mommy what's happening?!" cried Christopher.

He and Jillian were huddled together at the bottom of the stairs.

"Grab your coats! *Now!"*

Miriam urged Tyler again to keep moving, and hurry down the stairs. Janice was on her way up the stairs to assist him. Something blocked the hall light behind Miriam. The shadow caused Janice to look up. Her eyes grew wide with terror, and almost lost her footing on the stairs.

"Look out, Mom—she's coming for you!" shrieked Jillian, pulling away from Christopher to rush to her aid. She grimaced after slipping on the stairs.

Christopher trembled where he stood, watching the malevolent shadow descend upon them.

"No, Jill, just run!" screamed Miriam. *"Everybody run and get out of here!"*

A loud rustling noise followed Miriam's screams to her children. Once Janice reached the main floor with Tyler, he ran to the front door with Chris while she helped Jillian hop over to the door. Tyler and Chris fumbled with the doorknob, and didn't get it open until Miriam joined them, with the immense shadow bearing down. Janice threw the door open, and screamed for everyone to hurry. Miriam was the last one out, tumbling through the doorway and landing hard on the porch.

Janice and the kids stared fearfully at the house from the front lawn. The porch lights flickered as the front door began to close. Suddenly, the lights' collective glow intensified and the door crept open again. The sound of a young woman's snide laughter erupted from inside the house and emanated toward them, growing increasingly derisive.

Not waiting for what would come next, everyone ran, crying hysterically as they scrambled into the minivan. After nearly hitting an aspen in the front yard, Miriam guided the careening Chrysler down the driveway. She raced along LeClair Drive toward Janice's side of the subdivision.

A cackling shriek pierced the suburban stillness, followed by a shadowy mist drifting down the steps to the driveway. Leaving the house unattended, with the door wide open and most of the lights on, the mist rose into the air. It pursued the course of the minivan, where the line of exploding streetlights charted the mist's path all the way to Janice Andrews' townhouse.

Chapter Thirty-five

"Hello?"

The voice sounded anxious.

"Miriam?" For a moment, David didn't recognize her. He had frantically dialed Littleton for the past half-hour until the tips of his fingers grew numb.

"David, thank God it's you!"

"I'm calling from John's cabin. Christ, I've been trying to reach you for the past half-hour! What the hell's going on?"

"She's back!" Miriam's voice trembled, and it sounded as if the rest of his family cried nearby.

"Allie Mae?" He'd expected it, and he shot a look to John, confirming what they'd feared had happened.

"Who else would I be talking about?" she shouted into the phone, and began to weep.

"Miriam, darlin'… please calm down." He fought to remain calm himself. "Is she there right now?"

"Here? No." Her voice trembled. "She's in our house *again!* She attacked Ty less than twenty minutes ago, and then chased us out!" She sobbed harder.

"Is he all right?" David felt a large lump form in his throat.

"He got out okay, but he bruised his other arm trying to protect his shoulder!" she managed between sobs. "She showed up without any warning, David! We were ready to eat dinner…. There's *no* way in hell we're going back there!"

"Did you see her?" He asked tentatively, equating Allie Mae's strength and malice with her ability to materialize. He prayed he wasn't foolishly assuming the immediate danger for his family depended on how lucid her specter was.

"No, but everyone else did!"

"Shit!" he hissed into the phone.

"Ty won't talk about it, but Jill and Chris said they saw her chasing me! They said she has *no face!* And Jan described a huge shadow covering the ceiling as it came after us, with a blue eye glowing in the middle of it!"

David ran his free hand nervously through his hair, angry at himself for underestimating the spirit's wily ruthlessness. It sounded as if Miriam covered the phone to prevent him from hearing fresh sobbing from everyone in Jan's townhouse.

"I don't understand how this can be," he muttered, feeling increasingly helpless. "She was just here trying to force her way inside John's cabin!"

"What?" Miriam uncovered the phone. "When did that happen?"

"Right after it got dark," said David. "She finally stopped about an hour ago."

A loud hum suddenly interrupted their conversation. As the distortion grew louder, the kids and Janice began screaming.

"What the hell's happening?" he shouted into the handset. *"Miriam!"*

"Are you there, David?" Miriam shouted back. "I can't hear you! If you can hear me, do you hear *that?* Something's pounding at the door! Oh, *shit! The door's breaking, Davi—"*

The line went dead.

"Miriam! Goddamn it, answer me!"

John stood at David's side while he continued screaming into the phone. Terrified for his family's welfare, David slumped toward the floor… until a surge of rage seized him. He bolted for the front door, undoing the locks and throwing the door wide open before John could stop him.

"Come back and get me!" he screamed into the night, with John tugging on his arm. *"Allie Mae, come back you cowardly bitch!"*

A gentle breeze moved through the trees. The nocturnal birds and animals continued to make their territorial calls, along with a few hardy crickets and other insects that had somehow prolonged their summer lifespan. Defeated, David hung his head and turned to step back inside John's cabin, wondering what he could possibly do to save his family from the spirit's wrath and fearsome power he had misjudged horribly. Just before John closed the door, the nighttime creatures quieted their calls. Both men paused to listen, and at first David heard nothing beyond the muted activity. Then a subtle rumble emerged from the west, growing louder as it moved toward the cabin.

The heaviest wooded land in the national park's forest surrounded John's home, and the densely crowded tree line stretched for several miles in any direction. The tops of the tall pines and oaks along the western side of his property began to sway, creaking noisily as the wind forged a path toward them. As the source of the rumble approached, what sounded like an immense swarm of angry hornets aroused from a hundred nests now gathered in the darkness above the trees. Recalling the experience in his backyard a week earlier, David realized Allie Mae had come back. He stepped back out onto the porch.

She heard me!

"Get in here, David!"

John pulled harder on his arm, but David resisted.

"No, John! I need to face her!" He fought to shake free from the older man's powerful grip. "If she wants me, she can have me! I can't let her hurt my family anymore, and I can't let her hurt you either!"

He managed to free himself as the roar and growing swarm reached a small clearing separating the cabin from the forest.

"Damn it, David! *Listen* to me!" John pleaded over the growing din. "She's not going to stop with just you! When she's done with you, she's going back to get the rest of your family! She *won't* stop until she's taken both Tyler and Chris! It's not just about *you*, so get your ass in here *now!"*

David stared at him in disbelief. Although thorough in what he'd told John, he knew he didn't mention how Allie Mae threatened his youngest child. It's what brought him back to Tennessee.

"You'll have to trust me!" John continued to implore. "Your family will survive her anger tonight, but she'll kill you for sure if you don't listen and get back inside!"

Whether or not John's words about his loved ones' fates were true, Allie Mae intended to end his life. She had warned him, and Evelyn confirmed as much. His impetuous taunt brought her back, and unseen footsteps approached the cabin, crunching through pine needles and dead leaves in the darkness between the cabin's west side and the forest. John looked anxiously in that direction while restraining Shawn, whose instincts to protect his master were awakened.

Before the footsteps reached the front of the house, David allowed John to pull him to safety. As soon as the front door was closed and locked, the deafening menace gathered upon the front porch. The floor inside the cabin vibrated beneath their feet. It was as if the hostile swarm intended to gobble them up. The cacophony grew louder, forcing them to cover their ears until the noise ceased abruptly.

The unsettling silence that followed was absolute, without the faintest whistle from the wind. David and John stared wide-eyed at the front door for nearly a minute, the only sound coming from their labored breaths. John approached the curtained window next to the door. He pulled on the side of the curtain, attempting to peer outside. He moved his face closer to the edge of the window and opened the curtain a little further for a better view. A pale white hand reached in, grasping at his shirt. He pulled away in time, leaving the slender hand to claw hungrily at the window frame. When the edge of the curtain touched it, the hand hastily withdrew.

John hurried to where David stood, while Shawn snarled at the door. In response, a powerful force slammed against it, causing the door to rattle in its frame. Several items hanging on the wall dropped to the floor, and the feathers from the dream catcher above the door lifted into the air. The lights inside the cabin flickered and died.

Cast into darkness, except for the dancing flames in the fireplace and a few slivers of moonlight creeping in through the curtained windows in the rear of the cabin, David sought the kitchen light switches to no avail. John tried the lamp in the living room, which also clicked without a response. Worse, only three logs remained.

John kept a kitchen drawer filled with candles for such an emergency, since at least twice a year the cabin would be without power due to inclement weather. After grabbing a candle and lighting it, the two men remained crouched on the floor between the kitchen and front door for the next hour. In addition to the loss of electricity, the landline phone was dead. The logs in the hearth steadily burned down, where the dying coals popped intermittently within the fireplace. John eventually retrieved a dozen more candles, and placed them throughout the living room and kitchen, saving the last two for the hallway and bathroom.

"Depending on what she did to the circuits here, we'll likely have to wait until morning to get the power back on," John advised, when they felt safe to stand and move around the cabin again. "In the meantime, we can heat up some coffee the old-fashioned way, or make cocoa if you'd prefer."

He retrieved a kettle from the kitchen, along with a battery-operated radio/CD player. He returned to the fireplace after filling the kettle with water, and set the CD player on the coffee table. He hung the kettle from a metal rod beneath the mantel after they decided on cocoa.

"The reception on the radio's not so good," John advised. "I hope you don't mind country music, because that's all I listen to."

David nodded politely, despite his preference for rock n' roll. Deeply worried about Miriam and the kids, he glanced at his cell phone, hoping for improved signal strength. It showed zero bars.

John popped in a CD from a small stack on the coffee table. David had heard of the artist, Keith Urban. To his surprise, he enjoyed it more than he expected. Visibly pleased by his response, John played other CDs, ranging from older artists like Dolly Parton and Merle Haggard to newer ones like Brad Paisley and Taylor Swift. Impressed at the quality of the newer recordings, David grew saddened while listening to some of the tracks from Haggard's greatest hit collection.

"Brings back memories, eh?" said John, apparently noticing David's demeanor had changed.

"Unfortunately," said David. "My dad's favorite artists consisted of Willie Nelson, Loretta Lynn, and Mr. Haggard."

John nodded, his gaze thoughtful as he looked toward the dying fire. He got up and added the larger of the three logs, stirring the remaining embers to kindle the flames. He turned back to David.

"You've told me a good deal about Miriam and your kids, but nothing about your own father and mother," he observed. "Your sadness tells me it wasn't so good for you growing up in Chattanooga."

David nodded, staring into his cup.

"Let's just say I learned to hate Willie, Lorretta, and Merle for the same reasons I loathed my dad."

"Was he an abusive man?"

"It depends on how you define abuse," said David. "Did he hit me? Sometimes, but not enough to warrant a visit from a social worker. It was more neglect, since he was almost never around. The only time I'd ever see him was when he had a bone to pick with me about one thing or another." He raised his gaze from his cup with a faraway look.

"What about your mother?"

"I remember when I was young how much I adored her, she was so beautiful," he recalled. "I had no idea she didn't have long. As I grew older, she drank more and more. My folks used to fight a lot."

He turned his gaze to John.

"I think my dad used to hit her. She died when I was eleven. My aunt told me the angels came and took her, that she wasn't meant to stay here on earth. But I found out later she took her own life. She was found in their bed when my dad was away on business, with an empty bottle of Jack Daniels and what was left of her prescription sleeping pills on her nightstand."

"I'm so sorry, David," said John, his tone compassionate. "I'm sure she'd be proud to see what you've done for yourself."

"Maybe. Maybe not." David smiled weakly. "After that, my Aunt Ruth pretty much raised me, since my dad was home even less. I stayed with her and my Grandpa Elbert. When I was little, Grandpa used to beat the holy hell out of me and my cousin Celeste, until I got old enough to fend him off. Celeste was a year older. She died after falling down the stairs at Grandpa's house. She was fifteen at the time, and I was at a football game when it happened. It took Auntie several years to recover, which I'm sure she still hasn't fully. She hides it well, though. To this day, I think the old man did it."

He eyed John seriously.

"Maybe I should shut the hell up about all this."

"If you don't mind talking, I'm quite interested in the rest of the story that brought you to where you are today," John requested.

"Well, there's really not a whole lot more." David paused to pour more cocoa. He added peppermint Schnapps from a bottle John brought from the kitchen. "The old bastard finally died. My dad started spending more time in Chattanooga. Auntie and her husband were the only other folks living in the house besides me and him."

He blew on his cup and took a sip, while John waited patiently for him to continue.

"By then, I was a junior in high school. I earned all-city and second team all-state honors in both my junior and senior years playing football. On a recruiting trip during the spring of my senior year, I visited the University of Colorado and instantly fell in love with Boulder. The campus seemed so big to me, since I was a small-city kid from Tennessee. That's where I met Norm, since he was being recruited the same weekend. I played quarterback, and he was an all-state halfback from Mississippi. We hit it off immediately." He grew quiet.

"And you never left Colorado, I take it," said John. "It became your home."

"Yes, it did," he confirmed. "Miriam and I decided to stay after graduation. She sometimes misses San Francisco, where she's from. I've never missed Chattanooga."

John nodded. He exchanged the CD in the player for another one he fished out from the pile. A soothing arrangement accompanied by a beautiful voice resounded from the player.

"You mentioned to me a couple of days ago before driving up to Gatlinburg from Chattanooga that you visited with your aunt," he said, relaxing in his recliner with his cup of steaming cocoa in hand. "You've kept in touch with her, I see."

"Yeah, I have," said David. "But until this last visit, it's been mostly Miriam's efforts to stay in touch. I guess I've always blamed her for not protecting Celeste and me from our grandpa, since I'm sure Auntie had to see the way he watched her daughter. Celeste used to tell me how creepy he made her feel, and that he touched her on more than one occasion where he shouldn't have."

"Did you ever tell your dad about this?"

"I did. All that got me was a close-up view of his backhand coming across my face."

"Oh, I see." John's gaze shifted to the fire.

"It's all right," David assured him. "I got over it once I was the hell away from there. My dad died from a heart attack when I was in college. After graduation, I confronted my aunt with some questions I had about him. She had no idea how much I disliked him, and I told her then that I hated her father even more."

"How'd she take that news?" John looked at David, wearing a deeply curious expression.

"Actually, she took it much better than I expected," he said. "I frankly didn't care what she thought, assuming I'd never speak to her again after that day. But, she told me how she used to cry at night, worrying about my welfare after my mom died. I remembered then how she was the one to keep me in line with my schooling. To be honest, if she hadn't taken the time to make sure I participated in sports, my life would've turned out much differently. I could very well have turned into the asshole my dad and grandpa were, because she told me how her grandpa was even worse. In her mind, they were all trained from a young age to be abusers. She recalled how her grandfather was just as much the incestuous letch her father was."

"That's really too bad," said John, solemnly. "Sorry to have taken you down this road. I hoped to learn something that might link our current problem with Allie Mae."

David told him not to worry, and asked whom the beautiful voice belonged to as the song ended.

"That's Trisha Yearwood and the tune's called *Georgia Rain*, I believe." John moved over to the coffee table and the CD cover sitting on top of the stack. He picked it up, squinting in the dim light from the candles and the fire burning nearby. "I'll have to tell you tomorrow, when I can see it."

"It's a beautiful song," said David. "There are a few CDs here that I'll need to add to my collection when I get back to Denver. Who would've thought?" He smiled weakly.

"Maybe it'll help you not to forget your southern roots!" John chuckled.

"Maybe so."

The conversation about David's upbringing now finished, the two moved to other subjects, passing time while they listened to more music from John's collection. Midnight arrived, and then twelve-thirty, the visitation time favored by the ghost. David added the last log to the waning fire. For the next hour, they patrolled the main floor, listening for any unusual noises and keeping an eye out for anything else out of the ordinary. But other than steady cricket chirps and calls from the usual nocturnal creatures outside the cabin, all remained quiet.

They retired for the night around one-thirty. Leery of sleeping apart from the protection of one another, David took the couch while John grabbed another blanket from his room and stretched out in the recliner. They lit extra candles, and set them on the mantel and end tables in the living room.

David's dreams were vivid, filled with images both familiar and foreign. The strongest image he remembered the next morning was of John bending over him. Dressed in buckskins, beads, and a headdress, he shook a painted gourd and chanted strange phrases. A bright, ethereal haze surrounded him, and he wore a worried expression on his paint-streaked face, continually looking over his shoulder. Every time he turned to David, his words and motions grew more urgent. His efforts became increasingly frantic while an ink-like mist permeated the air behind him, emanating from the cabin's fireplace. Before long, the row of candles on the mantel had blown out, and a pile of dying embers and ashes were all that remained of the last log on the hearth.

Chapter Thirty-six

The dawn's light seeped into the cabin through the back windows, fending off the early morning coolness that penetrated the living room through the darkened hearth. Sometime during the night, the electricity returned, courtesy of Allie Mae's retreat. The recliner had tipped over. John and Shawn were absent.

Not fully awake, David struggled to sit up on the couch while he looked around the living room. Books, magazines, and other items lay scattered on the floor. The CDs had fallen haphazardly over the coffee table's edge, along with the player lying on its side with the hatch open. Broken candles were strewn throughout the room. Only the dream catchers remained undisturbed, along with Allie's bag, where seven runes still surrounded it on the dining table.

"John?"

There wasn't an immediate response. The commode flushed in the bathroom. Shuffling footsteps followed, and John emerged from the hallway next to the fireplace. He wore several bandages across his brow and left temple. Shawn tagged along behind him, favoring his right paw.

"Well, at least we look like twins."

He forced a wan smile for David while pointing to his brow. His clothes were disheveled, and he looked exhausted.

"What in the hell happened here?" David rose gingerly to his feet. His lower back hadn't responded well to the couch's unforgiving contours.

"I believe I underestimated the spirit's wiliness," John replied, limping to where David stood. "At least we've survived to see another day, eh?"

"She did all this?"

"Yes, and not just in here." John motioned to the kitchen, and the hallway he had just come from. "Allie Mae's got a nasty temper, and I hope she's not planning to extend her stay." Despite his haggard appearance, he managed a wan smile.

"When did all of this happen?" David couldn't believe he slept through the assault.

"She returned shortly after three o'clock this morning, but didn't become a true nuisance until the fire died out around four-thirty," John explained. "She came in through the chimney. I heard Shawn whimpering, and I awoke in time to see her shadow hovering above you. I recited prayers for protection my grandfather taught me long ago. She left you alone, taking her anger out on me."

He paused to look at the mess around them.

"She hurt Shawn, too. His right paw's tender. Her tantrum didn't end until a short while ago, around six o'clock. I hoped to have the place straightened up before you woke."

"Thanks for saving my life, John," said David, "but you should've woke me to help you."

He thought again of the strange dream images. At least he knew what inspired them.

"We're not out of the woods yet," said John. "She'll be back, but hopefully not before we're ready to face her."

He patted David's shoulder and looked away, turning his attention to the mess around the coffee table. David helped him clean, picking up other items and debris strewn throughout the main level. He also helped John restore the recliner to its original position.

"I need to try and reach Miriam." David stepped over several pots and pans lying in the middle of the kitchen floor, amid broken glasses and the emptied contents from the flour and sugar bins. "I'll help you clean this up once I find out what's going on back home."

"You worry about your family, and I'll take care of this myself," said John, limping to a narrow broom closet next to the pantry.

David called Janice's number. The first call went to voicemail, and when the second call reached the third ring he worried his next call would be to directory assistance to find the number to the Littleton Police Department. Just before the fourth ring, a woman's voice groggily answered.

"Hello?"

"Jan, it's David. I know it's early, but is everyone okay?" He felt hopeful once he heard her voice.

"David, we've been trying to reach you!"

Muffled voices followed as she placed her hand over the receiver.

"Thank God you're okay!" Miriam wept, her voice hoarse.

"Yeah, we are… at least for now." He shot a wry grimace toward John, who picked up the larger glass shards and placed them inside a trashcan. "Are you and the kids alright?"

"We made it through the night, but none of us slept much," she said. "It got really hairy around here after we lost contact with you. The front door to Jan's home will have to be replaced. I'm calling Detective Colby first, so he can come over and see it."

"But nobody's hurt?"

"We're okay... but if her attack had lasted any longer, it might not be the case. I'm keeping the kids with me at all times today, and I've already called Eileen to let her know I won't be coming in to the clinic for any makeup appointments I moved to this morning.

She and Jim have been very patient through this, even though I can't be truthful about what's actually going on."

How could she be? He doubted anyone would consider dealing with an angry ghost as a legitimate reason to miss work.

"I guess it helps to own a third of the practice," he observed, dryly.

"That's true, and I'm thankful for it. But still…. What about you and your friend John—are you both all right?"

"Allie Mae came back after you and I got disconnected last night. Then she struck again early this morning and physically attacked John…. I imagine she'll be by again before the day is over. John's granddaughter is planning a ceremony later today that should end this once and for all."

"I pray it works. But, what if it doesn't?" She sounded resigned it wouldn't.

"It'll have to work," he replied, sounding more confident than he felt. "Either way, I'm coming home tomorrow. I can't let her antagonize you, the kids, or Jan anymore!"

"Just be careful. Don't do anything stupid," Miriam admonished. "She's much more powerful than most angry spirits—and I didn't need Sara to tell me this to know it's true!"

"Evelyn's every bit as good at this type of thing as Sara," David assured her. "If what happens today doesn't fix the problem, nothing will."

"That's exactly what Sara said last night. She talked about the strength and wisdom of John's granddaughter."

An awkward moment of silence followed. He desperately wished to be on the other side of the line, to hold and comfort her.

"Call me on my cell phone once the ceremony is finished," she said. He could tell she was fighting hard to keep from crying. "We won't be staying here tonight. As soon as the door's repaired today, we're renting a couple of hotel rooms near the Tech Center. Jan booked our reservation immediately after the power came back on last night. If Detective Colby can find time to stop by here before we leave, great. But we won't wait on him once it starts getting dark."

"I promise to call you," he said. "Please be *very* careful. You and the kids mean more to me than anything, so remember that—regardless of what might happen to me."

"Please don't do anything foolish, David! You mean the world to us, too, so *please* listen to John's granddaughter and stay safe!"

He waited for her to hang up first. By then, John had almost finished cleaning. He had two tours at the visitors' center that morning, at nine and ten, the only ones he couldn't find someone to fill in for him. David insisted on taking him to a doctor once he revealed several large bruises along the outside of his left thigh and leg. John refused to go, stating he once experienced far worse injuries falling off a horse, and had "healed up just fine."

John showered and prepared for work while David whipped up some eggs and bacon for breakfast. Afterward, John called Evelyn to let her know what happened. Alarmed about his injuries, it took him another ten minutes to assure her that he didn't need a doctor. She insisted on speaking with David, and made him promise to forcibly take her grandfather to the emergency clinic in Gatlinburg if the wounds worsened. Evelyn advised him to be ready to begin the ceremony around four o'clock, and it consisted of two parts, the latter of which would be completed later that night.

Within the hour, John left for the visitors' center. Per his instructions, David placed Shawn on his leash behind the cabin. John had bandaged and stabilized the husky's wounded paw. Since there was very little swelling, he decided to wait and see if the injury improved before taking Shawn to a vet.

By 9:00 a.m., David returned to the Econo-Lodge in Gatlinburg. Rather than risk facing Allie Mae alone in the cabin, he promised John they'd meet at the visitors' center for lunch, and return to the cabin together. A pleasant surprise came when David found everything untouched in his hotel room, including the newly purchased wardrobe.

Making the most of the reprieve, he quickly trimmed his beard, brushed his teeth, and jumped in the shower. He repeatedly peeked over the shower curtain, expecting Allie Mae to be lurking in the bathroom. Thankfully, she left him alone. Smiling as he exited the hotel with his packed suitcase in hand, he felt grateful for the most mundane experience since returning to Gatlinburg. He hoped it was a positive omen.

David visited a fashionable clothing store on Gatlinburg's strip, where he purchased several turtleneck sweaters to hide the bandaged neck injuries. Once in the car, he changed into a beige sweater. With all of his personal business finished, he headed to Cades Cove.

"You're looking dapper," John observed, once David caught up with him in the gift shop. "Are you up for a bite to eat?"

David glanced at his watch, surprised it was almost noon.

"Sure."

"Evelyn is planning to cook a pot of chili for tonight, which should be ready around five o'clock. There's an excellent deli in town."

Riding in David's rented Buick, the two were soon on Gatlinburg's strip. Morrie's Sub Shop was located in the older section near the Uber Gatlinburg tram. Excellent club sandwiches and a couple of Heinekens reminded David of the lunches he often enjoyed in downtown Denver with Norm. Non-intrusive subjects dominated their conversation, such as the Vols' football fortunes and the steady flow of tourists that would taper off near Halloween, and pick up again around Christmas.

They returned to the park around one o'clock, where David followed John in his cruiser to the cabin. The place seemed peaceful under the mid-afternoon sun, with virtually no sign of the assault they endured from the spirit's nocturnal visit. John walked to the backyard to check on Shawn. John's limp was less noticeable, and the same was true for the dog. Shawn's tail wagged fiercely as he jumped on John's uniform with dirty paws.

The cabin sat atop a hillside, which David hadn't realized the day before. The woods' sloping expanse behind the property and the bluish mountain peaks provided a breathtaking view. John scanned the area, obviously looking for signs of Allie Mae. He nodded approvingly once satisfied she wasn't anywhere around, and led the way inside his home through the back door.

Hickory smoke and cinnamon from the previous day hung in the air with the bacon scent from breakfast. After John changed out of uniform into jeans and another flannel shirt, they spent the next couple of hours watching television. When Evelyn arrived, she had her hair pulled up and was dressed in a UT sweat suit. A bit harried, it appeared she had rushed about since getting up that morning. Along with her duffel bag, she carried two paper sacks filled with the ceremonial supplies she needed. After giving a warm hug to both men and setting the items next to the table, she scolded her grandfather again for not being more careful.

"We'll be ready to begin within the next half hour," she advised, glancing at the clock above the oven that read 3:37 p.m. "Grandpa, I hope you don't mind me using the small wooden bowls Grandma used for desserts."

She motioned to the cupboard above the refrigerator, and John nodded his approval. David assisted in retrieving the half-dozen black wooden bowls stacked neatly in the cupboard's corner, and Evelyn set them on the table in a row near the candle and Allie Mae's bag. From one of the sacks, she pulled out an assortment of plastic baggies containing a variety of leaves, roots, and seeds. The other sack held a pair of ceramic incense burners and three white slender candles. She emptied two small bags of incense into each burner.

Evelyn removed a pound of deer meat and folded the sacks, placing them beneath the table.

"This isn't part of the ceremony." She seemed to notice David's curious look as she moved into the kitchen holding the package of fresh meat. "I told Grandpa I'd cook up some chili tonight, which I hope you'll enjoy."

She smiled as she put the meat on the kitchen counter and moved to the pantry, where she retrieved two large cans of chili beans and the necessary spices.

"I haven't had venison in years," said David. "If tonight's meal is anywhere near as good as what you fixed us yesterday, I'm in for a real treat!"

"Why, thank you, David." Her smile widened. "If you'll take your seat again at the table in a few minutes, I'll soon join you."

While waiting, he studied the strange names of the various leaves, roots, and seeds.

"What you and I will do first is crush the roots and blend in the herbs," she advised, once she joined him. She tore open the first few packages. Immediately, the fragrances of each filled the air, some pleasant but others bitter and acrid. She lit the incense and the larger white candle from the previous day. "Some of the roots will really stink once we mash them up."

Evelyn opened the duffel bag and removed two small wooden mallets, handing one to him. Next, she set three of the bowls near him, placing several red fleshy stalks from a chickweed plant inside the first bowl. She added a pair of brown slender roots on top of the stalks, which she called delani, along with a funnel-shaped yellow flower named Carolina jasmine.

"Go ahead and finish blending them together," she instructed, after taking care of the initial mashing of the stalks, roots, and flower. "Before we eat dinner, I'll need you to thoroughly wash your hands, since the mixture is toxic."

He paused to look at her with a "Why in the hell are we doing this?" expression on his face. She smiled and patted his wrist.

"It's necessary for you to actually handle the paste as you create it, since your physical essence must be absorbed for the paste to have maximum effectiveness," she explained.

He nodded and returned to the task of blending the mixture. It took nearly ten minutes for him to break down the stalks, although the flower and roots became a pliable mush right away. Before long, the concoction became enough of a paste that Evelyn indicated suited their purpose. The paste's color was dark rust, and she set the bowl to the right of Allie Mae's bag, just outside the rune she had previously placed there.

She placed a handful of very small black roots inside the next bowl, which she called unaste'tstyu, or black snakeroots. In addition, she opened another bag containing a single dark brown root she called kagaskutagi, also known as 'crow skin'. She pressed the root in with the others, and spread seeds from liverwort, or skwali as she called it, on top. David blended these ingredients together, and formed a black paste. She set the bowl on the left side of the bag.

With two bowls in place, she pushed the third one to him.

"This one is the most important, since it will be the end result you seek," she said. "As we add in and mash the ingredients, I'll need you to focus your thoughts on what you want to happen tonight, both for you and your family, as well as the girl's restless spirit."

He agreed to do whatever she asked. She opened packages containing the three largest roots, breaking them into smaller pieces. One seemed almost carrot-like while the other two were gray and scraggly. Their names were dayewu, distai'yi and amadita'ti. They barely fit inside the bowl.

"Go ahead and combine them. Concentrate, David."

He struggled to keep the distai'yi inside the bowl. Meanwhile, she removed several fresh white lilies from the last two packages.

"The devil's shoestrings are always the hardest to get to cooperate," she said, surely noticing his growing aggravation to keep the damn things inside the bowl long enough to crush them.

She reached over and helped him hold the bowl steady, until he finally subdued them. The resultant paste was light gray. Evelyn handed the lilies to him, explaining he should be the only one to add them in. The paste was almost white when finished, and the aroma had become somewhat pleasant compared to a few moments ago. He thought about his beloved family, and how desperately he wished for Allie Mae to find peace, or at least leave them the hell alone.

"So far so good!" she enthused, moving the bowl to the lower edge of Allie Mae's Treasures, just below the runes. "We're now ready to break for supper. Before we do, let me explain what each of the bowls represent, so you can reflect on their meaning while we eat. The bowl with the red paste represents your success and triumph. It's for the victory we seek tonight. The bowl with the black paste, as you've already correctly guessed, represents death. But, remember it doesn't correspond to the spirit's intent or fate. Rather, it's the same as the Tarot Death card, or the rune's death symbol. It simply means the end of a journey, and hopefully the end of your struggle against her."

She waited for David's acknowledgement that he understood. He nodded.

"The last bowl represents the final result you desire, as I already mentioned, which is peace and happiness. The three together will provide protection as you return her treasures to where you found them."

"You mean I'll be taking the bag back to the ravine?" A chill seized his heart.

"Yes, David." She took his hands. "It's the only way to end this. I assure you, you'll be ready to do it by the time we complete the ceremony tonight."

John came over, placing his hand on David's shoulder.

"I've set up the TV trays in the living room, and the chili's ready," he announced.

Evelyn stood and David followed her to the kitchen sink where they both thoroughly cleansed their hands. They joined John in the living room. He poured them each a glass of iced tea to go with a steaming bowl of chili. Small loaves of hot bread were placed alongside each bowl, and after Evelyn recited a brief Cherokee blessing, the three sat down to eat.

It was shortly after five o'clock, and the sun disappeared behind the western hills. The cabin's security lights came on as they chatted quietly in the living room. When the topic turned to Allie Mae's attack from the previous night, John showed Evelyn his injured leg. She gasped when she saw the bruises, but held off giving her grandfather the stern lecture David expected.

John told again how the spirit crept in through the fireplace after the fire died, and loomed above David as he slept. If not for Shawn's prompting, he might not have been able to save David from Allie Mae, since he slept soundly in the recliner and was unaware of her presence. Once awake, John watched her shadowy form descend while the air around them became frigid. The vapors from David's breaths were being sucked up into the wraith's essence as Allie Mae moved closer.

John recited a prayer he had uttered only one other time since his teenage years, and that was at his wife's deathbed. It failed to appease the anisginas then, the evil spirits who brought her cancer, and he had feared it might not be effective in the present time. To his surprise, the entity lifted from David and faced him. The shadow seemed impenetrable, and the row of candles on the mantel blew out, as well as the others in the living room and kitchen. Being surrounded by complete darkness didn't deter him, however. He chanted the prayer more fervently. Books and magazines flew off the shelves, while pots and pans crashed to the floor in the kitchen.

John described how he pictured a dance his grandfather showed him long ago, and began to imitate it, moving toward David in the darkness and feeling the invisible iciness of the spirit's essence embrace him. Shawn barked angrily at his side while sacred items were torn from the wall, and ceramic dishes fell upon the pots and pans scattered across the kitchen floor. Despite the noisy racket, David slept.

As John explained to him earlier, the confrontation lasted about an hour. The ghost uttered her own chant, spitting out vehement threats as she sought to overpower John's prayer. He felt an icy spray as her shrouded face drew near, and he responded in kind, raising his voice to match hers. Finally, she let out a terrible scream and threw him against the recliner. It tipped over, and he landed hard on the floor and on top of Shawn. He expected her to try and finish him off, but it didn't happen. The lights in the living room flickered and came back on. She had left.

John laid still until certain the attack had ended. After a few more minutes, he got up and turned off the overhead light, so David could continue sleeping. He went to the bathroom, where to his surprise and horror, his face and shirt were covered in blood. He scrubbed his face clean and bandaged the cut above his eye, praying Allie's corpuscles and other matter hadn't merged with his own. He then took care of Shawn's leg.

"If not for you risking your own life, I surely wouldn't be sitting here now," said David. He decided to share the strange images he dreamt while John battled the spirit.

"Once a shaman, always a shaman," Evelyn observed, smiling proudly after David described the dream. John weakly returned her smile, stating he hoped to never face such a demon again.

After he and David helped Evelyn clean up after dinner, they returned to the living room. Since it wasn't time yet to move on to the next portion of the ceremony, they conversed on lighter subjects with the TV muted in the background. Around seven o'clock, Shawn scratched at the back door. Evelyn went to the door and opened it. She peered cautiously outside while removing the chain from his neck. Similar to the previous night, Shawn whined and repeatedly looked toward the darkness beyond the security lights. Evelyn shut the door and locked it, peering through the door's drawn curtain.

"Come here, boy!" John called. The husky trotted into the living room, his tail sweeping across the coffee table as he went by. "There, there, Shawn… good boy."

Shawn's response was a drawn-out whine. John glanced worriedly at Evelyn, who stood next to the back door. She frowned, shaking her head.

"She's back, isn't she?" David asked, worriedly.

"More than likely, yes," said Evelyn. "I'd planned on getting started around nine, since the actual ceremony takes about two hours. We'll need to arrive at John Oliver's homestead by eleven-thirty, which should give you plenty of time to reach the ravine by twelve o'clock. Most magical spells are strongest after midnight. You've noticed Allie favors the latter half of the midnight hour. Our spell will work the same way, but in the earlier half hour."

She peered through the back window again before moving over to the table, where she opened her duffel bag and removed a leather-bound book. She also produced a single white dove feather the size of her index finger and a smaller patch of deerskin, laying them alongside the book on the table near her chair.

"Grandpa, would you mind if I use your CD player?" she asked, removing a disk from the duffel before closing it and setting it beneath the table. "I'd like to set the mood."

John didn't mind, and checked the player to make sure it still worked. He brought it over to where Evelyn waited. She plugged the player into a nearby outlet, stating she wanted to recharge and preserve the batteries in case the power went out again.

"Both of you, please join me at the table," she said, and placed the disk inside the player.

The sound of soft drums, chimes, and a wooden flute playing a lovely, and yet haunting, melody filled the air. David returned to his seat at the table, as did John, after first placing two large hickory logs inside the fireplace and waiting for the flames to take hold. A dozen additional logs sat next to the hearth. Ready to begin, Evelyn poured them each a cup of fresh coffee first.

"I'd still prefer waiting until nine o'clock to officially start, but it might be helpful to discuss some of what you'll hear, David, and the meanings behind key phrases," she said, replenishing the incense in the burners and lighting them. "Grandpa is familiar with most of the Cherokee incantations I intend to use. Since I'll be completely focused once we begin, having some familiarity beforehand should help you stay focused and in tune with me, David. Grandpa should be able to tell you what's going on, and where we are in the ceremony once my guides take over. When that happens, I may not be coherent enough to be understood."

A gust of wind blew against the back of the cabin, rattling a few loose shingles on the roof. John grimaced. It appeared last night's visit from Allie Mae had left some undetected damage.

"Wait here, while Grandpa and I make sure everything is locked up."

Evelyn rose from the table and John soon joined her. Since the drapes covering the loft's window were still closed, they focused on the windows and doors on the main floor. The bathroom window turned out to be the only one unprotected, as the wooden shutters had been left open that afternoon.

"Stay focused no matter what happens, David," she said, after returning to the table. "I was thinking just now of what might help prepare us better for our ceremony. Grandpa, do you recall the 'Tale of the Lovers' as well as the other story you used to tell Hanna and me when we were young, about the Cherokee warrior sent to find the Great Antelope imprisoned in the land of darkness beyond the Three Blood Rivers?"

"I do," John replied.

"My guides told me that you should share them with David," she said. "After I closed the shutters in the bathroom, I heard them say 'Have him tell the stories, the ones from when you were a little girl.'"

Hesitant at first, John agreed to recite the tales. Evelyn turned down the volume on the CD player, so he could be clearly heard. A gifted storyteller, David already knew from the tour he and Miriam had taken at the Cable Mill that fateful Saturday, before the vengeful spirit invaded their lives. When John began to speak, the wind, which had been whistling against the eaves of the cabin, died down, as if someone else wanted to hear the stories, too.

The first story involved an Indian girl named Quia-sontha and a young brave named Ta-e-kita. Similar to the Shakespearian tale of Romeo and Juliet, the families of Quia-sontha and Ta-e-kita feuded within the Cherokee nation. Set in the early 1700s, when the white settlers still respected the Cherokee, the story centered on the healing of the feud, as the families finally saw the senselessness of the war. But, as in the legendary tale of Romeo and Juliet, the lesson came at a cost. Ta-e-kita died in a battle with one of Quia-sontha's older brothers who didn't want this peace, leaving Quia-sontha to grieve from her loss until she died of a broken heart.

David nodded politely at the story's conclusion, wondering what in the hell it had to do with his situation. If it was supposed to be a portent of things to come, then a serious ass-kicking awaited him by Allie Mae's ghost. Evelyn laughed.

"You must understand the ceremony tonight is not only intended for your salvation," she explained. "In some ways, your tormentor is like Quia-sontha. Allie Mae feels terribly wronged, and when she passed over to the other side she did so with a horrible wound and burden placed on her heart. I'm sure you'll find the next story more appealing."

She motioned for her grandfather to continue, and he moved on to the next tale. It dealt with a warrior named Sha-hinta, sent by Tsu'l'kalu, the Cherokee deity known as 'the Great Lord of the game'. Tsu'l'kalu sent Sha-hinta to the land of darkness to save the Great Antelope, kidnapped by an enormous mythic horned serpent known as Uktena. After a terrible struggle to reach this land, where he escaped death at the hands of a host of enemies waiting for him at the Three Blood Rivers, Sha-hinta defeated Uktena and returned the Great Antelope safely to the Great Mountains of the Blue Ridge. Tsu'l'kalu rewarded Sha-hinta by allowing him to lead the first hunt when the antelope grew plentiful again.

"You see, this one wasn't so bad," said Evelyn, smiling warmly.

David thanked John for sharing the stories, which took just over an hour to complete. The clock on the kitchen wall read 8:24 p.m., and as soon as John finished, the wind began to whistle again as it moved freely through the eaves, no longer hindered by whatever force had prevented it from reaching the cabin. He and Evelyn turned their heads to the back door, and David caught a glimpse of a shadow passing by the door's window, visible through the curtain.

"Let's make our final preparations. Would either of you like more coffee before we start?"

Evelyn's smile couldn't mask her nervousness. She returned with the coffee pot, setting it on a warmer near John's place at the table after replenishing everyone's cup. Once seated again, she handed a pad and pen to David.

"Write down the information I'm about to tell you, and refer to it while the ceremony is in progress," she instructed. "The first thing we'll do is try to loosen the spirit's grip on you, to disrupt her ability to haunt you at will. We'll use these items for that." She pointed to the white feather and the patch of deerskin.

"This first part of the ceremony is known as Tsigiu, which means *I eat* or *I take*," she said. "You may have heard of the Cherokee spirit eaters, which is where this ritual is taken from. The intent is to take the evil influence and bind it in the deerskin offering. The feather represents your desire for lasting peace, and it will be placed with the deerskin inside Allie Mae's bag."

She waited for him to finish writing, and then set the three slender white candles in front of the three wooden bowls containing the pastes. She opened the leather book, which contained a number of bookmarks.

"Once the binding is done, we'll set up your protection for when you enter her lair, the sacred ravine in Cades Cove," she advised. "Like the great warrior, Sha-hinta, you must go and face your nemesis. Allie is your Uktena, and like Sha-hinta you'll be after the thing you prize most. Your Great Antelope is the safety of your family and your own peace of mind."

She waited for him to make eye contact with her after writing it down.

"She's near…listening to us from outside the cabin," said Evelyn, her tone soft and serious. "No matter what happens, concentrate on what you want to accomplish, your freedom. I'll now give you words to remember, to watch for. Let them serve as a map to know where we are in the ceremony, so that you won't be distracted by whatever Allie brings our way. Rest assured, she'll try to stop us, and the best time to do it is before the ceremony is completed. Once the incantations are spoken and you're marked by the pastes we mixed earlier, she can't harm you."

Evelyn tapped on the note pad for him to turn to a fresh page. Then she turned to the first marked page in the book she held.

"When you hear the word Dunuwa in a succession of three, which means *it has penetrated*, the ceremony will be halfway over. The phrase Dayuha hinehi-hinida'we utsina wa will mark the beginning of the end of the ceremony."

She waited for him to finish writing the phrase, helping him spell each word. Then she moved to a bookmark placed near the end of the book.

"Listen for the word aduniga which means *relief has come*. The last incantation will end with yuhahi, yuhahi, yuhahi, which is sort of like an exclamation that we're finished. Afterward, I'll apply the empowered pastes to your forehead, cheeks, and hands. That's when the ceremony will end."

Evelyn returned to the first marked page in her book and laid it open. She lit the three candles, moving from left to right, and removed three small brushes and a vial of water from her duffel. After pouring a small amount of water into each of the three remaining wooden bowls, she placed the bowls in front of the candles with the brushes resting on the edge of each bowl.

"The water is pure, in case you're wondering," she advised. "We're ready to begin once nine o'clock gets here."

She glanced at her watch and back at the kitchen's clock. Both showed 8:49 p.m. For the next eleven minutes they sat in silence, listening to the same instrumental CD on its second run through. David thought of Miriam and his kids, hopefully safe and sound in a hotel. He regretted not taking a moment to call his wife, and knew it wouldn't be an appropriate time right then, with the ceremony about to begin. His thoughts turned to Allie Mae's ghost and when she'd strike. He wondered if she planned something dramatic, like shaking the cabin's foundation at nine o'clock. Or, would she wait until Evelyn became vulnerable under her guides' influence?

Nine o'clock arrived. Evelyn asked David to give her his right hand, which she took in her left. She closed her eyes and uttered a quiet prayer, waving her right hand in the air above the large white candle. A noticeable depression formed in its center, obscuring the flame. The flame shot up, rising nearly a foot to where her palm hovered. She smiled and opened her eyes.

"My guides are ready," she said. "Remember, don't be alarmed by what takes place during the next couple of hours."

She closed her eyes and passed her hand over the other three candles, the flames rising toward her palm as well. When she brought her hand back to the book, she opened her eyes.

Evelyn removed the first bookmark and set it to her right. She began reciting an incantation from the page. Soft at first, she became more ardent as she read the words. The wind became more noticeable. Gusts rustled leaves onto the back porch, and the whistling grew stronger.

She picked up the patch of deerskin and passed it over the large candle, its flame leaping to her hand again. She opened her mouth, imitating the act of eating the patch while bringing it down from her face to her chest. She repeated the incantation and set the deerskin on the left side of the book now resting on the table.

The feather came next, and she passed it over the candle. As before, the flame leapt toward her hand. She placed the edge of the feather against her forehead and over her heart while chanting the next incantation on the page. Once finished, she placed the feather on top of the deerskin patch and lifted the items together. While repeating the incantation with her eyes closed, she kissed the items.

"Hand me her bag."

David carefully lifted the bag and gave it to her. She loosened the leather strap, and a foul odor rose into the air. It seemed as if whatever caused the previous scents had died, and advanced decomposition set in. Everyone grimaced from the pungent smell, as Evelyn placed the deerskin and feather inside. She closed the bag and handed it back to him, and he returned it to its original spot on the table.

"We're done with the first part."

She turned to another page and read the next series of incantations, her finger showing she repeated some phrases over and over before moving to the next marked page. From what he could tell, she had between thirty to forty more pages marked. He flipped to the first page of the notepad and studied the words she told him to look for.

"It'll be awhile before she gets to those phrases," said John. "Right now she's undoing Allie Mae's web, removing it strand by strand." He looked up, and his eyes moved from one end of the ceiling to the other.

"You can see it?" David glanced up at the ceiling, but saw nothing.

"Yes, I can," John confirmed. "For several days, I've noticed it around you. It'd been there before, when you first arrived, but only faintly. Now it's pronounced, and I can tell you it's a terrible feeling to see something like this and be unable to do anything about it."

David thought of the spirit's visitations, wondering how terrible they would've been if he had John or Evelyn's ability to see beyond physical reality. Meanwhile, the ceremony continued. She stopped talking, and leaned her head back. He moved to keep her from falling, but John stopped him.

"Evelyn's guides are in full control now. Trust me… let her be."

She leaned back at what appeared to be a painful angle, but her body stayed relaxed and the chair stable. Slowly she sat up. As she did, her eyes rolled back.

Despite how impossible it seemed, she looked at the book and turned to the next bookmark. The voice emanating from her now was much deeper and gruff in timbre.

"One of her guides has chosen to take over," whispered John. "Don't be alarmed, since it usually means the guide feels they can provide additional help to vanquish the asgina."

The word dunuwa resounded three times from Evelyn's open throat, signaling they officially reached the ceremony's midway point. Three loud thuds shook the roof. John and David nervously glanced at the ceiling. Evelyn's visitor paid no attention to the disturbance, moving onto the next bookmark.

"The guide has broken through her web," said John. "And like a spider busy perfecting the rest of its snare, Allie Mae has returned to try and mend the break. But she won't be able to do it. Be prepared for her anger to escalate."

Evelyn's guide continued to move through the next few passages, speaking the incantations with ever increasing force and determination. As John predicted, the ghost fought hard to keep her ground, sending forth scratching noises and knocks across the ceiling in a desperate attempt to repair her trap for David.

Undeterred, the guide continued reciting passages with crisp enunciations of the ancient Cherokee spells. The confrontation between the guide and Allie Mae's angry responses grew more intense, until what sounded like a chorus of voices shouted a litany that ended with "Dayuha hinehi-hinida'we utsina wa!" The chorus resounded fiercely from Evelyn's throat while her body convulsed in her chair. Somehow, she clung to David's hand. He almost let go, but John urged him to hang on, warning it provided the only means for her guides to fight for him.

"Here's what they just told the entity," John advised. "They said, 'now your soul fades away—your spirit shall grow less and dwindle away, never to reappear. Let her be completely veiled in loneliness—O Black Spider. May you hold her soul outside the web, so that it never returns to thrive in the meshes. Forever she shall dwell in the depths of hell, oh evil one!'"

David found the incantation confusing. It sounded to him as if they called on some other menace, as what else could it mean to summon the aid of something like *O Black Spider* or *oh evil one*?

"There's good and there's bad, and both forces exist throughout the universe," said John. "There's a higher power different from what you or I might call upon, and it governs the realm where Allie Mae's spirit resides. It's part of the great mystery in our world."

Evelyn lurched forward and another chorus erupted from her, as if a stream of invisible vomit launched into the air. The convulsions increased until the chorus ended. Her body went limp, and her grip on David's hand was tenuous. She slumped with her head buried in her arms next to the book, with her eyes shut. She stayed like this for several minutes. Finally, she stirred.

"Where are we?" she asked, her voice hoarse from the recent abuse her throat endured. Her eyes had been restored to their normal position, the irises aglow from energy beyond her own.

"You're near the end." John smiled lovingly, and his expression revealed his relief. "There are only a few passages left, since your guides took care of the hardest part."

"So, Allie Mae hasn't forced her way inside the cabin yet?" She sounded hopeful.

"Not that we can tell," said David, looking to John for affirmation.

"Go ahead and finish the incantations, so we can get ready to visit the cove." John pointed to his watch, which read 10:38 p.m.

Evelyn sat up and took a sip from her coffee. After a few deep breaths, she rubbed her hands together and returned her left one to David's grasp. She found her place in the book, noticing only a few bookmarks were left. Before she finished reciting the first line of the incantation, three loud thuds shook the front door.

David turned to look, his anxious eyes scanning the front of the cabin. Evelyn paused long enough to draw his attention back to the ceremony, and resumed. The pounding resounded again… more fervently. She picked up the pace, moving swiftly through the passage while speaking the mysterious words clearly and with passion.

A similar assault visited the cabin's back door. When it failed to dissuade her from her task, both doors shook simultaneously. John cast an uneasy glance toward the fireplace. The fire burned strong, but for good measure he left his seat to grab another log and threw it onto the hearth. By the time he returned, Evelyn had reached the final incantation. She shouted the phrase containing the word aduniga with enthusiasm, and followed this with "Yuhahi! Yuhahi! Yuhahi!"

One last slam pushed the back door inward enough to creak painfully on its hinges, and a low, sad sigh followed. Everything became eerily quiet outside. Even the wind disappeared, leaving the steady pops from the fire as the most noticeable sounds.

"It's finished!" John announced triumphantly. He started to rise.

"Not yet, Grandpa," advised Evelyn, her weary voice revealing exhaustion. "We… we still must apply the pastes to David's face and hands."

John grimaced, glancing at the clock. It read 10:56 p.m.

"Turn and face me," she instructed David.

He turned his chair toward her. She picked up the brush resting on the edge of the water bowl in front of the rust colored paste. After dipping the brush in the water and pressing the bristles against the side of the bowl to remove any excess liquid, she pushed the dampened end of the brush slowly through the slender candle's flame. A tendril of smoke arose from the bristles, and once it disappeared, Evelyn dipped the brush into the paste. She brought the brush over to his face.

"Close your eyes and picture your success… your triumph over the entity."

David closed his eyes. The paste felt warm as Evelyn brushed it on his face, from the bridge of his nose to the middle of his right cheek.

"Without opening your eyes, hold out your hands with palms faced downward."

He felt the same warmth from the paste as she drew a cross on the back of his right hand. He heard the brush being returned to the bowl and another picked up.

"It's time for the end of things to come, the conclusion of Allie Mae's reign in the world of the living. May she return to darkness from whence she came. Think about this, David."

He pictured the black paste being administered to the left side of his face and left hand, the smoke rising from the brush's bristles as it passed through the next candle's flame. Surprised the paste felt cooler than the other one that was streaked onto his face, a similar cross soon followed upon the back of his left hand.

"We're almost done. May you find peace and be granted happiness. It's our sincere prayer that Allie Mae's soul also finds peace."

The stir of water and the soft crackle of another brush's bristles moving through the flame of the last slender candle confirmed the third step in the ritual. The warmest of the pastes touched his forehead, crossing from one temple to the other. He envisioned the white line, and how it contrasted with the other two streaks on his face.

"Go ahead and open your eyes."

Evelyn and John were smiling. She held up a small mirror, so he could see his reflection. The pastes had been brushed on thicker than he envisioned, and the white one was the most dominant on his face. Looking somewhat like an Indian warrior, the other two streaks met perfectly on the bridge of his nose and extended to his eyes' outer edges.

"I probably should've waited for you to put on your coat first, but I'll help you slip it on to avoid smudging anything," said Evelyn. "We need to get going, since it's already ten after eleven."

Evelyn blew out the candles, and John retrieved the coats from the guestroom. He helped her place the arms of David's coat over his hands to protect the ritual's marks. She placed Allie Mae's bag inside the coat's lower right pocket. Ready to leave, it took each of them giving Shawn an obligatory belly scratch to keep him from following them outside.

The temperature had grown colder since dusk, and now hovered in the low thirties, leaving a thin layer of frost on the windows of all three vehicles. The night was clear and tranquil, and a yellow-tinted moon just four days past its fullness illuminated the front of John's property.

"Let's take my car," John suggested.

David and Evelyn followed him to the cruiser and climbed in, she in front and he in the back. John started the engine, but it shut off after he let it idle. He tried again. The engine sputtered and quit again. Irritated, since the engine was recently tuned for the coming winter, he prepared to try one more time. The dashboard lights flickered and died.

"I don't think this has anything to do with the maintenance on your car, Grandpa," said Evelyn. "We'll take my car."

She climbed out of the cruiser and walked to her car, less than twenty feet away. With her keys pointed to disable the alarm, she reached for the Nissan's front door with John and David behind her. A shadowed figure suddenly sat up in the front seat, glaring at her through the frosted tinted glass.

David only caught a glimpse of the intruder's face peering out through the driver's side window, but Evelyn and John saw it clearly. She screamed in surprise and fell into her grandfather. They stumbled to where David stood, while the Nissan's horn blared loudly.

The car shook violently. The small dream catcher hanging from the rearview mirror slapped against the windshield, while napkins and other paper items floated in the air inside the vehicle. Evelyn and John froze. David could tell neither one had expected an outright invasion of Evelyn's personal property.

His shoulders slumped in defeat, and he wondered what else could go wrong. Then a strange sensation crept through his entire being, carrying a surge of power and malice unlike anything he had ever known. Along with this odd feeling came new thoughts... and a sudden determination to take charge of the situation.

"Come with me!" he told them, and ran to his rental car.

David unlocked the driver's side door and threw it open. He climbed inside and started the car, prepared for it to stall like John's cruiser, but believing for some reason it wouldn't. The engine revved to life and held steady while it idled. Evelyn and John joined him. She sat in the front passenger seat while John sat behind her. Immediately, the assault on the Nissan ceased.

"We've still got time to do this," said David, the tires screeching as he raced down the driveway toward the park's main thoroughfare. He looked in the rearview mirror expecting to see the Nissan or some vestige of the spirit's presence in pursuit, but saw only the empty moonlit road behind them.

"You'll need my directions, since it can be tricky to navigate in the dark," said John.

"No… I don't believe I will," said David. "I can get us there just fine."

His tone sounded cold, almost rude. He couldn't help it. David felt very strange, and sensed Evelyn staring at him. He wanted to try to explain what was happening, but couldn't. He could only focus on getting to the ravine.

He drove fast, taking several reckless turns on the park's road to the Oliver homestead. John started to chastise him, but Evelyn shushed her grandfather, as if understanding the transformation and that things could turn volatile if either one distracted David.

When they reached the parking area next to the trail leading to John Oliver's cabin, the car screeched to a halt, just inches from the wooden guardrail. It had taken under fifteen minutes to make the drive, and the clock on the dashboard read 11:58 p.m. The wind blew in strong gusts across the moonlit meadow, and the tall trees bordering the meadow's edge were bent severely from the weather's force.

"We'll wait here for you," Evelyn said quietly, as if privately second-guessing the decision to do this.

David didn't respond, staring through the windshield toward the meadow. John Oliver's cabin wasn't visible, just the entrance to the trail leading to the homestead. When he and Miriam visited two weeks ago, they had veered from that trail. They walked across the meadow to a break in the tree line, where another path, overgrown and forgotten, took them a mile into the woods to the ravine. He envisioned this moment for the past week with dread, but now felt relieved it had arrived. His troubles would soon be over.

He opened the car door once the clock clicked over to midnight.

"Y'all can wait here if y'all like, or y'all can move on," he said. John glared at him from the backseat. "I imagine this'll take thirty minutes or so. If I'm not back here in an hour's time, it'll mean she got the best of me, and y'all would be better off just gettin' on home."

David couldn't believe the deep country drawl and his casual indifference to the people who had so wonderfully befriended him. He hated himself, but couldn't override it. It felt so alien, and at the same time amazingly comfortable.

Without another word, he unfastened the seatbelt in irritation and stepped out of the car. A stiff gust from the meadow embraced him. The air quite chilled, he found it oddly comforting. He absently closed the driver's side door and stepped away from the vehicle. Before the dome light dimmed to where Evelyn and John's faces were no longer visible, he disappeared from view. He hurried along the trail to his destined appointment with Allie Mae.

Chapter Thirty-seven

The wind continued its assault, growing stronger once David veered from the path. His shoes crunched upon the frost-covered grass and weeds that served long ago as Mr. Oliver's pasture for his livestock. He smiled and picked up his pace with resolute purpose. No longer fearful, the isolated loneliness brought comfort, along with an unfamiliar solace while surveying the undisturbed countryside glistening in the moonlight. It mattered not that the tree line he headed toward stood ominous, immersed in deep shadows.

To his right sat the Oliver cabin. Its roof brightly awash from the moon's eerie glow, the rest of the one-time residence lay hidden in darkness. A small orb of red light danced near the porch and disappeared as it moved behind the cabin, reappearing at the edge of the woods before vanishing again. Seeing something like it thirty minutes ago might've sent him scurrying back to the car. But, at the moment, he merely grunted.

David kept moving. He was less than a hundred feet away from the break in the tree line, where Miriam and he took turns posing for snapshots. The tops of two wooden posts, the only remnants of a gate that once stood there, peered out from the bushes shrouding the overgrown trail to the ravine. A hazy figure stepped out from the shadows near the gateposts.

Another burst of energy surged through his being, bringing a wide, leering smile to his face. He casually glanced at his watch. The time was 12:06 a.m.

"Just like old times, ain't it, girl?" he called to the figure becoming solid as he approached.

It was a young woman. Barefoot and dressed in the blue gown he recognized, the moonlight formed a soft halo around her strawberry blonde hair. For the moment, her head hung down, hidden by her gorgeous locks. She didn't respond to his call.

"I'm about to teach you another lesson, Allie Mae, and give you what you've been waitin' for all these years," he told her, slowing his pace as he awaited her reply.

Less than sixty feet from where she stood, he pointed to her with his left hand. David shook his index finger menacingly while reaching inside his coat pocket with his right hand.

"I'll bet yer just achin' for…."

His words disappeared when he pulled her bag of treasures from his pocket. Once his fingers touched the stains from Norm's blood, the sensation that had seized his body and controlled his thoughts and words receded. An icy rush of tingles pricked the flesh along his lower back, as whatever force possessed him exited his body.

David's vision blurred for a moment. When it cleared, he found himself clutching the bag tightly. He couldn't remember why he held it, surprised to see tall grass and weeds. He looked around anxiously while zipping the coat up to his neck, until he saw the shrouded lonely cabin to his right.

Oh, shit!

He stood alone in the middle of Cades Cove… or did he? Fragmented images of what had brought him to the place began to trickle into his awareness, including the unfamiliar twang and careless words that flowed from his mouth. A wave of incredible terror and regret swept through him.

He slowly looked to where the girl waited, now solidified. Her head no longer hung toward the ground. Instead she faced him, the impenetrable dark shadow obscuring her features. The moonlit halo surrounding her shimmering hair made her head even more ghastly. The air around him grew extremely cold, and he noticed her bare, slender arms shook at her side. She was more than a tad upset.

"Allie… Allie Mae, I-I've come to return this t-to y-you," David stammered, taking a careful step closer. He raised his hand and took another tentative step, holding the bag out. "I'm sorry if I said anything to offend y-you. I just want to make peace—"

He didn't finish the words. Still more than fifty feet away, in the next instant her form appeared in front of him, inches away. He bumped into her frigid corpse. She grabbed him by the arms and searing pain ripped through muscle and bone, like a pair of buzz saws slicing through his coat and sweater's sleeves. Allie Mae rose off the ground and brought her face close to his. He feared being absorbed by the deep shadow shrouding her face. But, what he saw next made him wish for that shadow instead.

"Ya murderer-r--r! M-m-u-u-rder—r-r!" she shrieked.

The shadow drew away, and under the moonlight's illumination he saw her face clearly. Her right eye was like a glistening sapphire, and it accompanied the delicate features of a gorgeous young woman, despite blood splatter upon her right cheek. The eye was narrowed, and along with her quivering frown, it emphasized her wrath.

But, it was the left side of her face that caused him to fight to free himself from her ironclad grip. Her left eye was a ruptured mass, barely attached to the optic nerve lying exposed, along with a portion of her brain that oozed and pulsed through the destroyed socket. The bones from her forehead down to her chin had been violently crushed, and the flesh had been beaten to a bloody pulp of mashed muscle and sinews. Her lips had been partially torn away. Most of the teeth from a once spectacular smile were either missing or broken, while what remained was barely attached to the left side of her splintered jawbone. The carnage continued down to the top of her throat, where her carotid artery and windpipe had been torn through.

"Murderer-r-r! God damn ya, Billy Ray-y-y!"

An icy shower of blood drenched his face as she screamed, forcing him to his knees. Rather than the brave warrior Sha-hinta, he felt like a timid little boy, despite the fact the pastes on his face tingled once the blood touched them. Waves of warmth radiated through the rest of his body and eased the pain from her grip. However, the sound of steady breaths wheezing through her damaged throat easily overmatched the promise of supernatural aid. The pulsing gurgle told him her larynx filled with another round of blood, ready to be sent forth at any moment.

He fought harder to get away, but she effortlessly subdued him, pushing him onto his back and throwing herself on top. She embraced his body; her dead, cold flesh penetrating his garments as if intending to merge with his living tissues. He screamed in terror, and the ground collapsed beneath him, opening into a huge chasm. The wind from his rapid descent pushed the hood of his coat up to where the steel snaps slapped painfully against the side of his face.

The free-fall increased in speed, and he feared being sucked into the very core of the earth. But then his descent stopped, abrupt and painless. A mountain stream murmured to his right, and as he listened, other sounds filled his ears. A symphony of chirping insects and croaking frogs surrounded him, along with an owl's intermittent calls. He opened his eyes, terrified he might find that horrible face gazing at him and ready to send forth another shrieking rain of blood. Yet, Allie Mae wasn't there.

Lying on his back beneath a medium-sized oak, it took a moment for his eyes to adjust to the darkness. When they did, he recognized dim outlines from the ravine he visited twice before. Unlike his visit with Miriam, when the dried streambed told of decades when no water flowed through the ravine, the area looked similar to how it did when he observed Allie and her playmate, Zachariah, as kids.

The oak's foliage was sparse, and the sky beyond was almost fully visible through the branches. A thousand stars filled the night sky, where the moon had disappeared. He sat up, feeling the cool grass beneath his hands. The scents of daffodils and honeysuckle filled the humid night air. As he got on his feet, a bullfrog startled him as it flew past his waist. It splashed into the water before hopping to the other side of the stream. As he followed the sound, he saw the clumped trees he had hid behind in his dream from a week and a half ago. The trees were bigger, with more carved names upon the trunks.

It gave him enough information to determine his location in the ravine. He stood and turned toward the oak. Hard to be certain, since the tree appeared to be much younger and its trunk significantly smaller than when it shaded him and Miriam on their fateful picnic;

yet, logic said it had to be the same one. For the moment, its tender bark was clean, and had been spared the ritual butchery visited upon several of its neighbors. To the left of the tree, just five or six feet away, sat a large stone slab. Similar in shape and thickness to the one that formed the ledge over the ravine near its mouth, the slab sat upon a pair of small boulders. It looked as if someone had created a bench for sitting close to the stream.

A faint glow appeared at the top of the ravine, and the sound of footsteps announced someone was coming. David slid around the tree and ducked down. The yellowish glow grew brighter and the footsteps continued their approach. The top of a candle lantern was soon visible, and a young man stepped onto the ledge. Dressed in a white shirt and an old fashioned brown suit with a narrow black tie, his dark hair glistened in the lantern's glow as if wet from water or some sort of oil. The tips of his shoes were muddy. He looked around the ravine with the lantern held before him.

David gasped.

"Ty?"

The young man stopped to listen, and David stepped from behind the tree.

"Ty, it's your dad. *It's me!"*

The young man pointed his lantern toward the oak where David stood, but said nothing. He leaned his head out and squinted, perhaps trying to see who called, but shrugged. Another set of footsteps approached, much softer than his, and soon another lantern's glow appeared at the top of the ravine.

"What are ya lookin' at?"

The female's voice sounded youthful and sweet. The young man smiled sheepish and brought his lantern around. Allie Mae McCormick stood in the lanterns' collective glow. She wore a blue bonnet, with her hair in ringlets framing her face. Her face was stunningly beautiful, and she smiled serenely with an innocence David would've never guessed existed, based upon his experiences. Her deep blue eyes glistened in the candle flames' soft luminance.

"Nothin' I guess," said the young man, glancing away after eyeing her shapely form so deliciously attired in the blue gown.

She looked somewhat taller to David. When he noticed the laced, black boots she wore, it seemed she had gone to great trouble not only to look nice for the late-night meeting with her apparent beau, but she certainly endured some discomfort. Whatever foot pain or assaults from mosquitoes and gnats he saw swarming near them, she didn't let on that any of it bothered her.

"Well, I've come just as I said I would, Zachariah," she told him. "I've brought ya a present, too." She giggled.

"Oh, my God!" whispered David, after recognition of the moment fully hit him.

The night of Allie's death, somehow relived... but for whose benefit?

If the terrible event was being recreated for him, was the kid named Zachariah somehow involved? He marveled at how this teenage boy appeared a near-dead ringer for his eldest son. Even the kid's mannerisms were similar. Coupled with the fact Allie Mae wore the same gown, it all made sense.

Seeing the unmolested dress attested to tears and missing buttons that had previously escaped his notice. Obviously, the bonnet and shoes would disappear before the night ended. Could the innocent looking young man be capable of the powerful hatred and violence that at some point destroyed her face? He didn't think he could handle witnessing such a crime, especially from someone who so closely resembled Tyler.

She carried a bouquet filled with honeysuckle and lilacs and attempted to give it to Zachariah.

"Why don't ya wait on that," he said, seemingly pleased by the gesture but anxious to lead her to the stream. "I've got somethin' to show ya first!"

They moved down the side of the ravine opposite David and crossed toward his hideout. Eerily, the two followed the same course he and Miriam had taken when they first visited the ravine. Allie Mae held her gown as they stepped on flat stones above the stream's surface to reach the other side. As she did, part of the bouquet fell into the water. She tried to reach down and grab the flowers, and almost fell in. Zachariah caught her, guiding her up the bank to where the bench sat.

"My, oh my!" she exclaimed. "Since when did this get here?" She walked over to the stone slab, rubbing her hand against the top, admiring it under the lantern's glow.

"Billy Ray helped me set it up," he said, which drew a scornful look from her. "I needed his help when I first found this big ole rock, in the brush over yonder." He pointed to a spot, less than twenty feet away in the darkness, where the woods were dense. The look on his face showed he desperately wanted her approval.

She studied his eyes for a moment, and smiled.

"It's nice." She brushed her hand over the surface to make it clean enough to sit on. "I guess it ain't like Pa will be any madder if I sit on somethin' like this, after I've already muddied my shoes and splashed water on the bottom of the dress Momma made me this past Easter."

She laughed and motioned for him to join her on the bench. Once she sat down, she set the lantern on the ground next to her feet.

Zachariah hesitated in joining her after setting his lantern to the side of the bench closest to the oak. He wrung his hands together while opening and closing his mouth as if he wanted to share some secret, but either couldn't or didn't know how.

"Will ya sit down?" she playfully scolded. "It's not like I can stay out here all night. If Pa wakes up and finds me gone this late, I'll get the worst whippin' of my life!"

Zachariah nodded and sat down. When he did, Allie handed the bouquet to him. He thanked her and brought the flowers close to his face, smiling as he inhaled the powerful fragrance David could smell from where he watched, a dozen feet away.

"The bench is nice. I'm sure other folks would say it's handsome, too," she said. Zachariah alternated between sniffing the flowers and staring at his feet. "How was Reverend Tillis' sermon tonight at the Baptist church?"

"It was all right, I reckon," he said. "I missed half of it, though, 'cause Billy said we needed to leave if he was to help me get this set up. How was the sermon at y'all's church?"

"It was fine. A lil' borin', maybe, but Pastor Smith's gettin' better…. Set what up?" She eyed him curiously after glancing around. "This bench we're sittin' on, or are ya talkin' 'bout somethin' else?"

Zachariah laid the flowers on the bench, sighing deeply while rubbing both hands on his knees. He stood and moved to the tree's trunk, forcing David to duck further into the brush and overgrowth nearby. Burning up in his coat, David could tell Zachariah was overheated in his dress clothes as well. A trickle of sweat coursed down the side of the young man's face, and as he looked at the trunk, it appeared he closed his eyes and muttered a prayer.

Without turning around, he pulled out a small switch knife from the front pocket of his coat, the blade glistening briefly as he opened it. David worried it would be when the attack happened. If so, he would do whatever was necessary to prevent it, regardless of the personal consequences. Zachariah remained facing the tree. He lifted the knife to the height of his chest and began to carve into the oak's trunk. It took him a few minutes to finish, and he stepped back, admiring his handiwork.

"What do ya think?" he asked Allie.

She had waited expectantly for him to finish, but her reaction surprised David as much as it disappointed Zachariah.

"Oh, my dear Zach," she said, her smile fading. She released a mournful sigh. "Come over here and sit with me."

Hesitant to do as she requested, his hand holding the knife shook. She reached out and took it from him, pulling his arm to get him to sit down. She folded the blade shut and placed it in his palm, cupping his hand inside hers.

"I'll always love ya," she said tenderly. "Ya will always have a place in my heart. Friends forever. Remember?"

He looked down, shaking his head in dissent. His shoulders began to tremble, and he seemed on the verge of tears.

"Oh, darlin', don't cry." She wrapped her arms around him. "I love ya, I truly do. But my heart belongs to Seth. We've spoken of this before."

He pulled away and stood, his hands balled in fists as he faced her.

"Why?" he demanded. "Why *him* and not *me?"*

David prepared to jump out from his hiding place when things turned violent. Allie gazed into Zachariah's face. Calm and unafraid, the compassion in her eyes confirmed the sincerity of her words.

"He's the *one*, Zach," she said.

"The one, *what?!"* he replied angrily. "Is he the one who's been by yer side since we was younguns? Or the one who's always made time for anythin' ya wanted to do, includin' yer witchin's? God knows what his ma and pa'd think if they ever found out 'bout what ya often do out here in the mil' of the night!"

"And I trust ya never to tell 'em!" She stood, her look serious. The warmth and compassion from a moment ago dissolved in her rising anger. "Is this the reason ya brought me out here—to talk 'bout things we can't change none?"

"I'm every bit as good a man as Seth!" He moved toward the tree and pointed at what David couldn't see, although he pictured a freshly carved heart with her name on the tree's other side. "I can provide for ya! I can give ya all the lovin' ya need! Ain't *nothin'* he can give that I can't, and ya know it's *true!"*

She stood and faced him, and the softness in her eyes revealed she fought tears.

"Please, Allie… *please* put my name under yers!" he begged, wiping his eyes with a coat sleeve as tears began to flow.

"I-I can't. I can't and I *won't!"* she replied, seemingly offended.

David thought it had to be killing her, to tell her longtime friend those words. He wondered what might've happened had she survived and later experienced the terrible loss of her true beau dying overseas on a World War I battlefield.

"Allie Mae, please!" Zachariah cried harder and fell to his knees.

"No!" she shouted and turned to leave.

He fell to the ground, pounding his fists in frustration upon the unforgiving earth. David felt sorry for him. Allie Mae was likely Zachariah's first and only love, until that point in his life.

She picked up her lantern and stepped down the bank, and onto the stones leading to the other side of the stream. When she reached the opposite bank, she started to climb. Another man stepped out of the shadows and blocked her path.

"And where the hell do ya think yer goin'?"

The man's voice was gruff, and she looked up in surprise.

"Get out of my way, Billy Ray!" she hissed. "This ain't none of yer concern, and I've got no quarrel with ya… yet!"

"I think not!" he replied, laughing meanly. "My brother's pain *is* my concern, so yer quarrel's most rightly with me, too!"

He pushed her back, and she stumbled down the embankment. Before she could regain her balance, he grabbed her arm, yanking her behind him as he moved across the stream.

Zachariah sat up as his brother and captive approached, sniffling and wiping his face on his coat's sleeve. Allie Mae yelled a litany of threats at Billy Ray, who seemed unaffected by her taunts and focused only on the task of dragging her up the bank and over to the bench, where he threw her on the stone slab. The bottom of her dress became entangled on one of the slab's sharp edges and ripped. Rather than continue her verbal tirade, she glared at him while assessing the damage to her gown.

David tried to get a better view, peering around the oak. Until they reached the illumination provided by Zachariah's lantern, he couldn't see the infamous Billy Ray Hobson. Allie Mae's lantern had fallen into the stream when her assailant grabbed her.

A towering man, Billy Ray stepped into the lantern's glow. Ruggedly built with powerful legs and arms, a scruffy beard covered most of his face. Clad in a white, short-sleeve shirt open around the neck, he looked as if he might have earlier worn a suit similar to his brother's, with identical trousers. Unlike his younger brother, he wore heavy black boots, like those used by the region's early coal miners. A shadow cast by his brown fedora obscured his eyes.

"What are ya doin' here, Billy?" Zachariah rose to his feet and moved to the bench. "This is between just her and me."

"The hell you say, 'lil brother!" he huffed. "'Seems to me Allie Mae's got some carvin' to do, so I reckoned I'd lend her a hand!"

He yanked her up by the arm with more force than before, and she yelped in pain. Obviously furious, she glared at Zachariah while scooping up the bouquet he left on the bench.

"So, ya told him *when* we's meetin' here tonight?" she seethed.

"Billy ain't supposed to be here—honest!" he whined, shifting his anxious gaze from her to his brother and back again. "He was supposed to help me get set up and then leave! That's what he promised!" He narrowed his eyes at his brother, who grinned as if amused by the exchange between Allie and him.

"I ain't got time for this horseshit," said Billy Ray. "Let's get on with the carvin' of my brother's name, so Seth Sullivan will know who ya belong to when he gets back from the war."

He grabbed his brother's lantern from the side of the bench and dragged her toward the tree. She clawed at his hand to release her, and as before, David intended to come to her aid. He moved around the side of the oak and prepared to launch himself at the fiend once close enough. When the older Hobson came within a few feet away, and raised the lantern toward the mark his brother made, his face became discernible. In shock, David drew a sudden breath. Although fifteen years younger, the face he stared at was his own. He couldn't believe it, and moved away from the safety of the tree to get a closer view. Both Allie Mae and Billy Ray paused to look in his direction. She gasped as though she could see him, while Billy Ray narrowed his eyes, as if David's image was faint and too hard to discern.

"I'll have none of yer witchery!" he hissed, returning his attention to the task at hand.

David could come no closer. Something charged and unseen constricted tightly around him when within a foot of Billy Ray. It left him just near enough to feel the body heat and smell the sour odors of whiskey and sweat emanating from the man, but too far away to impact his actions. He panicked at the thought he might not be able to come to her aid after all.

Allie Mae's gaze remained fixed on David, and she smiled weakly.

"Woe to ya, Billy Ray, if ya persist in yer effort to forge a lie!" she warned, bringing her attention back to him. "Ya sense the spirit's presence, but know another far worse than this one is drawin' near. *His* vengeance will be realized if ya fulfill the evil in yer heart!" She raised her chin defiantly.

Billy Ray hesitated, nodding as if he believed her.

"All right, Allie Mae. All right," he said, pulling her closer to where she leaned away from his foul breath. "There's other ways to teach a bitch like ya a lesson!"

Rage suddenly seized her face, and she shook her arm free from his grasp.

"Don't ya call me no bitch!"

He chuckled, motioning for Zachariah to continue to stay out of it.

"Ya ain't nothin' but a bitch… and a whore, Allie Mae. Just a fuckin' sleazy whore!"

"Why ya bastard!" she shrieked, and slapped him across his face.

The sound ripped through the ravine, and at first Billy Ray seemed shocked. But the shock soon turned to wrath. Before she could strike him again, he grabbed her arms and threw her on the ground. He warned Zachariah again to keep out of their feud and jumped on top of her, pinning her arms under his weight while she fought to free herself. The bouquet of lilacs and honeysuckles flew out of her hand, with the majority landing next to her head.

He removed her shoes to keep her from kicking him with the sharp heel tips and pointed toes, throwing them to his brother to hold for safekeeping while he showed him "the only way to tame a back-talkin' slut like this-un."

"Now, ain't that better?" he told her once he straddled her torso to where she couldn't move.

"Let me go, goddamn ya, ya fuckin' snake!"

"O-o-oh! I like a gal with some fight in 'er!" He grabbed her arms near the wrists and held them fast to the ground. He bent his face down to hers.

"Don't do it, Billy Ray!" said Zachariah. "She's mine—not yers!"

"Ya disgust me! *Ow-w-w!"* She howled in pain as he tightened his grip on her wrists. "Make him stop, Zach! *Ah-h-h! Stop* hurtin' me!"

Zachariah moved to where they struggled on the ground, but seemed unsure what to do next. He circled the spot while pleading for Billy Ray to get off. Disgusted with the younger Hobson's response, David ran over and tried to knock Billy Ray off. The mysterious force prevented him from so much as grazing his body, although he turned his head in David's direction.

Allie looked toward David, too, and whimpered as if aware he couldn't save her. To Billy Ray it appeared she looked instead at the flowers strewn near her head.

"What's this, I see?" he asked, turning to his brother for an answer when she refused to give one.

"It's my present from her," said Zachariah, bending to pick them up. Billy Ray stopped him.

"It wasn't what ya was hopin' for when we went to all this trouble earlier tonight, now was it?" He pointed at the bench they created and back toward the tree where Zachariah had carved her name. "I've got somethin' right proper in mind for em in a 'lil while."

"Let me go!" Allie Mae squirmed more aggressively to free herself.

"Hold still ya goddamned bitch!" he hissed in irritation.

Billy Ray slapped her hard across the face, and when she shrieked again he slapped her harder, pulling her bonnet off and shoving it in her mouth. The act finally got his younger brother moving, to stand up like a man and rescue his beloved.

Zachariah grabbed him from behind by the shoulders. Slighter in build, he succeeded in lifting his brother off Allie Mae… but only for a moment. Billy Ray turned and slugged Zachariah in the gut, causing him to fall backward. His head landed hard on a thick root protruding from another, much older oak. With blood trickling down the side of his face, he laid motionless. Allie Mae screamed while David checked on him. He couldn't get close enough to be sure, but he thought Zachariah still breathed. *Definitely unconscious.*

"Ya killed him, ya bastard! Ya murderer!" she shrieked after spitting the bonnet out of her mouth.

Billy Ray secured her under his weight once more, shrugging indifferently. He laughed and tore open her dress, exposing her breasts. She fought harder, which made the leering smile on his face broaden.

"Get off me! Yer *hurtin'* me! *Please... let... GO!"*

Shocked and mortified for her, David tried to attack again, screaming at him to leave her alone. He managed to knock Billy Ray's hat off and witnessed the goose flesh rise on the back of the fiend's neck. But it only made him briefly look over his shoulder while squeezing Allie's breasts with his rough and dirty hands.

"Yer goddamned spirits can watch if they're so inclined," he told her. "But, one way or another yer givin' me what I've come for!"

She continued to squirm while he pressed his face down onto her right breast. He pulled up her gown forcefully, ripping her undergarments free and throwing them toward the woods. All the while, David desperately pushed his body against the invisible force to where the charged warmth became a fiery burn too painful to endure. She seemed to see him through her tears, sobbing while she pled for Billy Ray to stop.

He shoved her legs apart, and eyed the small bunch of lilacs and honeysuckles lying next to her head. He chuckled gleefully as he picked up the flowers with one hand while securing both of her wrists with his other. He brought them between her legs and wiped them around her sex. When he started shoving them inside, a look of horror appeared on her face. Enraged, she managed to free her wrists. With her left hand, she raked four fingernails against the tender spot just below the right side of his jaw.

"Get the fuck off me!"

David desperately sought to help lift her attacker to where she could slide out from under him. Again repelled, the invisible force sent him flying into the stream.

Billy Ray howled in pain, grabbing at her fingers while blood oozed freely from his wounds. Infuriated as much as she, he slammed her arm down against the ground. A soft crunch and snap announced it fractured on impact.

"Someone please help me! He's goin' to kill me!"

"Shut the hell up, bitch!" Billy Ray roared. *"Or, I'll kill ya now!"*

She ignored his threat and screamed louder. He warned her once more, and when she wouldn't stop, he began to pound her face with his fists. David managed to climb onto the bank, his clothing soaked. The left side of Allie Mae's face was bloodied from the blows from Billy Ray's hand, and she looked at David standing to her right, openly begging for him to save her. But he couldn't. The force that stopped him before now crackled with intense energy, and the invisible barrier extended to the edge of the bank's slope. He could only watch helplessly.

"Who are ya callin' to?" asked Billy Ray, sarcastically, following her gaze to David. "I told ya to shut the hell up!" He leered in David's direction, until his gaze fell on a sharp, pointed rock protruding from the ground a few feet away.

"Let's see if yer spirits can save ya from this!" he said menacingly, again securing her wrists with one hand while he dug out the rock.

David's heart dropped when he realized Billy Ray's intent. The force remained impenetrable. He fell to his knees on the bank, crying while he pleaded for Billy Ray to stop.

As if he could hear, the rogue whose likeness David bore paused to looked at him one last time and smiled. He then turned his attention to Allie Mae, whose eyes followed the course of the heavy, sharp-pointed rock he wielded above his head. She screamed again as he brought it down onto her mouth. Muffled cries followed, as crushed teeth and torn tissues fell inside her open throat. Again and again, he brought down the rock, and once it smashed into her left eye socket she quit moving. Billy Ray added a few more blows for good measure, and each delivered to Allie Mae's left side, away from David. When finished, he casually tossed the rock, barely missing David's head as it flew by and fell into the stream. The waning bubbles announced its arrival at the bottom of the stream.

The evil intentions of her attacker weren't finished. To David's horror, after loosening his belt and removing his trousers, Billy Ray savagely raped the corpse.

David looked away, unwilling to witness the continued violence. He laid on the edge of the ravine's bank weeping until something nudged him. Fearing Billy Ray would be leering at him, he was grateful to find him gone. Allie Mae's corpse lay a few feet away, and in the lantern's soft glow, he saw Zachariah stir next to the other oak.

The pasted streaks on David's hands were nearly undetectable. They had smeared and washed away during his struggle to save her life and his subsequent dousing in the stream. His watch, waterproof and still attached to his wrist, showed the time as 12:48 a.m. Allie Mae's passing must have been around twelve-thirty. He stood and carefully pressed his hands forward. The mysterious force receded, undetectable until he neared her body. He wondered if her spirit touched him, and worried what would come next. Billy Ray reappeared at the top of the ravine carrying a pair of shovels.

"We best move quickly," he said to Zachariah, after he returned to where the corpse lay, while his younger brother struggled to stand.

"What the hell have ya done?!" Zachariah cried out once he saw Allie Mae's violated and violently torn body lying nearby. He immediately ran to her side, gathering her body in his arms, his sobs heartrending.

"Ain't no time for cryin' over her, Zach!" Billy Ray responded harshly. "If she hadn't broke yer heart and put up such a fight just now, she'd be all right. But, once a bitch n' whore, always a bitch n' whore!"

He pointed to the bleeding wounds along his neck.

"Goddamn ya, Billy Ray!" shrieked Zachariah.

He laid Allie's body on the ground and ran to his brother, pummeling his back and shoulder. The older Hobson easily subdued his weaker sibling, gripping his wrists with enough force to bring him to his knees. Zachariah howled in pain and crumpled to the ground, wailing loudly.

"Yer goin' to hang for this!" he screamed. *"Sheriff Thompson's goin' to see to it once I tell 'em what you've done!"*

"You'll do no such thing!" retorted Billy Ray. "What do ya think he'd say when I tell em' how ya helped me kill Marshall Tillis? Once I show him where ole Marshall's buried behind Blake Casper's place… hmmm?"

His smile pompous, he brought the edge of one of the shovels close to his brother's face. Zachariah continued to sob, but he heeded his brother's threat and got back on his feet. He reluctantly took the other shovel and picked up the lantern, casting another sorrowful glance at Allie Mae's lifeless form. He followed Billy Ray as he moved to the woods on the other side of the bench. David crept close behind as far as the mysterious protective force would allow, causing Zachariah to look over his shoulder several times.

"Pay no attention to her conjured spirits," said Billy Ray, moving to the darkened woods across from the ravine. "Foller me over to where we found the makin's for yer bench. There's a hole we can use to bury her."

A few feet beyond the tree line lay a shallow depression in the ground, where the stone slab unearthed had been. Since it was only a foot or so below the surface, the two set out to make it deeper. After digging into the soil a few inches, the tips of their shovels met repeated resistance, as if the earth refused penetration into its thick clay.

They argued about what to do next; whether to dig a hole someplace else or to make do with the one they had. With Zachariah rapidly loosing his nerve, Billy Ray made the decision to bury the body in that spot, stating no one in the community would come looking for Allie Mae before sunrise.

They retrieved her corpse and carried it to the hole, picked up her shoes and other clothing, and the remaining stems from the strewn bouquet. They placed the corpse and everything else in the hole, and covered it. Zachariah noticed something glistening in the dirt, near the hole's edge. He reached down and picked it up, and as it glistened in the lantern's glow, Billy Ray snatched it from his grasp.

"Well I'll be fucked!" he declared, examining the oval object.

David drew as close as he could to see what he held. The precious stone, a sapphire, appeared polished, although covered in a film from many years under the earth's surface.

"'Anythin' else in there?"

Billy Ray dropped to his knees and dug his hands around the body while Zachariah stood by, grimacing. He pushed the corpse aside, throwing the limbs back as his fingers probed the soil. He soon recovered a handful of other non-faceted gems: a deeper purple stone, another green, one red, and one other with a yellowish tint that David guessed to be either topaz, or the off-color diamonds the region was known for. Billy Ray lifted the corpse and shook it, perhaps thinking the jewels were Allie Mae's and hidden in her garments. Only trickled blood fell from the body that had grown cold and stiff since her death.

He tossed her body aside and dug his hands even deeper, recovering several more gemstones. When at last he could find nothing else, he stood.

"We ain't got time to look for more tonight," he said, after placing the gems inside his trousers' front pocket. "Looks like we might've found ourselves some treasure!"

He picked up the corpse and threw it in the hole, where Allie Mae's limbs twisted grotesquely. Zachariah grimaced after seeing her mutilated face in the lantern's glow again.

"So, are ya just goin' to leave her here?" he asked sadly, his eyes swollen from tears.

"Yep. But, not like this," replied Billy Ray. "Lay yer shovel down and come with me."

They walked back to the bench. With tremendous strain, the two lifted the immense stone slab and carried it to the hole. Billy Ray's strength amazed David, since it appeared the slab weighed upward of three hundred pounds and Zachariah provided little help in sharing the burden as they moved it to the woods. When they arrived at the hole, Billy Ray guided his brother in positioning the slab directly over its original spot. They dropped it, crushing Allie Mae's remains beneath.

Zachariah looked at the slab entirely obscuring his love. His body shook until it appeared he might collapse again. Billy Ray grabbed him and turned his attention to the ravine.

"We need to clean this place up and make it look like it did before we was here tonight," he advised, moving to the small boulders that recently supported the stone bench.

He picked up one of the boulders and told Zachariah to gather up the rest of the flower stems and any clothing shreds he could find. However, Zachariah wouldn't help him anymore. His attention was drawn to an unusual sound emanating from the woods further downstream, well beyond the reach of his lantern's glow. It sounded as if a huge nest of hornets had been disturbed, and an angry swarm swiftly approached.

"Do ya hear that?" he asked anxiously, while his brother returned for the other boulder.

"Hear what?" asked Billy Ray, his tone impatient and his breaths labored from the recent exertion.

The noise grew much louder and filled the air in front of them, while an immense shadow crept onto the edges of the lantern's glow. Zachariah screamed and dropped the lantern on the ground. Rather than wait for his brother, he scrambled to the other side of the ravine, splashing up water and kicking his foot against Allie Mae's submerged lantern as he clambered to the other side. He frantically clawed his way out of the ravine, and his cries echoed into the night as he ran down the path toward John Oliver's homestead.

"Goddamn it!" Billy Ray hissed in anger.

He appeared only slightly concerned by the encroaching shadow until it reached the oak bearing Allie's name, where the angry buzz suddenly grew to a deafening roar. He raised his sullen gaze, and the meanness in his countenance softened. His eyes grew large and his lips quivered. In a panic he, too, fled from the ravine, leaving the lantern and shovels behind. David wasn't able to see what frightened him from within the dark mass, witnessing only the ominous shadow veer swiftly toward Billy Ray Hobson as it pursued him out of the ravine.

David listened to Billy Ray's terrified screams as the specter caught up to him. The echoes of that terror filled the night air as he fled along the same path as his brother. David wondered if it was the reason Tennessee's census archives contained no record of what became of the two men associated with Allie Mae McCormick's disappearance. Perhaps it was also the reason no one realized her corpse lay under the stone slab, despite the digging tools left behind by her murderer.

The buzz and screams disappeared into the night, and David returned his gaze to where the lantern lay. Allie Mae's blood glistened in a large puddle on the ground where she died. Near the puddle lay two objects, and he moved to them. The lantern's glow was fading, but in the fleeting light he saw the objects more clearly, and when he did he fell to his knees and cried again.

Allie Mae's little bag of keepsakes apparently had fallen out from inside her dress, and next to it was the broken bicuspid from when her face had been savagely crushed. David scooped up both items, holding them in his lap. The contents of the bag jingled softly.

Overwhelmed by terrible grief, he screamed into the night while he pictured what her family went through in trying to find their cherished daughter. He thought of his own daughter, Jillian, and how it would destroy him and Miriam if anything like this ever happened to her. He buried his face in his hands, dropping the bag and tooth on the ground. Bawling harder than he ever could remember, tears flowed freely through his fingers, dripping onto the light blue thread of the bag's cross-stitched letters.

Incredible despair and loneliness filled his heart, and the body heat created by his distress left him unaware that the temperature dropped rapidly. When cold enough to where his fingertips tingled, he peered through his hands. A figure with two bare nymph-like feet stood in front of him. He wiped away his tears to clear his vision, and saw the frayed inseam of a once-beautiful blue Easter gown.

"I'm so sorry, Allie Mae… s-so *very* sorry!" he said between sobs, reluctant to look up.

He felt her fingers graze his shoulder, and prepared for the worst. The figure withdrew her hand. As she stood before him, David gathered his courage and looked up. Her dress was still torn, but enough buttons were left intact for her to cover her bosom to her neck. She no longer bore the carnage inflicted upon her person. Her face was whole and radiant, and her eyes twinkled in the light he thought at first came from the lantern.

A nightingale called from somewhere nearby, distracting him. Still in the ravine, the colorful foliage and loose leaves strewn around said he returned to the present. His misty breaths had nothing to do with Allie Mae's chilled presence, but instead were caused by the cold, early-morning mountain air of late October. The moonlight's glow fully illuminated his surroundings.

He looked at her again, fearing what he might see. Allie's face remained beautiful, and her aura seemed like an angel's. She held him in her gaze for a moment and smiled, nodding approvingly. The ground shook beneath him, and he looked in time to see the bag and tooth pulled into the earth, the tender blades of grass separating to allow the items through. When he looked up again she was gone; the only vestige being her shimmering strawberry blonde hair and the bottom of her blue gown as she disappeared into the woods near where her body lay buried.

David waited a few minutes to see if she returned, but she didn't. Surrounded by songs from the early morning birds in the treetops he got to his feet. The multitude of weathered names on the surrounding oaks and pines were clearly visible under the moonlight. According to his wristwatch the time was 1:38 a.m. Weakened from the past hour and a half's emotional toll, he staggered into the deep grass and weeds of the ravine to reach the other side.

David followed the overgrown trail, grateful for the moon's abundant light. He soon had a clear view of the path's entrance framed by tall pines that once defined the northern boundary to John Oliver's property. As a precaution, he glanced over his shoulder. He remained alone, except for the nocturnal animals and birds busy foraging for food.

He stepped past the tree line and into the meadow. A soft breeze blew toward him from the darkened cabin, and when he glanced toward it this time it seemed lonelier than before. He pictured it long ago, in the spring of 1916, wondering if its occupants slumbered peacefully the night Allie Mae died, or if the screams and shrieks that pierced the night had awakened them in terror.

Grateful the Buick was still parked where he left it, John opened the driver's side door. He had awaited David's return with Evelyn by his side. They both shared their gratitude he remained among the living. He responded with a weak smile, and motioned for John to remain in the driver's seat while he climbed into the back seat.

John pulled the car onto Cades Cove's main thoroughfare. David's clothes were still damp, and once the warmth from the car's heater reached him, he shivered more than he had during his return from the ravine. He retrieved his cell phone from inside his coat, dismayed the screen received a slight crack from his fall into the stream. Luckily, the phone still worked. When he finally had two bars of signal, he dialed Miriam's cell number and waited while it rang, hoping she hadn't gone to sleep yet. She answered, and at first all he did was weep.

"It's finished," he managed to whisper into the receiver, and as he did, both John and Evelyn turned toward him. "It's finally over."

Chapter Thirty-eight

David told John and Evelyn what happened once they reached the cabin. Although not surprised, both responded with sorrow upon learning the details of Allie Mae's brutal murder. John commented again on the similarity between David's last name and that of the Hobson brothers. Since it wasn't so unusual to change last names during southern Appalachia's formative years, he suggested there might be a link that extended beyond the coincidence of his and Tyler's physical appearance closely matching that of Billy Ray and Zachariah. David admitted he thought the same thing after what he had witnessed that night in the ravine.

David insisted that John and Evelyn sleep in the bedrooms, and he would take the couch again. Shawn and a warm fire kept him company, and he fell asleep around three o'clock, after keeping a watchful eye on the picture window. Other than occasional gusts whistling through the eaves, no other disturbances visited the cabin.

He planned to be up at sunrise, but John didn't wake him until eight o'clock. After he showered and shaved, Evelyn surprised him with flapjacks and thick, sliced bacon for breakfast, along with a pot of fresh brewed coffee.

"Thank you for everything," he told her, once he finished packing up his rental car. A beautiful fall Sunday morning in the Smokies was in the making, with only a few wispy clouds dotting a blue sky.

"It's been my pleasure, David." Evelyn stepped down from the front porch to give him a warm hug. "Please be sure to keep in touch!"

"I will… I promise!"

He moved to John, who was dressed in his ranger uniform, complete with hat and dark sunglasses. He smiled at David; the corners of his eyes misted beneath the glasses.

"You'll be hearing from me very soon," David assured him. "I'm grateful for everything you've done for me, and I want you to know I consider you as my friend."

John nodded. They shook hands and seemed unsure of what to do next.

"Oh, come on you two. Give each other a hug!"

As Evelyn stepped toward them, they embraced, enforcing the bond forged during the past week. David fought tears as he got in his car, forcing a smile as he waved one last time. He kept an eye on John and his granddaughter through his rearview mirror until they grew faint, and the Buick soon merged onto the thoroughfare leaving Cades Cove. It took another three hours to reach Chattanooga, and along the way he listened to the handful of country CDs John had given him. He quietly marveled at how his music taste had been altered, and wondered how Miriam, and especially Tyler, would react when he opted for a country song the next time they took a spin in their sports car.

Almost noon when he pulled into the parking lot at Jo-Jo's Steakhouse in Chattanooga, his aunt's Taurus sat near the entrance. David parked a few spaces down from her. A family favorite just a few blocks from the airport, Aunt Ruth had suggested the restaurant might be nice to revisit. She reserved a booth for them, near the back of the restaurant.

"Well you made it here sooner than you thought you would, David, don't you know!"

She rose to greet him. Smartly dressed in a dark pantsuit, her hair and makeup looked as if she recently visited a salon. It touched him that she'd gone to such trouble on his account, and a new surge of guilt seared his conscience.

"My foot went a bit heavy on the gas once I was safely beyond Knoxville," he joked. "It's so good to see you again, Auntie!"

The sentiment was genuine, but it seemed to take her aback a little. He figured she had become accustomed to his preferred distance in their relationship.

"My, you look sharp today!" she said, as if looking for a distraction. She brushed her hand against his dark, blue velour dress coat. One of the few original garments spared Allie Mae's wrath, it lay hidden in the car's trunk when she attacked his wardrobe. "I don't think I've ever seen you wear a turtle-neck before."

"I just started, since it's been a little cooler than I expected this past week." David hoped the chocolate one he wore covered the scabbed scratches on his neck. "Maybe Miriam will like the look. If so, I plan on adding a few more when I get back to Denver."

"Honey, she might just buy a dozen once she sees you later today!" She laughed.

A waitress arrived to take their order, and afterward Ruth told David about Max's planned cataract surgery, since the dog often tripped down the staircase in her house. She feared he might break his neck if she didn't get it taken care of soon. David felt sorrowful her life consisted of so little now that she grew older. When eager to learn the details of his Gatlinburg meetings, he gave her a fabricated succinct summary of what happened, avoiding anything that might sound exciting.

Ruth mentioned she had called Miriam a few days earlier. Touched by the kids' school pictures, she accepted a previous invitation to fly to Denver at Christmas. He was thrilled to hear the news. If nothing else, the ordeal had softened his heart. Ready to bury the hatchet on past hurts and grudges, he hoped they could once again be close.

After lunch Ruth grew quiet and pensive, as if wanting to say something but unsure how to proceed.

"What is it, Auntie?"

Rather than reply, she lifted a leather tote bag from the floor next to the booth. It appeared quite old, and the corners of the brown bag were badly worn. David cleared away their dessert plates to allow enough space for it to sit on the table. She opened the bag, and removed a large photo album.

"Bobby wanted you to have this," she advised. "He set it aside when you were young, right after your momma died. I know you weren't so close to your daddy, but Bobby always loved you… in his own misguided way."

In the past, he would've refused the item. Sensing how badly she wanted him to have it, he smiled weakly and took it. Several page markers stuck out, and she explained they were for photographs of particular note. She stood and leaned over the table while opening the album's clasp, and David turned to the first page she had marked. Filled with an assortment of black and white photos, many were yellowed from age. Most of the images were clear, except for some of the oldest photos. These looked as if someone had wadded and torn them up, and then threw them in a musty box many years ago. One had been taped back together, and he recognized the image of the young man in the picture.

"Who's this?" His voice dropped to a whisper. He already knew, but needed her confirmation.

"That's my great uncle Zach," she said. "I thought of him when you showed me Tyler's school picture the other night."

The image was identical to the Zachariah he saw the previous night, including what appeared to be the same suit and tie.

"From what my pa told me many years ago, the picture was taken shortly before he went to Europe back in the summer of 1916, to fight the Germans in World War I."

"I didn't know we had anyone from our family participate in either world war," said David, surprised and staring at the picture. John's speculation turned out to be true.

"Your great, great uncle was one of the most decorated veterans from the First World War," said Ruth. "Pa once told us Uncle Zach received a Purple Heart and other medals for valor. There was a published story some years back from another Tennessee veteran that served with Uncle Zach, who said he'd never known a braver man. He said it was almost like he dared the German troops to kill him if they could. But he survived the war with only a minor wound to his arm."

She grew thoughtful again and David moved to the next marked page, featuring photographs from a farm.

"That's the farm up in Pigeon Forge I told you about last week," she said. "I was just thinking of Uncle Zach and the last time I ever saw him."

He looked up from the album's pictures.

"It was Christmas, and the year was 1946," she said. "He was fond of my pa. That year, he arrived after dark on Christmas Eve. It was very cold, I remember, and we spent most of the evening gathered around the fire. I'd only seen him twice before, and I had just recently turned seven. The previous times I'd seen him, he'd try to tickle me or find some other way to make me laugh. I could see why Pa loved him so…. But on that night he acted real strange."

She paused to take a sip of tea, and didn't immediately resume.

"What do you mean?" asked David.

"Well, for one thing he kept looking over his shoulder, like he expected someone to be there," she said. "That wasn't all. When we went to bed, Pa had Bobby and me share our bed with him. Now, I know you might think that's a bit strange by today's standards, but back then no one thought much of it—especially when a person's kin was involved, and there wasn't always a bed for them to sleep in. Uncle Zach kept us up all night, and I remember we worried Santa might not come to our home on account of it. He slept between us and kept sitting up in the bed, pointing at some invisible person and begging them to leave him alone. It was so pitiful."

"Do you think he saw someone, or was he losing his mind?" David tried to sound ambivalent. Ruth regarded him for a moment, smiling coyly.

"I guess it doesn't matter if you think I'm crazy or not," she said, chuckling. "I've always felt that he did see someone, or at least *sensed* someone. It was really soft, and I doubt your daddy heard it. But I'd be willing to swear on a stack of bibles that I heard a girl's voice speak to him from the darkest shadows in our bedroom."

"Do you recall what the voice said?" David's pulse suddenly picked up and he fought to keep his cool façade.

"Yes, I do. The voice said 'The time of my vengeance is nigh, and I'm coming for you real soon!'"

David was in the process of taking a drink from his iced tea, as his throat felt dry. He spat it out onto the table.

"Are you all right, dear?" Ruth asked, worriedly.

"Yeah, I'm fine," he replied, coughing and dabbing with his napkin to clean up the mess. Thankful nothing touched the photographs, most of it landed on the sleeve of his jacket. He brushed himself clean using another napkin. "Whatever became of Uncle Zach?"

"I never saw him again after that Christmas," she said, her eyes dreamy. "The next afternoon, Christmas Day, he and Grandpa had a bad argument in our front yard. They both were shouting, and Uncle Zach said something about how you can't escape God's vengeance, and that my grandpa's sins would curse us all. He must've truly believed it, because his body was found a few weeks later in mid-January, 1947, hanging from the rafters in an abandoned barn just outside Omaha, Nebraska."

"Zach was great grandpa's brother, correct?" asked David. "Was his name Billy Ray?"

It was bad enough to be blood related to Allie Mae's murderer. He wanted confirmation Billy Ray and Zachariah survived that night.

Ruth sat up straight and eyed him suspiciously.

"I know your daddy and my pa never mentioned his name when you were growing up, because that's how much they hated him. No one called him anything other than Will or William, except Uncle Zach. And I only heard him use the name Billy Ray one time, and that was during their terrible argument on the front lawn of the house I still live in to this very day. How'd you hear of that name?"

David wasn't sure how to respond. Until a few minutes ago he didn't know for sure they were even related. The sad truth was he never knew the name of his great grandfather, due to apathy while growing up in the shit haven of his highly dysfunctional family.

"I don't know," he said. "I must've heard it somewhere long ago, from someone who knew him, I guess." A twist on words, but honest enough.

Ruth nodded and pointed to the album.

"I know you've got a flight to catch soon, so I'll move through what I've marked quickly. The rest you can look over on your own."

She pointed to the pictures of the Pigeon Forge farm, which spanned several pages in the album. Most of the pictures were taken from the 1920s up to the 1950s. One featured an older man with one hand on the shoulder of the man David recognized as his Grandpa Elbert, when he was much younger. It might normally be hard to identify the elder man, since his face was shadowed beneath the brim of a straw sun hat. But, the four long scars that stretched from his jaw to the base of his neck made his identity unmistakably clear.

"Mean as a damned rattlesnake," remarked Ruth, after she noted David's horrified facial expression. "He didn't have many friends from what I understand, but Grandpa Will had a great many people who'd wait on him hand and foot. Everybody I knew hated him, especially my father. Your daddy hated him, too."

"How about you, Auntie?" He couldn't shake from his mind the terrible act he witnessed. "Did you hate him?"

"I'd rather we just forget about him and move on."

David sensed she kept a tight lid on that aspect of her upbringing. If her father's treatment of her daughter, Celeste, gave any indication, she certainly experienced similar sexual abuse growing up. Before he let her move to the last photos, he asked her how the old man received the scars along his neck.

"From a close encounter with a black bear is the way he always told it," she recalled. "If it'd only been a grizzly. The world would've been a much nicer place for me and Bobby growing up, not to mention what my Pa and his two sisters went through."

David reached over and grasped her hand, thanking her for the painful information she shared. She offered a wan smile, and moved on to the last sections she had marked in the album. These were mostly pictures from his early childhood, and he was amazed by how many there were.

"Like I said, your daddy loved you dearly, David," she said. "Even if he wasn't around much and had a difficult time showing his tender side, he'd play with you whenever he could, and take photographs of you along with your momma."

They visited together until one-thirty, when he needed to leave in order to get his rental car returned in time for his three o'clock flight. He helped her return the album to its tote bag and accepted the bag, intending to bring it on the aircraft as a carry-on to protect it. He then walked Ruth to her car. After a warm goodbye, and again letting her know he looked forward to her upcoming Christmas visit, he got in his car and headed for the airport.

The plane destined for Denver finished boarding by 2:45 p.m. While awaiting takeoff, he decided to view more pictures from the album. Some of the photographs came from the early years of the twentieth century, and possibly from the last decade of the nineteenth century. He regretted not asking his aunt when the name Hobson changed to Hobbs. Curious to learn the storied reasons behind the change, he already knew beyond any doubt what had inspired it.

While perusing the early pictures, he came upon one taken in front of the Methodist Church in Cades Cove. The year was 1915, and the photograph appeared to have been taken during the spring or summer. Likely a bake sale or similar event, an assortment of pies and cakes were piled on several tables in front of a few hundred people. Most of the men and women were dressed in their Sunday best. Near the front of the throng stood a pair of beautiful girls wearing light bonnets and whose hair hung in ringlets. One of the girls was Allie Mae McCormick.

David brought the image closer, admiring her unusual beauty. The girl next to her appeared to be just as pretty, and was certainly her sister, Emma Sue. As he scanned to see what the other family members looked like, he saw two other familiar faces nearby. Zachariah and Billy Ray Hobson stood less than fifteen feet to the right and a few rows back of the McCormick girls. Zachariah faced the camera, wearing a serious expression similar to most of the people in the photograph.

Only one person in the crowd smiled… *Billy Ray.* His sly grin told of his disregard for the photographer's instructions as he looked toward the McCormick sisters. If the picture had captured the front of his face instead of his profile, perhaps his lecherous leer would've also been obvious. The picture told so much in light of what would happen the next spring, as well as what befell David's family nearly a century later.

The plane taxied for takeoff, and he closed the album. He placed it inside the tote bag, and slid the bag beneath his window seat. Grateful the nearest seats were empty, it afforded him privacy to reflect. There was so much pain… so needlessly visited upon his loved ones, as well as upon Allie Mae and her family. All of it came down to the evil of one man, whose changed last name couldn't save his descendants from the curse of his wickedness.

David thought about the strange sensation that had taken him over the night before, and how his dreams during the past week brought similar experiences. The fact that one of the dreams and Allie Mae's rape and murder were eerily linked made him wonder if his great, great grandpa's spirit briefly took possession of his body.... Or, maybe it meant something far worse.

Once the plane was safely in the air, the hills of Tennessee became smaller and smaller in the window as the aircraft headed toward the immense mountain range to the west. David closed his eyes and buried his face in a pillow provided earlier by the stewardess. For the rest of the ride home he wept.

Chapter Thirty-nine

"When are we going, Daddy?"

"In a few minutes. Right after everyone's done eating their lunch. And that means your veggies too."

David moved through the kitchen, casting a playful look of scorn toward Christopher. His youngest child sat sullenly in front of his plate. The Sloppy Joe was gone, but the green beans remained untouched. Excitement filled the household on the second Saturday in December. The annual Hobbs Christmas tree hunt was set for that afternoon—depending on when Christopher finished his meal.

"Dad, can we take a rain check on waiting for Chris, and get out of here?" asked Tyler. "I've got something important to do later on, and I don't want to miss out on decorating the tree before I have to leave."

"Let's ask Mom," Jillian piped in. "She'll be right back!"

"Oh, where is she?" David grabbed a Coke from the refrigerator.

"She's outside checking the mail—here she comes now!"

Jillian limped briskly to the front door and opened it for her mom, whose hands overflowed with Christmas cards and an assortment of bills. Scattered snowflakes filled the air behind Miriam as she stepped inside. She removed her scarf, but left her coat on since they were about to leave anyway.

"Is Chris done yet?" Miriam asked.

"No, but Ty would like a rain check!" said Jillian, before David had a chance to respond.

Miriam moved into the dining room, setting the Christmas cards inside the antique crystal bowl Aunt Ruth gave them the year before. Pleased she finally found a good use for it, the bowl held nearly a dozen open cards that would later be hung along the banister in the foyer. She planned to fill the bowl with a mixture of glitter-painted pinecones and leftover ornaments from the tree before Ruth's arrival the following weekend.

"I think I can go for that," she said, as David joined her in the dining room.

He came up behind her, kissing her on the neck as she finished sorting through the mail.

"Yippee-e-e-e!" exclaimed Jillian from the kitchen. "Come on, Chris! You're *done!*"

Christopher joined his sister in celebration, while Miriam examined the return address on one of the last envelopes in the pile of mail.

"This one's for you from Gatlinburg," she said, smiling as she held it out for David to take.

The envelope was thicker than any of the others in the stack, and he eagerly tore it open when he saw that it came from John Running Deer.

"Are we ready to go yet? Daddy, get your coat!" said Jillian, bouncing into the dining room with Christopher. Sadie's high-pitched bark accompanied her eager tail wagging as she chased after them.

"Hold on, everyone," said Miriam, looking over David's shoulder. He sat down at the table after opening John's correspondence that came with a card. "Daddy's got something important to look over and then we'll be on our way."

The card was a specialty Christmas version from Gatlinburg. It featured Santa's sleigh being pulled through the air with a beautiful moonlit view of the Smoky Mountains in the background. In addition to the warm holiday wish inscribed inside, John and Evelyn had signed it together.

A letter addressed to David fell out and landed on the table. After Miriam quieted the kids once more with a promise of a definite departure within the next ten minutes, she urged him to open it so they could both read it. He laid it open on the table:

Dear David,

It was very good to hear from you again this past Thanksgiving, and both Evelyn and I look forward to your family's visit next April during your kids' spring break from school. We're already planning lots of fun things to do, and I've booked the week off from my normal tour duties. Evelyn plans to join us as well. She and her boyfriend broke up right after Thanksgiving. (She has been sad the past two weeks, but realizes it is better that it ended now instead of later, since they planned to marry next summer.)

The reason I included this letter with our card is mainly to let you know the latest news about Allie Mae. I realize we discussed some of this already, but in case you wanted the specifics of what has been going on and the important people involved, you'll now have a copy of that information.

As we discussed in early November, Micky Webster and I decided to visit the ravine just before Halloween. Following your description, we found the stone slab in the nearby woods. It wasn't easy to find, but we finally uncovered it, roughly twenty feet from the oak tree that bears her name. Since we had a pretty good idea what was lying beneath it, we contacted Dr. Peter Kirkland and his forensic specialists at the University of Tennessee in Knoxville. It was a decision I soon regretted, and now feel it would've been better to have left her remains undisturbed where they were.

Dr. Kirkland visited the site on November 3rd, and he brought a small hoisting machine to safely lift the slab. Underneath it was numerous smashed bone fragments, and a few traces of soiled blue and white fabric. He soon determined the bones were human, and his team carefully lifted the remains out of the ground. To be certain they got them all, they dug down nearly six feet into the earth. The professor wanted to be sure none of the remains had settled deeper into the ground, since the ravine has been flooded on several occasions since 1916.

The team was ready to place the stone slab back over the hole, when one of the graduate students noticed something unusual about the slab's underside. Once he pointed it out to the rest of us, I was surprised no one had noticed it sooner. Circular symbols had been carved in snake-like lines, moving from one end of the slab to the other. Dr. Kirkland was very excited about this. He contacted another professor at the university, named Dr. Walter Pollack, whose specialty I understand is archaeology. Dr. Kirkland called on his expertise because Dr. Pollack is supposed to know a lot about the Indians and other ancient races living in the southeastern United States, particularly my people, the Cherokee.

Dr. Pollack became quite excited once he saw the stone carvings, even more so than Dr. Kirkland. He believes complex civilizations lived in this region long before my people's ancestors, the Iroquois from up north, arrived around 1000 AD. From the way the symbols were carved, he stated they could be between two and three thousand years old.

The point of all this is that they dug into the hole again the next day, which I didn't object to. But I did object when they also wanted to dig into the surrounding area. Despite my concerns, they received official permission from the park service in Washington D.C. by the next afternoon, November 5th. Micky and I made sure the dig stayed within the permit's boundaries.

By nightfall on November 7th, a large section of the ravine had been dug up. Several more slabs were found, including the largest one that formed the ledge at the top of the ravine. Despite their irritation with my earlier protests, Dr. Kirkland and Dr. Pollack allowed me to see a curious artifact found almost ten feet below where the bone and fabric fragments were discovered. The only way I can describe the object is a golden scepter with a very sharp ivory edge on one end. The scepter is in excellent condition, measuring nearly four feet with many of the same symbols discovered earlier engraved along its length.

Bear with me, David. I needed to revisit some information so you'll understand the importance of what I tell you next. By the end of the next week, the human remains were verified as belonging to a young female, between the ages of fourteen and nineteen, which fits Allie Mae's description. The violence you described, David, couldn't be verified since so many of the bones were crushed when the slab was dropped on top of the body (that fact has now officially been confirmed by the forensic specialists). The most recent carbon dating test placed the bones' presence in the hole between seventy-five to one hundred years, which also confirms what you saw that night in the ravine.

Here's where this gets quite strange. Other bones were mixed in with the first skeleton, and Dr. Kirkland wondered if we had stumbled on the depository for an early twentieth century mass murderer. But, since some of the bones were found where the scepter was located, nearly a dozen feet below the surface, the mass murderer idea doesn't make sense. Dr. Pollack thinks that some of these older bones drifted to the earth's surface over the years while the rest remained deeper in the earth with the scepter.

That information alone was enough to complicate things, but then another two-dozen skeletons were found in shallow graves along both sides of the ravine. The immediate evidence suggests these bones were from white settlers—men, women, and children of European descent. If the artifacts found with these other skeletons are as old as they appear, then these people predate the early 1800's migration into Cades Cove by two hundred years. The deteriorated helmets, body armor, jewelry and muskets are similar to what the settlers of colonial Virginia wore and used in the early 1600s. It challenges what we've known about the early history of Cades Cove, especially since it appears these people died violently. All of the skeletons' upper neck vertebrae have been severed, which Dr. Kirkland stated was a sure sign of decapitation.

One big question for me is how did these settlers get here without any evidence they actually lived in the area? Executed and buried with their belongings, I now wonder if they encountered a legendary rogue Indian tribe that my Cherokee forefathers forced out of the area around 1650.

I thought about the jewels you said Billy Ray Hobson recovered from the hole and stuffed into his trousers' pocket. Do you recall seeing anything else that resembles what I described above? The gold and jewels would not be important to the vast majority of Indian tribes in North America, so I am very puzzled—both by the treasures found where Allie Mae was buried and the evidence of such violence upon the settlers' remains.

When I told Evelyn about the discovery and what happened afterward, she was immediately angry. Beyond the worry about the destruction of our Cherokee heritage, she's upset about the university dabbling in something they have little understanding of. The ancients often enlisted powerful spirits and magic to guard over their burial places. She feels certain the older remains and the scepter belong to the other entity she told you about, and which she firmly believes was the source of Allie Mae's exaggerated strength and wrath. Disturbing its resting-place could bring severe consequences, and set in motion terrible events for all involved. That's her strongest fear, and my heart tells me that she's right.

She contacted the NCAI (National Congress of American Indians) in Washington. When they heard what was happening, they sent their representatives to both Cades Cove and before Congress. They remain skeptical that any of the bones are from an ancient Native American race, for the same reasons I mentioned earlier. Fortunately, two small burial mounds that lie near the ravine predate my people's arrival by at least one hundred years. Using this information, Evelyn was able to get the digging stopped, at least until everything is sorted out. In the mean time, the items taken from the cove will remain in safekeeping within a secured vault at the University of Tennessee. The only thing released to us so far has been Allie Mae's remains, and it took considerable effort getting that done.

When we spoke on Thanksgiving Day, I briefly mentioned I had an eventful week. What I didn't tell you was that I revisited Allie Esther the previous Monday, this time with both Micky and Cheryl to assist me on 'official business'. She agreed to a DNA test, and the university's forensic folks did us a favor by making it a priority to find out if Allie Mae and the older woman are blood relatives.

Normally this takes some time, but they had the results within a week. The two are definitely related.

This past weekend, on Sunday, Allie Mae McCormick's bones were laid to rest in her family's plot at the old Methodist Church in Cades Cove. Allie Esther and her two grandsons, along with Dr. Kirkland, Micky, Evelyn, and myself attended. It was a mixture of Scottish and Indian traditions, and Evelyn put together a spell to insure Allie Mae stays at rest, and to also bind the force that empowered her—to keep it from returning since its tomb was plundered and desecrated.

Well, that brings us up to date. I'll keep you posted on any further developments. Until then, I look forward to our next telephone conversation, David. May the holidays be a blessed time for you, Miriam, and the kids.

John

"Wow," was all Miriam could say, watching David close the letter and place it back inside the card.

He set the card on top of the others within the crystal bowl, displaying the glittery depiction of Santa navigating the sky above a meadow that could very well be the one next to John Oliver's cabin in Cades Cove.

"I'm thinking we should avoid the ravine on our next visit," he said thoughtfully. "While I wouldn't mind seeing where Allie Mae is buried, I believe horseback riding would be the right choice in the spring." He looked up at her and smiled.

"That does sound like a much better idea," she agreed, returning his smile as she caressed his shoulders.

"Can we go now?" Jillian impatiently peered at them through the dining room doorway.

She was already dressed in her parka and mittens. Christopher and Tyler soon peered in with her, wearing their winter coats and gloves.

"All right," said David, getting up from his seat at the dining room table. He clapped his hands together. "Who's ready to go find us a nice big Christmas tree?"

"I am! I am!" shouted Christopher and Jillian together.

They each grabbed one of their dad's arms, dragging him to the foyer. Miriam picked up her scarf and put it on while David gathered his coat and gloves. He went outside to warm up the minivan, and the rest of the family soon joined him. Miriam and Christopher were the last ones outside. They both told Sadie sweetly they would be right back, and then Miriam set the alarm and closed the door.

Sadie stood in the foyer for a moment, listening to the excited chatter outside. Once the Chrysler headed down the driveway, she moved to her favorite spot in the living room, atop the sofa facing the TV. A Scooby-Doo cartoon episode was in progress, and she curled up with her head resting on her paws. Her eyes began to close, but suddenly her ears perked up. She lifted her head to listen.

Footsteps resounded from the dining room, the steady creaks moving from one end to the other. She grunted softly and jumped down from the sofa, the playful jingle from the bell around her neck announcing her tentative approach to the dining room. When she reached the room's doorway she stopped. A low growl grew within her throat until it erupted as a series of sharp, menacing barks. She refused to enter the room.

John Running Deer's card began to vibrate. The tremor grew more volatile, and as it did the bowl started spinning, wobbling on the table while the other cards moved to the bowl's sides as if pulled magnetically. When John's card drifted to the bottom of the bowl the phenomenon ceased. The others fell on top.

Sadie barked once more and scurried back into the living room, burrowing to safety beneath the sofa. Shifting her anxious gaze from the kitchen to the foyer and back again, she waited.... But nothing pursued the dog. Other than the cartoon still playing on the television and the steady purr from the heater, all remained quiet in the house. It remained that way until a solitary sound emerged from the dining room, emanating from the lead crystal bowl filled with Christmas cards. Loud and deep in its resonation, and frightening enough for Sadie to whimper, the noise announced that danger had returned to her home.

Pi-i-i-n-n-ng!

The End

To be continued in:

The Raven Mocker

Evil Returns to Cades Cove

(Cades Cove Series Book 2)

Available Now

~~~~~~~~~
~~~~~~~~~

About the Author

Aiden James is the bestselling author of *Cades Cove*, *The Judas Chronicles*, and *The Gabriel Files* (with J.R. Rain). The author has published over thirty books and resides in Tennessee with his wife, Fiona, and an ornery little dog named Pepper.

To learn more about Aiden and his interests, please visit the links below:

Website: AidenJamesNovelist.com

Facebook: Aiden James, Paranormal Adventure Author

Twitter:
@AidenJames3

Printed in the USA
CPSIA information can be obtained
at www.ICGtesting.com
CBHW080931061024
15321CB00098B/3515

9 780578 651743